M000221906

Other works by Robert J. Alvarado
www.youngpistolero.com

Non Fiction
Elfego Baca Destined to Survive
2013 Sunstone Press, Santa Fe, NM, First Printing
2016 Sierra Press, Albuquerque, NM, Second Printing

Fiction
Young Pistolero Series
The saga of Rafael Ortega de Estrada, a young Mexican peón on the run riding a stolen Appaloosa stallion after shooting the haciendero who raped his younger sister. Heading north, Rafael enters the United States in 1866 to find life on the other side of the border holds new dangers along with the promise of a new life. This gritty tale is set in the American Southwest as Americans and Mexicans struggle after the Mexican-American War.

Young Pistolero (Book 1) 2013 Sierra Press
2018 Finalist for Drama TV Series category, by the Latino Books into Movies Awards; by Latino Literacy Now #1 Fiction Book for 2015; by The Latino Author

Star of the Young Pistolero (Book 2) 2014 Sierra Press

Death Stalks the Young Pistolero (Book 3) 2015 Sierra Press
#1 Fiction Book for 2016; by The Latino Author

Legacy for the Young Pistolero (Book 4) 2017 Sierra Press
#3 Fiction Book for 2017; by The Latino Author

A Reckoning for the Young Pistolero (Book 5) 2018 Sierra Press

Dangerous Venture (Book 6) 2019 Sierra Press

Justified Vengeance (Book 7) 2019 Sierra Press

The Black Phantom (Book 8) 2020 Sierra Press

PRAISES AND AWARDS

Young Pistolero, Young Pistolero Series Book 1
2018 Finalist for Drama TV Series category.

The Latino Books into Movies Awards are conducted by Latino Literacy Now, a 501c3 nonprofit co-founded by Edward James Olmos and Kirk Whisler. The judges for these awards are screenwriters, directors, producers, and others from the entertainment industry. They have deemed these books worthy of consideration for future television and movie production.

Young Pistolero, Young Pistolero Series Book 1
#1 Fiction Book for 2015; by The Latino Author

Young Pistolero is a great fiction story that incorporates both history and a great story plot of a young man whose life spirals after avenging the rape of his younger sister. It has all the muster of a good western including gun fights, murder, and survival. The author does a fantastic job of incorporating the history of the United States and Mexico during a time when the Wild West was in full swing and struggles occurred on both sides of the border. The descriptions of history add much to the story and make the life of Rafael, the protagonist, really interesting.

Mr. Alvarado weaves a plausible plot and his setting descriptions and actions are right on. His graphic scenarios of land and territories make you feel as if you are right there alongside the rider as he heads through some rough terrain. His characters were exactly what you might expect of people living in the 'rough' west trying to survive the elements and mayhem of that time.

The writer incorporates Spanish words, which allows the reader to identify with the characters; however, he brilliantly illustrates the meaning after each and every word so non-Spanish speaking readers don't miss a beat. The book is filled with so much action that you can't put the book down. It has all the earmarks of a great western series. If you are looking for a good book to read, then this is one to put on your list this year. An excellent read! – Corina Martinez Chaudhry

Star of the Young Pistolero, Young Pistolero Series Book 2

You sir, are a great story teller! I am so anticipating the next book – just like Avatar! – Corina Martinez Chaudhry

Death Stalks the Young Pistolero, Young Pistolero Series Book 3
#1 Fiction Book for 2016; by The Latino Author

The author writes so skillfully that each book keeps you on the edge trying to figure out what will happen next. I would highly recommend reading all the series. This is just an amazing writer and a really great story overall. Would love to see it on the screen one day.

Legacy for the Young Pistolero, Young Pistolero Series Book 4
#3 Fiction Book for 2017; by The Latino Author

This is the 4th novel and saga of Rafael Ortega de Estrada. I can't emphasize enough how much I love these books. Mr. Alvarado is a story teller no doubt. Each book keeps you on the edge of your seat because you don't know what is coming next. As I've indicated before, I would love to see this on the screen one day soon. A truly great story! Can't wait for the next book.

A Reckoning for the Young Pistolero, Book 5

It's very rare that you find a series of books that will keep you on the edge of your seat throughout each chapter, but this sequence of the life of Rafael Ortega de Estrada (Rafe) does this and much more. You can't get enough of this western saga and the day the books end will be a disappointment for many readers. Mr. Alvarado's descriptions of history, the character's and their significance to the story, and the amazing dialogue quickly bring the reader into the author's fictional world. A reader couldn't ask for more and will feel as if they've entered into a whole new world. And they have!

There are so many twists and turns within the story, that you won't be able to put the book down. It is rare to find such a gem and a great fictional story in the immense literary library at our fingertips and especially one such that you just don't want it to end. It's much like the Harry Potter series where each character, plot, and overall story becomes ingrained inside the reader's head. What a great testament to this author whose creativity is beyond expression. Your readers await the next book with anticipation. – Corina Martinez Chaudhry

Death Stalks the Young Pistolero

This book is a work of historical fiction and is not to be construed as real. In all respects, any resemblance to actual persons, living or dead, or descriptions of events or locales is entirely a product of the author's imagination.

The material in this book is for mature audiences only and contains graphic content and language. It is intended for readers aged 18 and older.

A glossary of *italicized* Spanish words is provided at the end of this book, with the exception of words which are equivalent in both languages, such as *importante* = important, *Mamá* = Mama, or words of Latin origin found in the English dictionary. Other words, phrases, and sentences written in Spanish are immediately explained within the text itself.

Printed in the United State of America

ISBN-13: 978-0991477722

SIERRA PRESS

Published by Sierra Press
Phoenix, Arizona
First Printing, March 2015

Cover art and design by John Flinn
Graphic art by Daniel Alvarado and Lina Luna

DEDICATION

This book is dedicated to my maternal grandfather, Manuel Arambula de Velasquez, who was born in Torreón, Coahuila, Mexico in 1888.

My grandfather came to the United States as a teenager and with help from a local businessman opened up a pool hall in Chandler, Arizona, and then later many more around the Valley of the Sun. He was an inspiration to me and encouraged all his grandchildren to work hard and go after whatever goals we set for ourselves. I thank him for that gift.

ACKNOWLEDGEMENT

First and always, I owe more than thanks to my wife, Ellen, for her unending hours of critique, review, and clarity. To my friends and family who encouraged me to continue the saga of the Young Pistolero Series, thank you.

I would like to acknowledge the wealth of historical information which is weaved into this work to depict the places and events of this saga's time period. As a work of historical fiction, where real-life historical figures or actual locations are used, the situations, incidents, or dialogues concerning those persons or places are entirely fictional and are not intended to depict actual events or to change the entirely fictional nature of the work.

CHAPTER 1

Jed Clements promised himself to go to Round Rock, Texas, to find Luke Payton and tell him his brother, Butcherknife Bill, had been killed in New Mexico. Jed was back in Austin, Texas, and mighty glad. He and nine other John B. Sutton cowboys decided not to stay in San Marcial, in the New Mexico Territory, and work for Sutton's widow after the killings. It riled Jed the greaser got away with killing Butcherknife and Sutton. Ponyboy George got his too, but Jed never cared for Ponyboy and after all he did rape and kill a woman, so it was no matter.

Sutton's widow inherited it all – the land, the cattle ranch, and all of Sutton's money, making her a mighty rich woman. After Sutton's death, she decided to hire local Mexicans to work alongside the Texas cowboys to run the cattle. That was the last straw. Jed wanted no part of working with greasers.

On the long, cold ride back to Austin, Jed weighed his decision to find Butcherknife Bill's brother. Butcherknife often bragged about his older brother Luke, riding with the notorious Sam Bass gang, robbing and killing. Around the campfire, Bill told stories about Luke being caught after a failed bank robbery in Fort Worth and put in jail. Bill puffed out telling about how the gang had sprung Luke in a blaze of gunfire. Jed knew most of Bill's stories were embellished to impress the men and knew Luke had been sent to a federal prison in Kansas, but he never mocked Bill's lies.

Last thing Jed heard about Luke, he was living in Round Rock, a small town north of Austin, Texas. The town of Round Rock was where the Chisholm Trail crossed Brushy Creek. Jed had only been to Round Rock once when he was fifteen years old. It was not much of a place then, now the talk around saloons in Austin was it had grown and was a wild town where the law looked the other way.

It had taken almost a month for Jed and the other Sutton cowboys to make it back to Austin. Pete and Jake headed for Fort Worth, thinking they could rifle up with the Bar S Ranch. Jed was not sure what he would do, but sitting in the Devil Dog Saloon sure felt good. Jed was making up for the New Mexican drought, as he called it, drinking and howling at the moon – chasing Texas whores. Most of all Jed was thankful to be back in Texas.

After spending the last month drunk and gambling, Jed was running low on money. Summer was coming and he needed to get signed with a spread before the cattle drives started moving. Lingering in Jed's mind was the promise to himself to find Luke Payton and tell him about Bill getting killed. He thought maybe Luke would be obliged for telling him about the death of his brother and could put in a good word for Jed with one of the big outfits in the area.

It was near sunset when Jed arrived at the lawless town of Round Rock, approaching it on the south road from Austin. Not having a plan he hoped Luke Payton would be easy to find.

Piano music and laughter came out of saloons from both sides of the street as he slowly rode to the livery stable. Once he had his horse settled, Jed strode along the boardwalk, his Texas spurs jingling. His first stop was the Lucky Lady Emporium. It was surprisingly quiet with only a couple cowboys standing at the bar and one poker table with three players. He strolled over to the bar and ordered a beer. Looking the place over, Jed was pretty sure no one in this dull saloon could be Bill's notorious brother. Pondering how to find Luke, Jed decided to ask about Luke Payton.

"Anybody here know Luke Payton?" he asked loud enough for everyone to hear. The bartender's head jerked up and his eyes darted to the poker table. The two cowboys at the bar turned to look at him.

"Shur nuff do. Who's askin?" one of the poker players said not looking up from his cards.

"Spent time workin with his brother at the Circle B,"

Jed said. "I got sum news fer im."

The poker player turned and looked at Jed for a long minute. It made Jed uncomfortable, but knew the poker player was not going to tell him where to find Luke until he believed he was not a lawman. Cowboys had a sixth sense about law dogs and protected each other.

Finally, the poker player responded, "He hangs out mostly at the Golden Horseshoe Saloon."

"Much obliged," Jed thanked the man and started to walk out when the same cowpoke spoke up. "Yew bess be careful. He'll kill yew iffin yew cross im," he warned Jed.

Jed strolled the boardwalk toward the main part of the town of Round Rock looking to both sides of the street for the Golden Horseshoe Saloon. Jed went by the Red Dog and the Easy Time before he saw the Golden Horseshoe across the street. As Jed crossed the street, piano music and a woman's voice floated out greeting him before he pushed in the batwing doors. The saloon was cloudy with smoke and loud with talk and laughter. Thinking about the poker-playing cowboy's warning, Jed sided up to the bar and casually surveyed the room hoping to identify Luke.

The action in the Golden Horseshoe was typical for a Texas saloon. The saloon girls were decent, a couple even quite pretty. A large roulette wheel spun in the far corner. Two tables of Faro were surrounded by both players and watchers. At four poker tables there were no empty seats. Jed stood on the far end of the long bar with a direct view of the string of dusty cowboys leaning along the bar nursing shots or beer. A few of them looked at him knowing he was a stranger. What they saw was a compactly-built, thirty-year-old cowboy in worn chaps. Sandy hair curled from under a dusty, well-worn black Stetson and his beard was reddish. Jed's wiry physique made him look a lot less tough than his scrappy nature.

"Ain't seen yew round here before," the bartender said while his eyes suspiciously looked through Jed.

"Jes got in from Austin," Jed replied casually. "Worked for the Circle B." The bartender relaxed recognizing the Circle B name. Round Rock did not like strangers, especially law dogs or worse, bounty hunters. Bartenders were good at sizing up strangers and sounding the alarm to the local outlaws. The bartender served Jed a whiskey and a beer chaser and then moved down to the far end of the bar.

Jed tossed down the whiskey in one big gulp and then sipped the beer turning his attention to the action in the room. Five men sat at a poker table with chips piled high in the middle of the table. He could see two of the men's faces – hard and expressionless. A tall man in a black hat and black leather vest sat across from them, and Jed could see a large stack of chips in front of him.

"Cum on, yew bettin or foldin," the man in the black vest snarled to a young cowboy across the table from him.

"Yew cain't be that lucky, Luke," the cowboy retorted. "Ain't natchral."

The eyes of the other players flicked between the two men showing apprehension. Jed noticed most of the winnings were in front of the man called Luke. The cowboy called the bet, and Luke raised the bet a hundred dollars. The others, except the young cowboy, dropped out. He called Luke's bet and laid out his cards showing a full house – three aces and two tens.

"Got yew this time," he said to Luke with a big smile.

"Not good nuff son," Luke crowed with a roaring laugh. He put down four eights on the table. Luke began raking the pot toward him when the young cowboy pushed back his chair and stood up. Luke's hands went down under the table. Everyone around or near the poker table drew aside giving the confrontation plenty of space.

"Yew cheatin sumbitch! Nobody's that lucky," the fearless young cowboy said between gritted teeth as he went for his gun. As he drew his pistol, Luke pushed the table at the young cowboy causing the young man to stumble a bit. The kid had no chance. Luke's gun was out and two bullets hit the young cowboy in the chest, throwing him backward to the floor. Luke held the smoking gun up as he looked around the room, just in case any of the young cowboy's friends decided to step in. No one stepped up. Still holding his pistol, he ordered one of the other players to pick up his chips from the floor.

"Drinks are on me," he hollered out.

Jed watched Luke walk with a slight limp to the bar and immediately be surrounded by cowboys. Some patted his back, while others made a wide path for him. They all wanted free drinks. Luke puffed his chest and welcomed the attention. He was a tall man, over six feet, sporting a long mustache and a small beard under his lower lip, both showing bits of gray. He wore a fitted white ruffled shirt with a black vest and a small red bandana, setting him apart from the other dusty Texas cowboys around him.

"Hey Bart, cash me in and yew bess git someone to haul that jasper outta here, afore he stinks up the place," Luke ordered the bartender as he dumped the chips out of his black hat on the bar top. The bartender poured drinks for the greedy hands outstretched at the bar, before he gathered the chips and sorted the count. He handed Luke two thousand, four hundred dollars. Luke counted five bills and pushed them to the bartender to cover the bar tab.

Luke stood at the other end of the bar from Jed, sipping from a bottle the bartender left on the bar. Jed noticed the greedy cowboys began to drift away from him, leaving him standing alone at the end of the bar. The cowboys in this bar were not Luke's friends, of that Jed was sure. He knew the ways of cowboys and these men feared the man more than they liked him. After what he saw, Jed had second thoughts about telling Luke the news of his brother getting killed in New Mexico. He probably should just walk out and go back to Austin, however Jed stayed at the bar nursing his beer. Luke was a bully, but Jed was not afraid.

"So long boys," Luke said after another swig from the bottle in front of him. Picking up his hat and coat he headed for the door. Jed tossed back the last of his beer and followed. He waited until they were out the door before he said anything to Butcherknife Bill's brother.

"Luke Payton!" Jed called after Luke's back, hoping

Luke would not turn around with gun in hand. Luke stopped and turned to face a dusty sandy-haired cowboy. Looking at him up and down, Luke had his gun hand ready to pull and stood his ground.

"Yeah, whatcha want?"

"I'm a friend of yer brother Bill, worked for him at the Circle B," Jed said keeping his distance from the gunslinger. Jed was heeled, but kept his hands well away from his weapon.

"So, what yew want with me?" Luke asked keeping a keen eye on the man's gun hand.

"I cum to tell yew, yer brother was kilt by a Mescan over ta New Mexico way," Jed said in a matter-of-fact tone.

"What the hell yew sayin? Don't be bullyragging me," Luke Payton growled, grabbing Jed's shirt and pulling him eye to eye. Jed smelled Luke's breath on him. Not flinching he stared directly into Luke's bloodshot eyes.

"Like I said, a greaser shot Bill in New Mexico." Jed pulled himself away from Luke. "I'm not lyin. I rode all the way up here from Austin to tell yew what happened to yer brother," Jed added.

"What the hell was Bill doin in New Mexico?" Luke blurted out.

"We drove a herd to a town called San Marcial for John B. Sutton at the end of last summer," Jed said. Luke stared hard at Jed trying to process the information. His brother Bill was dead. Luke had not seen his brother for several years and he would not call them close, but Bill was his little brother and Luke had been raised to protect and defend the family. After what seemed like a long minute, Luke grinned and grabbed Jed around the neck and said, "Cum with me." Luke led Jed back into the saloon.

"Bring me a bottle and two glasses," Luke shouted out to the bartender as he and Jed walked to a table with a lone cowboy and a saloon girl. When they reached the table, Luke glared at the saloon girl. "Beat it," he said. Jed could see the cowboy bristle before the saloon girl jumped up and pulled on his arm.

"Jimmy, let's dance," she wisely told the cowpoke.

Tugging on his arm, the saloon girl pulled the reluctant cowboy onto the dance floor.

Luke sat down and Jed followed. Another saloon girl delivered a bottle to the table and two shot glasses. Luke slapped her butt for the effort. He poured two drinks and picked up a glass.

"Now tell me who yew be and what happened to my brother Bill," Luke demanded.

"Name of Jed Clements. I was a wrangler with the Sutton outfit down Austin way and I worked for Bill. Yer brother was the ramrod for the Circle B Ranch. The boss decided to take his herd to New Mexico for better range."

Jed took a sip of whiskey trying to read Luke's face, but Luke gave nothing away. Suddenly Jed was unsure what to tell Luke about the situation in San Marcial, after all Bill and Ponyboy bushwhacked the Mexican who killed them. It was a fair killing by the law, still Jed did not hold with Mexicans killing Texans.

"San Marcial's nuttin but a shitheel town run by greasers. One of em kilt Bill and another cowboy," Jed said.

"Why'd the greaser shoot im? Bill was mighty handy with a pistol."

"I warn't there. At the trial the greaser said Bill and Ponyboy dry-gulched im and he got the best of em."

"Why the hell would Bill dry-gulch a greaser. They're easy pickins. Mostly they be scart of Texans."

"It had sumthin to do with hosses. The boss, Mr. Sutton, wanted the greaser's hosses and Bill and Ponyboy went after em. All I know is they both ended up dead. Sutton ended up dead, too. Shot down in the saloon by the same greaser."

Luke pondered Jed's story and thought it sounded a bit fantastic. How could a greaser best his brother Bill? Suspicious by nature Luke narrowed his eyes to slits and asked, "Why'd yew cum here and tell me? Yew want money or sumthin?" he asked with a sneer.

"Bill was a friend of mine. We rode fer over ten years and he used to talk about yew round the campfire. He was almighty proud of yew." Jed was suddenly nervous, but tried not to show it. Luke did not respond to the news in the manner Jed expected. Any idea he had about Luke helping him find a job seemed to be evaporating. "Well I tol yew, so much obliged fer the drink," Jed said and stood up to leave.

"Not so fast," Luke growled. "Yer gonna take me to that town in New Mexico so's I kin take care of that greaser," Luke said after he took another shot of whiskey.

"I ain't going back to that shitheel town again," Jed complained thinking all he wanted was to land a drover job somewhere here in Texas.

"Yes yew r cowboy, yer gonna hep me find that greaser and I'm gonna kill im." Luke pulled his pistol and laid it on the table with his hand still holding the handle. "Or do yew want to taste sum lead?"

CHAPTER 2

A deep blue sky and a cold breeze in early February of 1871 greeted Rafael Ortega de Estrada when he saddled Rayo, his Appaloosa stallion. It was unusually clear weather for this time of year in northern New Mexico, and only a little snow decorated the rooftops and shadowed ground. Rayo needed a good run and Rafe was happy to oblige. Mounting the stallion and heading east at a gallop, Rafe felt the cold drive through his coat and into his bones and found it exhilarating. It reassured him he was alive.

Rafe arrived home to Santa Fe late last month after the trip to Torreón, Mexico, to rescue his mother and sister from *don* Bernardo Reyes' *hacienda*. It was the place where he grew up as a *peón* and his mother and sister were living like slaves to the *don*. He and his friend, Carlos Zuniga, planned the trip posing as horse buyers, and all went as planned until *don* Bernardo turned the tables on them. According to their plan, Carlos spirited Rafe's mother and sister, María, and her two children away from the *hacienda* and away from Mexico, while Rafe distracted *don* Bernardo to select horses from the stock in the canyons. Alone in a canyon, it was the *don* who turned the tables and shot Rafe leaving him for the buzzards. The greedy old *bastardo* shot Rafe in the chest and left him to die in a small canyon just south of his *hacienda* and told him it was for the gold, before he shot him point-blank in the chest.

Rafe would be dead, if it were not for two Chichimeca Indian boys who brought Xihuitl, a traveling Aztec medicine man to help him. By a twist of fate, the old *don's* bullet struck the turquoise stone mounted in the center of a silver star amulet Rafe wore around his neck. The amulet, given to him by Chief Letoc, protected him as the Tiwa Indian Chief had promised.

The Aztec Healer treated his wounds, but when Rafe regained consciousness, he had lost his memory. Falling backward from the force of the bullet, he had hit his head on a rock leaving a large knot and no memory of the past. Without his memories, Rafe went with the Healer on his journey. He was still not sure how long he and the Healer traversed the frontier of Mexico visiting many Indian villages on the Healer's work as a traveling medicine man. Finally his memory recovered, Rafe left the Healer heading north to Torreón to kill the *desgraciado,* the despicable wretch *don* Bernardo, who shot him and left him for dead in the canyon.

Rayo snorted and perked his ears jerking Rafe from his thoughts. He looked at the snow-capped Sangre de Cristo Mountains ahead of him and remembered the Copper Canyons of Mexico, where he and the Healer traveled. How different mountains looked in winter, and yet in summer the rugged peaks probably looked very much alike.

He had grown to love the mountains here in northern New Mexico over the past five years while he lived with his adopted family. He thought of Santa Fe as his home now, and George and Josefina Summers his adopted parents. Now, Santa Fe was truly his real home – a home for him, his mother, his sister, and her children.

He also owed Carlos a deep debt. Carlos willingly risked his life to bring Rafe's family to Santa Fe. George and Josefina Summers opened their home to them as family, and everyone was frantic when Rafe did not return. During the long months, while Rafe followed the Healer through the mountains of Mexico without his memory, the family began to believe the unthinkable – Rafe was dead.

Rayo slowed to a trot, steam blowing from his nostrils in the cold. The exquisite Appaloosa was bred at *don* Bernardo's *hacienda* in Torreón. *Don* Bernardo was a miserable wretch, a *desgraciado,* however he had been one of the finest horse breeders in Mexico. Rafe now owned Rayo and Santiago, both top studs and the foundation for Rafe's budding horse breeding business here in Santa Fe.

"There now," he spoke to the Appaloosa with a gentle tone and stroked his neck. The horse responded by perking his ears to Rafe's voice and lightly tugged on the reins. Sun bathed Rafe's face in warmth and he breathed deeply of the crisp mountain air. Looking at the tall mountains east of Santa Fe, he thanked God for returning his memory and for letting him live to see his family again.

"Gracias a Dios," Rafe praised God and crossed himself. He believed God saved him from certain death by sending the Healer to his aid. He owed Xihuitl his life, although the Healer gave credit to the Aztec Goddess Coatlicue. "The Goddess Coatlicue, the preserver of life, is with you my young friend," Xihuitl told him many times. While he was without his memory, the Healer gave Rafe the name Citlalin, meaning star in *Nahuatl,* in honor of the Goddess. The Healer followed ancient ways of the Aztecs and even though Rafe was unable to fully comprehend the Aztec Healer's beliefs, he owed the Healer for saving his life.

The Healer also taught him about Death. "Death is near you at all times and can grab you at any instant. Death was there the day I found you shot; only the power of the silver amulet and the Goddess' blessing saved you. There are incomprehensible forces on this earth," Xihuitl taught him. Rafe would never forget the lessons of the Healer and hoped someday to return to Mexico and thank him properly. He thought about him often and wondered if he stayed in the Aztec village at the bottom of the canyon.

His mind was still sometimes confused from the amnesia and seemed to have some blank spaces where time and places were missing, however there was one concrete memory in his mind. *Don* Bernardo was dead and Rafe's family was safe from the *haciendero.*

On his way home from Mexico, Death stalked him again in San Marcial, when he was ambushed by two Texas cowboys. They wanted his blooded horses, Rayo his Appaloosa and Santiago the black stallion. They bushwhacked him on the road out of town. Rafe killed them in the fight and brought their bodies back to San Marcial, where their boss, John B. Sutton, took issue with the killings and drew on him. Rafe had no choice, but to kill him too.

Since returning home to Santa Fe, Rafe started plans for a new house he would begin building this spring on the land he owned adjacent to the Summers' ranch. His mother, sister, and the children would have a good home and enough to eat. He could easily provide for them from the proceeds of the horse business. The children would go to school and his sister and mother would never have to work like slaves again.

"*Vamos Rayo,*" he kicked the horse gently in the ribs. They flew east toward the foothills on a path they had ridden so many times before. Rafe felt the horse's tremendous power beneath his thighs, the muscles straining with the speed.

Returning to the Summers' ranch late in the afternoon Rafe felt invigorated by the ride. Trotting into the barn, he saw Carlos practicing with his rapier at the back of the barn, thrusting the sharp tip into a haystack. Rafe slid from Rayo's back and walked closer to his friend.

"Why do you play with that old sword," Rafe cajoled Carlos. "Guns are the way here."

Carlos stopped and turned around, snapping the sharp point toward the ground. "Spaniards have been masters at the sword for generations. Using the rapier is part of being a Spanish gentleman."

"I want a pistol in my hand, not a sword, if there is trouble," Rafe chuckled.

"Perhaps," Carlos replied. "Using the rapier distinguishes you as a *caballero*. It makes the mark of a Spanish gentleman." In a swift move, Carlos thrust the sharp tip of the sword almost touching his best friend's neck before Rafe could move his hand to his pistol. Carlos' sudden movement astonished Rafe, but then quiet and reserved Carlos often surprised his best friend.

"Using a sword is more than fighting, it is discipline and agility. You should come and take lessons with me. You can be my sparring partner," Carlos coaxed him.

Carlos and Rafe were like brothers, but friends born on opposite ends of the Spanish *casta* system. Carlos' family were aristocrats from Los Lunas and Rafe a *peón* born and raised on *don* Bernardo's *hacienda* in Mexico. Carlos was educated in Spain, while Rafe was educated here in Santa Fe, after he came to live with George and Josefina Summers.

"When would I need to use a sword?" Rafe asked him.

"Perhaps never or perhaps a day will come when a pistol is not at your side." Carlos' words jarred Rafe. He had a recurring dream about Chiwiwi, the girl he had loved, and Carlos' brother Benicío. In real life Benicío killed Chiwiwi and Carlos killed Benicío. In Rafe's dream after Benicío killed Chiwiwi, he threatened Rafe with his rapier. The dream did not come every night as it used to, but it still often played in his mind.

"I'll go, then someday I'll best you!" Rafe's dark brown eyes glinted as he teased Carlos who still held the sharp tip of his rapier near his throat.

Carlos jerked the tip of the sword closer to Rafe, then swung it down to his side. "I'll speak to Maestro Luis tomorrow when I go to my lesson. I'm sure he will accept you as a student."

CHAPTER 3

Rafael's mother, Celiá, was working in the kitchen with Juanita helping to prepare the evening meal as she did most every day. Now that Rafael was back in Santa Fe, he scolded her for working, yet she liked to keep busy and it made her feel she was repaying the Summers for their kindness. Even though they thought Rafael might be dead, the Summers welcomed her, María, and María's children, Antonio and Alicia, into their home like family.

Today she was peeling potatoes while three-year-old Alicia played on the floor with an iron pot and big spoon. Antonio was outside in the horse barns or following George Summers around the big foundry. Celiá fretted five-year-old Antonio would be a bother, even though *Señor* Summers said the boy was a joy to have around.

Lolo and Lizzy, the Summers' teenage daughters, spent countless hours playing with the children and teaching them words in English. Sometimes it was difficult for Celiá to remember she was a guest in the Summers' home. She had been a *peón* on *don* Bernardo's *hacienda* near Torreón, Mexico, her entire life. Now she was free, however there was so much to learn about her new life.

Alicia pushed herself onto her tiny feet. She toddled behind Juanita, who was standing at the stove stirring a pot, after seeing the family's small kitten run under the kitchen cabinet.

"*Gatito,*" she called out happily. "*Nana, leche, leche,*" Alicia called to her grandmother to get some milk for the kitty.

"*No Alicia, no leche.*"

Celiá was used to watching María's children, her grandchildren. When they lived at the *hacienda*, Celiá spent most of her time raising them while María tended to *don* Bernardo. Now, María eight months pregnant with *don* Bernardo's third bastard child was tired and too sick most of the time to help with her two young children. She spent most of the day sleeping. Celiá was worried and hoped after the child was born María would feel better.

Sometimes, Celiá thought María was just being ornery, unhappy about coming to Santa Fe to live with Rafael. She complained about leaving the *hacienda,* even though the *don* abused her and worked her too hard. She misunderstood his sexual abuse as love. The three children, Antonio, Alicia, and the unborn baby were the result of his continued exploitation.

When Rafael returned to Santa Fe late last month, he brought the news *don* Bernardo was dead. He died of a heart attack. María wailed and beat her fists into her brother's chest saying he had killed the *don.*

"No *hermanita,* I did not kill him," Rafael told his sister. "I wanted to, but I did not."

María still pouted and barely spoke to Rafael and Celiá struggled to understand. Except for the cold winter, life here in Santa Fe was happy and good. They had more than enough food, warm clothes and blankets, and a real home. The children had real shoes for the first time. Rafael was planning to build them a new house on land not far away.

Alicia lay on the kitchen floor sticking her small arm under the kitchen cabinet to reach the kitten. She cooed and wiggled trying to reach as far as her little arm could go. Celiá smiled at the joyful play. Alicia's little pink cheeks were full after the almost two months of proper nourishment. Celiá thanked God the small child would never know the stark life at the *hacienda.*

The back door opened and George Summers and Antonio blew in with a cold wind. Antonio's brown eyes were alive with excitement and his cheeks were red from the cold.

"*Nana, Tata* let me ride the big black horse," Antonio almost shouted at her. He ran to his grandmother and threw two cold arms around her neck as she bent down. Antonio started to call George Summers, *Tata,* last month, although María scolded Antonio when she heard him call George, grandpa, in Spanish. Celiá could tell George

Summers was beginning to bond with her young grandson and thought it was good.

"You are so cold," Celiá said to him. "Sit at the table and I'll make you some hot chocolate."

"*Nana,* I rode really fast. *Tata* let me ride the horse without him holding on."

Celiá looked at George with a question in her eyes. "He's getting to be quite the horseman," George told her in his best Spanish.

"Are you sure it is safe?" Celiá fretted.

"I was riding younger than he is," George responded. "He has a gift, like Rafe. The horse responds well to him."

"You are too kind," Celiá told him.

"The boy must learn, Celiá. He must learn to ride and shoot," George responded.

"*Tata* is going to teach me to shoot a gun when I am older." Antonio pointed his index finger and cocked his thumb like a gun and pretended to shoot around the kitchen.

"Sit at the table Antonio and drink your hot chocolate. Shooting can come later. Much later," his grandmother said.

"Have you seen Rafe?" George asked Celiá. She had not quite gotten used to calling her son Rafe, instead of Rafael. It was his *Americano* name and she was trying to remember to use it.

"Rafe said he was taking Rayo for a run into the mountains."

"Ah, yes. When you see him, tell him to come to the foundry."

Celiá nodded in agreement before George turned and left the kitchen. While Antonio sipped the warm drink, Celiá made a plate of food for María. She had not come down for breakfast this morning. When the plate was ready, she said to her grandson, "Come Antonio, let's take this plate to your *mamá.*"

Antonio jumped from the table and ran ahead of Celiá to his mother's room. With five-year-old exuberance, he flung open the door and jumped on the bed with his mother.

"*Mamá,* we brought you food." María turned toward the boy slightly groggy.

"*Mamá, Mamá,* wake up." Antonio pulled on her arms with his little hands.

"*Mijo,* give me a hug," she said to him. Pulling Antonio into her arms, she held him as close as she could with her extended belly. She knew she should try to get up, but standing hurt her back so much, she preferred to lie down. This baby had been a problem from the very first day. Besides the baby's father, *don* Bernardo, her lover, was dead and she was stuck in this foreign land where she did not belong with his children.

Rafael talked of building them a home, sending the children to school, and learning English. She knew it would be a better life for them, but she felt lost. What worth was a young mother of three bastard *peón* children in this place?

She watched the Summers' daughters, Lolo and Lizzy, happy and chatting about dresses and boys. They went to the Christmas social at the church and came home with glowing reports of the boys who danced with them. The girls were only a few years younger than she, with a lifetime to live. Her life was over. *Don* Bernardo loved her and was a rich, important man. He would have married her and made the children his heirs. Now she had nothing.

"Please María, you must eat for the baby," her mother cajoled her.

"*Sí, Mamá.* I know I must, but my stomach always hurts."

"Try to eat a little," Celiá told her. "The baby will come soon and then you will be better."

Chapter 4

Three weeks later María's baby was born. It was a boy and she named him Bernardo. The baby was small and something did not seem quite right to Celiá, however the family was ecstatic with the newborn.

"Gracias a Dios," George thanked God. "He is a fine boy."

"Look at his little pink toes!" Lolo exclaimed. The two Summers' teenage daughters were instantly in love with the baby. They argued about who could hold him and who had to wait. Lolo, the older by two years, usually won over her younger sister, Lizzy.

Even Josefina wrapped him in soft blankets and cradled him with such a fuss. She and the girls were already planning his baptism in the spring and the girls were embroidering a fancy outfit for him to wear.

"He likes me better," Lolo told Lizzy. "See, he's already smiling at me."

"No he's not," her younger sister protested.

As the first few weeks passed, Celiá became more and more worried something was wrong with the baby. He wailed for hours and could not be calmed. Then, when María tried to nurse him, he promptly fell asleep seemingly uninterested in feeding. María showed him little patience. Any hope María would regain her energy was eroded by the wailing baby.

"Take him downstairs," she screamed at her mother. "I can't stand his screaming."

"He needs your comfort," Celiá admonished her. "He needs to nurse."

"Let the girls walk with him. I'm too tired."

It seemed to Celiá the baby was not improving and was not putting on weight. His eye sockets had dark rings and his skin looked pale and a bit gray. She tried to talk to Josefina and Juanita about the baby, but neither woman knew what to do. "I'll call the doctor," Josefina said at the end of the third week.

Rafe spent little time at the house, working long hours in the foundry and at the horse barn. He was happy the baby was finally born, except not particularly happy María named him Bernardo. He wished to forget the old *desgraciado*. He was dead and Rafe wanted to forget the past.

One evening the baby was wailing and Lolo was rocking him gently to soothe him as she walked around the parlor. Something about the baby and the movement reminded Rafe of the Aztec healer. He had diagnosed a problem with a baby at an Indian village, and cured him with herbs and goat milk. "The baby cannot tolerate her breast milk and it causes much gas in his belly," the Healer had told Rafe, speaking about the baby's Indian mother. Unlike the Indian woman, María was not eating native grasses, still Rafe thought perhaps the Healer's methods could help.

"Let me hold the baby," Rafe said to Lolo.

"Make sure to hold his head," she said as she handed the screaming baby to Rafe. Gently, Rafe laid young Bernardo on his lap and rubbed his stomach. He tried to remember how the stomach of the young Indian baby felt. He remembered it was extended and hard. Bernardo's belly was not hard and Rafe gently massaged it the way the Healer taught him. Bernardo continued to squirm and wail heartily.

Lolo vigilantly watched Rafe, making sure he was careful while holding baby Bernardo. At almost sixteen, Lolo was a young woman. She dreamed of the day when she was married and would be holding a baby of her own.

"Lolo, go to the kitchen and ask Juanita if she has any goat milk," Rafe said.

"Goat milk?"

"Yes, please go ask her."

Lolo scurried down the long hallway from the parlor to the kitchen returning in a few minutes. "There's no goat milk, but she has some fresh milk from this morning's milking."

Rafe stood up and handed baby Bernardo to Lolo.

He had been searching his memory trying to remember the herbs the Healer used in the goat milk to soothe the Indian baby in Mexico. He found it odd some of his memories during his time with the Healer seemed to be fading, almost as if replaced by his old life once his memory returned. All he could remember was the Healer carried pouches of dried leaves and powders. He had added something to the goat milk to soothe the baby.

Rafe headed toward the kitchen hoping to find his mother working with Juanita. She often treated the *vaqueros* at the *hacienda* and knew about herbs and potions. Stepping into the kitchen, only Juanita stood at the long counter chopping vegetables.

"¿Juanita, dónde está mi mamá?" he asked if she knew where his mother was.

"Con María," she replied she was with María.

Rafe took the stairs to the second floor by twos. He heard their voices before he got to the bedroom at the end of the hallway.

"You must get up," he heard his mother say.

"No Mamá. I'm too tired," he heard his sister's voice. He knew his mother was frustrated María had not started trying to regain her health after the baby was born. Most days María stayed secluded in the small bedroom with the draperies pulled down. His mother told him his sister ate little and cried often. When the baby wailed, it only made María worse.

Rafe knocked on the door and opened it slowly. The two women looked up as he entered. He had only seen María twice since the baby was born and was shocked at her appearance. Her once shiny flowing hair hung limply around her dull looking face. Her eyes were sunken and her skin a pasty gray. Her cheekbones jutted out showing how much weight she lost.

"Go away," his sister grumbled at him and Rafe ignored her comment. *"Mamá,* I need you to try some medicine for the baby."

"Yes, go with Rafael and leave me to sleep," María said gruffly to her mother.

Celiá followed Rafe out of the bedroom and closed the door. As they walked down the hallway, Rafe related the event with the Healer and the baby in Mexico and how the Healer had helped the young mother with goat milk and herbs.

"Do you know what herbs he might have used in the goat milk to soothe the baby's stomach?" he asked her.

"Acaso batamote," she replied, "but I do not have any herbs. When we left the *hacienda,* we took nothing. Perhaps Juanita or Josefina knows where to find such things here in Santa Fe."

A few days later Celiá obtained the herbs and goat milk for the baby and tried the milk potion. Bernardo was not soothed and continued his fussiness, however Celiá refused to give up. María had all but stopped nursing the baby boy, and Celiá was distraught at her daughter's behavior. María told her mother she cared little whether the baby lived or died.

"How can you say such a thing?" she admonished María.

"He will be better off," María grumbled. "He will never be anything here in this place. In Mexico he could have been a *don."*

"No María, he would only be a bastard in Mexico. *Don* Bernardo would never have acknowledged him. Here he can grow up to be like Rafael, a man with land and a life."

María blamed everything on her brother, Rafael. If he had not shot *don* Bernardo, she might have been the *doña* of the house, *don* Bernardo's wife and her children, his children, heirs to the *hacienda.* Now, Rafael stole them to this place and killed *don* Bernardo and she could never go back.

"Rafael, I spit on him for what he has done. Go away *Mamá* and leave me be."

A few days later Josefina called the doctor to the house, again. The baby continued to decline and now his crying was more like a whimper. Josefina had lost a child, a baby, their son Gregory, to influenza when he was eight months old and watching this precious little baby suffer was like reliving an old nightmare.

The doctor came and checked baby Bernardo from head to toe, unable to discern any medical reason for his distress, though it was obvious to the doctor the baby was not well.

"He does not seem sick," the doctor said, "however he does not respond like a normal baby." He asked the women what they had tried and they told him the remedies. "Where is the mother?" he asked. Celiá and Josefina took the doctor upstairs to the bedroom where María lay in bed.

"María, this is the doctor. He wants to check on you," her mother said.

"Go away. I don't want you to touch me," she almost screamed at the doctor.

"Your baby needs you," the doctor said kindly. "He needs his mother and the warmth of your breast."

"He needs his father and he is dead. God is punishing me for my brother's action." María began to writhe and sob, beating at the bed sheets by her side. "Go away and leave me to my fate."

The doctor and the women left the room closing the door behind them. "She is angry," Celiá told the doctor. She wanted to explain to the doctor about *don* Bernardo and how he abused her daughter, forcing her to bear his bastard children, but decided not to.

The doctor did not know if María was suffering from any malady or just hormonal sadness after childbirth. "The baby needs nourishment," he told them. "Perhaps a wet nurse can be found," he suggested.

"I will check at the church," Josefina answered. "Sometimes the priests know about such things."

CHAPTER 5

In late March the family stood dressed in black, lowering baby Bernardo's small coffin into the cold ground. Nothing had stopped his slow decline until he died two days ago. Lolo and Lizzy cried harder than María, who stood stolidly without much emotion. Celiá and Josefina stood crying and holding hands.

Josefina asked her husband if it was all right to bury Bernardo next to the grave of their son Gregory. "Gregory will take care of him," she said and George agreed. Beside the tree behind the house, the priest blessed the coffin and sprinkled holy water on it. A similar scene when they buried Gregory flashed in Josefina's mind. It was over twenty years ago, but today it seemed like yesterday. He was her first child and she still stung from the loss.

She looked at María and could not believe she stood dry-eyed as young Bernardo's body was put in the ground. Josefina remembered her grief and how her husband, George, retreated into himself when Gregory died. She wondered if perhaps María could not show the grief she must be feeling.

So much had happened in a few short months to María. First, she was pregnant when Rafe and Carlos went to Torreón and rescued the family from *don* Bernardo's *hacienda*. María felt she had been kidnapped, not wanting to leave. At twenty years old she had two children and the baby now in the small grave, all bastard children fathered by the *haciendero*. Celiá told Josefina this pregnancy was difficult from the beginning. María's last months of the pregnancy were no better than the first.

Even before the baby was born, Josefina watched María exhibit anger, especially toward Rafe. She blamed him for everything. It angered Josefina, wondering if the outcome of today could have been changed, if María tended to the baby properly. Josefina wanted to scream at the young mother, shake her. Then again, maybe she did not understand the mental anguish plaguing María, and could only hope time would heal her.

Rafe and Carlos lowered the small coffin into the ground and covered it with dirt. Saying a final prayer, the family returned to the warmth of the house. María went to her room and the Summers' teenage daughters played with Antonio and Alicia, María's two older children. At five and three years old, they were somewhat unaware of the tragic events of their young baby brother.

Rafe, Carlos, and George went to the parlor. George stood smoking a cigar in front of the fire.

"What's wrong with her," Rafe asked. "How can she not cry for him?"

"Grief affects people differently, son," George said. Rafe knew he was right. It was not long ago he mourned for Chiwiwi, the woman he had loved, who was killed by a bullet meant for him. He had raged against God and the world for months.

"She has not accepted the move from Mexico," Carlos interjected. "Remember, she did not want to come to Santa Fe. She fought me most of the trip north."

"Yes, she thinks *don* Bernardo loved her. She does not understand the evil in him and remembers only the good," George added.

"We must give her time to heal her soul," Carlos said.

Rafe said nothing. He could never accept María's love for the miserable old *don* who raped her when she was fifteen and continued to father her children. Her defense of him was beyond Rafe's ability to comprehend or tolerate.

George changed the subject. "I've received a telegram from an old friend, Bill Moore."

"Who is he?" Rafe asked.

"Bill was the commander of Fort Union just north of Las Vegas, New Mexico, during the Indian uprisings. I met him many years ago when I was talking to the Army about buying my original gun designs. He retired from the Army and is working a gold mine on Baldy Mountain," George explained. "He's been prospecting for the last five years outside of Elizabethtown. Bill wired me last week asking for weapons to protect his mine against claim jumpers."

"Elizabethtown? I've read it's a wild and rowdy mining town," Carlos said.

"Yes, so I've heard, too," George added. "That's why I'm worried about Bill. I want to take a load of rifles and guns to him next week and check up on him."

"You should not go alone, *don* Jorge," Rafe said using his personal name for George. "I'll go with you."

"No, you must stay here with the women. You have work at the foundry and on your house, besides I don't know how long I'll be gone."

"I don't like it," Rafe grumbled. "It's dangerous and the trip up into those mountains is treacherous." George smiled at Rafe's concern. It was only a few months ago George felt the same way when Rafe insisted upon going back to Mexico to rescue his mother and sister from *don* Bernardo's *hacienda.*

"Bill wrote the passes are just starting to reopen after the winter. If I leave next week, I can be home by Easter."

Rafe knew his adopted father was a sure shot as well as smart and cautious. George had invented the GSW double-action pistol. Though George was fast and a sure shot, Rafe did not like the odds. Elizabethtown would be full of outlaws, drunkards, as well as claim jumpers.

A week after baby Bernardo was laid in the ground, George Summers loaded the small wagon and was ready to go. Rafe shook his hand and told him to telegraph if there was trouble. Josefina stood in the courtyard waving until he was out of sight and then turned to go into the house with tears streaming down her cheeks. Rafe wrapped his arm around her shoulders.

"Stubborn old fool. I begged him not to go, and then begged him to take you with him. He said I worry too much. Elizabethtown is a bad place," her voice trailed off.

"He'll be fine. He won't take any chances," Rafe assured his adopted mother. "If there's any trouble, Carlos and I will go immediately."

CHAPTER 6

George Summers' trip from Santa Fe to Elizabethtown was hard even though the warming spring temperatures had melted most of the snow from the main trail, if you could call the steep rocky pass a trail. Above the treeline, snow and ice clung to shadowed crevices where the sun could not reach. The going was hard and George was frustrated with the slow pace. It would have been easier without the wagon, but George was carrying guns, rifles, and plenty of supplies for his friend, Bill Moore.

A stage line ran in the summer from Santa Fe to Elizabethtown, after the snowmelt and spring rains ended and the mountain pass was clear. When George checked, the stage was not scheduled until after mid May. George knew Bill needed the guns and supplies now.

Along the trail George met up with riders coming out of the mountains. They were miners who had been stuck in the mountains for the winter. The scraggly looking men stopped and talked a bit about mining and about Elizabethtown.

"My claim dun played out," one old timer said. "Been like livin in icy hell for months now." He told George he was going back to Oklahoma where he had some kin. "I's hopin they'll take me in. I can still work a farm iffin I git some food in my belly."

George saw the hollow look around the old miner's eyes and his sunken cheeks. Pulling out his food sack from under the seat, he handed the old timer what was left of his daily ration. The old man's eyes widened and his lips curled in a grin showing several missing teeth.

"I thank yew kindly. Yew bess be careful," the old grizzly miner told him. "They's plenty of trouble up on that mountain."

George expected to make the trip from Santa Fe to the mining town in three days, and was frustrated it took longer to reach the summit over the town. He arrived in

Elizabethtown, New Mexico, late Wednesday afternoon. Stopping at the summit, he looked down on the town nestled in a split between two peaks. George knew the story of how Elizabethtown started. His friend, Bill Moore, investigated a piece of glittering rock a Ute Indian brought to the supply store at Fort Union. Recognizing it as gold, Bill told the Indian he would give him supplies, if he showed him where he found the rocks. The Ute took Bill to Baldy Mountain and showed him the spot. Bill was able to make a claim before gold fever spread quickly and soon the fledgling town was booming. Elizabethtown was named for Bill's daughter, Elizabeth, when the town was incorporated in 1867.

As George overlooked the town, he was surprised. It was a lot bigger than he guessed. He clicked the reins and started down the ridge into the town. Main Street was lined with buildings – a church, assay office, printer, land office, stores, livery, bank, doctor, and several boarding houses lined the street. Numerous saloons advertised cheap liquor, pool, and dancing. The main street was a muddy mess due to the spring thaw, so people mostly stayed along the wooden sidewalk. At three in the afternoon, the town was bustling with activity.

Things seemed peaceful in town. Tinny piano music floated from the saloons and women walked along the storefronts carrying brown paper wrapped items. Children ran along the wooden sidewalk laughing. The General Store was busy with several wagons parked in front. For all the talk of violence, it did not seemed too much different than many towns George had been in over the years.

George drove the wagon past several brothels, the Pearly Gates Saloon, and pulled up in front of the Mutz Hotel. He had wired ahead to Bill saying he was coming, but did not expect Bill to be in town. More likely he would stay in the hills protecting the mine until George found him. He dropped the horse's tether weight, jumped to the sidewalk, and walked into the hotel.

"May I help you?" the desk clerk asked.

"I need a room," George replied. "And a hot bath if

that's possible."

"That'll be three dollars for the room and half dollar for the bath," the clerk said crisply. "How many nights you staying?" The clerk swung the hotel registry around to face it toward George.

"Several. I'm not exactly sure, yet." George picked up the pen and signed his name.

"George Summers?" the clerk asked when he read his name. "You be Bill Moore's friend from Santa Fe."

"Yes."

"Bill said you was coming. I'll send my boy to his mine in the morning to let him know you got here. Room seven at the top of the stairs and to the right," the clerk said brightly handing George a key. "I'll get the hot water boiling and let you know when the bath is ready."

"Much obliged. I have a wagon out front. Can you have your boy take it to the livery?"

"You don't want to put it up at the livery or it won't be there in the morning. I have a barn in the back where my boy keeps an eye on things."

George pulled a few more dollars from his vest pocket and handed them to the desk clerk. "You run a good hotel," he said.

"Like I said, I'll let you know when the bath is hot."

Later after a hot bath and a change to clean clothes, George walked down the wooden plank sidewalk to the Miner's Restaurant. George had not been in a mining town since he spent some time in Magdalena in '56, when he was a much younger and less cautious man. Pushing in the wooden doors of the restaurant, the stench of manly body odors greeted his nose, not much helped by the smell of wood smoke.

Inside the restaurant, men sat at long wooden tables with benches on both sides. A rotund woman carried bowls of something and sat the bowls in front of several men to his left.

"What is this shit?" one man yelled at the woman after taking a sniff.

"Yew know it's bear stew, Freddy. That's all we've

got til the supply wagon comes over the mountain," the woman retorted giving Freddy a slap on his head. "Jes yew eat it an sum of them biscuits and shut yer trap."

"That bear? The same one Bert kilt last week?" Freddy asked. The woman huffed and walked away.

George took a seat near the end of the table. Two miners sat across from him.

"Yew ain't frum round here?" one said to him.

"No, I'm from Santa Fe," George said.

"Oh yew must be Bill's friend. He said yew's comin. I'm Paul and this here's Stoney."

"Glad to know you. Name of George Summers." George extended his hand and the men each shook it.

"How's the stew," George asked.

"Terrible, but it's hot and it's all they got. Biscuits ain't too bad."

"Bill's been awaitin yew comin. We saw him at his mine this mornin."

"The hotel clerk is sending a boy to tell him I've arrived."

The woman shoved a bowl in front of George and dropped a spoon on the table before she headed toward the other end. George took a spoonful of stew, expecting the worst. Surprisingly, he thought it was tolerable and the biscuits were soft and flaky.

After a few spoons of stew George said to the men, "Seems pretty quiet here. I expected a ruckus."

"Iffin it's a ruckus yew want, jes yew wait till later. Things will start kicking up bout midnight when the saloons close," Paul told him.

Paul, Stoney, and George ate the bear stew and finished the plate of biscuits and butter.

"You two have a claim?" George asked.

"Yeah, if yew can call it a claim. We've been working for dust for almost a year. Yer friend Bill has one of the best veins," Stoney said. For the next hour, Paul and Stoney bent George's ear about life in Elizabethtown. George was tired after the long days on the mountain trail and finally stood saying his goodbyes to Paul and Stoney.

"Probly see yew up on the mountain," Paul said. "We git by Bill's from time to time."

"Hope to see you then," George said. Walking back to the hotel, George lit a cigar and looked up at the night sky. It was clear and millions of stars twinkled in the inky blackness. He was hoping good weather held, so he would not get trapped here too long by a surprise spring snow which could close the pass.

The clerk was not at the front desk when George climbed the stairs to his room. Closing and locking the door behind him, George took off his boots and hung his jacket on the chair. He hung his holster and pistol on the bedpost near his head.

Climbing under the blanket, he laid his head back on the pillow and promptly fell asleep. Later, three sharp barks of a pistol woke George from his deep sleep. The gunshots were close by, out on the street, under the window of his room. Instinctively, he grabbed his gun out of its holster hanging on the bedpost. He moved cautiously to the window and peeked out. The bluish light from the moon and dimly lit lampposts showed three men on horseback with guns drawn in the street below. On the street a man struggled to get up.

"Tol yew to sell," a voice below growled. George's stomach churned wondering whether the man lying on the street was his friend Bill. George knew he could easily kill the three men on the horses from his vantage point, however held back from taking matters into his own hands.

The man on the dirt grumbled something and raised a pistol at the horsemen. Two more shots rang and the man on the ground slumped dead. The three horsemen turned and rode hard out of town.

George watched from his window. Only after the horsemen were gone did lights start to peek from windows and several men moved out of the shadows and into the street. One knelt by the dead miner. "Jim Evans," he called to another man.

"Damn. He tol me Clay had threatened him," another said. George sighed in relief. The body was not his friend,

Bill Moore. He now understood why Bill was worried.

A plump man with a rifle walked toward the scene. "Alright, stand back," he barked. George guessed he was the sheriff. The man knelt and checked the dead man and then stood up.

"Anybody witness this killing?" he asked. The men in the street hung their heads and did not answer at first. Finally one man piped up, "Yew knows who dun this sheriff. It's Allison and his gang. They wanted Jim's claim and he wouldn't sell."

"Maybe and maybe not," the sheriff replied. "Gotta have a witness to a killing."

"Clay Allison don't leave no witnesses," another man said, "leastwise, no live ones."

"You men get this body off the street and then go on home," the sheriff barked and then walked away.

Standing in the window, George guessed it was sometime shortly before midnight because the Pay Dirt Saloon across the street was still open. The men below him on the street grumbled and did the sheriff's bidding, picked up the body, and carried it off. He watched as they slowly carried the body down the street. The lights burning in the windows across the street were extinguished in all except the saloon. George remembered Paul's remarks at dinner saying the ruckus would start around midnight when the saloons closed.

George shivered standing near the window. Even though the spring sun was warm during the day, at night the temperature still fell below freezing. Turning, George put his pistol in the holster and crawled back under the blanket. He stared up at the ceiling in the dark, his mind churning with questions, thinking about the scene in the street.

George thought the sheriff seemed less than concerned about the dead prospector. Why was there no real law in Elizabethtown? Did Clay Allison control the sheriff? How did the outlaws pick who to target? George knew the dead miner's claim would belong to the first person to file a new claim on it in the morning – claim jumpers. George hoped the GSW pistols and rifles he brought would be enough to protect Bill's claim.

From what George saw of the booming town when he arrived in the afternoon, it looked prosperous and earlier no one seem scared to be in town or out on the streets. One thing he noticed right away, most of the miners were not gun hands. Some carried a pistol tucked behind their belts, although most of them were unarmed. They would be easy pickings for the Allison gang.

George heard a few shouts from the street after the saloon closed, but no more gunplay. Finally he drifted off to sleep. When the sun peeked over the eastern peak of the mountain, George stretched in bed. After a week of sleeping in the back of the wagon, the soft bed was a pleasant comfort for his old body.

CHAPTER 7

Dressing, George wrapped his gunbelt around his waist before he walked down the hotel stairs. The clerk looked up and greeted him, "Good morning Mr. Summers. I sent Davey early this morning to tell Bill you arrived. He's not back yet."

"Much obliged. I'll be at the restaurant having breakfast if Bill comes looking for me."

"Yes sir, I'll be sure to tell him."

Walking out of the Mutz Hotel, George looked at the street where the miner died last night. Only a dark spot in the mud showed the spot where he died. People were starting their day and no one seemed concerned about the killing. George walked to the restaurant and swung open the door. The smell of hickory bacon filled the tented restaurant with a welcoming aroma. A few wary eyes darted his way and then the owner's of the eyes resumed their meal.

George sat at one of the long tables. Like last night, only one meal was being served – bacon and biscuits. Mounds of both were heaped on large platters on the tables. The large rotund woman stopped near him and asked, "Coffee?"

"Yes, please," George replied.

He helped himself to a plate and buttered two biscuits. He picked up a jar of jam and spread some on the biscuits and grabbed several strips of thick bacon from the platter. Breakfast was much better than the bear stew served last night. The bacon was salty and the biscuits soft and tender.

George's back was to the door and he jumped when a hand grabbed his shoulder.

"Hello you old coot," a familiar voice said. Bill Moore hurried into town after young Davey Lawson brought him the news that George had arrived yesterday. He had been expecting him for several days.

George stood and shook Bill's hand and Bill sat down beside him. George noticed dark circles under Bill's eyes and leanness in his face making him look older. Bill motioned the waitress and she filled his cup with coffee and filled George's up to the top.

"Heard there was a killing in town last night," Bill said between bites.

"Saw it out of my window," George responded.

"Jim Evans. He had a claim not far from me," Bill said. "Damn law is doing nothing bout the claim jumping. Jim was a good man."

Bill ate and told George about the Allison gang killing the owner of the Humbug Mine as he headed to town for supplies and the owner of the Pine Gulch Mine was killed in a gunfight behind the Rich Vein Saloon. In each case, Allison or one of his men ended up with the legal claim to the mine.

"What about the sheriff?" George asked.

"Sheriff Robertson is an older man, around fifty-five and he has a young deputy. Together they are not much of a law outfit, but they satisfy the territory's requirement for having a peace officer in town. The true law in Elizabethtown is Clay Allison and his vigilantes, taking advantage of the fast growing town, and taking the best claims for free. I think maybe the sheriff is taking payoffs from Clay."

After breakfast, Bill took George on a tour of Elizabethtown. Bill said the town was nicknamed E-town by the locals. Except for the Mutz Hotel and the bank, which were built with stone, the rest of the buildings were constructed of rough cut lumber. The bank and hotel were two stories, while the rest were low buildings. A small church stood on the left side with a cross on top of a short steeple. "There are about one hundred buildings and around six thousand people in E-town," Bill told George proudly showing off the town.

"Six thousand!" George exclaimed.

"Most are up in the hills working claims and not in town," Bill explained.

The early morning activity in the town was mostly quiet, except for shopkeepers opening their stores. George noticed a few Chinese men, seeming out of place, walking down the road with sacks thrown over their shoulders and asked Bill about them.

"Some poor Chinese are making their way here looking for work in the mines," Bill told George. "The Indians don't want anything to do with mines and resent the mining activity in the mountains they consider sacred. There have been a few raids by the Utes, but for the most part Indians just stay away."

"How about your mine? Tell me about it," George asked.

"Call it the Mystic Lode. I scouted these hills with an old Ute Indian when I was in the Army. Did a little digging and I was the first to strike gold back then. I used to have three claims. I sold two to a friend so I could concentrate on Mystic. I know I'm sitting on a big strike. I've already found plenty of nuggets to prove it to myself."

"I ate dinner with two miners last night who said you had a good claim, Paul and Stoney."

"They are my friends. Otherwise I try to keep a low head," Bill said. "It don't help to go busting your lips about finding gold in these hills, unless you got the gun power to back it up. By the way, where are the rifles?"

"They're in the wagon behind the hotel. The clerk said he would have the wagon watched, still I'll feel mighty relieved when we get them to your mine," George said.

George and Bill turned and headed back toward the Mutz Hotel. Some of the larger saloons were starting to open, even though it was not even ten in the morning.

"Kinda early to be opening a saloon," George mentioned.

"Some of the mines work shifts and the night shift will be getting to town soon." Bill told him. They finished touring Elizabethtown and were almost back to the hotel when a middle-aged man with a round belly approached. A dingy star was pinned to the pocket of his vest.

"Howdy Sheriff," Bill greeted him cordially.

"Hey Bill," the sheriff replied and stopped.

"George, this here is Sheriff Danny Robertson."

"George Summers. Glad to meet you sheriff." George extended his hand.

"Just got back from Spanish Bar Mine," the sheriff said. "Got word this morning, Ramon Matus was shot and his shack burned. Henry rode by there yesterday and found Ramon kilt and rode into town to tell me."

"Heard Jim Evans was killed here in town. Do you know who did it?" Bill asked, although everyone knew who was to blame.

"Naw, it happened when he came out of the saloon late last night. Nobody saw it happen."

"My friend George here, heard it and saw the riders shoot him dead before they rode off. He was watching from his room up there in the hotel."

Sheriff Danny Robertson raised an eyebrow. "That right mister, you seen who dun it?"

"Well not exactly Sheriff. It was three riders and I couldn't see their faces in the moonlight," George told him.

"Nobody never sees nothing around here," the sheriff grumbled.

"That's the third mine owner killed this week Danny and you know Clay's gang is behind it. You best get help from Santa Fe," Bill told the sheriff.

"I can handle it Bill, don't you worry none," the sheriff said. "Staying in town long?" the sheriff asked looking at George.

"A few days, then I'll head back to Santa Fe. I could take a message to the U.S. Marshal there to send you some help," George offered.

"Now that's a mighty fine offer, but I can take care of E-town myself." The sheriff tipped his hat and walked off.

"Shit, he won't do nothing. Everyone thinks he's in with the killers. That's why I wired you. My mine is one of the biggest and richest here. Clay hasn't hassled me yet because I have a voice in town, but I worry it's only a matter of time before they come after me." George heard bitterness in Bill's voice and saw worry in his eyes.

"So you think Clay Allison is behind all the killings?" George asked.

"Seems like. When one of the miners is killed, a new claim is filed and one of his vigilantes is suddenly in business. Clay doesn't bother with played out mines or newcomers until they make a strike. I heard some of the newcomers pay him a blood money percentage for protection. Clay calls his gang, vigilantes. Swears he's protecting the town and mines. Damn, he's just a vicious claim jumper from Texas. You saw some of his work last night first hand."

"Yes, they made sure the man was dead; shot him dead after he was down," George recalled with gritted teeth.

Arriving at the hotel, George stepped up to the desk clerk and asked about his wagon. "Can you have your boy hitch up the team and pull it around to the front?" he asked.

"You be leaving today, Mr. Summers?" the clerk asked.

"Yep," Bill replied. "He'll be staying with me out at the mine."

George went upstairs to pack his satchel and returned downstairs to wait for the wagon. Shortly, the wagon and team pulled up in front of the hotel. George tipped the young boy fifty cents and checked the cargo. "Seems to have made it through the night," he told Bill.

"I'll drive," Bill said climbing up on the seat and picking up the reins. George climbed into the seat next to him and Bill started the team. On the way to the mine they talked about old times. Bill asked George about his family. He never met Josefina or the girls and listened as George told him about meeting a young Mexican boy who saved his life in the Texas desert.

"Rafe is like a son to me now," George told him. "Where are Mary and Elizabeth? Are they here with you?"

Bill hung his head a bit. "Mary died of the fever two years ago. After that I sent Elizabeth to St. Louis to a school back there where she'll be safe. She's supposed to come home for the summer, but . . . well I hope things quiet down here."

George knew Bill adored both his wife and daughter. Mary was dead and Elizabeth gone and George paused trying to think what to say. "I bet she's darn pretty. She'd be ten or eleven?"

"Twelve," Bill grinned. "I got a picture back at the shack I'll show you."

Bill navigated a narrow trail around Baldy Mountain. When they arrived at the Mystic Lode Mine, located on the west side, Bill pulled the wagon in front of a wooden plank shack.

"Home sweet home," Bill laughed. The shack was made of rough sawn wood, looked sturdy, and the roof was layered in overlapping wood planks. A chimney poked up on the left side. George and Bill unpacked the GSW weapons from the wagon and carried them inside the shack.

Bill whistled as he handled one of the rifles. "They sure are beauties."

"I've made a lot of improvements over the past years. They shoot with a lot less recoil," George told him.

Bill and George unpacked the provisions from the wagon and Bill thanked George for thinking to bring supplies. "It's been a long winter and the regular supply train doesn't start hauling until May. A man gets mighty tired of beans and salt pork."

Bill unhitched the horses and led them to a small corral on the side of the shack. "Let's go see the mine," he said proudly.

Bill took a torch and led George to the tunnel. Wooden timbers held up the mine's main tunnel opening. As they entered the darkened tunnel, George stumbled in the dim light of the torch's glow, suddenly almost blind in the dark.

"Here's where the first vein ended," Bill shone the torch on the mine's wall. "And there's where we found a richer vein." Bill played the torch along the wall and George saw the cutting and evidence of digging. He followed Bill and the torch, his eyes getting accustomed to the dark. "We've pretty much played this vein out and are tunneling deeper looking for another," Bill pointed as they followed the tunnel.

Further into the tunnel they reached four men drilling holes with steel hand drills. One man held onto the drill, while the other pounded it with a heavy hammer. Before every hammer blow, they rotated the hand drill. Their work was precise and monotonous. The banging of the heavy hammers vibrated the tunnel and rang in George's ears.

"When they get the holes deep enough, they stuff a stick of dynamite into it with a long fuse. They do eight holes at a time and then will blast," Bill explained the process.

"Howdy boss," one of the men said to Bill. The others stopped their hammering and stretched their backs.

"This is George Summers from Santa Fe," Bill introduced him to Lefty, Mike, Jake, and Sam. "He's brought the guns we need."

"Howdy George," one of the men stuck out his dusty glove and George shook it. The others did the same. "We's mighty glad you come with the guns."

"How's it going Lefty?" Bill asked.

"Almost ready to blast," Lefty replied. "You best be getting outta here."

"Come on, we better head back." Bill led George back out of the mine. The bright sunlight was a welcome sight and George thought mining was not for him. Shortly, the rest of the men came out of the mine and crouching behind large boulders they waited for the blast.

"We're trying to find the next vein. Mike, my foreman, knows how to find them and I trust him," Bill said.

"Blooooie!" The explosion sent dust and some debris out of the mouth of the tunnel. The four miners covered their noses with a bandana and headed back in.

"So, you think you'll find another vein?" George asked.

"Yep, the first three were rich, but short. Everybody

thinks my claim is the richest around, still if we don't strike another vein this year, I may have to call it quits. I've had a good run of luck, so I'm happy either way."

"While we hid behind those boulders, I saw a rider up on that knoll. Looked like he was spying on us," George told Bill pointing to a ridge east of the mine.

"Yeah, I saw him too. As long as people think I have the richest claim, I'll be a target like those others who were killed. Sure am glad you brought those guns."

Later that night they all congregated in the cabin while Mike cooked up venison and potatoes, with green beans and peaches George brought. While Mike was cooking, George showed the men the GSW rifles and pistols. He explained about the double-action, where the gun would repeat firing without thumbing the hammer. George brought a dozen rifles and eight pistols, with plenty of ammunition.

The five miners ate like they were starving and talked excitedly through dinner about the new vein, the guns, and the food. George noticed Bill's face looked less tired than this morning. During the meal Bill told the men about the recent killings, but even bad news could not dampen their spirits.

"That's the best meal we've had in months," Lefty said. "We sure are glad you come, Mr. Summers."

"Call me George."

After dinner Bill told the men, "I want round the clock guard duty. We'll take turns in four hour shifts. Take some of those rifles to the shaft."

"Sure thing boss," Jake said and the others nodded in agreement.

When the men opened the door, a cold wind blew in. "We might be in for a storm," Bill said. "The weather can be pretty unpredictable this time of year. I'll go get some more wood."

Bill stoked the fire before he and George settled down for some sleep. "You take that cot over there," Bill said.

Silently, George said a prayer before he turned away from the fire and fell asleep. He did not hear Bill get up and leave in the middle of the night to take his turn at guard duty.

CHAPTER 8

A week after George left for Elizabethtown, Rafe, Lolo, and Lizzy attended the Palm Sunday Pageant at the San Miguel Catholic Church with Carlos. The Summers' family usually went to the diocese in Tesuque, which was closer to the Summers' ranch, however Carlos asked them to join him at the bigger church in Santa Fe. The girls were chatting excitedly, riding in the back of the buggy, about boys and fussing about their dresses. Carlos drove the buggy, while Rafe rode Rayo.

Carlos traveled the longer ride to Santa Fe to the San Miguel Mission Church, because it reminded him of the church in Madrid, Spain, where he studied at the Seminary for several years. His education was in Latin and Mathematics, and the years at the Seminary instilled in him a sincere faith. Last week he told Rafe, he finally found a teaching position at the San Miguel Catholic Diocese School starting next fall. "I'll still be able to work at the foundry and with your horses on the weekends," he told Rafe.

As Rafe rode beside the buggy, he saw small wildflowers beginning to pop up from the reddish-brown earth. Spring was beginning to warm the earth and new life was coming just in time for Easter. It was his sixth spring in Santa Fe and he now considered this his home. Whatever memories he might have of his childhood in Mexico were best forgotten now that his mother and sister were living here.

At the pageant, Rafe was surprised to see Carlos talking to a pretty girl and they strolled around the pageant displays, her arm linked in his. Lolo and Lizzy talked with some young teen boys. Lolo was sixteen and attracting a circle of young admirers, obviously attentive to her. Rafe thought she was getting more beautiful each day. When they arrived home, the girls jumped from the buggy and ran into the house, while Carlos and Rafe drove the buggy to the barn.

While they brushed and bedded down the horses Rafe said, "Carlos, did you notice Lolo was surrounded by boys at the pageant?"

"Uh, oh, I didn't see," he said and blushed.

"Yes, you were busy with the pretty girl in the green dress."

"Her name is Bibiana de Soto. I met her several months ago . . . our ancestors came to New Mexico with Diego de Vargas in the 1690s to reconquer the territory for the King of Spain. She wants me to attend an Easter fiesta and spend time with her family next weekend," Carlos said, his eyes beaming at Rafe.

"What! I thought you were afraid of girls?" Rafe questioned him putting a shocked look on his face to tease his friend.

"Why are you saying that? I'm not like you Rafe. You get them and drop them like hot tortillas," Carlos replied seriously.

"No I don't. You know I only loved one, only Chiwiwi," Rafe retorted mildly annoyed.

"What about the one you picked up at El Coyote Cantina, and Susan in Albuquerque, and that redhead named Sylvia, and María Cristina," Carlos named them off watching Rafe's eyes widen, before Rafe hung his head and looked down.

"Basta!" Rafe told his friend to stop it. "Tell me about the lucky girl?" Rafe asked as he put his arm around Carlos' shoulder.

"No I won't, *pendejo*. You will take her away from me."

"Amigo, you have me wrong. I would never do that. Well, I will if she's beautiful." Rafe quipped back at his friend with a wicked grin spreading a broad smile framing straight white teeth on his good-looking tan face. Carlos knew girls in Santa Fe considered Rafe handsome.

"Baboso," Carlos ruefully retorted calling Rafe a drooling idiot.

"So, where did you meet this lucky *señorita?"* Rafe

asked.

"I met her last month when we were helping Padre Valentino," he said.

"You devil, you enticed her into a dark corner and snuck a kiss?" Rafe teased his best friend.

"No! Of course not," Carlos retorted.

"When her direct ancestors came with de Vargas, they came here to Santa Fe. My ancestors settled south in Los Lunas, Belen, and Socorro. During the reconquest, splinters of families settled all over New Mexico and part of her family settled in Los Lunas. Bibiana's family came often to Los Lunas to visit relatives when she was younger. We met there at church festivals and she . . . she recognized me." Carlos was stuttering a bit trying to tell Rafe how he and Bibiana knew each other.

"And you didn't recognize her?" Rafe asked.

"No, not at first. She is so pretty now. We were just children then."

"And she thinks you are a handsome *caballero?*"

Carlos looked away for a moment touching the long scar down his cheek, then looked back at Rafe. "You know the years after my family lost our land grant have been difficult and . . . I . . . she does not know about Benicío. She does not know I killed him."

Rafe knew about the years Carlos followed his murderous brother, Benicío, and was there when Carlos killed him. He killed Benicío for shooting and killing Chiwiwi. It was a day neither would ever forget.

"She will understand what you did was right. So, are you going to marry the beautiful *señorita?*" Rafe asked changing the subject and lightening the mood.

"*Eh pendejo,* we have not started any formal courting arrangement, besides I don't have an official job yet," Carlos explained. "Her father probably will not allow any courting before I can provide for her. He is very proper and Bibiana is his oldest daughter."

"Those ways are dying," Rafe told him. "Besides you will start teaching in the fall and you work here at the foundry."

"No amigo, the old ways do not die easily. She is *criollo* and studied in Madrid, Spain, and the family has a solid land grant. Perhaps her father will not even allow me to court her."

Rafe knew the old Spanish *casta* system was still alive and well even now in 1871, but he also knew things were changing quickly in New Mexico. It was a territory of the United States now – they were Americans, not Spaniards.

"You said she wanted to introduce you to her family next weekend at the Easter fiesta. She sounds interested in you," Rafe said.

"Yes . . . she is so beautiful, I will probably trip over my feet and make myself a fool."

"Perhaps I can go with you to give you courage and keep you out of trouble," Rafe suggested.

"I will not introduce her to you," Carlos pointed a finger at his friend. "You . . . you . . . girls like you," Carlos cajoled Rafe and they both chuckled.

"Me? I'm not a *caballero*, I'm a *peón*. Her father would never allow it," Rafe reminded Carlos of his social status and his upbringing as a poor peasant. By the Spanish social *casta* system he would always truly be a *peón*, a *mestizo*, one of mixed Spanish and Indian blood. Only here in the United States could he be a landowner and a rancher of status.

"Yes, I guess I shouldn't worry. Bibiana will have nothing to do with a *peón* like you," Carlos added with a belly laugh.

"So we will go to the fiesta, pretending to be two *caballeros* of good standing, and you will sweep the girl of your dreams off her feet," Rafe said.

"Yes, and you will not be charming," Carlos told his friend with an emphasis on the word not.

Chapter 9

When George woke in the morning there was a deep chill in the shack at the Mystic Lode Mine. Bill was gone, so George stoked up the fire and started some coffee. Looking out the window, the sky was gray and heavy, and snow covered everything in a blanket of white.

George's heart sank a bit. It was Thursday morning and his hope to spend only a few days in Elizabethtown before heading back to Santa Fe was quickly evaporating. If snow closed the pass, he would be stuck here.

A little while later, Bill opened the door and snow with a cold wind blew in with him. Shaking his hat and coat Bill said, "Winter's not done with us yet. Coffee ready?"

"Coffee should be ready," he said trying to sound cheerful.

"Good. I could use some to warm up."

"The boys blasted some pretty good rock yesterday. Look, I sat a couple of the pieces there on the table."

George looked at the rock and could not tell if it was good or not. Bill laughed and picked up a rock and showed George a spidery shiny vein in the pinkish rock.

"We're getting closer to the lode," Bill said excitedly. "The men are setting more charges before they come for breakfast. Bill started a pan of bacon cooking and chopped potatoes and onions in another pan.

Suddenly the wooden shack rattled from the blast and the pans hanging on the wall clattered. Bill never twitched as the blast went off, but George almost jumped out of his chair.

"I guess you get used to the blasting," George said chuckling.

"We usually get eight charges set a day," Bill replied.

After the blast, the men came into the shack dusting snow off their heavy coats. "Still snowing hard," Lefty said. "Reminds me of that spring dump we got three years ago cutting us off fer most a month."

George tried hard not to react to the news, hoping Lefty was wrong. Mike poured coffee for the men and asked George if he wanted more. George noticed the men acted as equals, and each pulled their share of the load, including cooking and helping. It seemed more like a family of brothers, than a boss and his men.

It snowed hard for the rest of the day, through the night, and into the next morning. At least two feet of snow lay on the ground around the mine. The men continued their work and the blasting continued regardless of the foul weather. When George asked Bill about it, Bill said, "The temperature inside the mine is almost constant, summer and winter. The mountain insulates the rock. We can work in any weather; we just can't always get off this mountain."

The snow ended late Friday afternoon, yet the wind continued to howl through the mountain pass where the Mystic Lode Mine lay covered in white. Bill said they were lucky the snow was wet, not drifting in the wind. He told George of a time several years ago when snow drifts covered most of the shack and the men were stuck inside for two days.

Bill and the miners continued their work schedule of digging and blasting. George no longer jumped when the blast suddenly jolted the house. Trying to keep busy, George followed Bill into the dark mine. Borrowing some work clothes, he helped load the small wagon with rocks and pull it out to the rock pile outside. The work was brutal and George's back ached and his shoulders sagged after just a few hours. He marveled at the miner's fitness as they slung the heavy hammers and lifted rocks for countless hours each day.

At night they talked and laughed and George found he liked them all. Lefty was from Missouri. He met Bill in the Army, where Bill was his captain. When they left the Army, Lefty came with Bill to look for gold and they worked as a team until they struck the first vein. Mike was the head miner, a man comfortable with using explosives. He oversaw the drilling and placement of the dynamite. George noticed he was a very cautious and precise man. If the drill hole was not perfect, he would have the men start a new one. Jake was small and wiry and could outwork the others lifting rocks. He was quiet and did more listening than talking. The fourth man, Sam, was a local. He grew up in these hills and although George did not ask, he looked part Indian. Besides working in the mine, Sam set snares and traps and kept the men in fresh meat.

Chapter 10

It was Good Friday in Santa Fe and Rafe knew Josefina had not received any word from George. He should have sent a telegram if he was delayed, or better yet, headed home. The creases on his adopted mother's forehead told Rafe she was very worried.

He found her in the yard tending her budding roses. When she heard him, she rose and wrapped her arms around his shoulders. She tried hard not to fall into his chest and sob. She felt in her soul something was wrong.

"He said he'd be home by Sunday," Rafe told her. "He's probably on his way. Quit worrying and show me your roses. I see they are starting to bud now that the weather is warming."

The next day, Rafe and Carlos were working on a stamping machine in the foundry. "George should be home by now," Carlos said calmly with worry in his voice.

"Yes. Josefina is worried. It's not like George. He always sends her a telegram and lets her know when he will be home," Rafe replied. Rafe was trying not to worry, but the memory of the day he found George in the Texas desert, almost dead from an Indian's arrow, was still clear in his mind. If Rafe had not found him that day, George would be dead, and Rafe would not be in Santa Fe. His entire life would be different.

"If he doesn't show up tomorrow, I'll send a telegram on Monday to the hotel and see if we can reach him." Carlos looked relieved. Tonight was the Easter fiesta at Bibiana's and he was already nervous.

"Are you ready to be grand at the fiesta tonight?" Rafe teased his best friend and Carlos blushed.

"I'm just hoping I don't fall on my face or step on her toes when we dance," Carlos replied.

Late in the afternoon, Rafe and Carlos rode to Bibiana's family *hacienda*. Carlos looked dashing in the *traje,* the suit made for him in San Marcial before their trip to

Mexico last fall to rescue Celiá and Maria. Rafe wore the *caballero traje* he took from *don* Bernardo's house on that same trip. Sitting on silver studded saddles, they both looked like prosperous *caballeros,* Spanish gentlemen, Rafe on Rayo and Carlos on the black stallion, Santiago.

Riding to Bibiana's, Rafe began to fret. When they entered the archway to the *hacienda,* Rafe's stomach was turning in knots. "Carlos, I don't like this posing as a *caballero.* You said it yourself, I'm just a *peón.*" Rafe was *mestizo,* a Mexican from mixed blood, and not acceptable in high Spanish social circles. "I shouldn't have come."

"It's too late now, amigo. We're here. You may not be a *caballero,* but you have *machismo.* You are a tough man. Just stick your nose up in the air and act like you own the world," Carlos told him.

They were met by two *vaqueros,* who took their horses and directed them to enter the courtyard surrounded by a high wall with the main house on the far end. Music came out from a small orchestra located under the shade of a large cottonwood tree to the left of the courtyard.

"Bienvenidos a mi casa Carlos," Bibiana greeted them and Carlos bowed slightly and kissed her extended gloved hand.

"Bibiana, I wish to introduce to you *mi amigo,* Rafael Ortega de Estrada."

"Gusto en conocerte," Bibiana said it was nice to meet him.

"Igualmente, señorita," Rafe returned the customary greeting before he bowed and kissed her gloved hand.

Bibiana linked one arm with each of them on either side of her and led them to where her father and mother gathered with guests. Rafe scanned the courtyard and saw a group of young men standing proudly dressed in their best *trajes.* Even the older men wore their splendid *trajes,* with paunchy bellies straining under the sash, betraying their easy life and eating habits. He squared his shoulders as he and Carlos walked beside Bibiana.

Bibiana introduced Carlos to her mother and father, *don* Pedro and *doña* Agustina de Soto. *"Señor, soy Carlos Zuniga de Armijo de Los Lunas de Nuevo México,"* Carlos made his introduction in the formal and customary way. He continued to give his family's social credits, explaining his origins in both Spain and Los Lunas. He reminded them of fiestas in Los Lunas, where they may have met when he was a child, and of his parents.

While Carlos talked, Rafe panicked. He had no social linage to recite upon introduction. He was not a *caballero* as were Carlos and the others. He was *mestizo* and would not be accepted in traditional Spanish social circles, even in Santa Fe.

When Carlos finished, he bowed and kissed *doña* Agustina's gloved hand. "Where did you get such an unusual scar?" *doña* Agustina asked referring to the scar etched in Carlos' face from the corner of his eye to the tip of his lip.

"A most unfortunate incident in Madrid, *señora*. I was protecting the honor of a young woman from a *hombre malo* when I took the tip of his sword, however I assure you I protected the woman's honor," Carlos lied with a smooth elegance. Rafe gave Carlos a quick glance, surprised by the lie. Rafe was there the day Carlos' brother, Benicío, gave him the scar on the streets of El Paso.

Carlos then introduced Rafe. "May I present Rafael Ortega de Estrada, recently arrived in Santa Fe from Torreón to breed Appaloosas and other fine Mexican breeds. The *hacienda* in Torreón is known around Mexico for the best blooded horses." Astonished at Carlos' words, Rafe quickly bowed formally to Bibiana's parents. Hopefully they would not notice the sweat popping out on the bridge of his nose and forehead.

"*Sus caballos son sementales finos,*" *don* Pedro complimented Rafe on the fine stallions. "I would like to see them closer, perhaps later."

Doña Agustina was about to ask more questions, when they were interrupted with more guests arriving. Bibiana took Carlos and Rafe by an arm and led them off. A small orchestra played music and a woman in a long red dress danced. Across the courtyard a group of young *grandees,* sons of Santa Fe's aristocrats, stood together. Long tables were set on one side of the courtyard heaped with large platters of food. The fiesta reminded Rafe of ones *doña* Carmela gave at the Reyes' *hacienda* in Torreón. When Rafe was a child, he would climb a tree and watch the ladies in fancy dresses swirl to music with the men in their elaborate suits.

Bibiana led them to the long tables of food and excused herself. As she walked away toward the entrance to the courtyard Carlos looked dejected. "She'll be back," Rafe said. A servant offered each of them a drink and a plate. Rafe took several pieces of meat and pieces of fruit, while Carlos set his plate back on the table and turned away.

"Why the long face," Rafe chided him. "You should pretend to be less available. I hear girls like that."

"She is so beautiful and I . . ."

"You are a great liar," Rafe finished his sentence. "You made up the most elegant lie to *doña* Agustina about your scar and made me a *caballero.*"

"Here you can be whatever they believe you are," Carlos replied.

"You told them I came from a *hacienda* in Mexico. What if someone finds out I'm a *peón?*"

"Mexico is a big country. Don't worry," Carlos grinned.

Rafe and Carlos stood at the far end of the courtyard. Bibiana, along with her sister, was performing her hostess duties escorting newly arriving guests to be greeted by her parents.

It was more than an hour later when Rafe saw Bibiana approaching them with a young woman in a red and black gown. Their arms were linked and their gowns swished to the beat of the orchestra.

"Carlos and Rafael, this is my *prima,* Ana Teresa de Soto from California," she introduced her cousin.

"A su servicio," Carlos said, bowed, and kissed her lace-gloved hand. Ana Teresa was dressed in a lacy red silk dress trimmed in black with a black lace shawl around her shoulders.

"Igualmente, señorita," Rafe bowed formally and said he

was also at her service. His knees shook a bit as he bowed and kissed her hand and when he rose, his eyes met hers – they glinted a soft golden brown. He did not release her hand as a sharp pang shot through his heart right down to his groin. Just then the orchestra began playing music for the Fandango dance.

"Do you dance *señor?"* Ana Teresa asked Rafe.

"Yes," he responded and gave her his right elbow turning her toward the dance floor.

Rafe and Ana Teresa put their hands up above their heads looking into each other's eyes, before they began the dance. The Fandango started with a slow tempo, gradually increasing into a quick rhythm. They snapped their fingers and clicked their heels while they circled each other, never taking their eyes away. Ana Teresa clicked the heels of her shoes with the rhythm.

His adopted mother, Josefina, had taught Rafe to dance, explaining to him it was a vital part of New Mexican culture and acceptance into society. She told him the Fandango was danced like a chase, where boy sees girl, girl snubs boy, girl chases boy, and then runs away. Thankfully, Rafe knew the dance well and noticed Ana Teresa responded to him.

With the Fandango completed, the orchestra started the Bolero. Rafe took Ana Teresa at arm's length and began the dance. In the Bolero' slow tempo, the partners never turn, facing each other while taking slow steps forward and then long sideway steps. Rafe and Ana Teresa locked eyes during the dance.

While they danced, Rafe felt lost in the golden glow of her eyes and wondered if she felt the same. Not since Chiwiwi, had feelings sparked in him and it confused him. He believed no one could ever take the place of his beloved Chiwiwi in his heart, now he was not sure.

After the dance she walked to a quiet spot in the gardens and Rafe followed. She asked him to get drinks for them. Returning with two cups of punch, he asked her about California. Ana Teresa felt a calm and ease with Rafe, although she was not sure why. He was not arrogant or aloof, like the other young *grandees* of Santa Fe.

"My family had a rancho near Rancho Simi, just north of Los Angeles. It was taken by lawyers. My father could not produce the original Spanish land grant documents awarded by the King," she explained. "We were forced to leave the rancho, everything we owned, and I came here to live with my uncle and his family."

"*Lo siento,*" Rafe said he was sorry. "It is so with many families here in New Mexico."

"*Gracias,* my family is lucky, because we have family here in Santa Fe. Many families in California lost their land and have nowhere to go. Some are ending up working their own land, now owned by gringos." Ana Teresa had told no one in Santa Fe about her status, which was precarious at best. When she met other *caballeros,* she pretended to be on holiday visiting her aunt and uncle's family. Rafe's quiet manner and obvious empathy with her plight made her feel comfortable with him.

"So, if you now live here in Santa Fe, I am the lucky one," Rafe told her looking into her golden eyes. Blushing, she quickly fluttered her fan and turned her head away.

"Tell me about yourself," she said still hiding part of her face behind her fan. Rafe steeled himself knowing the question was coming, remembering what Carlos told him. "You can be whatever they believe you are."

"I was born in Mexico and learned to breed horses at the *hacienda.* I moved to Santa Fe and I have a horse breeding business. It is small and just starting to grow. Someday I will breed the best horses in New Mexico."

"I love to ride. Perhaps you can take me riding one day," she said to him.

"I would be delighted to take you riding," Rafe responded and bowed slightly to her.

"There you are," Bibiana called to her cousin. "We have been looking all over for you two. Come, they are starting the games."

During the evening both girls were commandeered by several other young *caballeros* to dance and talk. Rafe watched Ana Teresa dance with several *grandees,* who he was sure were part of the Spanish aristocrat society of Santa Fe. She dazzled all of them in her red and black dress and black lace *mantilla*.

Riding home after the fiesta, both Rafe and Carlos were lost in their separate thoughts – Carlos was thinking about Bibiana and Rafe was thinking of Ana Teresa. Though customs were changing, the old ways did not die easily. If Ana Teresa was *criollo*, Rafe doubted she or her father would consent to a courtship. He was *mestizo*. It would never be allowed, even in 1871.

"Tell me more about Carlos," Ana Teresa said to Bibiana after the fiesta ended and most of the guests were saying goodbye to Bibiana's parents. Bibiana told her a special man named Carlos was invited and she knew Bibiana was very interested. "I think he's very handsome, except for the scar," Ana Teresa added.

"I think it makes him look daring, don't you?" Bibiana giggled with her cousin.

"How did he get it?"

"He told me he was saving a young woman's honor in Madrid. Don't you think that sounds so romantic?"

"Yes. I wish someone would defend my honor," Ana Teresa said and laughed.

"Perhaps Rafael would. Carlos said he's very good with a gun. I saw him following you around like a puppy at the fiesta."

"*Estás loca,*" Ana Teresa told her she was crazy, but remembered seeing Rafael often watching her during the evening.

"No, Rafael was taken with you. I could see it in his eyes," Bibiana reassured her.

"Well, he is handsome and was a good dancer, better than Diego or Frederico, and his manners were impeccable, but there are many *caballeros* here in Santa Fe, Bibiana. You know it is very important for me to marry well, now that my family has lost our wealth. I will not have a large dowry like you," Ana Teresa said.

CHAPTER 11

After Sunday Mass of the Resurrection, the Easter afternoon meal was quiet and subdued at the Summers' home. George had not returned and no telegram would be delivered on Easter Sunday. A deep worry line creased Josefina's forehead.

Lolo and Lizzy played with Antonio and Alicia after dinner. Celiá helped Juanita clear the table and María ate little and went to her room. After dinner, Rafe stopped Josefina and held her gently by her shoulders.

"I'll ride to town in the morning and send a telegram to the hotel and to the sheriff. We should know something by tomorrow afternoon," he told her. "Try not to worry."

"I can't help it. I know something has happened to him," she replied.

After breakfast on Monday, Rafe rode into Santa Fe to the telegraph office. He sent two telegrams – one to the Mutz Hotel and another to the Sheriff in Elizabethtown. He decided to hang around town and wait for a reply, hoping it would be good news.

To pass some time, he stopped at the saddle shop and talked to Timoteo Florentino, the best saddle maker in Santa Fe. Timoteo's ancestors started the saddle shop when Santa Fe was a young city in the early 1700s. He had made several saddles for Rafe's young horses, and one for Rayo.

"Buenos días, Timoteo," Rafe said.

"Buenos días, Rafael. Is the new little Appaloosa ready to wear a saddle yet?" Timoteo asked.

"Not quite yet. He's a mighty spirited horse, though. He'll need a special saddle," Rafe told him. "He has a lot of his father's pride and spirit." Rafe's horse, Rayo, was the sire and the young colt reminded Rafe of Rayo when he was a colt. As the weather was getting warmer, Rafe was letting the foal run in the pasture. He could tell the young one was built for speed and would be a fine horse. He planned on training it and giving him to Carlos. Rafe owed him for bringing his mother and sister to Santa Fe. Besides, if Carlos married Bibiana, he needed a fine horse to assume his gentlemanly life.

"Timoteo, can you make an *Americano* saddle for Rayo?"

"Por supuesto," Timoteo replied he could. They talked about the differences in Spanish and American saddles for almost an hour before another customer arrived. Rafe said his farewells promising to bring Rayo for a fitting soon, and walked back to the telegraph office. He walked in hoping for good news.

Jim, the operator, looked up as he closed the door. "The lines are down. Tried and tried, nothing will go through." Rafe's shoulders slumped and then he thought perhaps George was on his way home and could not send a wire.

"Can you keep trying off and on," Rafe asked.

"Sure will. I'll try every couple hours," Jim replied.

"Much obliged. Send someone to the ranch if you get through."

When he arrived home to the ranch's courtyard, Josefina was out the door and standing on the veranda before he was off Rayo's back.

"The lines are down," he called out to her. "George can't send a telegraph."

"Gracias a Dios," Josefina cried out and crossed herself looking up to heaven.

Rafe bounded up the five steps to the porch and grabbed his adopted mother in a huge *abrazo.* "Jim will keep trying to send out a wire. He'll send word when he gets through." Rafe held her in the hug, each feeling the relief of what they thought was good news.

CHAPTER 12

Yesterday, Easter Sunday, the sun finally broke through illuminating the crystal white snow in millions of sparkling glints like diamonds at the Mystic Lode Mine. However, the shack, mine, and mountain were covered in deep, heavy snow. Standing on the porch, George looked out on a sea of white, not able to distinguish the rutted trail from the rocky slope near the shack.

He kicked himself for not sending Josefina a telegram when he arrived in Elizabethtown, letting her know he was safe. He promised her he would be home by now and she would be worried out of her mind. Stuck here at the shack, it might be days before he could get back to town to send her a wire.

Work at the mine continued regardless of the day or holiday. Sunday was a day of work, even Easter Sunday was no different. George put his frustration into lugging rocks.

This afternoon, Mike yelled excitedly. He called to Bill and the others to follow him outside. Out in the bright sunlight, Mike extended a hunk of rock. It glittered in the sun. Through the center ran a three inch vein of pure gold.

"Yeehaa!" Jake and Lefty yelled in unison. "She's a beauty," Lefty whistled. Bill took the rock, turning it over several times, and lit up in a huge grin. "Gold boys and good quality. We're close, very close to the mother lode." Jake did a little quirky dance in the excitement and the others laughed.

"Show us where this came from," Bill told Mike. They followed Mike back into the mine. Deep inside, Mike stopped and shone his torch on the wall of the tunnel. A thick vein of gold ran down the stone. "We're rich!" Lefty touched the gold vein and the others chimed in with joyous enthusiasm.

"We need to shore up this tunnel, before we start working on the vein," Mike said.

"Lefty, Sam, you go get the timbers. Jake, clear the

rubble," Bill ordered.

George followed Mike and Bill back to the shack where they huddled over the kitchen table in a discussion on the steps to extract the gold vein. George was interested in how the process needed to be changed, now that the gold vein was found. Smaller dynamite charges would be used to carefully work the edges of the vein. It was important not to blast the gold to smithereens.

They worked tirelessly, excitement displayed in each of their actions. Heavy timbers were hauled into the shaft. Every attempt to make sure the tunnel was secure and safe was being executed. Bill divided the GSW rifles and pistols between the men and stashed extra ammunition in the tunnel. George overheard him tell them to keep a constant lookout and to keep the rifles with them at all times. When George asked him about the extra precautions, Bill explained, "I swear these hills have eyes and ears. When someone hits a new vein, it is telegraphed all over the mountain. If Clay Allison gets wind of this strike, he may come after it."

Later when George stood on the front porch of the shack, he thought the sun had melted some of the snow pack. Maybe he'd be able to ride to town in the morning and send Josefina a telegram.

The next morning George looked out of the shack's window hoping to see a bright sunny day. Instead gray clouds hung heavy in the sky. Mike opened the door and a freezing wind blew in before he could shut it out.

"Looks like more snow coming," he said.

George cursed to himself knowing he was not getting off the mountain today. Bill and his crew talked excitedly about the gold vein. They had no cares about the weather – rain, snow, or sun. Just as Bill told him, inside the tunnel the weather was always the same. Outside the new storm added several more inches of snow to the already thick layer on the ground.

CHAPTER 13

Tuesday morning started with an expectation that George would magically appear driving the wagon into the courtyard of the ranch. As Tuesday night approached, worry sat like lead in their hearts. At breakfast on Wednesday, Rafe told Josefina he was riding to town again to check if the telegraph to Elizabethtown was working yet.

Josefina sent Celiá with Rafe to do some shopping at the general mercantile in town. Rafe had not spent much time with his mother since George left. His days were busy in the GSW weapons foundry and he and Carlos spent most evenings in the horse barn. Celiá spent most of her days helping in the kitchen and caring for her grandchildren.

Rafe helped her up into the wagon seat and clicked the reins. The sky above was a brilliant turquoise with puffy white clouds scuttling along the horizon. The sun was warm on their faces as they rode down the lane.

"You look tired *Mamá,"* Rafe said to her.

Celiá smiled a bit. *"No mijo,* I'm not tired. I like to be busy."

"You cook, clean, and look after Antonio and Alicia. I brought you to Santa Fe to rest. María stays in bed all day and does nothing." Rafe tried hard not to be angry at his sister, but it had been almost a month since baby Bernardo died and she still secluded herself in her room. She would hardly talk to him.

"She is grieving," his mother said.

"Grieving? She didn't even cry when we buried him."

"She's not grieving the baby. She's grieving her life. All her dreams of living as *don* Bernardo's wife and the *doña* of the *hacienda* are gone."

"Grieving that *desgraciado!"* Rafe grumbled calling the old *don* a miserable wretch.

"She loved him. Her life was in Mexico," his mother said simply.

Rafe grumbled a curse under his breath. He could not understand how his sister could love the man who raped her and stole away her youth. He would never understand.

"What about the children? Doesn't she love the children?"

"Yes, but they remind her of him. You should not be so hard on her, *mijo.*"

"How can you defend her, *Mamá?* You have raised those children. They look to you for love and caring, not to María."

Celiá did not respond. She did not know how to make Rafe understand the feelings of a young girl's heart, even if it made no sense.

As they approached town, Celiá changed the conversation to happier thoughts, asking Rafe about the buildings in town. She had only been to Santa Fe a few times and enjoyed the red chilis hanging from the *viga* beams and the Indian women wrapped in their colorful blankets with geometric designs. Rafe pulled the wagon in front of the mercantile and helped his mother down.

"I'm going to the telegraph office while you do the shopping. Mr. Burgess will help you load the things into the wagon. I'll be back shortly."

Rafe opened the door for his mother and then turned and headed down the street. The telegraph office was several blocks away. He pushed in the door and waited while Jim helped another customer.

"Good morning, Jim. Any news on my telegraph to Elizabethtown?"

"The lines are still down. I caught a message from Denver yesterday saying the lines are down all over the mountains north of Taos. They had a big snowstorm blow through Denver and then south. Some miners were lost in the mountains. No stages or supply wagons can get through the mountain passes."

Rafe's heart jumped to his throat. Miners lost in the mountains. George should have been returning when the snow storm hit.

"Keep trying the telegraph, Jim. Much obliged for the

information." On Rafe's walk back to the mercantile, his heart hung heavy. His brain exploded with possible scenarios, many not good.

Mr. Burgess had loaded the wagon by the time Rafe reached the store. Thanking the shopkeeper, Rafe helped his mother up onto the wagon seat.

On the way back to the ranch, Rafe told Celiá he would have to go to Elizabethtown and look for George.

"Is it a dangerous trip?" she asked.

"Yes, especially if the mountain passes are icy, but I have to go look for him. I will take Carlos with me, but that leaves you, María, and the children alone."

"We have been alone before," she replied. Rafe swallowed hard knowing he had left them for more than four years in the hands of *don* Bernardo, alone and defenseless.

"Yes, I know. I do not want to leave you again."

"We are not alone. *Doña* Josefina and the girls are there, and so is Juanita," his mother said.

"Josefina is distraught about George and the girls are, too."

Celiá knew Rafe was right. Josefina and the girls struggled to act gracious and she felt it was a great burden for them to cope with María's hostility.

"Perhaps I can take María and the children to visit Lupe and Jose in El Paso. We could take the stage, no?"

Rafe was shocked by his mother's intuition. Visiting family in El Paso might be good for María, a change from the unknown surroundings of Santa Fe. Perhaps being there would help her overcome her mood.

"Yes *Mamá*. The stage takes three days to El Paso. Do you think María will agree?"

"*No lo sé,*" she replied she did not know.

By the time they reached the GSW ranch, plans swirled in Rafe's head. After helping his mother with the supplies, he drove the wagon to the barn. Not unhitching the team, he strode directly to the foundry to look for Carlos, finding him in George's office. Carlos looked up from his work when he heard Rafe's footsteps at the door.

"Any word?"

"No, the lines are still down. There was a spring blizzard in the mountains and the word from Denver is there are some miners lost."

Carlos did not need more explanation. Both he and Rafe owed George Summers a great debt, as well as being treated like part of his family. "When do we leave?" he asked.

"Tomorrow or Friday."

"We taking the wagon?" Carlos asked.

"No, it will slow us down. We'll take the pack horse. We'll talk later tonight, but we should expect trouble." Carlos nodded in understanding – they needed cold weather gear and guns. Carlos was a peaceful man by nature. Schooled in Madrid, Spain, at the seminary, he disliked killing. It was against God's rules, however living in the often lawless New Mexico Territory made him have to modify his beliefs. He would defend himself and his family and he would pack the guns they needed.

Rafe found Josefina in the parlor sitting beside the unlit fireplace. She had her head in her hands. Rafe lifted her gently and wrapped two strong arms around her.

"He's fine, Mother. Carlos and I will find him. He's probably sitting in the nice warm hotel drinking coffee," Rafe said lightening the mood. "We should not expect the worst. The storm has knocked out the telegraph, so anything can be possible."

"I know," she replied. "When will you leave?"

"Tomorrow morning, if you can see my mother, sister and the children to the stage for El Paso."

"Why?" she asked.

"My mother thinks the change might be good for my sister."

Josefina nodded in agreement accepting the decision. "Yes perhaps she is right. I must get some things prepared for their trip . . . and yours."

Rafe found his mother in the kitchen. "Have you talked to María, *Mamá*? The stage leaves tomorrow at noon for El Paso."

"*Sí,* she wants to go. She is upstairs packing her things." Rafe was surprised by his sister's reaction, and pleased it would not be a fight to get her on the stage.

Thursday morning his mother, Josefina, and the girls kissed and hugged Rafe and Carlos as they stood next to the horses in the courtyard making the final checks on the gear. Celiá, María, and the two children would leave shortly for the stage to El Paso.

"Be careful," Josefina told Rafe. Then she said, "Bring him home safe."

"We will," Rafe replied.

They rode down the ranch's lane with a heavily laden pack horse in tow. Rafe rode Rayo and Carlos rode Santiago. Carlos disagreed with taking Rayo and Santiago, the two best studs in the barn, however Rafe insisted. "They are both smart and surefooted," Rafe said, "and besides they can outrun any trouble we might encounter."

Rafe and Carlos rode hard out of Santa Fe heading southeast around the Sangre de Cristo Mountains. Carlos thought they should take the shorter route through Rancho de Taos maybe saving them as much as a day's travel, but Rafe disagreed. "George would have taken the road through Las Vegas and then north with the wagon. Perhaps we'll meet him on his way back."

They followed the stage road, spending the night at the Eagle Inn stage stop.

Before noon on Friday they reached Las Vegas, New Mexico, and stopped at the Stapp & Hopkins Mercantile. Rafe knew Will Stapp from previous trips with George to Las Vegas. "Hello Mr. Stapp," Rafe greeted the merchant when they walked into the store.

"Well now, hey Rafe. Whatcha selling today?" Will asked.

"Nothing today sir, we are on our way to Elizabethtown to meet up with George. Did he stop here on his way?" Rafe asked.

"Sure did. Said he was going up there to see his friend Captain Moore."

"This is my friend Carlos, Mr. Stapp."

"Glad to meet ya son," the merchant shook hands with Carlos.

"Can I do anything fer you boys today?"

"A pound of your elk jerky will do," Rafe replied.

"Have to tell ya boys to be careful when ya git up there to E-town. Word is there's been a whole lotta trouble there lately. They say Clay Allison is behind all the trouble up there," the merchant warned.

"Much obliged, Mr. Stapp. You have any idea why Allison is causing trouble?" Rafe asked.

"I heard say he works for someone who wants to own all the gold and silver mines on the mountain. Allison and his vigilantes just do the dirty work." the merchant explained.

"Anyone know who that someone is?" Carlos asked.

"Naw, we guess it's some big shot in Santa Fe. You should follow the foothills to La Cueva and over the pass. I heerd the shortcut route through the reservation is impassable. You bess be real careful now," the merchant warned.

"Much obliged, Mr. Stapp. If you see George tell him we came by," Rafe said as they left the store.

CHAPTER 14

When Jose and Lupe received Rafael's telegram in El Paso saying Celiá, María, and the children were coming, they were delighted. Lupe cleaned the baby cradle and made the back bedroom ready for their arrival, knowing María's baby should be born by now. Jose drove the buggy to town on Saturday morning to meet the stage.

Waiting near the stage office, Jose watched the driver help Celiá, María, and her two children step out of the coach. Neither woman held a small baby. Jose's heart fell. He did not need to be told, the baby did not survive. He and Lupe lost two children shortly after birth, and the forlorn look on María's face was all too familiar.

"Celiá, María, aquí," he called and waved. Seeing Jose, Celiá's face brightened.

"Ah Jose, hola."

"Bienvenidos," Jose welcomed them and hugged the children. Alicia held a blanket tightly in her fist and did not return his hug. Antonio said, *"Tío,* I want to ride up front with you."

"Sí, mijo," Jose replied smiling at Antonio's exuberance at life.

When they were all settled, Jose clicked the reins and slowly drove down the streets of El Paso. Antonio was fascinated with the tall and brightly painted buildings. He read some of the signs in English – bank, hotel, sheriff. "I'm learning English," he said proudly. Looking at Antonio was almost like looking at Rafael when he was five or six and just like Rafael, Antonio radiated a zest for life.

On the trip to the ranch, Antonio continued to talk to Jose and point to the birds, trees, and rocks along the way. When they arrived at the ranch, Lupe came running from the house waving hello. Behind her, Martín and Ita's two young sons toddled. Caught up in the moment, Lupe did not immediately realize María held no small baby, then a lump caught in her throat.

"Bienvenidos," she welcomed them. *"Ustedes deben estar cansados."* Lupe said they looked tired and led the two women into the house to the kitchen where she made them sit down.

"I wish to lie down, *tía,"* María said.

When Lupe returned to the kitchen from showing María to the bedroom, Celiá was holding Alicia in her lap rocking her. Alicia clung to her blanket.

"The baby died," Celiá said simply. "He would not nurse and María had a hard pregnancy." Lupe understood. It was heartbreaking to lose a child, though not uncommon.

"She is well?" Lupe asked. "She looks so tired."

"María is unhappy. She did not want to leave Mexico and now the baby . . . " Celiá's voice trailed off. "We thought perhaps some time here would help her to recover."

"You are welcome to stay as long as you like," Lupe told her.

That evening, the entire family surrounded the dining room table, including María. For the first time in many months, Celiá saw her smile. Ita, Martín's wife, was talking to her and they were laughing.

After the meal, Jose poured glasses of tequila to celebrate their visit. María sipped from her glass. When Alicia started nodding in Celiá's lap, Ita picked her up and she and María took her to the back bedroom, returning shortly with their arms linked.

Celiá looked at her daughter and smiled with hope. Being here in El Paso with Jose's family might be good medicine for her.

Over the next week, Celiá saw a dramatic change in María. She ate heartily and helped with chores. Her cheeks looked fuller and there was color to them. Martín and Ita invited her to ride to town. They saddled a gentle horse for her and the three rode off.

"I cannot believe the change in her," Celiá told Lupe. Although Celiá watched her daughter blossom, María still ignored her two older children. Antonio and Alicia came to

Celiá for their needs, while María gave more attention to
Ita's two boys.

A few days later, María and Little Jose came in
breathless. She and Little Jose snared a rabbit and María
held the prize by the neck. Celiá saw her daughter, like a
young girl, laughing and happy. It had been five years since
she saw such a look in her eyes. She was beautiful. Her long
black hair flowing down her back and a smile stretched
across her face.

On Saturday, Ita and María went to town to buy
supplies. Both came home with a new skirt and *camisa*.
María twirled around and around in the wide flowered skirt,
pretending to dance.

CHAPTER 15

At the Mystic Lode Mine, the sun on Friday morning lit up the small canyon. George Summers asked Bill Moore whether he thought the trail to town was passable and Bill told him it would be treacherous at best. A horse could slip on the ice sending the rider and horse over the side. George decided to stay put.

Saturday morning dawned cold and sunny. The clear turquoise sky was a promising sight. As George looked from the Mystic Mine's shack, all he saw was snow. In another week it would be May, but it looked like February.

"Sorry George," Bill patted his shoulder. "I know you must be wanting to get home."

"Do you think I might be able to ride to town tomorrow and send a telegraph to Josefina? I don't want her to worry."

Bill studied the landscape. "Maybe, if the sun warms up some. I'll go with you."

Bill and George joined the men in the tunnel. Mike was carefully exposing the gold vein. "Lookee here Bill. The vein heads off to the left," Mike said and illuminated the thick streak of gold.

George noticed progress was much slower now that the gold vein was found. The daily blastings were fewer and lighter. He was no longer needed to help push the heavy cart full of rocks from the tunnel to the rubble pile, which made the long hours of the days stuck on the mountain even more tedious.

It was early afternoon and George was standing on the porch of the shack in the sunshine, allowing the sun to warm him. The hills and crevices were still filled with white. A few light puffy clouds scuttled along the ridgeline. He looked at one of the clouds which seemed darker than the rest and was not blowing along with the others. George studied the gray cloud formation, hoping it was not more snow coming. The single gray cloud continued to plume upwards. Suddenly George realized it was not a cloud, but smoke. Running to the tunnel, he grabbed a torch and headed in to find Bill.

Hearing of the smoke plume, all the men came running out of the tunnel.

"There," George pointed.

"Looks like it's coming from Paul and Stoney's mine," Bill said.

"Whew, sure do look like it," Lefty whistled. "Whatdaya think?"

"I don't like it. With all this snow, it would take a might big blow to start a fire that big," Bill replied. Bill looked at the sun almost over the peak of the mountain and shook his head. "It's getting too late to ride over and check it out. Couldn't make it over this snow in the dark. Jake, you should ride over there in the morning and see what happened."

A few hours later, George was peeling potatoes in the shack while the men worked in the tunnel. He heard a voice yelling outside. Dropping the potato, he grabbed the rifle by the door and ran out. A horse and rider had stopped just outside of the tunnel.

"What do you want?" George demanded walking quickly toward the rider with the rifle at the ready.

"Claim jumpers burned us out," the man said sliding off the horse. He shook himself off and seeing the rifle held up his hands. "Don't shoot mister." The man pulled off his hat and George recognized Stoney from the Miner's Restaurant.

"Stoney?"

"Yes, who you be?"

"I'm George Summers. We met at the restaurant in town last week. I'm Bill's friend." George lowered the rifle.

"Golly be, yes you are."

"Stoney, what happened? Claim jumpers?"

"It was Clay's vigilantes. Ambushed us and shot Paul. They burned the cabin. I couldn't do nuttin about it."

"We saw the smoke cloud and Jake was going to check it out in the morning. I guess that won't help now. Is

Paul dead?"

"Yep. They shot him dead and left him at the mouth of the tunnel. I hid and I guess they thought I wasn't there. Paul never had a chance."

"Let's go get Bill." George grabbed a torch and led Stoney into the tunnel, yelling Bill's name into the dark. About halfway in, Bill came running out. Stoney repeated the story for Bill and again for the rest of the men who followed them out of the tunnel.

"Come on, Stoney, let's get you a cup of coffee and something to eat. Are you hurt?"

"Naw, I twisted my ankle some slipping on some ice, but I ain't hurt."

Inside the shack, Bill's Army training surfaced and he barked orders. They would be ready, if the Clay Allison vigilantes came to Mystic Lode. "We'll split up. Stoney, you, George, and Lefty will stay in the cabin. Mike, you, me, Jake, and Sam will stay in the mine. We can't let them catch all of us in one place."

They took turns eating supper and Bill ordered a rotation for guard duty. He was sure the Allison gang used the blizzard to an advantage. They knew it made getting any help from town impossible. Bill thought they might be next.

Rafe and Carlos pushed on out of Las Vegas trying to make as many miles as possible wanting to reach Elizabethtown. The east side of the mountain was covered in snow. Rising with the sun on Sunday morning in La Cueva, they pushed the horses up into the mountainous trail, picking carefully over the ice and deep snow. Finally, cresting the ridge they saw Elizabethtown below them. The town looked prosperous, the main street lined by buildings constructed of new lumber, with a few made out of stone. The town was covered in a thick coating of deep white and the snow on the main street was visibly trampled. As they walked their horses down the middle of the street all seemed quiet. It was almost noon and most of the restaurants and saloons were open.

They stopped in front of the Mutz Hotel, tied the

horses, and walked into the main lobby.

"Good morning," the clerk greeted them. "You come over the pass?"

"Yes sir."

"Well now. You be the first to make it over in a week," he said. "That's good news for the town. We've been cut off."

"Is a George Summers staying here?" Rafe asked.

"He was here, but I ain't seen him since before the storm. He left with Bill Moore and headed to the Mystic Lode Mine," the clerk replied. "Do you need a room? I only got one left for tonight with all the miners holed up causa the blizzard."

Rafe looked at Carlos and let out a relieved sigh hearing George was at the mine.

"Can you give us directions to mine," Carlos spoke up.

"Certainly. Follow the main road outta town heading north and just follow it till you come to a fork. The northwest road will take you right to the mine. I ain't seen nobody coming from that direction, so it might not be passable yet," the clerk added the warning.

"Much obliged," Rafe responded.

They rode out of town at a slow pace. The road was not exactly flat and there was a crust on the snow where it melted and then refroze. As they worked further up the mountain, it became impossible to tell the trail from the cliff. The snow piled higher and higher as they headed north. In many places the horses were thigh high in the snow. Rafe and Carlos pressed on knowing one slip could be disastrous. Rafe trusted Rayo's sure feet, but the packhorse was heavily loaded and not as stable. Finally, they came to what they thought was a fork in the trail and Rafe held up his hand, looking up the northwest road leading even higher up the mountain.

"What do you think?" he asked Carlos. Carlos sat on Santiago and studied the sea of white. A cold eerie stillness surrounded them. Rayo perked his ears catching Rafe's attention. "Shhhh," Rafe whispered. Straining, they heard the reports of gunfire in the wind.

"Come on," Rafe said kicking Rayo forward up the snowy trail.

Tugging on the pack horse, Rafe set a reckless pace. Explosions of gunfire became clearer at each curve in the trail. Rayo and Santiago twitched their ears hearing the reports in the distance. Finally, Rafe saw a trail of thin smoke coming over the next rise.

"Up ahead, around the bend. Let's take it slow," Rafe said and pulled his rifle from the carrier in his saddle.

When they got to the bend, they worked their way around a boulder and the mine came into view. They heard rapid reports coming from near the entrance to the mine tunnel. "That sounds like a GSW rifle," Rafe said and Carlos nodded in agreement. "Looks like they're shooting up to those boulders," Carlos said pointing to boulders on a hill several hundred yards away from the mine entrance.

They watched for movement near the boulders and saw the flash of a gun and heard the report. The shooters behind the boulders had the miner's trapped in the mine tunnel. If the men tried to leave the safety of the mine, they would be sitting ducks.

"Carlos, take your rifle and work your way up behind those trees and I'll stay here behind this cover. Maybe we can start a cross fire and flush them out. You fire the first shot when you get to a safe position."

Jumping down from the horses, they sank up to their thighs in snow. Working slowly to his position, Rafe waited behind a boulder. He watched Carlos working his way around through the trees, keeping his location in sight. He watched as Carlos' rifle barrel flashed several times toward the shooters hiding below him. Rafe trained his rifle where the shooters were hiding and carefully aimed at the spot. When a head and rifle barrel popped up, he squeezed the trigger four times. His GSW repeater barked in his hand and the shooter spun and dropped. Rafe put two more shots toward the boulders and he heard shots from Carlos' position.

"Jack's hit," Tom yelled to the rest of the vigilantes.

"Who the fuck is shooting at us?"

"Is he bad?" a voice yelled. More shots peppered their position from the east, not from the mine.

"Yeah, he's down. Go tell Charlie," Tom ordered.

Mickey worked up to where Charlie was sitting near his horse. "Somebody's got us in crossfire," Mickey said. "Jack's down."

"Damn, where'd they come frum?"

"Dun know."

"Let's git outta here," Charlie ordered the men. He was cold and tired of this fight. Even though the Mystic's men were pinned in the tunnel, Bill Moore's men forced him to keep his distance. Charlie had underestimated their firepower.

"What about Jack?"

"Jes leave im. He'll probly die anyway," Charlie growled and started to mount his horse. Leaving a good man bothered Mickey, but he knew Charlie had no patience for the sick or dying. More than once Mickey saw him shoot a man rather than try to save him.

Carlos and Rafe kept peppering the boulders. Inside the tunnel, Jake and Sam were taking their turn guarding the tunnel entrance. They had been rotating positions and then resting since this morning. Sam caught a rifle flash from the east and then another from trees on the far hill. He shaded his eyes into the sunlight trying to see if the claim jumpers were on the move, circling around them. He and Jake heard the report of bullets not coming toward the mine entrance.

"Whatdaya think?" Sam asked Jake. "Someone's shooting, but it looks like they're a shooting at the claim jumpers, not at us."

Jake peeked from the mine entrance and saw a bullet chip into a rock near where he knew the shooters who had them pinned down were stationed. "Maybe we finally got us some help from town."

Carlos saw seven horses and riders crest the hill above the treeline and head away from the mine. Cautiously, he worked his way back to Rafe's position. "I think they left. Saw riders go over the ridge."

Lefty and Bill joined Sam and Jake at the tunnel entrance hearing the gunfire and then the sudden quiet. Crouching at the tunnel entrance they waited. Rafe and Carlos approached the mine from behind the shack, hidden from view to the tunnel.

"Don Jorge! It's Rafe and Carlos," Rafe yelled out.

"Who are you?" Mike yelled back from the tunnel.

"We're looking for George Summers. I'm his son," Rafe hollered. After a brief pause, the voice yelled, "Show yourselves."

"Don't shoot. We're here to help." Rafe yelled.

Rafe and Carlos rode slowly to a spot in front of the mine entrance. They held their rifles pointed up. A tall man came out with a GSW rifle pointed toward them.

"Is George here?" Rafe asked the man.

"You said you's his son. Aren't you boys Mexican?" the man asked not taking his eyes off of them.

"Yes, I'm his adopted son, Rafe. This is my friend Carlos," Rafe answered understanding the man's skepticism under the circumstances. Finally, the tall man smiled. "Rafe? George has talked a lot about you. How the hell did you two get here?"

"Came looking for George when he didn't get back to Santa Fe. Where is he?"

"George is inside the tunnel with the others. He got shot this morning."

Rafe followed Mike into the tunnel. Behind them he heard one of the men talking to Carlos about securing the horses. As Rafe's eyes adjusted to the dim light, the tunnel seemed to widen. Up ahead he saw several torches burning. George was stretched on the tunnel floor, with his back propped against a pile of blankets.

"Don Jorge." Rafe dropped to his knees using his personal name for George Summers.

George smiled at him. "You always have good timing when I'm hurt. They've had us pinned down all day." Rafe was pleased to hear George joking.

"What happened. How did you get shot?"

"They surprised us. I was in the house with Sam and Stoney. Everyone else was here defending the mine. Sam and I got hit when we made a dash for the tunnel. The bullet went through without hitting bone, but it's still bleeding some. Bill cleaned it best he could and put a tourniquet around my leg."

Rafe pulled back the blanket covering George's leg and studied the wound with the light of the torch. It did not look infected, but it was still leaking blood. "Looks like the bullet may have nicked a vein. Can you stand and walk?"

"It starts the bleeding more when I try to get up. I've already lost some blood," George told him.

Rafe looked at Bill and said, "We have to get him out of here and to a doctor."

"I doubt he can ride. How was the trail on the way up from town?"

Rafe sighed. He knew the trail was icy and treacherous. There was no way he could get the wagon over the hill, with or without the claim jumpers shooting at them. "We got through, but the going was hard," Rafe responded.

"Daylight's fading anyway. We'll see what tomorrow brings," Bill said. "Mike'll make some grub at the shack and we'll all stay here overnight. You sure mustta put a scare into the gang to get them to light out," Bill chuckled.

"Put them in a crossfire," Rafe said. "I think I got one of them. Who are they?" Rafe asked.

"Clay Allison's gang, he calls vigilantes. They're just a pack of thieves, claim jumpers. I think they figured we couldn't ride to town for help with the blizzard and that's why they hit us. They burned Stoney out and killed his partner."

By the time Rafe emerged from the tunnel, Carlos and Jake were carrying a dead body into the camp. "Looks like they jes left him to die," Jake grumbled.

"Well that's one less. The ice will keep him. We'll take him to town when we go," Bill said.

The miners of the Mystic Lode relaxed and enjoyed a

hot meal inside the tunnel. Rafe was surprised the temperature inside the mine was a lot warmer than outside. With the hot food and knowing the Clay Allison gang was not outside, the men laughed and joked. George seemed in good spirits, even with the pain of the wound in his leg.

Chapter 16

Monday morning the sun burst over the mountain with a promise of warmth. "I think we can litter George down the mountain," Rafe told Bill. "Do you think the vigilantes are likely to strike us?"

"I'm more worried about the litter skidding off the icy trail," Bill replied.

Rafe told Bill of an idea to stretch a sling from the back of Rayo's saddle to the front of Santiago's to carry George. Bill nodded in approval. "I will go with you and take the dead man to the sheriff and your pack horse down for you," Bill told him.

Rafe and Carlos quickly designed the sling litter with ropes and several blankets. While the men draped the dead man over the pack horse, Bill saddled his. When they were ready, George limped to the sling and was helped up and into it and then covered with a blanket.

The small procession slowly wound down the narrow snow covered trail with Rafe in the lead. They passed the fork in the trail where he and Carlos heard gunfire as they rode to the mine yesterday. Again, Death was present, almost taking George's life. Luckily he and Carlos arrived in time to save George, but Death forced Rafe to kill. Death was slung across a horse and was being taken to town. Rafe pondered how Death seemed to stalk him, tickling and teasing him, and he did not know why. All Rafe wanted now was to get George home, before Death showed itself again.

It was late afternoon when Rafe and Carlos led the small parade into Elizabethtown. Several people gawked at the ingenious sling carrying George Summers. They also pointed to the dead body. They were not to the hotel before a portly man strode toward them. A sheriff's star was pinned on his shirt.

"Sheriff, we have a dead body for you," Bill told him.

The sheriff grabbed the dead man's hair to pull up his

head and looked at his face. Rafe noticed a slight hesitation in the sheriff's eyes, as if he recognized the man. He let go of the head and looked over at Rafe and Carlos.

"Who killed this man?"

"I did," Rafe admitted. "He was one of eight who were shooting at Bill Moore's mine. Seven of them got away."

"That's right," Bill said. "The vigilantes had us pinned down in the tunnel and shot my friend here." The sheriff walked over to the sling recognizing Bill's friend from Santa Fe.

"How do you know who was shooting?" the sheriff asked.

"You know it was the Clay Allison gang, sheriff. Do you know the dead man?" Bill asked with frustration at the sheriff's nonchalant attitude.

"Naw, never saw him before. You got any proof it was Clay's men?"

Bill knew the sheriff was lying. "You know this is Clay's doin. They killed Paul and burned his mine the day before they came for us," Bill groused.

"What? I ain't heard nothing bout that. How do you know?"

"Stoney was there when they killed Paul and burned the mine. Now he's up at the Mystic."

"He got proof?" the sheriff asked.

"This here's proof." Bill jerked his head toward the dead body. "He's one of Clay's men."

"I ain't never seen that dead jasper around here afore," the sheriff gruffed back. He knew it was Jack Braddely, one of Clay's vigilantes, but Clay would deny it.

"Let's take him over to the undertaker, sheriff," Bill said knowing the sheriff could not be pressed. Looking at Rafe he said, "Boys, soon as I'm done at the undertaker I'll meet you at the Miner's Restaurant. The doc is just up the street. You can't miss the sign," Bill told them.

Bill pulled on the pack horse's reins. He and the sheriff led the packhorse toward the edge of town to the undertaker.

When Rafe and Carlos arrived at the doctor, they helped George limp inside. "My father's been shot," Rafe told him. Rafe noticed the doctor look at George and then back to his brown face and shrug his shoulders. The doctor told his wife to heat up water and prepare the examination table. Rafe and Carlos waited in the kitchen where the doctor's wife directed them to the coffee pot.

After a little while the doctor came out wiping his hands. "The bullet nicked a vein in his leg. It doesn't look infected and I tied off the vein. He lost a lot of blood and is mighty weak, but with some rest and food, he should come out of it. I cleaned the wound and dressed it with ointments. Leave him here under my care and come back tomorrow. We'll see how he is in the morning," the doctor said.

"Thank you, doctor, er . . . " Rafe realized he did not know the doctor's name.

"Carson Lowe," the doctor filled in his name.

"Thank you, Doctor Lowe. We'll be back in the morning," Rafe said and they went out to their horses.

"I guess we better go see about getting a room at the hotel, before we meet Bill at the restaurant," Rafe said.

Crossing the street, they walked into the Mutz Hotel. The clerk looked up and said hello. "You boy's back?"

"We need a room. Do you know if the telegraph is up yet?"

"Ain't heard it is," he replied. "Number twelve, up the stairs."

Leaving Bill Moore after taking Jack Braddely's body to the undertaker, the sheriff rushed to the Golden Shaft Saloon. He looked around, then went upstairs, and tapped three times on a door to a room at the top of the stairs.

He tapped again, three sharp taps. Slowly the door cracked open.

"I gotta see Clay," the sheriff said. The door swung open and five men sat around a poker table. A man dressed in a gray suit sporting a heavy black mustache sat facing the door.

"What yew want, Sheriff?" the man drawled. "I'm

busy beatin these no good crooks at poker, so make it snappy."

"You went too far this time Clay," the sheriff said. "No one in this town will allow Bill Moore to be killed. He founded this town. I told you to leave him alone."

"Whatcha talkin bout Sheriff," Clay said in his thick Texas accent.

"Bill and two Mescans brought Jack's dead body into town and a friend of Bill's got shot in the leg. They said your men burned out Paul and Stoney, killed Paul, then had Bill and his men pinned down at the Mystic."

"Well now Sheriff, what's that got do with me? I've been here in town playing poker."

Sheriff Danny Robertson knew Clay never dirtied his own hands. His vigilantes did all the dirty work. "You give the orders," the sheriff groused.

"I never ordered anyone to do what yew jes said. Had to be them claim jumpers who's causing all the trouble round here. Don't yew worry Danny, I'll get my vigilantes up on the mountain and get them jaspers. I'll have my boys bring them jumpers right to your jail," Clay retorted never taking his eyes from his card hand.

Sheriff Robertson was hot under the collar. He knew Clay and his gang were guilty. The vigilantes and claim jumpers were one and the same. When Clay convinced him to take bribes to look the other way, Danny accepted the money. Now, he wondered if maybe he had let this go too far. He also knew Clay might shoot him in the back and find another chest to pin his star on.

"Just stay away from the Mystic." The sheriff turned on his heels and left the private poker room.

When the sheriff left, Clay barked an order to find Charlie. Charlie was supposed to kill Bill Moore up at the Mystic Lode Mine while it was isolated by the snowstorm. "Find Charlie and bring him here," Clay barked.

About an hour later, Charlie knocked on the private poker room at the Golden Shaft Saloon. He had been keeping away from Clay after the fiasco at the Mystic Lode Mine. When he was let into the room, Clay looked up from the game.

"Bill is in town along with two Mescans, the ones who killed Jack. Git the boys and kill all three of them, legal like," Clay growled. He asked no questions about what had happened at the Mystic, nor did he expect an explanation. Clay Allison only wanted results. Charlie nodded his head and turned to leave.

"Don't fuck it up this time. Git it done tonight," Clay spoke to Charlie's back.

Charlie Peters knew Clay was plenty mad about the mess at the Mystic and Charlie was mad because Jack Braddely had been a good friend. They came together to Elizabethtown from Houston about a year ago.

One of the Mexicans killed Jack and then swore it was self-defense. Charlie did not need any urging from Clay to want to make the Mexican pay – pay with his life.

CHAPTER 17

After cleaning up a bit at the hotel, Rafe and Carlos walked the few blocks to the Miner's Restaurant, which was crowded for the dinnertime meal. Bill waved a hand from a table near the back. "How's George?" he asked as they sat down.

"Doctor Lowe said he should be fine with some rest and food," Rafe said. A woman put bowls of stew in front of Rafe and Carlos and spoons. A plate piled with biscuits sat on the table.

"Elk stew and it sure is good," Bill told them and grinned. Suddenly ravenous, Rafe and Carlos dug into their bowls.

A short time later, Sheriff Robertson came in and sat beside Bill, raising his hand to be served. "Just got done talking to Clay. Says he had nothing to do with the shootin at the Mystic Lode Mine and the killing of Paul up there on the mountain," he reported hoping to convince Bill with the information.

"Danny, that's bull crap. Who else would be causing trouble around here, if not Clay and his so called vigilantes?" Bill asked him.

"Clay says it coudda been claim jumpers, the ones who've been killing owners and taking their claims. He said he's sending the vigilantes up on the mountain to protect the miners and to catch the claim jumpers," the sheriff said.

Listening to Bill and the sheriff, Rafe was confused wondering the difference between vigilantes and claim jumpers. Bill talked as if the vigilantes were the claim jumpers.

"What a load of crap, Danny. Everyone knows Clay's so-called vigilantes are the claim jumpers, one and the same," Bill said and laughed at what the sheriff said. Danny knew it too, but was struggling to keep up the ruse.

"I gotta have proof, Bill. You know that. A miner turns up dead and I don't have no witness to see who dun it," the sheriff gruffed.

"Proof? When a miner is killed, one of Clay's vigilantes ends up owning the mine rights. How about that for proof?"

"You know anybody can refile on an abandoned claim, Bill. Ain't no law against that."

"Danny, don't you find it strange how Clay and the vigilantes know first when a claim is abandoned? The next day they refile on it," Bill continued to press the sheriff. "I think we should call for the U.S. Marshal from Santa Fe to get back up here and help you."

Sheriff Robertson knew the Clay Allison gang was killing miners and jumping claims. He had been getting kickbacks for turning a blind eye. At first it was just a few grizzled miners who met their fate and lost their mines. Lately, Clay turned his murderous vigilantes into a full-fledged gang of outlaws, out to get all the big mines on the mountain.

"I can handle this Bill, no need to bring the Marshal back. Last time he was here, he found no evidence against Clay. There's no proof of wrong doing by him or the vigilantes," the sheriff calmly added.

Bill wanted to haul off and slug the sheriff for not upholding the law here in Elizabethtown. Instead, he stood up and looked at Rafe. "I'm gonna stay in town tonight and see about getting you two and George off this mountain in the morning. Let's get on over to the hotel and see about a room for me," Bill said. Rafe and Carlos got up from the table, leaving the sheriff alone and made their way out of the restaurant following Bill.

Charlie and four vigilantes sat on their horses across the road from the Miner's Restaurant. The sun sank over the mountain to the west of Elizabethtown and a light breeze blew through the valley bringing the chill of the evening. Charlie pulled the collar of his jacket up around his neck, cursing under his breath, "How fucking long does it take to eat a bowl of stew?"

"Whadidja say Charlie? They comin?" Tom asked.

"Jes be ready when they cum outta there," Charlie

grumbled. He and the boys were getting tired of waiting when Charlie saw Bill Moore leading the two Mexicans from the restaurant.

It was dusk and the mountain shadows were covering most of Elizabethtown. As he walked out of the restaurant, Bill turned right down the sidewalk. He was still grumbling to himself about the sheriff's lack of truthfulness about the vigilantes when he heard a voice.

"Which one of yew Mescans shot Jack up on the mountain?" a voice hollered out.

Rafe whirled toward the sound of the voice. In the shadow, he made out five men sitting horseback across the road. Bill heard the voice too, and pulled his GSW pistol before he turned toward the voice.

"Who's asking?" Rafe asked.

"Dun yew get uppity with me greaser. Answer my question cause I'm jes ichin ta kill whichever one of yew did it." Charlie sneered stepping his horse a few paces closer. His shotgun was in his right hand aimed at Rafe's chest.

"What was he doing up there shooting at us," Bill interrupted. As the speaker walked his horse closer, Bill recognized Charlie Peters. Bill always thought Charlie, a tough Texas gunslinger, was Clay's right hand man and responsible for most of the murders.

"Yew know we was protectin yer mine, Bill. We came up on some claim jumpers shootin at yer mine and fired at them to drive them off. Then these two Mescans came up from behind and killed Jack in cold blood," Charlie added.

"You know that's a load of bull crap, Charlie. Your men had us trapped in the tunnel firing on us. You just got some of what you deserve," Bill yelled back at him. Charlie saw Bill's pistol was already pulled and pointing his way. The two Mexican's pistols were still in their holsters.

"Yew know us vigilantes are here to protect yew and all the miners, Bill," Charlie said smugly. "Now yew Mescans drop yer gunbelts. We're agonna take yew in fer Jack's murder, all legal like." Bill knew Charlie and the vigilantes would kill Rafe and Carlos, probably string them up from a tree on the edge of town. He had no intention of letting that happen.

"You're not going to take these boys, Charlie," Bill told him. "Jack got what he deserved and the sheriff deemed it self-defense." Bill could see the hammer on Charlie's shotgun was not cocked. One of the other men held a pistol in his hand and Bill prayed it was not already cocked. The other three were slightly behind and sat their mounts with their pistols still in the holster.

Charlie glared at the Mexicans from his horse hoping one of them would draw. Then he and the vigilantes could shoot them down in the street, legal like Clay had told him.

"You're not taking them, Charlie, and if you thumb that hammer you're gonna get shot before you pull the trigger on that shotgun," Bill warned him. Bill's right hand held his GSW pistol. Now that he learned to use the weapon, he had faith in what he was saying.

Rafe felt Death tapping him on the shoulder and felt its cold breath on his neck. He scanned the five men on horseback, formulating a shooting plan if they decided to go for their guns. His hand rested by his gun's butt still in his holster, but he held back waiting for Bill's move.

Carlos, on Rafe's left, kept his eyes glued to the two men to the left of the man who was talking. There was no plan and no time to make one, if shooting started.

Charlie grew impatient with the standoff. He knew Clay wanted the Mystic Mine and wanted Bill Moore dead. With Bill dead, the two greasers would be easy pickings.

Of the three, only Bill had his gun out of the holster, which assured Charlie he had the upper hand. Hell, it was getting dark enough so no witness could tell who shot first. Charlie was sure, he and the boys would be telling the story of how the Mexicans pulled on them and they fired in self-defense. Turning his shotgun toward Bill, Charlie went to thumb the shotgun's hammer. Bill saw Charlie's thumb move to the hammer and squeezed off two shots into Charlie's chest knocking him off the horse.

Rafe saw the movement of Bill's hand and instinctively drew. Four well planned shots at the vigilante's horse's hooves skittered them. The spooked horse's movement jerked the riders so they could not take aim at Bill.

Sheriff Danny Robertson heard the shots coming from the street. Jumping up from the table, he stormed out of the restaurant and onto the street outside.

"The rest of you better put your weapons down, or next time we'll aim to kill," Rafe warned them. The four vigilantes stared at Bill and the two Mexicans. Charlie lay dead in the street.

"That's enough," the sheriff yelled out as he came running up. He saw four men on horseback and one on the ground, who he recognized as Charlie Peters.

"You'all put down all the guns," he barked.

"Glad to see you sheriff," Bill said. "These men seemed to think they wanted to do your job and arrest my friends for the murder of Jack."

Danny Robertson knew Clay had sent Charlie and the other men to string up the Mexicans, not arrest them. They might have even killed Bill and called it a fair fight. Sheriff Robertson finally had enough of Clay Allison and his murdering outlaws.

"You scum get on outta here!" the sheriff yelled at the vigilantes. "And tell Clay I ain't gonna stand for it anymore."

"Bill, you and these boys are spending the night in jail," the sheriff said looking at Bill with his gun pointed at him.

"No we're not sheriff. Don't be pointing your gun at me," Bill groused and raised his gun at the sheriff.

"Put them guns away, I ain't arrestin you. I just want to keep you safe from them varmints," the sheriff said holstering his pistol.

Bill, Rafe, and Carlos slept fitfully on the small hard cots of the Elizabethtown jail. Morning came without incident and the sun's rays illuminated the small cells. Rafe awakened with the sunlight. He pushed Carlos' shoulder, "Time to wake up amigo."

The sheriff came to the cells a little after sunup and

opened the doors. Rafe and Carlos stepped out of their cell and Bill from the other. "Hello boys. Sorry you had to be stuck in here. I felt it would be safer for you. The deputy and I kept watch all night," the sheriff stretched his arms looking haggard and tired.

He poured cups of coffee and had brought some biscuits and jelly from the Miner's Restaurant. "Thanks for protecting us, Danny," Bill told him slabbing jelly on a biscuit.

"I let Clay go too far. I'm sorry, Bill," the sheriff said. "I'll support you and the miners from now on. You best get these boys and your friend off this mountain right quick before those vigilantes wake up."

Rafe and Carlos followed Bill out of the jail. "You go gather your things from the hotel. Meet me at Doctor Lowe's house," Bill told them. "I'll go git the horses saddled."

Doctor Lowe was sitting at his desk when Rafe and Carlos walked in. "Hello boys. He's been asking about you." The doctor led them back to the kitchen where George sat at the table eating. He smiled broadly when they walked into the room.

"*Don* Jorge, you look much better," Rafe said.

"Yes, Carson and Judy have taken great care of me," he responded.

"Would you two like breakfast?" the doctor's wife, Judy, offered.

"Sure sounds good, ma'am, but we need to leave now," Rafe said knowing they needed to get out of Elizabethtown as soon as possible.

"He probably should have another day's rest, but the sheriff came last night and told me about the trouble with the vigilantes. I think he can travel, but it has to be slow going," Doctor Lowe warned. Just as the doctor finished talking, Bill walked into the kitchen and said hello.

"I'm ready to go," George declared.

"Don't blame you, George. I guess you're ready to leave this shithole," Bill said and laughed.

"Doc told me what happened last night and that all

of you spent the night in jail," George said.

"Yep, I need to get you all off this mountain this morning," Bill responded. "The sooner the better." Rafe and Carlos helped George stand and limp toward the door. They were surprised to see Rayo, Santiago, and a wagon waiting outside the doctor's office.

"I figured it was a fair trade for your wagon stuck up at the mine," Bill explained when he saw the surprised looks. "The doc told me it would be easier for you to ride in a wagon and not on a horse."

George gave Judy a big hug and shook the doctor's hand heartily. He thanked them for their help and hospitality. Turning, he limped down the porch steps and walked to the wagon. Carlos and Rafe helped George climb into the back, where he could stretch out his legs.

"I can get on," George grumbled, but they gave him a hand anyway.

"Tell me if your leg bothers you," Rafe told him, but knew George would not complain.

As Carlos was tying Santiago behind the wagon, Sheriff Robertson rode up. "I figure I better ride in this little parade for a ways," he said.

"Appreciate it if you do sheriff," Bill responded.

Rafe was anxious to get moving. The nagging feeling that Death was lingering here in Elizabethtown would not leave him. All he wanted was to get George the hell off this mountain and safely home. Death can have this place he thought to himself.

Carlos started the wagon with Santiago tethered to the back while Rafe towed the packhorse. Bill was in the lead and the sheriff rode behind. The doctor and his wife waved goodbye from the porch.

The small procession wound down the street and out of town climbing to the first ridge above Elizabethtown. George, riding backwards in the wagon watched the town disappear as they crested the ridge. Bill and the sheriff rode with them a little while longer before Bill raised his hand, pulled up, and turned his horse around.

"I guess this is far enough. I think you'll be safe from

here into the village of Cieneguilla. The sheriff and I are going to clean up this town. We're going to organize the miners and merchants and drive Clay and his gang of vigilantes back to Texas," Bill said. "Clay and his gang are finished in Elizabethtown, but he just might not know it yet. Besides, I have the best guns to back me up," he said patting the GSW pistol on his hip.

"I'll go to the U.S. Marshal in Santa Fe and make sure he sends a deputy here to help you and the sheriff," George said. "If the telegraph gets fixed, I'd appreciate if you'd send Josefina a note to tell her we are all safe," George told him.

"I will George. I'm so sorry about what happened." Bill said extending his hand to George. "I owe you." Bill and the sheriff turned and rode back toward town.

Rafe rode ahead setting a slow, but steady pace. His eyes scanned the hills looking for the trickster called Death. Death had stalked him in Elizabethtown, teasing him with its grim coldness. He still felt Death's eerie presence and thought about the lessons from the Aztec Healer, "Do not leave anything to chance and be aware of everything around you. Death will take you in an instant when you least expect it."

The going was slow on the snowy trail and Rafe stopped several times to make sure George was not in pain. By early evening they finally arrived at Cieneguilla's stage stop. George's face looked haggard. They could probably make Santa Fe in a few days at the slow pace, but time was unimportant – George was safe.

CHAPTER 18

Rafe, Carlos, and George arrived in Santa Fe on the first Tuesday in May. Josefina fussed over George, catering to his every need, and tucking a blanket over his legs as he sat by the fireplace in the parlor. She fussed and fidgeted until he finally groused at her. "Enough woman!"

Josefina ordered a feast for the evening meal including duck, which was one of George's favorites. The house was buzzing with joy.

Having delivered George safely home, Rafe and Carlos brushed and tended the horses giving them an extra portion of oats. Rafe noticed the pregnant mare had grown more rotund while they were gone.

"Looks like she's almost ready," Rafe told Carlos.

"Yes, it could be any day now," Carlos replied. Carlos was fascinated with birth. Nothing filled him with joy as the promise of a new life, which he believed a miracle from God.

"When are you going to see Bibiana? She has probably dumped you for another while we were gone," Rafe teased.

Carlos blushed a deep red. "I guess I'll see her Sunday at Mass."

"Why wait so long?" Rafe chided him. Carlos did not answer.

"You should go calling on her," Rafe urged.

"I . . . I can't." Carlos was shy and still not sure if Bibiana or her father would reject him.

"Friday is *el día de la Batalla de Puebla*. There should be a big fiesta downtown," Rafe reminded Carlos of the Mexican celebration of the fifth of May, when the French were defeated at the town of Puebla. "Do you think she will be there?"

Carlos brightened. "Yes, I think so. She mentioned it the last time I saw her."

"I bet she wanted you to ask her to go," Rafe

chuckled.

"Will you go with me?" Carlos asked. "Ana Teresa should be there, too."

Rafe thought a lot about Ana Teresa on the long trail to and from Elizabethtown. He also thought about Chiwiwi, his first and what he thought was his only true love. Chiwiwi was dead. The pain of her death still hurt in a deep place in his heart, but there was something about Ana Teresa. She dulled the pain and her eyes glinted gold, her smile lighted the sky.

"Yes, let's go to the fiesta and dance with all the pretty girls," Rafe said laughingly.

After dinner when the family celebrated George's safe return, Josefina caught Rafe in the hallway and grabbed him in a big hug.

"Gracias mijo." Tears cascaded down her cheeks. Rafe wiped at them gently and told her not to cry. *"Tú eres su ángel de la guarda,"* she told him he must be George's guardian angel.

In El Paso, Celiá had been at Jose's for almost three weeks when Jose received the telegram saying Rafael had returned from Elizabethtown. George Summers was safe. Rafael wanted them to come home to Santa Fe.

When Celiá told María she riled, *"Por qué, yo no quiero ir."* She refused to go. "I am staying here with *tío's* family," she said. "There is nothing for me in Santa Fe, only heartache. Rafael killed *don* Bernardo and our son lies dead in the yard. I will not go back and live with him and the gringos."

"What about the children?" her mother asked her. "We cannot all stay here in El Paso."

"Take the children," she said. "I need more time away from you, Rafael, and the children to decide what I want to do with my life."

Celiá was astonished at María's attitude. "I have looked after them when you were too tired, but they are your children, *mija.*"

"They will be better off in Santa Fe. I'm not a good mother to them now, *Mamá.*"

Celiá tried to argue with her daughter, but María would not budge. She intended to stay in El Paso and seemed to care little about the children. Later when Celiá talked to Lupe about the situation, Lupe said, "Perhaps she still needs time. She will miss the children when they are gone and realizes what she is doing."

The following morning Celiá tried to talk to María again, finding no change in her attitude, and knew the children would be better off in Santa Fe. While Jose and Lupe were family, they already had many mouths to feed. Celiá knew Rafael would see the children had a good life.

Without María, Jose drove Celiá and the two children to El Paso to catch the stage. "Give her time," Jose said. "She is safe here and we will treat her like a daughter." Jose gave Celiá and the children a big *abrazo* before they boarded the stage. "Do not worry. All will be well."

Chapter 19

Twenty-year-old María enjoyed her newfound freedom living with her uncle Jose's family. She never understood the concept before – free. She was free to do as she pleased, free to go to town with Ita, free to ride a horse, free to go to a dance in town, and free to be a young girl.

Her cousins, Martín and Ita, treated her like a sister, introducing her to their friends. Her aunt and uncle were kind and generous. Her brother Rafael bought the ranch for them and they gave thanks to him at every evening meal. At first she would cringe when they said it, but now she was beginning to understand his motives were good, even his motive to kidnap her from the *hacienda*.

Life in El Paso was so different than her life had been at the *hacienda* in Torreón, Mexico. *Don* Bernardo made her work every day, tending to his needs. Sometimes he beat her when he was in a foul mood or when he was not happy with her work. Other times he was generous and gave her beads and coins. María thought he loved her, but now watching Martín and Ita respond to each other, she realized she was wrong. Her mother and Rafael were right, *don* Bernardo had used her.

Friday, the fifth of May was *el día de la Batalla de Puebla* and the Mexican town of El Paso was celebrating Mexico's victory over the French at Puebla. Ita helped María shop for a new dress for the fiesta. Friday morning María could hardly contain her excitement. She and Ita took a long, hot bath and brushed each other's hair until it was dry and shone brightly. Her aunt let her use a silver comb for her hair.

When Martín, Ita, and María rode the buggy to the fiesta, María wanted to sing with joy. Arriving in El Paso, they parked the buggy and tethered the horse. Together they walked toward the plaza and as they got closer the music of Mexico filled their ears. The plaza, near the old Ysleta Mission was teeming with people. Vendors sold sticks of candy, flowers, sweet cakes, tamales, small tortillas filled with meat, and empanadas filled with fruits. María was enthralled.

Children ran and laughed without any cares. On one end of the plaza, a puppet theatre was setup to entertain them. Children laughed at the puppets wielding cardboard swords at another dressed in a French uniform.

As the evening festivities began, dancers in bright skirts of red, yellow, and green began swirling the perfectly circular skirts to the rhythm of the *mariachis*. The dancers each wore a braided headpiece of woven fabric matching the skirts. As they danced and twirled the skirts, they pulled at each side in a dipping motion. María could not help but to sway along and wished she might be one of the dancers in the plaza.

Later everyone danced and several young men asked María to dance. At first she was shy, but grew more bold. Ita gave her encouragement saying, "Go have fun. You are young and the night is warm." María danced every dance, even when no boy asked her. She danced with old men, with children, and with Ita and Martín.

On the way home to the ranch, her face glowed as she talked excitedly remembering every detail. Later in her bedroom, she smoothed her dress over the chair and twirled around and around in her undergarments. Later she tried to sleep, but the images of the fiesta replayed in her mind.

CHAPTER 20

Friday Rafe and Carlos spent the morning at the foundry catching up on gun orders. George was still not able to do much more than oversee any work, but was getting stronger every day. George overheard the boys talking about the fiesta and about several girls they hoped would be there. It brought joy to his heart to hear his adopted son carry on about a girl. George had not heard him talk about any girl since Chiwiwi died. Carlos was obviously enamored with a girl named Bibiana, and Rafe, Ana Teresa. George smiled to himself, wanting both to settle down and start families someday. Perhaps that time had come.

When Lolo asked her mother about the upcoming fiesta on Friday for *el día de la Batalla de Puebla,* Josefina fussed about the girls going without her and George. "They are too young," she argued.

"Carlos and I are going. We'll chaperone them," Rafe said. Carlos glared from across the table and Rafe winked so neither Josefina or George could see. Josefina reluctantly agreed.

It was already late afternoon when they were able to begin getting ready for the fiesta. Lolo and Lizzy were dressed and stomping around the house impatiently waiting for their chaperones.

"You are too slow," Lolo called to Rafe who was dressing.

"Calm down," Rafe told her. He put on his *caballero traje* and adjusted the sash. Before he dressed, he neatly trimmed the mustache and small beard under his lower lip. Carlos waited, sitting in the overstuffed chair in Rafe's room, ready to go. "You look more like a *grandee* than I do," Carlos laughed at him as they walked downstairs and out the door.

The buggy waited in the courtyard with Rayo and Santiago tied to the rear. Lolo and Lizzy were already sitting in the buggy talking excitedly.

The girls chatted happily on the way to town. Rafe pulled the buggy to a stop on the far end of the plaza. He helped the girls down and then caught them by an arm before they ran off. "You stay on the plaza," he admonished them sternly. "Lolo, do not let Lizzy from your sight."

"Oh Rafe, you sound just like Father. We're not little girls anymore."

"That's exactly what makes me nervous," Rafe replied. "Carlos and I will be riding on the *paseo* or walking in the plaza. If you need us, you will be able to find us."

After the girls skipped off, Rafe and Carlos untied the horses from the buggy and they mounted Rayo and Santiago.

In the early evening sky of May 5, 1871, a few planets were just becoming visible in the clear sky. The plaza was lit with hundreds of candles and oil lamps hanging from the *viga* posts and strung around the plaza. People milled around enjoying the mild evening, stopping at the vendors, or just strolling with friends. Vendors sold sticks of candy, flowers, sweet cakes, tamales, small tortillas filled with meat, and empanadas filled with fruits.

In the center of the plaza, *mariachis* played and dancers performed for the crowd. The strums of the guitars floated over the plaza. The women wore elaborate skirts of red, yellow, and green. The perfectly circular skirts swirled to the rhythm of the *mariachis*. Each dancer wore a braided headpiece of woven fabric matching their skirt wound into the braids of their hair. As they danced and twirled the skirts, they pulled at each side in a dipping motion.

Children laughed and ran in joy and excitement. On the near end of the plaza in front of the San Miguel Church, a puppet theatre was setup to entertain them. Children laughed at the puppets wielding cardboard swords at each another, one dressed as a French soldier and the other a Mexican soldier.

Rafe and Carlos slowly entered the *paseo* allowing their horses to strut. Around the *paseo,* carriages carrying *señoritas* rolled slowly along. Young *caballeros* rode on their best horses sporting silver tooled tack and pranced, wanting to catch the attention of the young ladies. It was an age-old ritual of Spanish aristocrats, played out in most any Spanish city or village around the world. By the old Spanish caste system rules, only aristocrats dominated the *paseo* ritual. Available *señoritas* from the best families, paraded in decorated carriages tempting the young *caballeros* in what was almost a courting dance on horseback. In Santa Fe, though it was now a territory of the United States, many of the old Spanish caste rules still applied. Both Rafe and Carlos knew *mestizos,* those born of mixed Spanish and Indian blood, were not welcome on the *paseo* during the ritual.

Watching the elegant formal custom, Rafe was torn. He was *mestizo,* and would never be anything better under the old Spanish *casta* system. But, this was not Mexico, nor Spain, this was New Mexico. He was a New Mexican man – educated, a man with money, and soon to be a full-fledged businessman with a horse breeding business. In his heart he knew he was probably a better man than many of the Spanish *grandees* strutting around the plaza.

Entering the plaza, Rafe knew Carlos was looking for Bibiana's carriage. "There they are," Carlos pointed to a carriage. Several *caballeros* followed the carriage as it moved slowly along behind others. Carlos bristled, annoyed Bibiana was flirting with the young *caballeros.* Dandies, he called them, *caballeros* who did little work and lived off their family fortunes – the lucky ones, who were able to keep the family's Spanish land grants, or still had connections to politicians or the church.

"*Vamos,*" Carlos grumbled spurring Santiago, but Rafe stopped him. "*Cálmate, amigo.* You must be calm and play the game. You cannot just barge up to her, or she will dismiss you. You must let her see you and ask you to talk."

Instead, Rafe led on Rayo, with Carlos following on Santiago. He pulled the reins to keep Rayo's head high. The horse snorted and flexed its powerful muscles as he pushed smaller horses aside. Moving toward Bibiana's carriage, young *caballeros* struggled to get control of their mounts as Carlos and Rafe muscled their way through the moving horses.

Bibiana's open air carriage was driven by an older Mexican man. Bibiana sat on the left side, her cousin Ana Teresa on the right. Two younger girls sat on the smaller seat facing backward. Rafe saw several flowers gripped in Ana Teresa's hand.

A horse to her side snorted and Ana Teresa jumped in her seat. She turned and glimpsed a *caballero* riding an Appaloosa coming up from behind the carriage. As they approached behind the carriage, Carlos moved to the left side where Bibiana sat. Only one *caballero* pranced beside Ana Teresa. Rayo nudged his rump and the *caballero* took a hard look at Rafe and Rayo. Rayo nudged again and the horse jerked up his head. The *caballero* rode on to catch up with his friends.

"Buenas tardes, don Rafael," Ana Teresa's voice sang from behind her red laced fan before she giggled.

"Buenas tardes, señorita," Rafe responded in formal Spanish. He held his head high, keeping his eyes calm and only glancing at her as Rayo pranced alongside the carriage. This Spanish custom was similar to an orchestrated dance. The young *caballeros* boasted and the young ladies pretended to be aloof and disinterested, when in reality this was a flirting ritual.

"I see you are not wearing your *pistolas* today," Ana Teresa said from behind her fan.

"I have no need for them here on the plaza, unless you are going to hurt me. Are you, *señorita?"* Rafe said and laughed, though still not looking directly at her.

"We heard you and Carlos were shooting *desperados* in Elizabethtown. I understand it is a wild mining town. Did you shoot anyone, *señor?"* Ana Teresa continued teasing Rafe. She did not believe Rafe was capable of such gunplay. In Ana Teresa's somewhat sheltered world, she idealistically thought gunplay was reserved for duels.

"We traveled to Elizabethtown on a family matter. The matter is finished now," Rafe replied keeping his response vague, not looking directly at her.

"Then I am happy you have honored me with you presence tonight, *señor.*"

"I am the one who is honored to see you *señorita.*"

"You ride a fine horse *señor.* You drove off all the other *caballeros.*"

"They will get over it, *señorita.* You should not be worried."

"You still owe me a day of riding," she said lowering her fan from her face. Rafe took a long look at her and saw her beautiful golden brown eyes glint in the twinkling lights.

"It would be my pleasure to take you riding *señorita.* Do I then have your permission to call on you?" Rafe asked.

"You must ask my uncle. He is acting as my guardian here in New Mexico. He has allowed other *caballeros* to take us riding."

Rafe sucked in a breath and suddenly felt overwhelmed by his ruse. Her uncle would never allow him courting privileges, but her invitation showed interest in him and telling him of other interested *caballeros* annoyed him. Was she trying to make him jealous?

They had only met once and danced several times. Rafe really did not know her, only knew she was a *Californio* visiting her cousin here in Santa Fe after her family lost their land grant in California. Why did his heart long for her? Was she toying with him or was she interested? Trying to shake the feelings, Rafe felt caught by her eyes. He felt them staring into his soul and he wondered what she saw. Even in her tenuous position, she probably would never even look at him, if she knew he was *mestizo.*

"*Rafael, vámonos,*" Carlos' voice startled him. Carlos and Santiago came around the carriage and rode along at Rafe's right.

"*Adiós señorita. Hasta que nos encontremos de nuevo,*" he wished her goodbye until they met again tipping his head slightly. He pulled on Rayo's reins and followed Carlos.

On the north end of the plaza, Alvaro Gutierrez and

Benjamin Pacheco rode to where Diego de la Torre stood beside his horse. Diego and several other dandies gathered in a group watching the traditional Spanish ritual.

"Baboso," Alvaro cursed as he dismounted.

"¿Qué?" Diego asked him what he was talking about.

"Carlos and that *caballero* riding the big Appaloosa pushed us out of the way."

"You are a *culón*. No one would ever push me aside," Diego bragged. Believing he was the most important *caballero* in Santa Fe, Diego de la Torre bullied his friends and enemies alike. The dandies who drank and rode with him feared him and some had scars to prove it.

Diego's ancestors were part of the first Spanish colony to settle Santa Fe with Juan de Oñate in 1598, making them one of the few original Spanish families who settled New Mexico. Diego was named after *don* Diego de Vargas, leader of the reconquest of New Mexico in the 1690s. He was the eldest son and as such rightful heir to the de la Torre Spanish land grant and status and someday would carry on the responsibility of running the *hacienda* for the next generation of the family.

Although not particularly handsome, Diego was thirty years old and dressed impeccably in the latest style. The short suit jacket of his *traje* was buttoned with elaborate silver clasps. Matching silver buttons ran down the sleeves. His tailored pants flared at the bottom with inset red ruffles matching his neck tie and sash. A rapier hung at his side, sheathed in a black tooled leather belt.

A *gachupín*, a pure-blood Spaniard born in Seville, Spain, Diego relished his position of authority with the other *caballeros,* most of whom were *criollo,* born in New Mexico. Diego and his friends were the current *paseo* dandies, the best and most eligible bachelors in Santa Fe. They ruled the *paseo* and Diego ruled them.

Diego scanned the carriages and spotted Rafe and Carlos beside the carriage carrying Bibiana and Ana Teresa. He knew of Carlos, but the other young man beside Ana Teresa rode a magnificent Appaloosa. Diego was proud of his black stallion that stood sixteen hands high, but even from a distance he could tell the Appaloosa prancing next to Ana Teresa was in a class above anything he had seen in Santa Fe.

Diego knew Bibiana and her family well. He considered Bibiana a sweet, yet uninspiring girl who would make someone a good wife. Him perhaps, if her father offered enough dowry. She would be the type of wife who performed her wifely duties and asked few questions about mistresses and money.

However, it was Ana Teresa who caught Diego's interest. She was Bibiana's cousin from California, who came last fall to live with her aunt and uncle. Diego made inquires until he found out her family lost everything in California. She had no money, so Diego knew marriage was irrelevant, but the fire in her golden eyes intrigued him. He knew she would gratefully accept his advances, thinking he would be a superior catch. Diego watched the two *caballeros* prancing beside Bibiana's carriage and bristled. He had plans for the beautiful *señorita* from California and he would not let some *pinche* dandy riding an Appaloosa spoil his plans.

"*¿Quién es ese hombre con Carlos?*" Diego asked his friends if they knew the man with Carlos prancing beside Ana Teresa on the Appaloosa, but no one knew him.

"He was with Carlos at the de Soto fiesta," Alvaro spoke up.

"*El traje del hombre es de México,*" another of the dandies said the suit the man wore was Mexican. Diego nodded in agreement thinking the *traje* looked a bit old fashioned.

"Alvaro, find out who that man is," he ordered his most trusted friend. Diego signaled and the other dandies followed him as he rode off to join the Spanish tradition on the *paseo*.

It was typical for Diego to let his *compañeros* do his dirty work, while he drank and gambled at the cantina. After all, he was *gachupín* and he was master of his world.

"Had your *señorita* missed you?" Rafe asked Carlos after they were well away from Bibiana's carriage.

"Yes. She said she was worried when I was not at Mass last Sunday."

"When are you going to ask her father if you can court her?" Rafe asked.

"Soon, I hope, maybe."

"Don't be so timid," Rafe told him. "Bibiana loves you."

"Yes we love each other, but it is not the way of Spaniards. It is her father who will decide who she will marry. I have no land or money to offer her a good life," Carlos said.

"The old ways are changing, amigo," Rafe reminded him. "Many families lost their rightful ownership to their Spanish land grants, not just you."

"Yes, that is true, but Bibiana's father is old fashioned and will not change easily. She has told me so. He wants her to marry well and has mentioned Diego de la Torre. Bibiana hates Diego and refused, but her father rules the family with an iron fist. He may force her to marry him."

It grated Rafe to see his best friend, Spanish by birth, caught in the same stupid social limitations he had felt all his life. They were Americans, not Spaniards, not peasants, but men in the new world. Why was it so difficult for things to change? His mother's words often rang in his mind, "Nothing can be done," but Rafe had learned it was not always so.

"Ana Teresa asked for us to take them riding and *don* Pedro might allow it. He was greatly interested in our horses, remember? You can be my partner in the breeding business and he will be impressed," Rafe suggested.

"It is not like when we went to *don* Bernardo's in Mexico pretending to be horse buyers," Carlos replied. "Her father will know the truth."

"You can be whatever they believe you are," Rafe said using Carlos' own words.

"Come on, we better find Lolo and Lizzy and make sure they are behaving."

CHAPTER 21

Celiá and the children arrived in Santa Fe on Saturday afternoon. When she and the children stepped out of the stage, Rafe was waiting and gave her an *abrazo*.

"Where's María?" he asked peeking inside the stage and finding it empty.

"She is staying in El Paso," his mother told him. "She needs more time, *mijo*. She was doing so much better there and wanted to stay," his mother added. "The change was good for her. Being around *tío* Jose and the family made her feel much better."

"What about her children?" Rafe asked.

"They will miss her, but she needs more time."

"More time," Rafe grumbling under his breath. The lazy ways of his sister riled him. Before he could protest, his mother added, "I'm sure she will miss them and be home soon."

Rafe accepted his mother's excuses and loaded her and the two children into the buggy. On the way to the Summers' ranch, they talked about his adventures in Elizabethtown and about the plans for the new house.

That same morning in El Paso, Lupe asked María if she enjoyed the fiesta, when her young niece sat down for breakfast.

"*Oh, sí.*" María excitedly told her aunt everything she could remember and Lupe smiled at her niece. This was not the same depressed girl who came here about a month ago. María asked her aunt why everyone was allowed to go to the fiestas in El Paso, but in Torreón the *peóns* were only allowed to watch.

"Yes it is for everyone, but Mexico is still caught in the old ways. The *mestizos, Indios,* and people without land are still treated as peasants." Her aunt struggled to explain, but thought María understood. "You were not slaves at *don* Bernardo's *hacienda,* but without money he could treat you so."

"Why is it so different here?" María asked.

Lupe paused trying to find words to explain to her niece. "America was founded on freedom. There are people who have more money or power, but we are free – if we work hard there is hope our children will do better. Jose works hard on our ranch and so does Martín, and the younger children are going to school. Tomás wants his own *rancho* and Little Jose hopes to be a doctor. Here they can have those dreams."

"I am just learning about freedom. I had no choices living at *don* Bernardo's *hacienda*. He told me what to do and I did it or I was beaten."

"Life for *peóns* in Mexico is still very difficult," her *tía* said.

"Do you think it will ever change?" María asked.

"Someday, I think. The desire to be free is in everyone. The power to be free takes money or courage. Your brother took his freedom at the point of a gun. He risked his life for you, twice."

"Yes, I now understand better what he did. When I get back to Santa Fe, I will put things right between us."

Later that night in her room, María pondered the discussion with her aunt. To be free took money or courage, her aunt said. She did not feel courageous, but María had a secret. A secret not even her mother knew. Over the years she tended *don* Bernardo, she had been stealing from him. At first it was only one gold coin, then later more coins. She checked his pockets after he made love to her and slept, and early in the mornings when she folded his clothes. She took the coins for the children, thinking she could buy them things when *don* Bernardo would not. She hid all of it behind a loose stone under the fireplace in the *casita*.

María had no idea how much money she had stored away, only knowing she had been stealing since before Antonio was born. When Rafael kidnapped her, her treasure was left behind. *Don* Bernardo was gone and now she was glad, but what about her treasure?

Over the next week, María paid closer attention when

she and Ita went to town. Mexican women walked the sidewalk beside gringo women. They shopped in the same stores and the children went to school. María was surprised she had not noticed it so clearly before. When she and Ita shopped in the mercantile, the shop owner treated them kindly.

On Sunday when the family went to Mass at the church in town, both Mexicans and gringos filled the pews. They tended to sit separately, but María saw the altar boys were light skinned or brown skinned.

For days, an idea percolated in María's brain. She must go to Torreón and retrieve her fortune. Only then could she start a proper life here in Texas. Her aunt and uncle were kind, but she wanted a life of her own for her and her children.

One night at dinner she announced, "I'm taking the stage to Torreón. I must go see to *don* Bernardo's grave and pay my respects," she lied.

"No María, it is not necessary," her uncle said.

"Yes, I must do this. It is my duty for the children, his children. Afterward, I will return to Santa Fe and fetch the children." María knew *tía* was anxious for her to return to her children as her aunt mentioned it to her many times.

At the news, Lupe crossed herself and kissed her thumb, *"Gracias a Dios."*

Two days later, María packed a satchel with several nice dresses. She wore a green dress with a small green and tan hat for traveling. Her uncle drove her to the stage depot in El Paso and bought her a ticket.

"Take this Mexican money," her uncle said handing her a fist of *pesos.* "You will need it in Torreón. *Don* Pablo should still be at the *hacienda* and will help you, if you need anything."

As the stage pulled out of the depot heading south across the border, María was not afraid. Across the seat from her, a young Mexican man and woman held hands. The woman held a baby in her lap. Next to her a man dressed in a gray suit tapped his fingers on a black bag.

María spent many long hours watching through the

small stage's window as the countryside changed. She realized it was the same trail Carlos drove when he was taking them north last fall. After three long days in the bumpy coach, María arrived in Torreón. She had butterflies in her stomach as she stepped down the two steps off the coach to the sidewalk. Would someone recognize her? If so, then what?

It was late morning and the town was busy with shoppers and *vaqueros*. The stage driver asked her where to take her bag and she told him she would carry it herself. Clutching her *mochila* knapsack and picking up the satchel, she walked to the livery stable.

"*Buenos días, señorita,*" the liveryman said.

"I need a horse." she said. "I wish to go riding. I am expected at the Santos *hacienda,*" she lied to him. María had formulated the lie on the trip, not wanting to start any rumors about her true destination.

"Riding *señorita?* Perhaps a buggy would be better. You are not dressed for riding."

"Yes, a buggy would be better," she agreed.

"*Un momento,* I will get a buggy ready for you, *señorita.*"

A bit later, María drove the buggy down the main *paseo* holding her head high. She drove down the road to the northeast and turned on the road leading to *don* Bernardo's *hacienda*. It was a road she had taken many times with her mother, but she had never driven this path by herself. As she crossed the marker to the *hacienda,* she swallowed a lump in her throat, but clicked the reins a bit harder.

When she drove up the lane, María was filled with mixed emotions. The once proud *hacienda* was empty. Weeds grew in the yards and in the gardens. Small *jacals,* huts made of mud and straw, stood empty on either side of the road. She drove by the *jacal* where she grew up. She could picture herself standing in the doorway the day *don* Bernardo first raped her, crying and watching Rafael mount the Appaloosa and ride to the main house with their father's flintlock pistol. He shot the *don* in revenge and then fled. It was only a little over six years ago, but it now seemed a lifetime.

When she pulled into the courtyard where the main house stood silent, a man walked from the barn to greet her.

"Buenos días, señorita," Pablo greeted her. "There is no one here." Pablo wondered who the young woman was. She was not dressed like the young women from town or any of the surrounding *haciendas.*

"Don Pablo ¿No me reconoces?" she asked if he did not recognized her. *"Soy María Ortega de Estrada."*

"¡María!" Pablo exclaimed.

"Yes, it is me."

"Why have you come? *Don* Bernardo is dead. No one is here, but me."

Although she had stopped caring, María needed to know one answer. "Did my brother kill him?" she asked the old horse master.

"No mija, he was not well. *El jefe* died of heart failure."

"¿Por qué has venido?" he asked her again why she had come. "There is nothing here for you."

"I need to pay my respects to his grave for my children," María explained. It was the custom and seemed like a good excuse. "I hoped to find some of my things in the *casita.* I left with nothing, not even the picture of my father."

"Everything there is gone. *Bandidos* took your things. I am the only one left to tend to the horses. Come, I will show you the grave I made for the *don."*

María and Pablo climbed a small knoll behind the house. At the top, a mound of dirt was surrounded by stones.

"I do not have the money to buy a proper fence," Pablo told her. A cross made of wood marked the spot where *don* Bernardo lay. María knelt and folded her hands. Inside she cursed his spirit and hoped he burned in hell. *"Que Dios tenga compasión,"* she said and crossed herself asking God for his mercy.

Pablo led her to a small log to sit down. *"Gracias, don* Pablo," she said.

"You do not have to call me *don,*" Pablo responded to the automatic use of the term *don* used as respect and not as status. "We are both *peóns.* How are Rafael, Celiá, and the children?"

"They are well. *Mamá* and the children are in Santa Fe with Rafael." María told Pablo about baby Bernardo's death and about life in New Mexico.

Pablo looked at the sky. A storm was brewing in the hills and the sun was hidden behind the clouds. "You can stay here tonight, but then you should go. It is not safe," Pablo told her.

"Why is it not safe?"

"*Bandidos* roam these hills, especially at night."

When they walked back from the gravesite, Pablo took the horse and buggy to the barn, and María walked to the guest house. Ducking under the doorframe, she stopped. Trash and broken furniture littered the floor of the empty rooms. The once clean and tidy home was in shambles. Remnants of clothes and broken dishes were burned in the fireplace.

The small wooden bed frame was still in the back room, the mattress was gone. The dresser stood on the far wall with the drawers pulled open, empty. All the gifts *don* Bernardo gave her were gone. Her father's picture gone also. An eerie silence filled the room. She peeked out the door to make sure Pablo had not followed her, then she went to the kitchen fireplace. Working the loose rock on the left side of the hearth, she worked it out of its notch. Reaching her small hand into the cavity, she felt the cotton sack where she hid the gold coins. She sucked in a breath of joy as she pulled the pouch out. The coins clinked inside.

Desperately she wanted to count the money, but quickly stowed her treasure in the *mochila* she carried on her shoulder. She pushed the pouch to the bottom and secured it tightly in her belongings making sure it did not jingle. Carefully, she replaced the rock in the hearth, stood, looked around, and walked out the door.

María crossed the Reyes *hacienda's* courtyard and found Pablo in the barn cooking over a small fire. "Come and eat. You must be hungry," he told her. As they ate, the rain began pounding on the roof of the barn. Water dripped through unfixed cracks and ran off the edges of the roof. Lightning cracked in the distance.

In the fading light María and Pablo talked. She was surprised she felt no shame in talking to the horse master. He was kind and understood the dilemma of a young girl born into servitude in Mexico, and she told him her inner secrets, except for the stolen coins in her *mochila*.

"The *don* was an evil man. He felt it was his birthright to treat us *peóns* so," Pablo said. "You must return to Santa Fe and start a new life."

"I do not feel comfortable there," she said.

"You cannot live here. There is nothing here. I am taking care of a few horses until I can sell them. After that, I too will leave. Rafael asked me to help him at his horse ranch in Santa Fe. You must go with me. It is not safe for a young girl to be traveling in Mexico alone," he said.

"No, I will not go back to Santa Fe," María pouted.

"María, *don* Bernardo is not the only *haciendero* who will exploit you," Pablo warned her. "If you stay in Mexico, you will have to take work on a *hacienda*. You are a *peón*. What else could you do?"

María listened knowing the horse master was right. Even the small fortune in her *mochila* could not sustain her for long and then she would just be a *peón*. Slowly she nodded to Pablo, "Yes, I will go with you."

Chapter 22

Rodolfo Guerrero sat around a small fire with a ragtag gang of thirteen *bandidos* chewing on a piece of cooked rabbit. The storm clouds brewed darker in the distance and shadows of the coming rain could be seen sheeting on the horizon. Rodolfo and his *bandidos* found shelter along the ridgeline of a canyon near the Reyes *hacienda's* land where an overhang of rock protected them from the oncoming rain.

Twenty-three-year-old Rodolfo was a *mestizo,* born on *don* Bernardo Reyes' *hacienda* northeast of Torreón, Mexico. As a child he accepted life as a *peón,* knowing nothing else until his best friend, Rafael Ortega de Estrada, shot *don* Bernardo who raped Rafael's younger sister María. Rafael then fled on the *don's* Appaloosa horse and Rodolfo began thinking differently. He grew bitter against the *haciendero* for meager rations, unnecessary punishments, and most of all for raping María. He used to lie awake at night and dream about escaping, like Rafael, but it was fate that set him free.

Rodolfo studied the jewelry and coins stolen earlier in the day from the carriage carrying *doña* Salinas and her two daughters on the road near the *hacienda* of *don* Felipe de Salinas. It was a small take, but the *doña's* emerald and diamond ring would fetch a good price in Chihuahua. He rolled the jewelry into a small pouch and counted the gold coins, separating thirteen and pocketing the rest.

"Javier," he called out.

"*Sí, jefe.*" Javier walked to where Rodolfo sat.

Rodolfo handed the coins to Javier, who took them and distributed the coins to the men. The men laughed and grinned with their new fortune. Most of the gang were illiterate *peóns* from *haciendas* surrounding Torreón. Hector and Kico were from a *hacienda* south of Chihuahua. They looked to Rodolfo as their leader. He planned the raids and made sure they had food and crude weapons. They stole from the *hacienderos,* taking the spoils of their raids, and at times helped struggling *peón* families they encountered along the way.

Living off the land as a free *peón*, meant living as an outlaw. Life was dangerous and hard, but these men believed it was better living as free men than as slaves to a *haciendero*. Pepe was the youngest at fifteen, the younger brother of Pancho. The rest were in their early twenties, young men without a future in their own country run by Mexico's upper social aristocrats while *peóns*, peasants, provided the labor force. The system ensured *peóns* could never get an education, buy land, or gain any political power, sowing seeds of discontent which were slowly being nourished, especially in the rural areas of Mexico.

Last week they were near San Pedro and came upon a young family. Their cart had broken a wheel and the young father was struggling to pull the wheel off. Javier and Kico jumped from their horses and helped the young man pull the wheel. It took several hours to get the cart back in order. Rodolfo decided to set camp and asked the young family to join them in a meal.

"Where are you coming from?" Rodolfo asked the father as they sat around the campfire.

"We left the Madero *hacienda* west of Torreón and are going to my wife's family in San Pedro," the man said.

"You are coming from Torreón?" Rodolfo asked.

"*Sí.*"

"Do you know the Reyes *hacienda?*"

"*Sí.*"

Rodolfo's interest peaked wanting to ask the young man more about the *hacienda,* because he had not seen his family for years.

"Do you know the Guerrero family at the Reyes *hacienda?*"

"No one is there, amigo."

"What do you mean, no one is there?"

"*Don* Bernardo Reyes *está muerto.*"

"*Don* Bernardo is dead?" Rodolfo asked shocked.

"*Sí,* many of the *peóns* have gone to the Santos *hacienda.* Some to others. The *hacienda* is deserted."

The news of *don* Bernardo's death delighted Rodolfo. Hopefully the *desgraciado* was burning in hell, as he deserved. Rodolfo had not seen his family since he was released from prison over two years ago. He wanted to see his parents and sister Consuelo, but did not want to bring shame to them. Now, if *don* Bernardo was dead and the *peóns* scattered to other *haciendas,* he wanted to find them.

"How did he die?" Rodolfo asked.

"I do not know."

The young family rested with Rodolfo's gang for the night and in the morning Rodolfo gave him a handful of coins. *"Gracias,"* the young father stammered.

"Vaya con Dios," Rodolfo told the family to travel safely.

For several days he led his band of *bandidos* toward Torreón through the canyons. The ridgeline where they were camped was only a short distance to the edge of the Reyes *hacienda's* land. Rodolfo planned to ride alone to the Reyes *hacienda* in the morning, and if necessary, the Santos *hacienda* to find his family.

Leaving the Reyes *hacienda* in the morning, Pablo went to deliver a mare to the livery stable in Torreón and to return the buggy María had driven to the *hacienda,* leaving María alone. She had been at the *hacienda* for three days. Living at the deserted ranch was eerie, but she felt safe with Pablo. Leaving the barn, she walked down the path to the nearby lake.

Pablo told her once he sold the horses, they would leave for Santa Fe. Yes she would leave Mexico, but she had not told Pablo she decided to go back to El Paso and live with *tío* Jose and *tía* Lupe's family. She would start a new life in El Paso, not Santa Fe.

On the path to the lake she passed a *jacal* where her friend Benita had lived. The little hut, like the others, was empty. A bit further the garden lay full of weeds, except for a few stalks of corn growing wild. Nearer the lake the *jacal* where her friend Lydia had lived was falling into ruin. She wondered where her friends had gone. Pablo told her many of *don* Bernardo's *peóns* were now working on the Santos *hacienda* not too far away.

Wishing she could visit them, she heeded Pablo's warnings to stay close to the barn. He warned her of roving bands of *bandidos*. "You are not safe here," he told her.

Reality about her situation began to sink into María's brain. She felt at home in Mexico and she loved the skies and the hills. Above her a hawk lazily circled on the light breeze. She felt at peace, but she could not stay. She was a *peón,* a peasant, and though she had some money it would not keep her from a life of servitude.

Arriving at the small lake, it glistened in the morning sun. María knelt by the side of the lake catching her reflection in the glassy water. The water was cool, but not cold. All was quiet except for the birds chirping in the trees. Stripping her dress and hooking it onto a branch of a nearby tree, María dove into the lake.

The water was cold at first, but as she swam it warmed. She had not had a proper bath since the day before she left El Paso, over a week ago and the water felt good. Her long dark hair clung to her back when she ducked under the water and then rose again to the surface.

Rodolfo rode slowly toward the Reyes *hacienda.* He left the *bandidos* this morning several miles east catching stray ponies running wild in the canyons. He rode cautiously, for he was a wanted man and he always kept up his guard, keeping to the trees and winding his way to the *hacienda* past the lake.

When he neared the lake, he heard splashing and giggling. Quietly he walked the horse to a nearby tree and slipped down off the saddle. Stepping closer to the lake he caught sight of a young girl swimming. Her long dark hair cascaded dripping wet down her back when her head popped above the water. Looking around, he saw no one else. Rodolfo studied the young girl for a few minutes and decided she was not so young, perhaps twenty, but he did not know her.

Crouching near the edge of the lake, he watched her enjoy the freedom of the water. She swam with abandon and he envied her.

María sucked in a breath and swam under the water feeling the ripples wash along her nakedness. She cut to the surface and the bright sun blinded her. Wiping water from her face, she gasped seeing a young man crouching at the edge of the water. Across his chest was a leather strap with bullets and a pistol hung at his side. A hat shadowed the top of his face, and a dark beard covered his chin.

"*Buenos días, señorita,*" Rodolfo greeted her politely. "There is no one here, but me. Please continue your swim. I am enjoying the show."

María tried to cover her nakedness turning her back to him. "It is not proper. You need to go," she gruffed.

Rodolfo was rather enjoying her predicament. "And who will make me?"

"*Don* Pablo will come looking for me," María said hoping the young outlaw would believe her.

"*Don* Pablo? You are from the Reyes *hacienda?*" Rodolfo asked surprised.

"*Sí.* He will be looking for me."

"*¿Cómo te llamas?*" he asked her name.

"*Yo soy María Ortega de Estrada,*" she said with as much defiance as she could muster.

The name struck him like lightning. No, it could not be María. She was no longer the young girl as he remembered in his mind, but a lovely young woman. Suddenly, the man began to laugh and María yelled at him, "Why are you laughing at me?"

"*María, soy Rodolfo Guerrero.*"

"*¿Rodolfo?*"

"*Sí.*"

Tired of treading water, María told him, "Turn around. I need to get out."

"Wait," Rodolfo said and ran to his horse. He pulled a blanket from his saddle and returned to the lake's edge. He dropped the blanket on the ground and walked behind a tree. María swam to the lake's edge and stepped out of the water, picked up the blanket, and wrapped it around herself. Peeking around the tree, Rodolfo watched her lithe body step out of the water. Her breasts were round with dark nipples and she was surprisingly slim around the waist for a woman who bore two children. Between her legs dark hair massed in a triangle.

"*Gracias,*" she said. "You may come out now."

Rodolfo walked out from behind the tree removing his hat. María looked hard at his face lit fully now from the sun. It was lean and hard, but she saw her brother's best friend walking toward her.

"You are still here? I heard the *hacienda* was deserted." he asked.

María answered his question with another, "Where have you been? I heard you were in prison?" Then they both laughed.

They talked for hours sitting in the sun at the edge of the lake, laughing and talking about old times and new. When María told Rodolfo that Rafael was alive and living in Santa Fe, Rodolfo praised God. Somehow he had known in his heart his best friend, Rafael, was alive.

"He is wealthy. He has been raising horses sired by Rayo and others," she told him. She told him about the baby dying and how her two children were learning English.

He told her about roaming the countryside with the band of *bandidos,* stealing from *haciendos.* "We are free," he told her.

"Rodolfo, why did you turn to the *bandido* life?"

"After Rafael shot *don* Bernardo and fled, life changed at the *hacienda.* You know how the *don* struggled to keep control over the *vaqueros* and *peóns* after he was hurt and *doña* Carmela left."

"*Sí.*"

"My friends and I skipped our chores and played in the hills and canyons. Sometimes we killed a deer or rabbit or pilfered from the gardens. No one was looking after us, so we did what we pleased."

"*Sí,* I remember you were young and wild," María said remembering him as a teenager, full of swagger and bravado.

"I made friends with Joaquin Moreno. You do not

know him. He grew up in town and would come to the lake fishing with his friends. I remember Rafael did not like him, because Joaquin was a thief and a bully. One afternoon several years ago, I was fishing when Joaquin and his friends came wanting me to help them hide. They had robbed the mercantile in town and *la policía* were after them. Before we could hide, *la policía* came riding up. Joaquin told them I was with them when they robbed the store. I spent six months in prison."

"But then, you were innocent!" María exclaimed remembering when the news spread through the *hacienda* that Rodolfo was a thief.

"It did not matter to *la policía,* we were just *peóns.*"

"Why didn't you come home after prison? Why didn't you try to clear your name?" she asked.

"When I got out of prison, I was ashamed. I could not come back to *don* Bernardo's *hacienda* and bring shame to my family. I tried to find work, talking to *vaqueros* from other *haciendas.* No one wanted me," he said with a sigh. "Then I met Hector and Kico on the trail outside of San Isidro. They had left *don* Luis's *hacienda* after their father was shot in cold blood and the *haciendero* turned them out into the cold. They were living in the hills in a small cave eating rabbit and mesquite seed pods and stealing from neighboring *haciendas.* With nothing to lose, I joined them."

María's heart ached for him. Life was not fair. Not for her and not for him. "What happened to Joaquin?" María wanted to know hoping he was dead.

"I don't know. Maybe he is still in prison. If I ever find him, I will kill him," Rodolfo said with bitterness in his voice. Rodolfo looked into María's face as he spoke. Her dark eyes bored into his heart and reminded him of a time when they were both young and innocent. Her still damp dark hair flowed down her back, framing her tan face. When she laughed, her dark eyes danced, lighting up her face. His heart ached.

"How do you live?" she asked.

"We travel the back roads and live off the land and off of what we steal from the *hacienderos.* If we can, we help other *peóns* we meet along the way. There are places we find shelter and where free *peóns* can live without fear."

"There are others?" she asked.

"Yes, many others. Someday we will join together and raise a true army and fight again for our freedom. When that time comes, we will win!" His voice grew with passion and María felt the power of his conviction. She felt drawn to him and drawn to his cause, but she was a girl. She wondered if girls could be *bandidos*.

"I must go soon. Pablo will get worried, if he gets back from Torreón and I am gone."

Rodolfo held her by the shoulders staring into her eyes. "I've always loved you," he blurted out giving into his heart's passion.

"¿Qué?" María was shocked at his admission.

"Yes, but you were taken by *don* Bernardo. I could never tell you," Rodolfo grumbled. "You deserved so much better." Rodolfo pulled her close and kissed her gently. Expecting to be slapped, he was surprised when she responded and kissed him hard and strong. She wrapped her arms around him, clasped in an embrace.

Passion and lust consumed him, but he controlled himself. He wanted nothing more at the moment than to grab the blanket from her naked body and take her at the lake's edge. Pulling back, he ended the kiss.

"Are you leaving? Can you meet me again tomorrow?" she asked him. Rodolfo knew he and the men should move on, but stared at her face. "Meet me here again in the morning, if you can," she said.

He stood and helped her up. He kissed her cheek and walked off to his horse. María dressed, folded the blanket and placed it in the curve of a tree branch, and then ran back to the *hacienda*.

She found Pablo in the barn. He looked relieved when she ran up. "I took a swim at the lake," was all she told him.

CHAPTER 23

Jed Clements peeked up at the ceiling through squinted bloodshot eyes assaulted by daylight streaming in the window. Maybe he would be able to move without the room spinning. Last night he had way too much to drink. He remembered winning a couple of big hands at a poker table, but he also remembered losing most of his stake, before he really hit the bottle with a vengeance. Trying to focus on the design in the ceiling, his head pounded and he felt like puking. He heard a soft snore and rolled his head to see a naked young woman curled up, half covered next to him.

It was his second week in Round Rock, Texas. He came looking for Luke Payton, Butcherknife Bill's brother, wanting to tell him about Bill's killing and maybe getting a job on a cattle drive. Now, Jed regretted his decision and wished he had never come here in the first place. Luke was forcing him to stay in Round Rock until he settled his affairs, then Jed had to go with Luke to New Mexico and find the greaser who killed Bill. Jed thought about just packing up and leaving, but the more he found out about Luke, the worse that idea sounded. Luke was a murderous lout, and Jed knew if he crossed Luke there would be hell to pay.

At least Luke gave him money to get a room and money to spend on whiskey and women. It was May and Jed was getting tired of loafing in Round Rock. The big cattle drives would be starting soon and Jed was watching his chances to get signed onto a drive evaporating. Luke said he had business to finish before they left for New Mexico, but Jed had no idea what he meant. As far as Jed could tell, Luke mostly gambled and drank.

Jed carefully swung his legs over the side of the bed trying not to awaken the sleeping girl. Looking closer at her, he recognized her from the Golden Horseshoe Saloon. She was one of the saloon girls who caught his fancy. She hustled watered-down drinks and flirted with the cowboys coming through Round Rock. She told him her name was Bonnie Brunel and she grew up in Austin. Tendrils of light brown hair fell around her pale face. After the red lipstick wore off, Jed thought she was pretty.

Her blue dress hung over the chair and she lay naked from the waist up in the tangle of sheets. Sitting on the bed his head thumped from the hangover, his throat raw from the rotgut whiskey. After he started losing at poker, he started drinking. The more he drank the more he lost. Vaguely, he remembered Bonnie talking to him and refilling his glass. He was no good with women, unless he was drunk and unless they were whores. Mostly whores just wanted your money for a poke and talking was not required. Looking at the sleeping whore, he wished he could remember if he fucked her or not.

Quietly he tried to wash his face and dress before the girl woke.

"How yew feelin this mornin Jed?" a female voice startled him. Jed slowly turned and looked back to see Bonnie yawning, while stretching her arms above her head. Her ample white breasts with pink nipples stared at him above the sheets.

"I ain't feelin right," he answered.

"Well, I'll tell yew boy, yew shur was feelin happy last night," she said. "Yew shur put the whiskey down."

Bonnie was happy after a long night of peaceful rest. Jed paid ten dollars for the whole night, in advance. Not many cowpokes in this area had that kind of money. By the time she got him to his hotel room and helped him out of his boots, he lay down on the bed and passed out while she made ten dollars for getting a good night's sleep.

"I have ta ask yew Bonnie, did we, yew know, did we?" he nervously asked not finishing the question.

"Naw honey, we shur didn't. Yew was too damn drunk and passed out on me. I still owe ya."

"Damn," he cursed.

"Don't yew worry honey, I ain't agonna let yew get away without yew givin me sum of that thar between yer legs."

Jed blushed and Bonnie sat there looking at him turn red. She liked what she saw – a thirty year old Texas cowpoke, with shaggy blond hair, and a good looking face through a thin beard and mustache. He was a bit leathery for his age, but had a smile including all of his teeth. He stood about five foot nine with muscular arms and legs.

Jed was new to Round Rock, and had only been around for a couple weeks. Most of the men in the Round Rock saloons were drifters and outlaws. The sheriff had a reputation for looking the other way when it came to the law. Bonnie was tired of the hardened rangy outlaws treating her as tough and mean as they wanted. The law looked the other way on that too.

Jed was different. He told Bonnie he worked cattle for several big outfits, the last one in New Mexico where the owner was killed.

"I wern't gonna stay and work with no greasers," he told her last night. "I'm agonna get on with a big ranch here in good ol' Texas."

Bonnie had a pretty good instinct for outlaws and Jed was not one. She was already thinking about catching this cowboy for her own.

"I won't be any good ta yew, at least not til I git my stomach to stop turnin," he said still blushing. He liked Bonnie and felt real good about her wanting him. He did not feel as embarrassed and shy with her like he did with most women.

"Let's go git sumthin to eat girl," Jed said as he finished washing. Bonnie threw off the blankets and got up stark naked. Jed could not help staring in the mirror as she pulled on her petticoats and a blouse. Walking to the dresser, she splashed some perfume on her arms and in her hair, before she put on her dress. Jed enjoyed the show and felt his groin respond to Bonnie's reflection. As they left the room, she took Jed's arm and led him down the stairs.

At the Round Rock Cafe they ordered breakfast, even though it was almost two o'clock in the afternoon. Jed noticed the way Bonnie's cheek dented into a dimple when she smiled or laughed. She only wore a little makeup on her face and looked really pretty in a blue dress. The dress made her eyes look slightly bluer, although Jed thought they were more gray than blue, like a dusky blue sky in the morning.

They were halfway finished when Luke Payton strode into the cafe. He walked directly to their table. "Hey thar Jed, been lookin fer yew," Luke said yanking a wooden chair from the adjacent table and sat down with them.

"Hello Luke," Bonnie greeted him in a strained voice. Bonnie knew Luke only too well and had some scars to prove it. He was a mean one and one Bonnie would rather not have to service. She was surprised Jed knew him.

"Hey Bonnie, yew been takin care of my boy here?"

"Shur am," she chimed in hoping Luke would move along and let them finish their meal.

"Lookee here Jed. We need to git goin on down to New Mexico and look fer that greaser what kilt my brother."

"When do yew want to git goin?" Jed replied taking a bite of eggs.

"Rat now. Go git yer gear and meet me at the livery stable. I'll have our hosses ready to go." Luke stood knocking the chair over as he kicked it away and strode out the door of the cafe.

Jed stared after him in astonishment, then looked at Bonnie with a sorry look. "I gotta go," he said.

Bonnie put a hand on his arm and said, "He'll wait, finish yer breakfast."

As soon as they finished their meal they hurried back to the hotel. Bonnie owed Jed one and she intended to earn her pay, hoping he would come back when he and Luke were done in New Mexico. In his room, she wasted no time hiking her skirt and bent over with her elbows on the bed. Jed dropped his pants, surprised he was already hard and pushed into her. Bonnie moaned and moved to his thrusts until Jed could not hold back and exploded, buckling his knees, and falling forward over her back. His face fell into her hair and the smell of her perfume filled his nose.

"R yew dun honey?" Bonnie said looking back at Jed.

Jed, a bit embarrassed, pulled up his pants and began gathering his gear. Bonnie got off the bed, grabbed Jed around the chest, and kissed him. "Yew bess come back to me when yew finish yer bidness with Luke, yew hear."

"I will Bonnie. I'll come back," he said and gathered his saddlebags. She kissed him once more before he left the room and hurried to the livery stable.

At the stable Luke waited with the horses saddled. "What took yew so long. I said I was ready ta go," he snarled.

"I hadta pay my bill," Jed lied as he tied his saddlebags and bedroll to the horse. Luke grumbled, but said nothing else.

When he finished tying his gear to the saddle, Jed mounted up and followed Luke out of the livery and down the main street of town. Just past the last building on Main Street, Luke headed south.

"Where yew goin? New Mexico's west," Jed shouted pushing his horse to catch up.

"We'll git the stage to El Paso in Austin," Luke said before kicking his horse sharply in the ribs and taking off at a gallop. Jed had no choice but to try to keep up.

Finally, Luke slowed the pace. His horse was breathing hard and sweat beaded along the animal's flanks. Jed fell in beside him.

"Tell me bout that town San Mercel, or whatever the fuck its name is and tell me about the greaser dun kilt my brother," Luke demanded gruffly.

"San Marcial is just a shitheel village bout a hunerd miles north of El Paso. It's full of greasers, but I'm not shur the greaser who kilt Bill lives there," Jed said.

"What the fuck yew mean he don't live there."

"His cousin is the mayor there in San Marcial. Think the greaser comes to visit him," Jed guessed.

"Well, what's his name," Luke asked.

"I don't rightly member," Jed replied.

Luke visibly bristled. The dumbshit cowboy did not

even know the greaser's name. He toyed with the idea of pulling his pistol and shooting Jed. His hand dropped to the top of his holster and touched the butt of his pistol.

"He rode a mighty fine Appaloosa. I'd rekenize that hoss anywheres."

Luke let out a long breath. "Whar ya hail frum Jed?"

"My pa had a dirt farm just north of Fort Worth. Didn't like farmin, so I joined a cattle outfit when I was fifteen. Been pushing them nasty critters ever since. What bout yew? I always heard Bill talk bout Tupelo. Did yew boys grow up in Mississip?"

"Shur nuff. I took Billy outta thar and we ended up in Austin. We got jobs as drovers. I never did like sleepin under the stars, but Billy liked it and stayed. I took up with some jaspers. We robbed a couple stages and pulled small jobs. Ventualee we hooked up with the Sam Bass gang. That was the bess time of my life, afore I got sent to prison."

"Why yew livin in Round Rock," Jed asked.

"Round Rock has lotsa range cowboys who think they knows everythin. They's easy pickins fer me. Whilest I was in prison an old gambler teached me how to play poker. He always said poker was a job, not a game, and iffin I treated it thataway I'd win more'n I'd lose. Course he teached me how to cheat, but I won't cheat less I'm alosin. I kin spot a man acheatin and most times he'll end up dead."

Riding beside Luke Payton, Jed wished he never went to Round Rock. All he wanted was an easy ticket to a cattle job, not to follow a gambler and killer back to New Mexico.

"I cain't be livin offa yew Luke. No tellin how long ittil take to find that greaser. I got to git me a cattle job when we git ta Austin."

"Dun yew worry bout no job now. We goin to New Mexico and find the greaser dun kilt my brother. I got nuff money ta hold us till we git back to Texas."

CHAPTER 24

Luke and Jed arrived in Austin late at night. "Let's git on over to the Crystal Palace and git us couple of them good lukin whores," Luke Payton told Jed Clements. The stage to El Paso did not leave until early the next morning.

"Naw, I jes want a beer," Jed said tired from the long dusty ride from Round Rock.

It was Friday night and by the Palace's standard, it was slow. Cattle drives were just starting for the summer and many of the local cowboys were already on the trail.

It had been a couple years since Luke darkened the door of the Crystal Palace. He used to win against the high-rollers at the poker and Faro tables regularly. One night he shot a cheater and while the sheriff could not charge him with murder, Luke was escorted out of town. "Take yer gamblin sumwheres else," the sheriff told him. Luke wondered if that sheriff was still alive and if he would remember him.

Jed knew the Crystal Palace was the highest priced saloon and brothel in Austin. He and his cowpoke friends could not afford the uppity prices. Walking into the saloon with Luke, Jed whistled under his breath at the lavish surroundings. The saloon girls sitting and walking around were young and pretty, not like the wornout whores at the Devil Dog Saloon where he often hung out.

Luke and Jed strolled up to the Crystal Palace bar. Luke ordered a bottle of whiskey and Jed a beer. Four men played poker at a table near the back of the room. Several saloon girls circulated, talking to the cowboys and smiling at their attention.

Luke scanned the room for an auburn haired beauty, Cinnamon Baker. Cinnamon was a rare whore, one who really made a man feel good. Her stunning looks, reddish hair and green eyes, were real easy to look at. When Luke was on a winning streak, he always asked for Cinnamon. She was high class, but worth it and tonight he had plenty of money with him. He won a small herd of cattle from a smart-ass cattleman in a poker game at Round Rock about a month ago. He sold the herd for ten thousand dollars before heading on this trip. He had plenty enough money to buy Cinnamon for a whole month.

"Where's Cinnamon?" he asked the bartender.

"Don't work here no more," the bartender replied.

"Damn. Where'd she go?" Luke asked thinking she might have moved to a different saloon.

"New Mexico."

Just then the madam of the Crystal Palace walked up and said, "Why Luke Payton. Ain't seen you for quite a spell. You back in Austin?"

"Jes passing through thisa way," Luke replied to Madam Marta.

"The barkeep jes tol me Cinnamon's gone," Luke said. "That's too bad causa I got me plenty of money."

"No, she doesn't work here anymore, but I got a real young one you'll like. She's as fresh as the dew. Come over here, honey," Madame Marta called out to a very young dark haired girl in a red and pink dress. Marta had brought the young girl from Dallas to take over Cinnamon's clients. The young whore's face was beautiful and she had enormous breasts. Marta thought she was a bit slow of mind, but no cowboy cared about her mind. She came from a country farm and her real name was Ramona Gutierrez Rafferty. Her mother was Spanish and her father Irish, but Ramona looked white. Marta gave her the name Romie and told her never to tell anyone she was half Mexican.

"Yer joshing me bout Cinnamon, ain't yew? She was yer best whore. Why'd she leave?" Luke demanded.

"Well she went off and got herself married. Look at this pretty little ol' thing."

Marta pushed Romie by the shoulders in front of Luke. "This here's Romie," Marta said. Romie smiled at Luke, showing a mouth with some crooked teeth, but Luke looked down from her teeth to the milky breasts bulging from her red velvet dress.

Without asking a price Luke said, "I guess I'll take her. Yew got one fer my friend, here?" he asked Marta.

"Sure," she replied, but Jed waved her off. All Jed wanted tonight was beer and a bed. All the way to Austin Jed thought about Bonnie, and how inviting she looked bent over the bed waiting for him. He decided he would keep his memory of her with him on the long trail to New Mexico, and then he'd return to Round Rock.

Luke followed the young whore upstairs to Cinnamon Baker's old room. She closed the door and stood there with her hands behind her and her right foot crossed over her left. She was young, probably not more than seventeen. Looking at her, Luke saw an awkward little girl with her head slightly bowed and her eyes looking scared behind loose dark tendrils of hair falling over her eyes. Luke removed his gunbelt and hung it on the bedpost.

"Cum here girl," Luke demanded. "I don't bite." He was leaning against the footboard of the bed looking at her breasts full to bursting from above the neckline of the dress.

Nervously, Romie walked over to him, her hands still behind her back. She made no move to remove her dress and her eyes still looked at the floor. Madam Marta had found her at her uncle's small store south of Dallas. Ramona liked to sing and people told her she had a pretty voice. The day Marta showed up, Ramona was tending the store and singing a tune.

Marta promised her she would sing every night at the saloon in Austin. "The cowboys will love you," Marta told her. Ramona thought it was her chance to go someplace in the world. When they arrived in Austin, Marta gave her pretty dresses and this nice big room. She never had a room for herself. She always had to share with her two sisters.

Ramona was exuberant. She was seventeen and the cowboys whistled and catcalled when she sang for them. For several months, Marta paraded her around the saloon and gave her the name Romie. She watched some of the other girls go up to their room with a cowboy poking at them and kissing them, but Marta did not allow anyone to touch her.

Then one day a couple weeks ago, Marta came to her and said, "It's time for you to start earning your keep."

"I sing for you," Ramona said.

"Singing don't pay the bills, honey. It's those two beauties on your chest that'll earn your keep," Marta told her. "Why do you think I've been showing them off?"

"What are you saying?" Ramona asked naïve to the world.

"I'm saying this is a brothel and you need to earn your keep by keeping the men happy. I've arranged a mighty hansum price for your first time."

Later that night, an older man took her up to her room. He took off her dress and fondled her breasts. He kissed and sucked her nipples until they stood up and she felt funny between her legs. He kissed her and talked nice to her. Then he sat her on the bed and removed his clothes. His hard penis stuck out straight. Ramona had seen her little brothers' running naked when they were children, but this man's penis was huge and hard. He made her kiss and suck on it and while she did, he groaned.

Turning her around he made her get on her hands and knees with her breasts hanging down. He rubbed her back and bottom and then suddenly she felt herself being torn apart between her legs. With a single thrust, he pushed himself inside of her, pulling her shoulders back into him as he pushed. Ramona screamed. Pain shot through her belly, but the man held her tightly by the shoulders and he continued to push and thrust into her.

"Shhhh, little one," he said. "It will not hurt for long." But it did hurt and she cried out.

Finally, the man pushed into her in a faster rhythm and groaned loudly. When he stopped, the man slapped her on her bottom. "Now you are woman," he said. Dressing and then walking out the door, he left Ramona lying on the bed crying. A little while later Marta came and showed her how to clean between her legs. The cloths she used to wipe herself were bloody, but not as bad as during her monthly bleed.

Marta gave her five dollars. It was more money than Ramona ever had at one time. "You will earn much more than this, but you will work for it," the madam told her.

A few days later Marta took her upstairs and explained to her what she would have to do to earn her keep. "You will sing early in the evening and then later the men will pay handsomely for your body," Marta told her. Ramona tried to protest and told Marta she wanted to go home, but Marta only replied with a sharp slap of her hand.

Now, this man named Luke, leaning on the bedrail, was the fifth. Each time it hurt a little less, but she was embarrassed when she was naked and the last man smelled bad.

"Cum on girl," Luke said. "Dun be shy, take yer dress off," he told her.

Ramona nervously removed her red velvet dress, but left on her black stockings which were attached to a lacy garter belt. Her firm breasts hung like overripe cantaloupes on her chest. Luke leaned back watching her. She stood by the bed looking down at her feet. Luke turned her all the way around to have a better look at her, before he removed his shirt and trousers. Marta was right, she was young. He was going to take his time and enjoy tonight.

When he dropped his pants, Ramona gasped. Luke's engorged member was bigger than she had ever seen. It was long and thick, with a mass of brown curly hair around his balls. He sat her down on the bed facing him and grabbing his stiff manhood rubbed it on her cheeks. She closed her eyes, not wanting to look at it. Slowly he rubbed it between her breasts, pushing them together to surround it in a soft pillow of flesh. Luke felt her soft breasts caressing his penis and knew tonight was going to be special. Pulling his penis up, he wiped it across her lips.

"Kiss it," Luke demanded. "Kiss it gentle, then suck it hard."

She tried to do as she was told, but choked back a bit from the odor of his unwashed penis. He noticed her hesitation and grabbed her by the hair to hold her in place.

"What's the matter darlin, don't yew like it?" he sneered at her. She said nothing and restarted kissing the foul smelling penis. Luke moaned as she tentatively kissed it and brushed her dark hair around it.

His penis was throbbing, anxious for the tight treasure between her legs. It had been a long time since Luke poked a fresh young cunt. The old whores in Round Rock were so big and flax you could barely feel them.

Pushing her back on the bed, he spread her legs wide. One of her garter's snapped and her stocking drooped. Thinking only of his pleasure, Luke grabbed his rock hard penis and pushed it between her legs figuring it would find its own way to the treasure. Scared and not ready, Ramona tensed as he pushed.

"Aaaiii, me duele," she cried out in Spanish as he hurt her.

Luke stopped in his tracks. "What the fuck did yew say? Yew a damn greaser bitch?" he yelled out and grabbed her by the throat.

"I'm sorry. Don't hurt me," she tried to yell out coarsely with his tight grip on her throat. Luke's penis went limp and he cursed at her. "Yew lyin bitch."

Luke drew back and backhanded her across the face, sending her petite body back toward the headboard of the bed. Her head crashed into the mattress.

"Ayuadame! Ayuadame!" Ramona screamed for help.

"Yew jes a fuckin Mescan greaser whore," Luke yelled jumping on top of her and punched her in the stomach and across the face. Blood spurted from her lip. Ramona's screams were heard downstairs. Luke lifted her off the bed and threw her against the wooden headboard.

"Fuckin greaser bitch," he screamed. "I hate greasers." Pulling at her legs, he pulled her toward him. Grabbing her by the throat he growled, "I ain't gonna fuck no damn greaser bitch." Suddenly a large black hand grabbed him and pulled him away from Ramona.

"Dat be nuff, saa," a large black man said. It was Moses, Madam Marta's bouncer. Moses stood six-feet-two and weighed about two-hundred and fifty pounds. He could handle most any trouble and he could handle Luke. "Ya bess be gittin yer pants on and a leavin this here place," Moses warned.

"She's a fuckin Mescan whore?" Luke screamed. Marta appeared at the doorway.

"What the hell yew doin, Luke?" Marta screamed at him, when she saw Ramona sprawled out on the floor with her lip bleeding.

"It's yer damn fault, yew tricked me an gave me a fuckin greaser whore," he said glaring through his evil eyes at Marta. "Give me my money back."

"Git the hell out of here, Luke, and don't ever come to the Chrystal Palace again," Marta told him. Moses kept a good hold on him and Luke could not move. His nostrils flared with anger, but the big man had him in a tight hold.

"Git yer clothes on and git going, or I'll have Moses break yer neck," Marta warned him.

In the mirror above the bar, Jed saw Luke stumbling down the stairs holding his gunbelt and boots. Finishing the last of his beer, he strolled to the bottom of the steps.

"What the hell happened to yew?" Jed asked.

"We're leavin," Luke said.

After Luke got them thrown out of the Crystal Palace, Jed decided to just bunk down with his horse. Jed slept little, tossing in the scratchy hay. He had no idea where Luke went, and he hoped he would not show up in the morning. If he was late, Jed had decided to start riding fast south – alone.

The next morning Luke walked into the livery about a half hour before the stage was to arrive with a smile on his face. "Shudda come with me," he said. "I won us a hat full at the Diamond Jim."

Luke sold their horses to the livery man and then they went to get the stage to El Paso.

CHAPTER 25

Diego de la Torre sat impatiently on his horse waiting for his *compañeros* to at arrive at his *hacienda*. Today was Saturday, their day at the Palacio. They would spend all afternoon until the cantina closed, drinking, gambling, and having their pleasure with *putas*. The Palacio was a sanctuary to Santa Fe's *caballeros*. *Indios* and *mestizos* were not allowed, not even *Americanos* were welcome there.

Fuming, he slowly pranced his horse in circles around the courtyard. Diego was anything but patient. He was *gachupín* and in the world, his world, everything revolved around him. Finally, Alvaro and Vicente rode into the courtyard.

"Están llegando tarde," he growled at his companions for being late.

"Perdóneme," Alvaro apologized. "You asked me to find the *grandee* bothering Ana Teresa at the *paseo.*

"¿Qué aprendiste?" Diego asked what he had learned.

"El hombre se llama Rafael Ortega," Alvaro told Diego. Alvaro had done Diego's bidding and found out Rafe's name.

"¿Algo más?" he asked what else Alvaro found out.

"El hombre es de México. Nada más," Alvaro told him Rafael was from Mexico and he knew nothing else.

Diego turned his black horse in a circle around his friend, his eyes glaring a dark hole in his chest. Alvaro squirmed in his saddle. Friend or not, Diego was a man with a terrible temper.

"Vámonos." Diego kicked his horse and galloped out of the courtyard with Alvaro and Vicente trailing behind. Riding off he filed the information about the *caballero*, Rafael, to memory, but needed to know more about the man from Mexico. They rode to the Palacio Cantina located in Santa Fe's oldest Spanish neighborhood, called *barrio de Analco*. It was a place where *caballeros* celebrated their heritage given to them by their ancestors – Spanish

conquistadores. In Santa Fe, the Palacio was a Spanish bastion, not yet ruined by the *Americanos.*

Diego hated *Americanos* almost as much as he hated *mestizos* and thought of them as stupid and inferior. At least *mestizos* usually knew their place, but the *Americanos* had been taking land, starting businesses, and making laws over the Spanish in New Mexico. All over Santa Fe, old Spanish families were losing their Spanish land grants and left penniless. Diego swore it would never happen to him.

As Diego rode into the *barrio,* he slowed his horse to a trot. Riding toward de Vargas Street, Diego sat straight, proud, and tall in the saddle. Red chili *ristras* hung from the *vigas* jutting from thick adobe walls of the houses. Graceful archways covering a sidewalk ran in front of several buildings, which were part of the San Miguel Mission originally built in 1610 during the settlement of Santa Fe by Juan de Oñate and his colonists. Most of the buildings in the *barrio* were over one hundred years old. Breathing in the air and the sights of the *barrio,* always filled Diego with pride. He turned the corner and rode down the street to Burro Alley. Taking the narrow alley, Diego rode to the cantina's corral.

Diego dismounted and dusted his *traje.* Leading Alvaro and Vicente, he pushed open the Palacio's door and walked from the bright sunlight into the dimly lit room. A man playing a Spanish guitar hesitated momentarily, several sets of eyes assessed the trio, and then the music continued. If Diego and his *compañeros* were not accepted, they would have been facing a pistol barrel or the tip of a sword in an instant. Diego strutted over to the bar. Before he got there, the bartender poured three glasses of brandy.

The Palacio Cantina proudly catered to *caballeros* from families of pure Spanish ancestry since it was established in the early 1800s. The smooth stuccoed walls of the cantina were decorated with *conquistador* weapons and murals of Spanish explorers and conquerors. Large paintings of Cristóbal Colón, discoverer of the Americas, Gonzolo Pizarro, conqueror of Peru and the southern Incan empire graced the right wall. Hernán Cortés, discoverer of the mainland of Mexico and conqueror of the Aztec empire, and Francisco Vázquez de Coronado explorer of the northern territories of New Spain, including Arizona and New Mexico, were painted on the left wall. The far wall was filled with a grand painting of Juan de Oñate on horseback, the first governor of the Kingdom of New Mexico.

The floors of the Palacio were covered with the finest thick European carpets. Elegant etched mirrors reflected the paintings. Crystal chandeliers, rich draperies, and imported furniture from Spain had been brought up the Chihuahua Trail by wagon from Mexico City. Although most of the furnishings were old, they sparkled from the laborious care given to polishing and preserving them.

The Palacio Cantina was run and owned by Virginia Barceló Verdugo, adopted daughter of María Gertrudis Barceló. María, nicknamed *La doña Tules,* had built a reputation of catering to Santa Fe's Spanish aristocrats. A shrewd businesswoman, she meticulously took care of a *caballero's* needs – drinking, gambling, and *putas.* Known also as *Madame La Tules,* she ran the finest whores in the *barrio.* Her *putas* were blonds, redheads, blacks, Spanish, *Indias* and *mestizas* catering to all *caballero* desires. She served only the finest liquors from Mexico.

La doña Tules' gambling tables were considered clean. She dealt Monte, and was known as the best Monte dealer throughout the territory. She did not allow any form of cheating, and if caught, cheaters were summarily thrown out of the cantina and not allowed to return. She also disdained any rough play or fighting, except for the occasional display of swordsmanship.

Virginia ran the cantina like her infamous mother with an iron fist. Also like *La doña Tules,* Virginia was a beauty. Tall and well proportioned with raven black hair, alabaster skin, and gray-blue eyes, she was a thirty-year old goddess. Rich and unmarried, only because she invested all her time in running the cantina and brothel, Virginia was highly desirable. Several *caballeros* died in duels over her hand, but only one *caballero* interested her a bit – Diego de la Torre. He exuded machismo and dominated the young *caballeros* in Santa Fe. She admired his power.

"*Bienvenido, Diego!*" Virginia called out as she floated downstairs. She was dressed in a black, old fashioned, high collared Spanish dress. The elaborate black bustle crowned a rippled red underskirt. A long lace *mantilla* hung past her waist. Although the style of the dress was old fashioned, Virginia looked anything but. Today, as every Saturday, she wore her heavy gold necklace, heavy with jewels around her neck, and six gold rings on her fingers. They were pieces of her mother's valuable jewelry collection which Virginia inherited.

"*Buenas tardes, querida,*" Diego waited for her to come all the way down to the main floor, then walked over and kissed both of her cheeks. Diego was not ignorant, nor impervious, to Virginia's interest in him and he took advantage of her attention.

"I got a new shipment of the Sauza you like," she said looking him in the eyes and brushed his right cheek with her perfumed hand.

"*Gracias,* bring a bottle to the card table," he said. He knew she wanted him, but the night was young and she would only want him more later. He kissed her cheek again and said, "*Más tarde, querida.*" Later when he was tired of playing cards, he would look for a signal from her to meet upstairs in her room.

Alvaro and Vicente drifted to the Monte table. Young *caballeros* were taking their turns at the table trying to win at Spanish Monte. Monte was a simple card game, played with forty cards after eliminating the 8's, 9's and 10's from a full deck. After the cards were shuffled and cut, the Monte dealer pulled the bottom two cards, called the bottom layout, and placed them face-up. Next he took the top two cards and placed them face-up. This was called the top layout. Players chose which layout to bet, top or bottom, and made their bets accordingly. Once the bets were placed, the dealer turned the deck face-up. The card showing was called the 'gate.' Players won if the gate was of the same suit of either card in the layout they bet. Diego squeezed in between Alvaro and Vicente and placed his bet on the bottom layout, showing a king of hearts and a seven of clubs.

At a table in the back, several older, white-haired *caballeros* sat drinking and laughing. The old *dons,* retired from their *hacienda* duties, were engaged in animated conversation. They discussed one of their favorite topics – politics.

"The governor burned the papers to give the *Americanos* control over Spanish land," *don* Armando grumbled. "He's a Methodist and a friend of *el Presidente* Grant. How can you trust a man like him?"

"*Sí, Armando,* he is no friend to *caballeros.* He does nothing when *dons* complain about the courts voiding our Spanish land grants."

Don Armando and his friends remembered a life before New Mexico became a territory of the United States. They or their fathers were part of Governor Manuel Armijo's army that drove the Texans out of New Mexico when the Mexican-American war started. They fought with Governor Armijo at Apache Canyon, the narrow pass about ten miles southeast of Santa Fe where they were setup to ambush the United States Army commanded by General Kearny in 1846.

It was when they were young, but it seemed like yesterday. They would have destroyed the invaders, but Governor Armijo turned into a *culón,* a chickenshit, and ordered the New Mexican Army to retreat to Santa Fe. General Kearny marched into Santa Fe and took New Mexico without firing a single shot. Governor Armijo saved his skin by fleeing to Mexico and escaped capture by the Americans.

These old *caballeros,* the old Spanish *dons,* never forgave the cowardly governor. Now they spent most of their time at the Palacio reminiscing about old times, sipping brandy, and taking a *puta* when they could get their old *penes* to cooperate. The Palacio reminded them of the good days, the days when Spaniards ruled the Kingdom of New Mexico. All they wanted now was to hand their land to their sons and drink in the Palacio where they did not have to deal with gringos.

It was almost midnight when Virginia signaled Diego to give her a half an hour before he came up to her room. Diego was ready, the cards were not falling his way tonight, and the thought of partaking of Virginia's moist treasure stirred his *garrancha*. He lost the next hand and stood up, collecting the small pile of money sitting in front of him.

Anxious, he made his way up to her room. Virginia was propped on silk pillows, her raven black hair spread on the pillows and her alabaster body only covered in a sheer black nightgown. She said she was thirty, but Diego knew it was more like thirty-six. Either way, her body was *magnífico*. Her breasts popped under the sheerness of the nightgown and showed aroused nipples. She beckoned Diego to come to her. Slowly he unbuttoned his waist length jacket and hung it carefully, teasing her with his deliberate movements. He was in no hurry.

She stared through half-opened eyes at his muscular chest covered with dark curly hair. She knew he was trying to taunt her, but she could also see his *garrancha* straining in his pants.

Diego sat on the bed and removed his boots. Virginia ran her hand lightly across his back. Turning, he bent over and pulled her nightgown away from a breast. He kissed and licked the exposed nipple until Virginia moaned and tried to grab his arm to pull him down, but he moved away. Unhurriedly, he unwrapped his red silk sash from his waist and used it to bind her hands to the bed post. She squirmed and playfully pretended to try to escape the tight sash holding her arms above her head. He pulled up her gown exposing the moist black haired treasure between her legs.

He teased it with his tongue until she begged him to take her. *"Diego dámelo,"* she groaned.

Diego knew what Virginia liked and he was happy to give it to her. As he finally engulfed his *garrancha* to the hilt, she moaned with pleasure. While he serviced Virginia, his thoughts wandered to Ana Teresa. He wondered if the *Californio señorita* was as pure as she seemed. Yes, he wanted

the young, pure *señorita*. He would take her virginity as a
conquest and he would not to be denied. He would take it
until he grew tired of her and then he would toss her away
for someone with money or land.

CHAPTER 26

It was now mid May and Rafe felt he was way behind schedule for getting his ranch house started. He and George had laid out the location with stones back in February. George recommended a master builder, Joaquin Castillo, who specialized in Spanish colonial architecture and was known in Santa Fe for excellent work.

Today was the second meeting between Rafe and Joaquin. On the first meeting, standing on the location, they discussed the general idea Rafe had about the house he wanted, and now Joaquin was coming to the Summers' home with renderings. Rafe poured over the designs, asked questions, and was very impressed with Joaquin's ideas. He wanted him to get started as soon as possible.

"Señor, it is already late spring and it is important to me to have the house built before winter comes again," Rafe advised the builder.

"Yes, I understand. With your approval, I will get a crew started this week," the builder replied. "It should be completed by November."

"Bueno," Rafe agreed. He was disappointed in the wait until November, but his family was safe here in Santa Fe. María was still in El Paso, but his mother and the children were comfortable and the Summers were gracious. As much as his adopted family enjoyed having Celiá and the children at their house, he knew his mother longed for her own place.

His plans for the house changed several weeks ago. He added two more bedrooms to the design, connected to the main house by a large breezeway. He made sure the design allowed for more space to be added in the future. He tried to tell himself it was just more prudent to build a larger house now as one project, but the truth revolved around Ana Teresa.

Rafe found her constantly in his thoughts. He tried to push the thoughts back; he was *mestizo,* she from an aristocratic Spanish family. It would never be allowed, but she was penniless and why did it matter anymore. This was New Mexico, not Spain, or even Mexico. They were free to marry whomever they pleased.

After the builder left, Rafe found his mother in the kitchen and told her about the plans.

"November will be a good time, *mijo*," his mother said cheerfully. "María will be home by then and we can all move together."

"Are you sure María is not a burden on *tío* Jose and *tía* Lupe? What if she does not come home until the house is built?"

"Your *tío* and *tía* are happy to have her. She, Martín, and Ita were getting along well. They are just a few years older and are a good influence. They have two children and María will soon be missing Antonio and Alicia."

"I hope so," Rafe said still trying to understand his sister's detachment from her children. His mother seemed content to raise them and the children looked to her for love. Last week Rafe signed papers at the diocese school in Tesuque for five-year-old Antonio to start primary school in September. Young Antonio called George Summers, *Tata*, and Alicia seemed happy and content. Neither cried for their mother.

"Jose will write soon and tell us she is well," his mother said. "Give her time, *mijo*."

A week ago when María left El Paso for Torreón, Jose and Lupe did not write to Santa Fe. "She will be home in a week," Jose told his wife at the time. "If we write, it will only worry them."

Lupe was worried. "She is so young, and so many things could happen," Lupe said to her husband. She knew communications with anyone in Mexico was difficult, if not impossible, and she found it difficult to sleep worrying about her young niece.

"You worry too much, *querida*," Jose told her. "*Don* Pablo is at the *hacienda* and will take care of her. It will be good for her to be alone and make decisions. Celiá babied her too much and made her feel weak. She is a woman and needs to make up her own mind about what is right and what is wrong. She needed to go to Torreón to free herself from the past." Jose patted his wife's shoulder.

Later in bed, Lupe said extra prayers for her niece. She understood what her husband said, but something was nagging at her. If anything happened to María in Mexico, she could never forgive herself for letting her go.

At the Reyes *hacienda,* curled on a small cot in the back of the barn near where Pablo slept, María could not get Rodolfo out of her mind. She was afraid to tell Pablo about Rodolfo and told him only about taking a swim at the lake. Was Rodolfo an outlaw or fighting for *peóns?* María wanted to believe him, but could she? He told her he had always loved her.

Last night he came in her dreams – young, strong, handsome. He held her and kissed her tenderly, then he was ripped away from her arms by a man wearing a uniform and carrying a long gun. She reached for Rodolfo, but he disappeared. This morning she felt shaken.

She found Pablo crouched over the small stove cooking potatoes.

"Buenos días," he greeted her. Over breakfast he told her he would be gone most of the day surveying the small canyons for the last strays. "If I find none, then we can be headed to Santa Fe in a couple days," he told her. "I only have one more horse to sell, or perhaps I will take it with us."

Mindlessly nodding in agreement, María was thinking about whether Rodolfo would be at the lake. After Pablo left the *hacienda* riding into the canyons, María walked to the lake. Birds chirped in the trees, calling to one another as the sun was bright and beginning to get hot. It was mid May and spring was turning into the hot, dry summer. When she got to the lake, all was quiet and Rodolfo was not there.

She sat on a small boulder near the water. The lake spread before her, glassily reflecting the sunshine. María had not made many decisions in her young life. Her mother and then *don* Bernardo made decisions for her, or perhaps life made the decisions. She had not wanted to be raped by the *don* and bear his children, but she had no power against him. Her mother decided they should escape to Santa Fe and live with Rafael, not her. The first big decision she made for herself brought her here to Torreón.

When she was young she dreamed of having a husband and children. In her naïve mind, she only wanted a bigger *jacal* to live in. She knew nothing of the world outside the *hacienda*. Now she had been to Santa Fe, El Paso, and saw a world so different than Mexico. In El Paso her uncle's family owned land and cattle. The children were going to school. Martín and Ita's two young sons would grow up never knowing what it was like to be a slave to a *haciendero*.

In just a few short years, her brother had become a horse breeder in Santa Fe, a businessman. It almost seemed impossible. In Santa Fe her children, Antonio and Alicia, would go to school and learn English. Soon they would forget their lives in Mexico, but María could not forget. Mexico was her home. She felt connected to the land here and felt a connection she could not explain.

She was surprised at her feelings. A few short weeks ago she was still angry at Rafael, thinking he killed *don* Bernardo. She thought of the *don* as her life, but her love turned to hate and she spit on the *desgraciado* and hoped he was burning in hell. He stole her virginity, as well as her youth.

When she left El Paso last week, she only came to Torreón to retrieve her fortune and then planned to return to El Paso, or perhaps Santa Fe, and start a new life. Now everything was different. A branch cracked nearby and María looked up to see Rodolfo tying his horse to a tree nearby. She stood up and ran to him.

Rodolfo pulled María to him, her warm body cradled in his arms. He came only to tell her to go back across the border where she would be safe. He wanted her. He wanted her more than life itself, and it was why he had come to a decision. He could not ask her to join him in the *bandido* life on the frontier. It was no life for her and would eventually mean only death. He knew it. Someday *la policía* would catch him or worse a *haciendero* would make an example of him.

"*Querida,*" he whispered over and over. Tangled in her embrace, all he wanted was her. María cried for joy in Rodolfo's arms. She smelled his breath and tasted his lips. Her breasts could feel his chest, his heart beating against them. Her hands reached around his neck and held him close.

Rodolfo whispered in her ear as he held her tightly against him. He could feel the spots where her erect nipples pressed against his chest and they felt like hot pokers.

"*Mi amor,*" she murmured into his cheek, kissing his face and neck. Rodolfo picked her up in his arms and carried her to a grassy spot under a tree. He laid her gently on the ground. She looked up at him, her eyes burning into his soul. María watched as he stripped his shirt. His bare chest glistened in the rays of sun cutting through the trees. She wanted him more than anything on earth.

Lying beside her, he took her in his arms. For more than two hours they found each other, touching everywhere, and joining in a long lost love. María found she knew nothing of love, only the pitiful mounting by *don* Bernardo. Her body responded easily to Rodolfo, spiking in ecstasy, and rippling waves of passion flowed through her. She wanted him inside her forever.

Finally, they rested in the warmth of the sun. Her head lay on his chest, her arm wrapped lightly across him and around his neck.

"Tell me how you make the *hacienderos* pay for the grief they bring to us *peóns,*" she said.

"The rich *gachupíns* and *criollos* stole most of their land from the peasants many years ago. They have no rights to the land, they just have money. They keep *peóns* ignorant and penniless to make them subservient." María did not understand all the words he used, but understood the passion in his voice.

"*Mi mamá* said *don* Bernardo stole my grandfather's farm. It is how we came to be in this place," she said.

"It is so for many. Padre Hidalgo fought for freedom

from the Spanish for the *mestizos* and the *peóns,* but little has really changed."

"How do you make the *hacienderos* pay?" she asked.

"We steal their horses and cattle and sell what we steal for money and give to poor families. We have helped many families escape to the north."

As his voice grew in passion, María felt it grip her heart and her soul. Rage for her former life at *don* Bernardo's *hacienda* swelled in her. How many young girls had been raped by the *dons* and made to bear their children. The *don* had not loved her; he had used her for his pleasure and as revenge against her brother, Rafael. She now wished for the courage of her brother, and wished she had killed the *don* herself.

"Where will you go, now?" she asked Rodolfo.

"West toward Durango," he said. "There are many *haciendas* along the way."

"I am going with you."

Rodolfo's heart sank at her words. He wanted her desperately, but knew it was no life for her. He wanted to think of her safe and away from this terrible life.

"*No querida.* It is no life for you, only running and sleeping on the hard ground."

"My life is here with you. I am not afraid. *Don* Bernardo stole my life and now you are giving it back to me. Sleeping beside you on the hard ground is a blessing, if we are free." María knew she finally found her home. She belonged in Mexico, beside Rodolfo.

He tried to reason with her, but she was determined. They made love again in the sunlight under the trees and then she said, "I must go gather my things at the *hacienda* and tell Pablo."

Rodolfo swung his leg up over the horse's back and pulled María up behind him. They walked the horse slowly down the lane from the lake to the horse barn. On the left side, the dying garden lay untended. A light breeze blew a few tumbleweeds along the dirt. Stopping the horse near the barn, Rodolfo lowered María to the ground and then slid off. Together they walked into the barn.

Pablo looked up seeing María and a young *bandido.*
He picked up the pitchfork and stood ready.

"Pablo, it is Rodolfo," María called to him.

"Rodolfo?" the horse master asked. He looked at the
young man, tall and lean, and did not see the young boy
who once lived here at the *hacienda.* He saw a *bandido.*

"*Hola, don Pablo,* where are my parents and
Consuelo?" Rodolfo asked.

Pablo lowered the pitchfork. "They are at the Santos
hacienda."

Rodolfo, Pablo, and María sat in the barn and talked
about what had happened at the Reyes *hacienda. Don*
Bernardo was dead and the *vaqueros* and *peóns* scattered to
neighboring *haciendas.*

"Where did you go? Some say you are a *bandido?*"
Pablo asked Rodolfo.

"Yes, so some say, but I take little for myself and
fight for the *peóns* who cannot fight for themselves. We
steal from the *hacienderos* and help *peóns.* We do not steal for
profit."

"How do you live?"

"We live off what the land gives us and a meager
income from what we are able to steal."

"You are playing a dangerous game my young
amigo," Pablo said.

"I cannot live in a world where the *peóns* are treated as
slaves. They must see how to take up the fight against the
hacienderos. We meet many others along the way who are
already picking up the fight."

"Where are you going?" Pablo asked.

"West toward Durango," he said.

"I am going with him," María proclaimed.

"NO!" Pablo bellowed aghast at the thought. "You
are going with me to Santa Fe, back to your children!"

"My children are well in my mother's care. She and
Rafael will raise them better than I. My place is here in
Mexico. My place is here fighting, so other young girls do
not end up as *putas* for the *hacienderos.*"

"It is too dangerous," Pablo told her and Rodolfo

nodded in agreement.

"I will gladly give my life, if even one other young girl does not end up raped like me," she proclaimed adamantly.

As they talked it became apparent to Pablo, María could not be swayed. He understood her vengeance, thinking of his life serving the *don* with only a small cot and leaky roof over his head.

"You can take the gray horse," he finally told her. She is gentle, but swift. "When will you go?"

"We should go now," Rodolfo said. "My men wait for me in the hills."

"Have some food and then you can go," Pablo replied. "I'll get the horse ready."

About an hour later, María was sitting on the gray horse. She tied her *mochila* containing her secret coin sack to the saddle. Pablo handed her a sack with food.

"Vaya con Dios," he blessed them to go with God and then walked nearer Rodolfo's horse and whispered, "Take care of her Rodolfo. You must send her to Santa Fe when she realizes this is no life for her."

Rodolfo looked into Pablo's eyes and nodded an understanding, then reached down and pressed several gold coins into Pablo's hand. "Get these to my mother," he said. "Tell her I am well."

Chapter 27

Rafe had not seen Ana Teresa since the fiesta *el día de la Batalla de Puebla,* on the fifth of May. Rafe and Carlos were working extra time at the weapons foundry to meet orders. George was still nursing his injuries from Elizabethtown, and Josefina grumbled at him if he tried to do too much. Rafe thought Carlos was uncharacteristically glum for several days.

"Have you seen Bibiana?" Rafe asked Carlos while they were shoveling coal into the furnace.

"No. She was not at church last Sunday. Usually she goes to the morning Mass, but I did not see her or her family," Carlos replied.

"So, Ana Teresa was not there either?" Rafe asked.

"No."

"You need to call on Bibiana," Rafe said.

"It is not proper," Carlos replied. "I have not asked her father if I may court her."

"It is not courting. It is business. We can ride Rayo and Santiago and talk horses with her father," Rafe suggested.

Carlos brightened. "Yes, he wanted to see the horses at the Easter fiesta, but there was no time. We could take the unbroke yearling sired by Rayo." The young mare was golden brown with white spots with Rayo's dark liquid eyes.

"We can get most of this work done today and go tomorrow," Carlos said and dug his shovel into the coal pile with renewed vigor.

The next day, Rafe and Carlos bathed and donned their *trajes,* taking extra care on every detail. Rafe shaved and trimmed his mustache and the small triangle beard under his lip.

When they reached the de Soto *hacienda,* they rode into the courtyard. A servant greeted them and Carlos asked if *don* Pedro was at home. After a few minutes,

Bibiana's father walked out the front door and down the steps of the veranda.

"Hola, Carlos. I see you have brought horses for me to look at. *Bueno."*

Carlos reintroduced Rafael, explaining Rafael was the owner of the horses and the breeder.

"Magnífico," he said running his hand down Rayo's dark brown flanks and across his distinctively white splotched rump. *Don* Pedro noticed the horse was much taller than any of his blooded horses. "I cannot remember when I have seen such fine Mexican horses."

"Perhaps you would like to ride him," Rafe suggested. "Only by riding can you truly feel his gait."

"Sí. Let me get my hat and jacket." Bibiana's father spoke to a servant who went into the house returning a few minutes later with a coat, hat, and riding quirt.

Rafe held Rayo while *don* Pedro mounted. Carlos climbed onto Santiago's back and they rode from the courtyard, leaving Rafe alone. The May weather was warm, not hot, but Rafe was sweating in the formal *traje.* He stood awkwardly holding the reins to the young mare.

"Buenos días," he heard a woman's voice say. Whirling around, he saw Ana Teresa standing on the veranda. Bibiana was standing at her side.

"Buenos días, señoritas." Rafe swept his hat down as he bowed to the girls.

"You promised to take us riding," Ana Teresa said, "but you take my uncle instead."

"We only hope to convince him of our expert horsemanship, so perhaps he will allow it," Rafe retorted.

Ana Teresa watched Rafe nervously fidgeting from foot to foot. He stood about six feet, with broad shoulders that filled out his *traje* nicely. His face was tan and when he smiled his teeth were white and straight. She thought he was handsome, but not dashing.

Ana Teresa walked down the steps and tentatively walked closer to the young mare. Rafe held the bridle tighter when she reached out to stroke its neck. The young mare shied, and then relaxed to her touch.

"She is pretty," Ana Teresa said trying to make conversation. She knew nothing about horses, except how to ride. Some were fat and some were tall, some were gentle and others rough to ride.

"She was sired by my Appaloosa," Rafe explained. "She will be a fine riding horse, sleek and fast."

"Do you think Carlos and my father will be back soon?" Bibiana interrupted from the veranda.

"Yes, your father is only testing the Appaloosa. They should be back shortly."

"How many horses do you have?" Ana Teresa asked Rafe still stroking the young mare's neck.

"Nine. Three are yearlings, like this one. By fall I will have two more," Rafe said proudly.

Hoof beats sounded outside the courtyard as *don* Pedro and Carlos rode in. They pulled up and Rafe helped the *don* dismount.

"Magnífico," he said handing the reins to Rafe. "Carlos has already explained he is not for sale, although I would pay handsomely for such an animal. He responds to the slightest movement. Such power, *magnífico,"* the *don* repeated his appraisal of Rayo.

Rafe smiled. *"Gracias.* I would be honored to train one of the yearlings, such as this one, for you."

"Yes, that would please me, but I prefer a colt. Then the old *dons* of Santa Fe will be most envious." *don* Pedro grinned.

"I have a young colt. I will bring him for your appraisal," Rafe offered.

"Fine. I understand you promised to take the girls riding. Is this so?" he asked raising his eyebrows.

"Yes sir. May we have your permission to do so?"

"Sí, por favor papá," Bibiana blurted out in a pleading voice.

Don Pedro turned to his daughter and smiled, "Tomorrow, *mija.* I will ask your brother to escort you."

"But father, we do not need a chaperon. We are only going riding." *Don* Pedro raised his hand to silence her and Bibiana knew her father would not change his mind.

"We will bring the colt for your inspection tomorrow," Rafe said. *Don* Pedro turned his back and strode back to the house in a dismissive, aloof manner which irritated Rafe. He stood in the courtyard staring at the *don's* back disappear into the house. Rafe felt his face burning by the insult and turned putting on his hat. He hoped Ana Teresa did not see.

Stepping up into Rayo's saddle, Rafe said simply, "Until tomorrow then, *señoritas.*"

Rafe spurred Rayo out of the courtyard and Carlos followed. Rage burned through Rafe's body. "Slow down," Carlos called to him riding up beside him.

"Nothing changes," Rafe muttered. The shame and feelings of inferiority from his youth as a *peón* and the treatment by *don* Bernardo enveloped him.

"*Cálmate, amigo.* His bluster was more for show. He was gracious on our ride and I asked if we could take the girls riding. He agreed," Carlos said.

"Gracious to you, but not to me," Rafe grumbled. "You are a *caballero.*"

"He knows nothing about you. Don't be so hot-headed. He was just asserting his rights over the girls. It is the way of a father."

Rafe relaxed a bit, taking a deep breath slowing Rayo to a trot, realizing Carlos was right. *Don* Pedro was allowing them to take the girls riding tomorrow. Still, it angered him to be dismissed in such a manner.

Chapter 28

The next day Rafe and Carlos took the yearling colt to the de Soto *hacienda*. *Don* Pedro was impressed when he inspected the young horse. Barely a year old, the colt was still shy and skitterish when the *don* approached.

Rafe spoke to the horse and stroked his neck. The shy colt pawed the ground.

"These are high-spirited animals," Rafe said. "Each with a unique personality. When he is trained, you will be pleased."

"Bring him back when I can ride him," the *don* said.

Bibiana and Ana Teresa ran down from the veranda dressed in riding clothes. Both wore split skirts and high leather riding boots. Bibiana carried a quirt in her hand.

"Ana Teresa is not an experienced rider. You must not allow them to gallop the horses," the *don* warned.

Bibiana's brother, Emilio, led three horses from the barn and stopped near his sister. Carlos quickly went to help Bibiana up and into the saddle, the split skirt allowing her to ride forward and not sidesaddle. Before Rafe could move, Ana Teresa mounted the darker horse in a manner showing she was not as inexperienced as *don* Pedro indicated.

As they rode from the courtyard, Rafe noticed Ana Teresa looked quite comfortable in the saddle. "I believe you have more experience on a horse than your uncle believes," Rafe said to her.

"My uncle feels responsible for me, promising my father to keep me safe. We had many horses on our rancho in California."

"I noticed you had a soft touch with the mare yesterday," Rafe replied.

"I like horses. I've ridden since I was a child." Ana Teresa kicked the dark mare in her flanks and the horse jumped to a gallop, her long dark hair and the horse's tail flying behind them.

"Hey," Rafe yelled kicking Rayo into a gallop and following Ana Teresa.

Bibiana laughed. "I knew she would disobey my father," she said to Carlos.

By the time Rafe and Rayo caught up with Ana Teresa she and her horse were breathing hard, but a look of joy was written all over her face. Rafe rode up beside her. "Do you want to race, *señorita?* I assure you, you will lose."

Ana Teresa slowed the horse to a cantor. A bright smile lit up her entire face and at that moment Rafe realized he loved her. He glanced back and Carlos and Bibiana were still far behind. He longed to say something witty, profess his love for her, or just to be gallant, but the words escaped him.

"When will you return to California?" Rafe asked her instead.

"Never, I fear. My father is in Spain trying to obtain copies of our family's original Spanish land grants here in New Mexico," she said and Rafe saw sadness in her eyes.

"You must miss California?"

"*Sí,* all my friends are there, my life is there. I was betrothed to marry," she replied looking straight ahead. Rafe's heart fell. She was betrothed to someone, probably a wealthy landowner's son.

"I did not know you were betrothed," Rafe said.

"The *caballero* no longer wants me, because my father has no dowry to offer his family. He left me for another, who's father has a large vineyard," she spit out bitterly. "*Desgraciado.* I hope he chokes on her father's wine." Rafe was shocked to hear her say such vile thoughts, but then chuckled never hearing such talk from a woman.

"Do not be bitter. New Mexico is a wonderful place for a woman, such as yourself. You can be free of such *desgraciados* here. I hope you will stay," Rafe told her.

"You would like me to stay?" she said lightly tipping her head to the side. Rafe did not get a chance to answer as Carlos, Bibiana, and Emilio caught up with them.

"My father told you not to gallop," Emilio said sternly.

"She was in no danger. She is an expert horsewoman," Rafe told him. Emilio grumbled something Rafe could not hear. He was bored and angry his father asked him to chaperon his sister and cousin.

"Let's ride to the creek and rest the horses before we go back," Bibiana suggested. They followed her to a small grove of trees not far ahead where a shallow creek ran over rocks. Rafe knew by the end of June, the creek would be dry until the summer monsoons started. Carlos helped Bibiana dismount, while Rafe helped Ana Teresa. This time she allowed his help.

Emilio stayed mounted. "Bibiana, you and Ana Teresa stay here until I come back," her brother told her firmly. He turned his horse and rode off. Bibiana and Carlos were elated. They walked off together arm in arm, leaving Ana Teresa and Rafe standing under the trees.

"Bibiana, you ride very well," Carlos stammered.

"*Gracias*. Father is very impressed with the horses. He told mother at dinner last night, Rafael's Appaloosa is the finest horse he has ridden in years. Father said the horse is from Mexico."

"Yes Rayo is a special horse."

"Is Rafael from Mexico?" she asked. "How do you know him?"

"Rafael saved my life," Carlos said. "Our lives have been intertwined by God since the day I got this scar."

"You told my mother you got the scar in Spain protecting the honor of a young girl," Bibiana said looking a bit bewildered.

Carlos turned to the woman he loved and took both her hands in his. "Bibiana, you need to know the truth. You deserve to know. My brother, Benicío, gave me this scar when I fought him in El Paso. It was over the honor of a woman, but not a young girl in Spain. My brother was a bad man who tormented people, women particularly. He became a murderous outlaw after our family lost our land grant. At that time, I had no choice, but to follow him. I have done some bad things."

Carlos could see the words registering in Bibiana's

mind. "I met Rafael the day I got this scar and then four years later Benicío left me for dead on the Chihuahua Trail north of Socorro. I would have died, but God intervened and Rafael found me. Because of him I am alive."

Bibiana let the words sink into her brain, though they made little sense, except Carlos owed Rafael his life. "I owe him too, then," she said. "I owe him for bringing your love to me."

"I killed my brother, Bibiana. I killed Benicío," Carlos blurted out, finally relieved to be free of his secret from her. "I did not do it in revenge for me. He killed two women and several others, and was going to kill Rafael." Carlos eliminated the part about the women were Indians, not knowing if she would understand.

Bibiana stood still for a moment, stunned. "You killed Benicío?"

"Yes." The silence hung like a curtain between them, but Bibiana did not remove her hands from his.

"I'm telling you this because I do not think a man and his wife should have secrets."

"Wife?"

"Yes, wife. I love you Bibiana. You know that. I want you to be my wife when I am able to support you. I am not a rich man. I have no land or property, but I will honor and love you forever as the Bible teaches."

Bibiana threw her arms around Carlos and clung to him. After a moment he gently pulled away from her and lowered his lips to hers. She responded to his kiss. When she broke the kiss, there were tears in her eyes.

"I want to ask your father for your hand," Carlos said. Bibiana's face darkened, her joy evaporating quickly.

"My father is old fashioned. He wants me to marry well, someone with land and money, someone like Diego de la Torre. I told him I would never marry Diego."

"We must wait until I have my teaching job in September. At least then I have something to offer," Carlos said. "If I ask him now and he refuses, he might never reconsider."

Bibiana knew what Carlos said could be true. Her

father was stubborn and once he made a decision, his honor would not allow him to change his mind. Desperately she tried to think of ideas.

"Carlos, my love, let me talk to my father," she said.

"What! I will not hide behind your skirts. What kind of man would he think I am, if I let you talk to him of our marriage?"

"Carlos, he has never refused me anything. It's 1871 and the old traditions are changing. I will talk to him."

"No! He will think me weak, a coward. He would not want a coward for your husband. We must wait until I have my job and then I will approach him for your hand. It is proper. Tell no one, not even Ana Teresa, or your father might overhear rumors. Promise me."

Bibiana agreed, but in the back of her mind plans to approach her father still played. She wanted to marry Carlos and her father would have to agree.

Chapter 29

As María and Rodolfo rode away from *don* Bernardo's *hacienda* heading toward the hills, she tingled with joy. She was free. Free from the chains of servitude and oppression. She sensed she would be a burden to Rodolfo, a worry, and swore to be strong and brave, vowing to fight to her last breath, if that became necessary.

Rodolfo watched María beside him on the gray horse, her dark hair flying in the wind. He wanted her so much, but worried he was leading her into danger. So much changed in the last two days. He was used to living without fear; now he was charged with keeping her safe. As much as he longed for her, he wished he had made her stay.

When they arrived at the small camp in the hills in the late afternoon, Pepe was cooking a rabbit over the fire. Javier was the first to hear the horses and grabbed his rifle. When he saw Rodolfo, he lowered the gun. The men stopped talking and gawked at María as she rode in on the gray horse behind Rodolfo.

Rodolfo dismounted and helped María down from her horse. *"Chicos ella es María,"* he announced.

"A beautiful *puta, jefe*. She can serve us well," Kico snarled. The rest of the men laughed and sneered.

"Silencio!" Rodolfo commanded. "She is not a *puta*. She is a fighter. One of us."

"She is a woman," Javier said. "She cannot fight. Maybe she can cook and spread her legs, but that is all."

"Chingate," María cursed at the man telling him to fuck himself.

Rodolfo stood there shocked and then the other *bandidos* laughed. One of them yelled out, *"Eh jefe,* you have brought us a wildcat," Paco chuckled and more good-natured laughter erupted from the men.

Rodolfo introduced the men one by one. María looked each one in the eyes unafraid and noticed their shabby *pantalones* and *camisas* and raggedy sombreros. Most only wore *huaraches* sandals. What few weapons she saw were old and rusty and their horses were as lean as they were.

The men shared the rabbit and the small stew cooking over the fire. María noticed Rodolfo took less than his fair share. She could tell the men respected him, but from the looks the *bandidos* gave her, she felt unwelcome.

Later when the night swallowed the small hillside in darkness, Rodolfo unrolled her blanket on the ground on a small level spot near the fire. He set his saddle leaning against a rock nearby. Some of the men left and took up their positions to guard the campsite for the evening. María longed to lie with Rodolfo, but he made no move to touch her. Tired, she stretched on the blanket and soon fell asleep.

In the morning, the men broke camp with only weak coffee to drink and nothing to eat. They erased their tracks, mounted, and Rodolfo led them west. Kico rode out ahead of the group, and came back riding up to Rodolfo. Rodolfo made a series of signals and the group turned left. María followed. They rode slowly, seeming in no hurry, but pulled up near a stand of small mesquite trees. They dismounted and held the horses quiet. Shortly, high on the ridge, the shadowed outline of three men appeared. María could only tell they wore the hats of soldiers. The small military scouting group continued on the ridge and rode east. When they were gone, Rodolfo signaled and the group mounted and continued heading west.

When they camped in the evening, Rodolfo allowed no fire to be built. He shared what little was left from the food sack Pablo gave him, each person getting only a few bites. María noticed none of the men complained. When she lay curled in the blanket on the rocky ground, her stomach growled. The reality of her decision was enveloping her and she struggled to be strong. She tried not to look at Rodolfo, afraid he would see it in her eyes.

In the morning, María woke to the squawking of a chicken. Pepe proudly held the struggling bird by the feet. He and Javier stole five chickens and some vegetables from a local *hacienda* during the night. Rodolfo told the men to break camp and mount up. He came over to María and gently took her hand.

"I know you are hungry. We will stop at midday. We must leave before the *hacienda* sends *vaqueros* to find us," he told her.

She nodded in understanding, trying to keep a hold of his hand a bit longer. He looked into her eyes and whispered, *"Querida."*

Putting many miles behind them, Rodolfo finally gestured to the men to stop at a well treed refuge near a small stream. María slid from the horse, stiff and sore from the riding. She welcomed any chance to rest and sat on a rock. She watched the men apparently going about their assigned chores. No one complained and soon a small fire was built and one of the chickens lost its head. Pepe was attempting to pluck the bird.

María stood and walked over and said, "Give me that bird. You do not know how to pluck a chicken." Taking the chicken to the stream, she dunked it and in no time the bird was defeathered. Skewering it she put it on the fire to roast. Taking over the cooking chores, María barked orders for more water. Rummaging through the cooking supplies, she found a pot and cooked some of the vegetables taken from the *hacienda,* leaving more than half for another meal. She directed one of the men to find some wild *orégano.*

A little over an hour later, the men ravenously devoured the food she prepared. *"Sabroso,"* they all agreed it was the best meal in months. The native *orégano* flavored the meat and vegetables with a slight woodiness. María sizzled the chicken skin over the fire until it was crisp.

"We will keep her, *jefe,"* Javier declared to Rodolfo at the end of the meal and the men agreed with laughter. María felt herself blush and smiled.

"Next time steal me some onions and coffee," she teased. "If you bring me flour and corn, I will make you the best tortillas. Better than your *mamás* ever made."

"We will steal everything you ask for and more," Kico said, "if you continue to cook for us."

Later, stealing quietly to the small stream María washed herself as best as she could. Bending over the stream she splashed water on her face, arms, and neck trying to wash off the grime of the several days of riding. It was almost dark and the stars were popping out in the night sky. Suddenly two strong arms wrapped around her. His lips kissed the back of her neck.

Rising and turning, she rose to be wrapped in the arms of Rodolfo. He kissed her hard and strong, sending jolts of passion to her groin. She wanted him, needed him, and in her passion pulled at his shirt and tried to loosen his belt.

"Querida," he said as he picked her up and carried her to a flat area not far away. There they made love twice. First, hurried and rough, then tender and languishing.

"Te amo," María told him over and over that she loved him. Finally, Rodolfo helped her dress and they walked back to the camp. That night he put his blanket beside hers, knowing the men had accepted María into their group.

CHAPTER 30

Pablo looked at the shabby curtains in the dining room of the main house at *don* Bernardo's *hacienda* and sighed. He remembered when it was sparkling and full of life, lit with hundreds of candles. *Doña* Carmela and *don* Bernardo entertained often, filling the house and courtyard with music and dancing. Now, the curtains were torn, some stolen and dust covered the once lovingly polished tabletop. *Bandidos* stole anything they could carry, but the heavy Spanish colonial table stood as a reminder of better days.

He turned and walked to the foot of the stairs. Along the wall going up the staircase to the second floor, the large paintings of the Reyes family still hung on the wall. Pablo stopped to look at a painting of *don* Bernardo's grandfather, *don* Rafael. He stared intently picturing young Rafael, dressed in the same *traje,* riding north after *don* Bernardo died last December. The resemblance was undeniable. Even after *don* Bernardo's death, Pablo kept his promise to Celiá and did not tell Rafael *don* Bernardo was his real father and *don* Rafael his great-grandfather. Pablo pulled the painting of *don* Rafael from the wall and carried it with him back to the barn.

Three days ago a letter came from the federal government in Mexico City. The authorities were looking for heirs to the Reyes property. If none were found within a year, the *hacienda* would be sold to the highest bidder and the proceeds taken by the government. Pablo knew María's two children were rightful heirs, but they were only children and it was not likely they would be allowed to inherit, but Rafael was an adult and the oldest son of *don* Bernardo. Rafael's mother, Celiá, raped and pregnant by *don* Bernardo at sixteen, made Pablo promise not to tell anyone. She cried in Pablo's arms that day so long ago telling him of her dilemma. Four days later she married Antonio Ortega de Escalante, another young *peón* at the *hacienda.* Pablo had kept his promise for over twenty years, but now the *don* was dead and the *hacienda* was at stake.

Although the main house and small *jacals* were mostly ransacked by *bandidos,* the once gracious property and barns were mostly intact, the extensive lands of the *hacienda* lush and valuable. Pablo's problem weighed heavy in his mind. Telling Rafael of his heritage would break his old promise to Celiá, but letting the *hacienda* be taken by the government seemed foolish.

It was over a week since María and Rodolfo had gone. This too hung heavy in Pablo's heart. María was a young woman and Pablo let her go with Rodolfo, a wanted *bandido,* but she had a mind of her own and he felt helpless to stop her. After they left, Pablo took the coins Rodolfo gave him to Rodolfo's mother and sister. They cried when they heard he was safe. His sister, Consuelo, was married and pregnant and they both wished Rodolfo had been able to come to visit them. Pablo told them Rodolfo was not a *bandido,* as generally thought. "He is fighting for freedom and justice for *peóns,*" Pablo told them. "You should be proud of him."

Pablo planned on telling Rafael and Celiá about María and Rodolfo when he arrived in Santa Fe. It would not be easy to make them understand María would have gone with Rodolfo, whether Pablo approved or not. He saw love in her eyes and a fire in her heart. He made Rodolfo promise to send her to Santa Fe, if there was trouble, but Pablo knew trouble could mean death to *peóns* fighting for their rights.

Slowly he walked out of the main house to the barn. Two horses stood near a pile of hay. The tall roan was broken and he found the smaller Appaloosa running in the canyon yesterday. It reminded him of Rayo, Rafael's Appaloosa stallion.

Stirring a pot containing the last of a few roots he made into a stew, Pablo allowed his mind to wander back to the past. When Rafael was a boy he helped him in the barns and with the horses. Rafael had an innate way with horses, which Pablo recognized and nurtured. Horses responded to Rafael and he was a good worker and he was helping him on the stormy night Rayo was born. The mare was having trouble. Pablo felt the foal was a bit sideways in the birth canal and tried to correct the position, but still the mare struggled. Suddenly a *rayo*, a thunderbolt, struck just outside the barn. The tremendous crack and brilliant flash of light jolted the mare enough to force the foal out like a shot. Pablo and Rafael stood staring at a beautiful newborn Appaloosa foal and Rafael named him *Rayo*, after the powerful thunderbolt.

Rafael was about fifteen the night the Appaloosa was born. When the young colt was not nursing or following the mare, Rafael played chase and grabbed the colt's tail. Rayo would whinny and play the game. They ran with each other, sometimes for hours. For two years, Rafael spent his free time caring for the Appaloosa colt, brushing its mane, and keeping the young colt's stall clean and full of hay.

When the colt was ready for riding, Rafael broke him gently, stroking his neck and getting him used to the bit. Rayo barely bucked when Rafael finally climbed up onto his back. Together they flew into the fields and canyons of the *hacienda*. Pablo had broken many horses, but Rayo and Rafael seemed to be able to communicate in a special way. Rafael taught the young horse to respond to a series of clicks and whistles, in a type of unspoken language. He thought it appropriate Rafael stole Rayo after he shot *don* Bernardo for raping María and fled north.

Pablo finished his last meal and packed his few belongings. He opened a trunk he kept hidden under a hay pile which contained silver candlesticks, an emerald necklace, and some gold coins. It was meager pay for twenty-nine years of work here at the *hacienda*. Removing the small booty, he put a couple coins in his pocket and everything else he wrapped in an old pair of *pantalones* and pushed them to the bottom of his saddlebag. He lay down on his small cot and tried to sleep.

When the light of morning cut through the gaps in the barn door, Pablo saddled the roan, tied the tether rope of the young Appaloosa to his saddlehorn, and rode down the lane. Reaching the edge of the *hacienda's* land, he stopped to look back. The main house was barely visible behind him. He turned the horses north toward the United States. The letter from Mexico City was tucked in his saddlebag. When he reached Santa Fe he would decide whether to disclose the secret of Rafael's birthright and his legal claim on the *hacienda*.

CHAPTER 31

Don Pedro de Soto stretched on his bed watching his wife brush her hair. From this angle, she looked exactly as he remembered her on their wedding night, perhaps a few pounds heavier, but her dark, waist length hair cascaded down the curve of her back. He remembered the first time they met at church when they were only in their teens. He stared at her through the Mass, imprinting her face in his mind.

She was petite, barely over five feet. Even dressed with her tall *peineta* hair comb draped with a lace *mantilla,* she was shorter than most girls. Her face was finely featured and when she walked it looked like she was tip toeing.

Pedro asked his friends, but no one knew her. Following Mass, the *Fiesta of San Miguel* carried on into the afternoon. Pedro followed the girl and her family, trying to catch her name. Finally, her father introduced his wife and two daughters to a portly man and Pedro heard the name of the girl as Agustina.

Her father was a large, imposing man and Pedro could tell the family deferred to his wishes, as was the traditional Spanish custom. His wife and the girls only spoke when their father allowed it, otherwise standing quietly beside him.

Pedro trailed near the family, trying to act interested in the ongoing activities. Finally, Agustina stood behind her sister while her father was talking. Pedro strode closer and whispered, *"Hola señorita."*

Agustina jumped at the sound of his voice. Turning she stared at Pedro with her light gray-green hazel eyes. *"¿Qué?"* she whispered back at him.

"Soy Pedro de Soto y estoy a su servicio, señorita," Pedro bowed slightly as he introduced himself. Before she could answer, her father barked to his wife and the family followed. As Agustina followed her father, she looked back

and smiled at Pedro, lighting up the room like a hundred candles.

It was several weeks later when Pedro learned her father owned a large *hacienda* south of Espanola, a town some miles north of Santa Fe, where he raised bulls. Pedro's uncle told him *don* Lorenzo was respected, but considered a hard man. The family rarely came to Santa Fe, except for holidays and the annual bull auction. His uncle knew little about the family and was surprised the *don* had two teenage daughters.

For months Pedro watched for *don* Lorenzo's family and Agustina, but never saw her again. He and his friends strutted their horses around the *paseo* on warm nights, attended the church's festivals, and went to church every Sunday, but *don* Lorenzo's family never came.

Late in August, Pedro and his friends went to the annual Santa Fe rodeo. It was a weekend of drinking, riding, and festivals. Vendors cooked meats and sold fruits and candies to the children. Cooled beer was sold everywhere. In the traditions of old Spain, *toreadores,* bullfighters, wore *traje de luces* in vibrant colors, elaborately embroidered. Their swords were decorated with paper flowers to hide the sharp blades.

Pedro and his friends downed several cups of beer and wound their way to the arena. A great cheer erupted *olé,* then gasps came from the crowd as they watched a young bull charge at the *toreador*. Much like a dance, the bull charged and the *toreador* dodged the lethal horns. The bull was intent upon the colorful cape the *toreador* waved.

When the bull was finally killed, the bull's owner was cheered. Pedro saw Agustina's father rise to be recognized and beside him sat his wife and Agustina. Pedro's heart jumped. He had not seen her since the festival of San Miguel. The bright sun shone off her dark hair and she sat clapping for her father's pride.

Perhaps it was the beer or the bright sun beating on his head, but Pedro purposefully worked his way to the far side of the arena to find her father. The beer filled him with bravado. Finding *don* Lorenzo, he arrogantly stood before the man and said, *"Soy Pedro de Soto. ¿Me puede dar su permiso para cortejar a su hija Agustina?"* The *don* drew back as if struck, but his wife held his arm. This arrogant young fool just told him he wanted to court his daughter.

"Querido, have you noticed how Bibiana looks at young Carlos?" Agustina turned from brushing her hair to speak to her husband interrupting his memories.

"¿Qué?"

"She is in love with him," she said.

"She is too young to be in love," he retorted.

"Was I too young? I was only sixteen when you asked my father to come courting."

Don Pedro grumbled under his breath, but knew his daughter was growing up. "Are you sure?"

"A mother knows her daughter. Carlos is a good man."

"He has no land, no money," *don* Pedro said. "He is a fine young man, but Bibiana deserves the best we can buy. Diego de la Torre, for instance."

"Bibiana does not love Diego. Besides he's a *pícaro* and would not truly love her." Agustina heard the rumors about Diego and knew he was a womanizer. "He will only bring heartbreak to the girl he marries." She stood and walked over to her husband lying on the bed.

Sitting beside him she said, "Carlos has a good heart, a devout man educated in Spain. You, yourself, said he comes from a fine family in Los Lunas and his uncle is involved in politics. It is not his fault the *Americanos* stole his family's wealth. It has happened to many of our friends."

"Sí, it is true. His great uncle Manuel was the territorial Governor and Manuel's son, Armando, is regent to the new Governor. The Zuniga name is well respected in Los Lunas, but he has not asked to court her."

"Perhaps, he is ashamed of his status since he has no land." Agustina smiled a knowing smile at her husband. "Possibly we can allow Bibiana to invite him to supper next Sunday after church?" she asked in more a statement than a question.

"Do I have a choice?" he responded with a smile knowing the answer already and thinking he might consider Carlos as a possible suitor for Bibiana. Having family connections to the Governor and new territorial government could be helpful in the future. New Mexico was changing and the control of the Spanish *dons* was being overruled by *Americano* laws and governmental controls.

"No." Agustina kissed him lightly on the lips and then with more passion. He wrapped his arms around her and drew her lithe body close and his *garrancha* responded quickly to her warmth.

The next morning Bibiana was overjoyed when her mother suggested she invite Carlos to supper after Mass on Sunday afternoon. "Ask him to bring his friend, Rafael, for Ana Teresa," her mother told her. "Perhaps the four of you can go riding again." Bibiana threw her arms around her mother and then literally danced out of the room. *Doña* Agustina watched as her daughter twirled. Yes, she was in love. There was no doubt.

Bibiana found Ana Teresa in the parlor sewing. "We can invite Carlos and Rafael to supper Sunday. Mother told me," Bibiana exclaimed.

Ana Teresa looked up from her sewing. Her cousin looked to be riding on feathers. "Why are you so excited?"

Kneeling in front of her cousin Bibiana whispered, "Ana Teresa, can you keep a secret?" Her cousin nodded, yes. "Carlos asked me to marry him," Bibiana blurted out with tears of joy streaming down her cheeks.

"Has he asked your father?" Ana Teresa whispered back.

"No," Bibiana shook her head from side to side. "You must promise not to tell anyone. Promise me."

"I promise. *Felicitaciones,"* Ana Teresa congratulated her cousin, but wondered if her uncle would approve of Bibiana's choice. Carlos owned neither land nor money to offer for the marriage. Bibiana was naïve to think they could live on love. Ana Teresa knew what it meant to be penniless after the *Americanos* took her father's land in California. She would not be called to love without money or station to back it up.

On Friday Carlos came bursting into the horse barn waving a letter. "Rafe, Rafe," he called out and Rafe looked up from Rayo's stall.

"Bibiana has invited us to supper after church on Sunday," Carlos told him beaming with joy.

"Us?"

"Yes, she writes I am to bring you, also." Rafe was elated knowing he would get to see Ana Teresa again.

CHAPTER 32

Pablo arrived in Santa Fe on Friday afternoon. His trip north was long and thankfully uneventful. He stopped at Rafe's uncle Jose's ranch to tell them about María. They were worried and not happy when he told them she went with Rodolfo. He tried to paint Rodolfo as a free man, not a *bandido* and told them she would be safe with him. He could tell they did not really believe him.

The trip north from El Paso surprised Pablo. New Mexico had tall flat-topped mountains and the dirt ranged from tan to reddish. The Rio Grande ran near the Chihuahua Trail with large cottonwoods and willows growing along its banks. The river and the trees gave Pablo plenty of shade and camping spots for his evening stops. He did not hurry, enjoying the beautiful early summer days. During the day the sky was an intense aqua blue, sometimes with white puffy clouds. It only rained once in the several weeks since he left Torreón.

Pablo stopped at a cantina on the outskirts of Santa Fe. He paid for a beer and asked the bartender if he knew George Summers.

"No se." The bartender asked several men at the bar, but no one knew a George Summers.

Pablo finished the beer and mounted his horse. The young Appaloosa nickered and tugged at the rope, then fell into the familiar pattern of being pulled. As he rode further into town, Pablo saw a tall mountain range circling the town to the east. The top of the mountains looked white in spots or light gray. He rode down the main road into town and found himself near the San Miguel Church.

The church was made from red earth adobe bricks covered with a brownish stucco facade. A rather small cross stretched into the blue sky above the two-story building. Pablo tied the horses to the rail outside of the church's courtyard. The church building was completely surrounded by a high adobe wall, only accessible by a wide gated entrance leading into the large courtyard.

Pablo could tell the church was very old and he never saw a church built with such a defensive wall. Walking to the large carved front doors, he pulled on the handle. The thick wooden door creaked as it swung open. Pablo removed his hat, knelt, and blessed himself using the holy water near the door.

The sanctuary was long and narrow with wooden pews lining both sides. At the front of the chapel, tall carved pillars graced paintings of the Blessed Virgin, Jesus, and San Miguel. Light filtered into the long room from high windows.

A woman in black knelt in the second pew with her head down, but otherwise the chapel was empty. Pablo sat studying the paintings behind the altar. They depicted scenes from the Bible and the carving of San Miguel was decorated with gold. Pablo bowed his head and thanked the saints for his safe trip and asked for their continued blessings.

The sound of heels clicking on the hardened floor made Pablo turn. A young woman walked out of the confessional near the back of the chapel. Pablo blessed himself and walked down the aisle and into the open confessional booth.

"Bless me Father for I have sinned," he said in Spanish. Pablo confessed his sins and the padre responded. When he was done, he asked the unseen padre if he knew a George Summers.

"*Sí,* I know *Señor Summers,*" the padre replied. Pablo asked for directions to the Summers' ranch and the padre told him to take the road north about an hour to the GSW Ranch.

"*Gracias, Father,*" Pablo responded.

"*Vaya con Dios,*" the padre told him to go with God.

When Pablo exited the church, the bright sunlight almost blinded him. It was afternoon and the padre said the ranch was about an hour out of town. Pablo gathered the horses and rode along the main street of town heading north.

Riding under the GSW arched sign reminded Pablo of riding to *don* Bernardo's *hacienda* in Torreón. The meandering lane led to a sprawling ranch house. The home was constructed of whitewashed adobe and smooth round river rock used in the foundation and for accents. Large pine poles supported the porch. The peaked roof ran lengthwise covered in red tile. The roof line was interrupted in the center by a second story, which stretched along the middle third of its length. Large windows and double doors opened to an extensive second story balcony.

The main house was only one of many buildings on the ranch. There were many outbuildings to the east of the ranch house yard, the largest building with a substantial chimney spewing thick black smoke. Pablo stopped the horses and dismounted. A woman came out of the front door.

"*Buenos días. Bienvenidos,*" she said.

"*Soy Pablo Medina de Torreón,*" he answered her.

"Pablo, welcome. Rafael has been hoping you would come. He is in the foundry. Come, you must be tired from your trip." Josefina led Pablo into the house, ordering a servant to find Rafe.

Josefina led Pablo to the parlor where an older man sat near the window. "*George, este es Pablo Medina de Torreón,*" she announced.

"Pablo, Rafael has spoken often of you. Welcome. Come, please sit down," George said. Pablo nervously perched on a chair across from George Summers. Now finally here in Santa Fe, Pablo felt awkward, shy, and not knowing what to say. Shoes clicked in the hallway and Celiá ran into the room.

"Pablo," she ran to him and gave him a big *abrazo*. "*Bienvenidos.*"

Excitedly she reintroduced Pablo to George and laughed and talked about Torreón. Josefina and two teenage girls came to the parlor door. In the back of the house a door slammed shut and then a voice rang in the background. In a moment, Rafe burst into the room.

"*Hola don Pablo, bienvenidos,*" Rafe welcomed him with

a huge bear hug. Pablo was surprised by the excitement of his arrival. Josefina and the girls headed to the kitchen to talk to the cook about supper. Rafe and George talked to Pablo about the trip.

"I had no problems," Pablo told them. "Rafael, I brought you a young Appaloosa. It is a yearling, and not as fine as Rayo, but he will be a good horse."

"Bueno," Rafe said. "Come, show me and we will take him to the barn." Rafe and Pablo found the young Appaloosa standing quietly in the courtyard. Rafe felt its flanks and talked gently to the colt. It was still young and would not grow to be as tall as Rayo. He had one brown front shoulder and leg and one white, with large brown spots on his haunches. The markings were unusual.

"He is a fine horse," Rafe said. "Come let's take your belongings into the house and then we'll take the horses to the barn."

"I can stay in the barn," Pablo said. "I will be comfortable with the horses."

"No, *don* Pablo," Rafe replied. "You are our guest and not a servant. There are many rooms in the main house. When I get my house built, I will have a private *casita* built for you." Rafe grabbed up Pablo's satchel and headed for the house. Following behind him, Pablo watched the square of Rafe's shoulders and heard the authoritative tone in his voice. The young *peón* boy who worked with him at *don* Bernardo's *hacienda* was gone and instead he walked behind a proud man.

They walked the horses to a large barn behind the building with the smokestack. Rafe told him it was the weapons foundry and the smokestack used for the large fire needed to melt metal. I will show you the foundry tomorrow; today I want you to meet my horses.

The rest of the afternoon, Pablo and Rafe talked horses and Pablo was impressed by the foals already sired by Rayo and Santiago. The barn was twice the size of the one at the *hacienda* and smelled of fresh hay. Behind the barn, a fenced hillside stretched for as far as the eye could see where the horses could run. Two mares were pregnant and the herd numbered nine, not including Rayo and Santiago. The young Appaloosa would make twelve.

"You have done well," Pablo said.

"You taught me well, *don* Pablo," Rafe replied.

"Please do not call me *don,*" Pablo said quietly. "I am only a man, not a *don.* You are the *jefe* here."

Rafe smiled knowing he had called the horse master *don* Pablo his entire life. It was a way of showing respect, not station. Here in New Mexico they were equals, as men. "Pablo, you are the horse master, I still have a lot to learn."

At the evening supper, the family circled the table before eating. George said the evening prayer.

"Lord, bless us your humble servants. We give thanks for this food which you have provided. We give you praise for bringing Pablo safely to us and for keeping us all safe in your arms and let us be servants of your will, Amen."

"Amen," they all chimed in. The aroma of the roasted pork, chilis, and potatoes permeated the dining room and the girls, Rafe, and Carlos dug into the heaping plates of food.

Pablo stared at the abundant portions heaped on the serving platters. Celiá helped the children fill their plates and took a hearty portion for herself. Shyly, Pablo filled his plate as the serving platters were passed. He had been eating jerky and camp food for weeks and living off meager rations in Mexico since the *don* had died. To him, this meal was a feast.

The girls talked excitedly about teaching Alicia new English words. They tried to get her to say, apple, showing her a red apple sitting on the table, but Alicia shook her head back and forth. Carlos and Rafe talked to George about the new Appaloosa pony.

"Did you stop at Jose's, Pablo? Is the family well?" Celiá asked.

"Sí, están bien," he replied they were well. Pablo's stomach turned knowing Celiá's next question. He dreaded this moment since he left El Paso.

"How is María? Is she getting better?" Celiá asked.

"Sí, ella está bien en Torreón" he replied she was well in

Torreón.

"*¿Torreón?*" Celiá questioned his response. Suddenly the room was quiet as the others listened to Pablo.

"*Sí,* she came to Torreón to pay her respects to *don* Bernardo."

"She went alone?" Rafe asked.

"Yes. She came on the stage from El Paso."

Celiá was shocked to think her daughter could manage to travel to Torreón by herself. She had never been an adventuresome child, usually timid and shy. Rafe was angry she felt any need to pay any respect to *don* Bernardo.

After several awkward silent moments trying to sort out the new information, Celiá asked, "She returned to El Paso with you?"

"No, she is in Mexico," Pablo replied.

"Mexico! You left her in Mexico?" Rafe uttered the question in a shout. Pablo's shoulders slumped. He knew the news would be hard to comprehend and only hoped he could make them understand.

"Calm down, son," George said to Rafe. "Let us hear what Pablo has to say." Pablo related the events in Torreón. He described how María came to the *hacienda* and planned to return with him to Santa Fe. He told the family she met Rodolfo Guerrero and they left together. Rodolfo will be responsible for her. They are in love."

Rafe was shocked, but happy his best friend Rodolfo was alive and well. He knew Rodolfo always liked his sister and knew he was a good person, however he was still confused about what transpired in Mexico.

"You said the *hacienda* is empty. Where did they go?" Rafe asked sorting through the facts, assuming Rodolfo must be working on another *hacienda*.

"They went to live in the hills. Rodolfo is a freedom fighter. He fights for the cause of *peóns* against the *hacienderos,*" Pablo responded.

Celiá gasped. "No!" Rafe slammed his napkin on the table in a thump and pushed out his chair and stood up scaring the two young children.

"Perhaps we should discuss this in the parlor,"

George said calmly. "This is not talk for the children."

In the parlor, Pablo took a high-backed chair, George and Rafe stood by the fireplace, Celiá sat on the sofa. Pablo related every detail he could about the situation in Torreón and in general about the desire of the *peóns* to be free of the oppression of the *hacienderos*. Rodolfo was only one of many fighting this fight. Rodolfo stole from rich *hacienderos* and helped *peón* families in need. "He is a good man and he loves María. He will take care of her."

"He is a *bandido*," Rafe said. "He may be fighting a good cause, but he can be shot on sight or worse. María is in danger."

"María said *don* Bernardo stole her life and standing beside Rodolfo in the fight to give freedom to others was a blessing from God," Pablo related the feelings María had told him. "She is happy and full of spirit."

Celiá could not believe her shy daughter was living off the land and fighting for a cause. It seemed preposterous, and yet somehow Celiá was proud of her. The *don* had stripped her of her childhood and of a life filled with love. Perhaps Rodolfo could give her these things.

"What about the children? Did she not think of her children?" Rafe asked.

"She said the children were safe and happy here in Santa Fe. She said Celiá was a better mother to them and you would see they were educated. She hoped they would not remember their life at the *hacienda*," Pablo said.

"I must go find them," Rafe said. "She is only twenty and does not understand what she is getting into."

"*No mijo*, let her go. Give her freedom, as you have taken yours," Celiá said wisely, even though her heart was breaking. "She was unhappy here in Santa Fe. Let her find her own dream."

The next morning, Pablo found Celiá alone near the barn and took her aside. He lay awake most of the night struggling with his dilemma about the ownership to the Reyes *hacienda*.

"Celiá, we have to talk. I may have a solution for

María and Rodolfo, but I may have to break my promise to you," he told her with hat in hand.

"What promise?" She did not immediately think about the secret he knew.

"You told me to never tell Rafael that *don* Bernardo was his real father," he reminded her.

"Yes, you must never tell him," she whispered looking around making sure Rafael was not nearby to hear.

"Hear me out. It could help María and Rodolfo," he insisted.

"How can it help them now?" she asked.

"The laws in Mexico have changed. Now, the first born of a *haciendero* can inherit the property, even though he is a bastard son. I can prove Rafael is *don* Bernardo's first born," he explained.

"How can it be proved? He did not get the Reyes name," she asked.

"When Rafael was born I went to the padre at the *hacienda's* chapel and told him what happened to you and he made a secret record of Rafael's birth as a Reyes. Before I left Torreón, I went to him and he still has the record." Celiá looked at Pablo aghast. The padre in Torreón knew *don* Bernardo raped her and that Rafael was the *don's* bastard son. All these years, she thought no one knew.

"We can take the record to the government and Rafael can inherit the *hacienda,* but Rafael must be the one who takes the proof to the government in Mexico City. So, we must tell him. I think he could sell or give the property to María and Rodolfo so they can leave the *bandido* life," he said studying Celiá's reaction. Her face turned dark, as if the shadow of a demon hovered over her.

"No Pablo . . . " she cried. "He must never know."

"We must, if we want to help María. She and Rodolfo will surely be killed or jailed as *bandidos,* you know that. Having them live at the *hacienda* is a good thing," he continued.

"What you say is true, but I cannot face Rafael when he learns the truth." She fell into Pablo's arms and sobbed, almost like the day she made him make the promise. "How can we tell him? How can we tell him he is not who he thinks he is, but is the son of the man he hates most in the world?"

"Rafael is a good man Celiá. He will be hurt and angry, but he will do the right thing," Pablo reassured her.

CHAPTER 33

It was six long and uncomfortable days ride by stage to El Paso, but Jed knew it was an easier trip by stage than by horse. Luke seemed to have no trouble sleeping in the cramped coach seat, while Jed squirmed on the hard wooden bench. The stage rolled in at two in the afternoon and Jed, Luke, and four other passengers got off the dusty stage from Austin.

Luke got them rooms at the Stratton Hotel. Jed wanted a hot tub and soft bed, but Luke wanted whiskey and a woman. "Wake me in a couple hours," Luke told Jed. Heading down the hallway, Jed grumbled to himself. He hated Luke Payton and routinely kicked himself for getting into this situation. If Jed knew he would be going back to San Marcial, New Mexico, with a crazy man like Luke Payton, he never would have gone to Round Rock. He tried to figure a way to get out of his predicament, but they all ended in Luke hunting him down and killing him. Luke was a man who would not be crossed.

"Git up." Jed pushed on Luke's shoulder several hours later. Luke's snoring sputtered and he rolled over. It was twilight in El Paso and the lights beside the saloon doors were starting to twinkle. Luke splashed his face with a bit of water before he dressed and slipped on his boots. Wetting his fingers, he slicked down his hair and perched his hat on his head.

"Let's go see what's goin on in this here town," Luke said heading out the door. Tinny piano music floated from a nearby saloon urging them toward the sound.

"That'd be Lilli Jean's Saloon," Jed spoke up. "Been there afore an it ain't a bad place."

"Howdy boys," Lilli Jean hollered out as they walked in the saloon. "Ain't seen yew boys here before. First one is on the house," she said. Lilli took notice of the taller man dressed in a black brocade vest and a white ruffled shirt. A thin black tie was knotted at his neck and he wore a tailored black jacket and a black flat-crowned hat. Even from across the room, she could tell he had a presence about him. She liked what she saw, then turned to mingle with a group of cowboys playing cards.

Luke and Jed stood at the bar and were set up with a shot of rye. Jack, the bartender, smiled and poured Luke and Jed the free drink of the good stuff. "Howdy boys."

Lilli Jean liked giving new customers a shot of her best whiskey. A shrewd businesswoman, Lilli Jean usually made ten-fold the profits from the single free drink. Luke savored the shot of rye and tasted the quality of the smooth whiskey, while Jed just tossed it down in one gulp and nodded to the bartender for a refill. After a little while Lilli Jean sauntered to where they stood at the bar.

"Where kin I go fer a high stakes game?" Luke asked Lilli Jean.

"Not round here hansum. There's a game always goin on over at the Gem Saloon and Billiards Parlor. Don't think they'll let yew in, yew gotta be introduced to get in ta that game," Lilli Jean told him sliding up to his side and bumping him with her enormous breasts. Forty years old and painted up to try to make herself look younger, Lilli Jean was not a half-bad looking woman.

"What about yew honey, can yew do an introduction? I kin make it worth yer while, like partners," Luke asked pushing up against her bosom and placing his right knee between her legs. Lilli liked the tall, brazen gambler's attitude.

"Shur nuff honey. I'll git yew into the game, but then yew gotta come back to finish what yew jes started," she said slowly grinding on his knee.

"Cum on Jed, we goin to a poker game," Luke said.

"Yew go," Jed responded. "I'll stay here."

"No, yew comin with me. I want yew to have my back in case there's trouble," Luke ordered. It was exactly what Jed was afraid of – trouble. And trouble had a name – Luke Payton, but Jed had no choice and went along.

Walking through the door to the Gem, the large room was busier than Lilli Jean's. All the pool tables were busy and a Faro game drew a crowd. The roulette wheel spun as betters leaned over willing the ball to land on their number or color as the croupier leaned back waiting for the ball to land.

Lilli Jean walked them over to a well-armed man holding a shotgun cradled in his arms near a door. "Got players for Mick's game," she purred to the guard. "Tell Mick I sent them."

The man looked at Luke and Jed before he led them to a door behind the roulette game and knocked twice and then twice again. When he opened the door, smoke poured out of the room. In the center of the room five men sat around a large round table with a pile of chips in the center. In a corner a man stood with a shotgun cradled in his arm.

"What's up Ken?"

"Lilli sent em." The man named Mick looked up over his cigar and his eyes wandered up and down Luke and Jed. "Don't look like they got nuff dough," he grumbled. "Later boys, go have a drink on me." Mick turned back to the game dismissing them.

"Got enough to play." Luke pulled a wad of bills out of his vest waving them in the air. Mick looked at Luke again.

"We ain't got room for two, maybe tomorrow."

"He's not playing," Luke jerked his head toward Jed. "Jes me."

Mick waved an arm and told Ken to get another chair. "Yer friend has to leave."

"See ya tomorrow, Jed." Luke said without turning. Jed was happy to leave Luke to the card sharps. Maybe he'd try to cheat and they'd shoot him. Right now, it was everything Jed could wish for.

"Come on let's finish this hand afore the cards get cold," the oldest man at the table grumbled. He was sure he had a winner.

"I'll call yew Steve," Bob threw in a fifty dollar chip and laid down two kings and two queens.

"Not good enough this time, Bob. I got yew." Steve laughed and put down three fours and raked in the big pot.

Luke sat down and pulled out five hundred dollars. The dealer converted it to an appropriate assortment of chips and handed them to Luke. "Name of Herman Hills. Yew ain't taking my money, but I sure am willing to get some of yers," a slightly overweight balding man said while shifting his stubby cigar from one side of his teeth to the other, then smiled showing big teeth holding the cigar.

"Luke Payton from Round Rock," Luke said.

"Al Butler," another player said. Al wore a vested gray suit and his suit coat was hanging around his chair behind him. "This here's Bob Gibbons," he said pointing to his left, "Mick McDonald and Steve Gregg over there."

Howdies were exchanged. "Game is five card draw, five to ante, ten to open and no limit. We like to keep it simple round here." Herman spoke to Luke.

"Deal em," Luke said.

Luke sized up the competition. They looked like good old boys from El Paso, local businessmen. Bob Gibbons wore a tailored suit over dusty well worn boots, probably a rancher. Mick McDonald was a red haired Irishman with a ruddy complexion. He might be a politician or lawyer or something Luke thought. Herman kept his cigar firmly planted between his teeth. Steve Gregg, an older man with a full head of white hair, was wearing rimless spectacles. He kept his eyes glued on his cards.

"Ante up gentlemen," Herman said as he shuffled the deck of cards. Everyone pitched in a twenty dollar chip. Herman dealt five cards each, then picked up his cards and sorted them into a fan. Luke subtly studied their faces looking for any clue to help him read the players. He did not see much, but enough to help him.

The game went on with Luke wining some and losing some and after four hours Luke had a handle on all the players betting habits and tricks. He gave up his own actions and tricks, only those he wanted them to see. Luke was good at reading people and these men were not professionals.

It was now time for him to press the game. The next

hand Luke took four hundred dollars. A few hands later, he raked in two-fifty. He bluffed a hand and took a big pot of eight hundred and sixty dollars.

Bob Gibbons perked up and began paying closer attention to the newcomer. Bob noticed Luke spun the ring on his left hand when he held a good hand. He definitely had not spun his ring on that last hand. He could not be cheating, because Herman was doing all the dealing and they played with an unmarked deck. Bob decided it must be pure luck, until Luke won the fifth hand in a row and raked in nine hundred dollars. Herman peered over at Al and Mick with raised eyebrows; they got his signal and nodded.

"What the hell's goin on here, yew cain't be that lucky," Bob confronted Luke.

"Yew callin me a cheat?" Luke sneered. "Yer boy there is doin the dealin."

"Yew boys know I deal a straight game. We never seen this gent before." Herman put his hands up looking around the table at the players.

"What's wrong, ain't yew'll ever been beat afore?" Luke spoke up with a big grin on his face. "Yew boys playin or dun in?"

"Deal em," Bob grumbled at Herman.

Luke folded the next three hands, even though the second hand was probably a winner. No need to irritate the players into quitting. Each had money in front of them Luke wanted to win.

After the three losing hands, Luke took a four hundred dollar pot. Over the next hour, he took well over two thousand dollars from the group of men.

"Yew's cheatin, mister. Nobody is ever that lucky," Steve yelled back at Luke throwing down three queens to Luke's full house. Luke anticipated the move, and moved his hand to his gun when he stood up and backed away from the table. Out of the corner of his eye, he saw the guard who stood in the corner all night, raise his shotgun and level it.

"Take yer money and git outta El Paso," Mick said. "Get out by noon tomorrow or yer a dead man on the street."

Luke scraped his winnings into his hat and said with a grin, "I thank yew boys for the game."

CHAPTER 34

Life with Rodolfo and the *bandidos* was not what María bargained for, however her love for Rodolfo made the harsh living tolerable. Most days were spent on the back of a horse, moving from place to place. Rodolfo told her staying in any one place put them in greater danger from *la policía*. She washed herself in small chilly streams, catching herself missing a nice big hot tub of water and soap. They ate whatever the land gave them, sometimes good, sometimes meager.

Several days ago Rodrigo and Javier stole three young steers from the Jimenez *hacienda*. They took them to a camp of *mestizo* squatters trying to grow corn by stealing water from a nearby spring on a *hacienda*. Rodolfo gave them the steers and told them to butcher them quickly and conceal the hides and meat, in case *la policía* came looking for them. He brought back a small portion of meat for the men's supper. María was impressed with Rodolfo's generosity, but disappointed with the skimpy ration he brought for them.

"If you bring meat, I will smoke it," she told him.

"It is too dangerous," he told her. "We need to travel light and free." María cooked the beef into a hearty stew for supper, also making a high stack of tortillas, and the men raved. They treated her with respect, telling her *gracias* with each meal. In the evenings, Rodolfo would tell stories and rile the men to fight the *hacienderos*. Freedom for *mestizos* and *Indios,* he would tell them. María loved to hear him talk and wished she could be of more help – she wanted to fight.

They were traveling west, never stopping more than one night as they continued to move. One evening she was bent over the cooking fire, when shots rang out. The men scrambled to grab the few weapons, sticks, and clubs they carried. More shots rang in the air and then a scream. María ran to the bushes, grabbing her *mochila* from near her blanket as she went to hide. Rodolfo had told her to run and hide, if there was trouble. María scrambled into a thorny dense bush, scratching her arms and legs as she crawled.

Rodolfo and the others walked into the campsite with their hands up. Five rangy *bandidos* pushed them along.

"We are not your enemy," Rodolfo said to the man who seemed to be the leader of the *bandidos*. "We have no money. We give it all to the *peóns* and keep nothing for ourselves."

"Que pendejo," the man grumbled calling Rodolfo stupid.

"Search if you like," Rodolfo said. "We only have a few guns and a little meat."

The leader of the *bandidos* jerked his head to one of the other men and he quickly rifled through the bags and blankets. María clutched her *mochila* tightly in her arms, barely breathing. She had not even told Rodolfo of the fortune lying in the bottom of her backpack, afraid he might give it away.

One of the intruders looked at the meager meal cooking on the fire and laughed. "They are poorer than most *peóns, jefe*. There is no meat in this pot."

The leader pushed his rifle barrel into Rodolfo's back. "Leave this place in the morning," he barked. The *bandidos* grabbed the two pistols from Rodolfo's men and mounted their horses. When they had ridden off Javier said, *"Desgraciados,* I will go after them. They took our guns."

"No amigo, we will find other weapons." Rodolfo held him back.

María waited until she was sure the *bandidos* were gone, then carefully crawled out of the thorny bushes. Dots of blood popped through her *camisa*. Rodolfo saw her and his heart sank. He was only leading her into trouble. He wanted to take her in his arms, but barked orders at the men to organize the camp instead. "As soon as we eat, we ride."

They rode all night in the darkness, lit only by a sliver of a moon. In the distance, María heard coyotes howling. She wrapped her blanket around her shoulders and kept riding trying to just follow the horse in front of her in the dark.

Late the next morning they stopped in a rocky area with an overhanging cliff, which gave them some protection from the wind. Paco caught a small rabbit, and María was grilling over the fire. At least they had meat. After the meal, Rodolfo finally came to her and wrapped her in his arms.

"*Lo siento,*" he said he was sorry. "María, you should go to Santa Fe. It is not safe for you here. We do not even have pistols to kill a mountain lion, if one attacked."

"We can buy guns," she said defiantly.

"María, *peóns* cannot buy guns in Mexico, even if we had the money."

"We can go to El Paso and buy guns," she told him.

"El Paso?"

"Yes, my *primo* Martín can help us buy the guns we need." Rodolfo started to rebuff her and then stopped. Yes, they could buy guns across the border. There, anyone could buy guns, even *peóns,* as long as you had money.

"We would need money. It will take me some time to steal enough, especially without any guns."

"I have money." María said. "I stole gold coins from *don* Bernardo for years. I do not know how much, but it is in my *mochila.*" Shocked, Rodolfo stared at her. He took her aside away from the men and said, "Show me."

María dumped the contents of the *mochila* behind a tree. She unwrapped the gold coins and laid them out and Rodolfo counted them.

"We could go north to Juárez, south of the gringo border, and then cross to El Paso. *La policía* are not looking for a young couple. We will tell them we are going to my uncle's ranch to stay for awhile."

Later Rodolfo told his band of *bandidos,* he and María were going to El Paso to buy guns. "Javier, you will be in charge. Go back and stay close to Torreón and we will find you when we return."

The next morning Rodolfo and María headed to Chihuahua on horseback. There, they traded the horses for a broken down wagon and two old mules. On the way north they talked and argued about how to obtain the guns. They planned to make contact with Martín, María's cousin. She begged Rodolfo to go directly to her uncle's ranch, but Rodolfo was wary. "He will not let you return to Mexico with me."

"My aunt and uncle must be worried why I did not come back from Torreón," she told him. "I need to tell them I am well and to not worry." After arguing for days, Rodolfo finally decided to let María go to her uncle's ranch, while he stayed outside of Juárez.

When María and Rodolfo arrived in Juárez driving the old wagon, they posed as a young couple looking for a place to start their life and raise children. Rodolfo found a campsite near the border about a mile northwest of Juárez, but not yet across the border.

In the morning, María put a blanket over the back of one of the mules and kissed Rodolfo. She crossed the border heading north to her uncle's ranch.

Lupe was working in the garden on the side of the house as a woman on a mule rode up. The woman was dressed in a *camisa* and red skirt with a shawl half covering her head. Lupe looked up into the sun and did not recognize her niece.

"Hola tía," María called to her.

"Gracias a Dios," tía Lupe praised God when she recognized María. "We were so worried. Jose. Jose," she screamed. "It is María."

After hugging her aunt and uncle, her aunt said, "Pablo told us you left the *hacienda* with a young man, a *bandido*. We have been so worried."

"Rodolfo is not a *bandido*. He is fighting for *peóns* to be free," she explained with a defiant tone in her voice, then paused and asked, "Pablo was here?"

"He came here to tell us before he rode on to Santa Fe. He knew we would be worried. He will tell your mother and brother when he gets to Santa Fe."

María quietly cursed to herself. If Rafael knew she was in Mexico with a *bandido,* he might come looking for her. "I am a grown woman, *tía*. I have chosen a life for myself. Rodolfo is a good man."

"Where is he?" her *tío* asked. "Why did he not come with you?"

"He is in Juárez visiting with friends. I rode north to tell you I am well." María decided to lie to her aunt and uncle, but now realized they would have wanted to meet Rodolfo. "I'll stay a few days and hopefully he will come and join me."

"Come, rest," her *tía* led her to the house. "You must be tired."

When Martín and Ita returned from town and saw María sitting in the living room with their mother, they grabbed her in a hug. Later after dinner, María and Martín took a walk in the warm night. María explained to Martín about Rodolfo's passion and how he fought for *peóns*, not wanting to paint Rodolfo as a *bandido*.

"It sounds dangerous," Martín said.

"I am not afraid. I only have to think of *don* Bernardo and how he treated me and I am full of courage." María told him. She swallowed hard, knowing the question she needed to ask her cousin would put her in a precarious position.

"Martín, we want to buy guns, many guns. In Mexico *peóns* are not allowed to own or buy guns."

"Guns! Why do you want guns?" Martín asked totally surprised by his cousin's request.

"*Primo,* we need the guns to fight for our freedom in Mexico. You speak English and can buy the guns here in El Paso. Can you help us? It is important to me and you must not tell *tío.*"

"María, it is not easy to buy a load of guns in El Paso. It would cause me a lot of trouble."

"Why? This is Texas. You are not a *peón*. You are allowed to own a gun here."

"Allowed to own a gun, yes. To buy a load of pistols and rifles . . . no one would sell a load of guns, especially not to a Mexican." María's heart sank. Even here in El Paso they could not buy the guns they needed.

María fell to her knees. She had been so sure they could buy the rifles and pistols they needed here in El Paso. Even with her gold coins, their cause was fruitless.

Martín was filled with empathy for his cousin's passionate plea. He remembered a time, not too long ago, when the Reynolds shot up their ranch, burned the barn, and almost killed his little brother. The Texans came with guns and he and his family had none, nothing to fight back with. The doctor saved his younger brother's leg, but he would forever walk with a limp. Now, he and his father carried GSW pistols and rifles, sent to them by Rafael, and they carried them always ready to defend themselves. The memory gave Martín an idea.

"Rafael can give you guns. We could wire Santa Fe and ask him to bring a load of guns here."

"No! Rafael will never allow me to return to Mexico with Rodolfo." María cried. "He will force me to return to Santa Fe."

"*Sí*, Rafael would take you away from this foolishness."

"I won't go back to Santa Fe. I want to fight *hacienderos* who rape young girls like me."

Martín knew the *haciendero* had raped María and forced her to bear his bastard children. He felt her anguish and decided to see how he could help.

"*Bueno,* I want to meet Rodolfo. I want to understand what he needs." Martín's words gave her hope.

María explained to Martín where to find Rodolfo's campsite outside of Juárez. The next morning her cousin rode to Juárez with a description of Rodolfo and the wagon. Finally, Martín spotted a young man standing under a tree near a broken down wagon.

"*¿Eres Rodolfo Guerrero?*" he asked the young man.

"*Sí*"

"*Yo soy Martín primo de María,*" Martín explained he was María's cousin.

"*Me alegro de conocerte,*" Rodolfo said he was glad to meet him.

"*Igualmente,*" Martín responded greetings. He then

explained to Rodolfo how María wanted him to come to her *tío's* ranch. He would be welcome.

As they rode the rickety wagon through the outskirts of El Paso and toward the ranch, Martín grilled Rodolfo about his life.

"I was Rafael's best friend at *don* Bernardo's *hacienda*. I knew María when we were growing up. I watched the *don* abuse her and I was there when Rafael shot the *don* and fled. After years of watching *don* Bernardo continue to hurt María, I fled to the hills and swore revenge. Now we help *peóns* giving them stolen goods and food. They need us there. These people lost their farms, and now have to work their own land for *hacienderos* who stole it from them. Some are beaten and others killed if they resist. They work for nothing, only meager rations of food."

Martín heard the passion in Rodolfo's voice. He had not been raised on a *hacienda* and did not truly understand life as a *peón*. He knew from talking to Rafe and hearing stories of others, even life here in Texas was easy compared to life on a *hacienda* in Mexico.

"But María is just a young woman."

"I love her. I loved her when she was young, before the *don* raped her."

When they reached the ranch, María ran to Rodolfo and threw her arms around him. Martín looked at the young couple clinging together in the yard and knew he would help them. He would find a way to buy the guns they needed. He was thinking about his friend, Jerry Carr.

Jerry dropped out of school in the fifth grade, preferring to ride his horse in the Texas mountains. Jerry would grab an old gun and take Martín to the mountains south of El Paso to track bobcats and mountain lions.

Once they stowed away on a wagon going to Las Cruces, just for fun. Jerry's family was from Oklahoma and Jerry never made no mind that Martín was Mexican. He would say, "Friends was friends no matter the color." Jerry was a crazy one sometimes and Martín worried he would do something to get them into big trouble, but he was his friend.

When they were older, Martín saw little of Jerry, but heard rumors of various scrapes with the law. If anyone knew how to buy a load of guns, it was Jerry Carr.

CHAPTER 35

María and Rodolfo spent several days resting at her uncle's ranch north of El Paso. María helped her aunt prepare meals and worked with her in the small garden. Rodolfo helped her uncle in the hay field. Lupe could see a big change in her niece. María was strong and proud, not the downtrodden young woman who came with Celiá several months ago. Her eyes shone with passion when she talked and Lupe could tell Rodolfo loved her.

At supper, Rodolfo told stories of life in Mexico and the young cousins listened intently. He made the stories sound exciting and funny, but in her heart Lupe knew there was danger in what they did. When asked, Rodolfo said they were anxious to return to Mexico soon.

Lupe tried to think of a way to broach the subject of what to do about María to her husband. As she brushed her hair before bed, she spoke to Jose. "He is a passionate young man. He has a good heart."

"*Sí, querida.*"

"They are in love," she continued.

"*Sí,*" Jose mumbled. Lupe could tell Jose was barely listening to her.

"It is not safe for her to return to Mexico. We should not have let her go before and now . . . " her voice trailed off.

"She is a grown woman, Lupe. We cannot stop her."

"You must send a wire to Rafael and Celiá," she continued and Jose grumbled at his wife's nagging. He knew María would run away, if she thought Rafael and Celiá were coming to El Paso to find her. "Be joyous in her health and happiness," he told his wife.

"We owe Rafael so much. He will be angry if you do not tell him," Lupe continued.

"Silence woman, you worry too much." Lupe knew the conversation was over. That night she prayed to Saint Christopher to keep María safe.

In their room Martín counted María's gold coins and was shocked it amounted to over a thousand dollars. This past week he got to know Rodolfo and liked him and could see the love in his manner toward María. He thought about what María and Rodolfo told him, how peasants were treated in Mexico and knew first-hand it was not much different here in Texas. It was reason enough for him to want to help them get guns for their cause.

Saturday afternoon he lied to Ita, telling her he was going to help Padre Antonio break a young horse. She told him not to hurt himself and to be back in time for supper. Martín hated to lie to her, but could not tell her the truth.

Guiding his horse up the path through large cottonwood trees near the Rio Grande just southwest of El Paso, Martín approached the house where his friend Jerry Carr lived. A small unkempt house, not much better than a shack, about five miles from the edge of town, it was well hidden amongst the tall trees. He knocked on the door and an elderly woman opened it.

Not recognizing the older woman, Martín said taking off his hat, "I am looking for my friend Jerry Carr."

"Thar ain't no Carrs livin here no mo," the old woman said, her voice raspy and low.

"Do you mean they moved away?"

"Yep, they gone an moved on to town."

"Sorry to bother you ma'am."

"Tain't no bother yung man," she said and closed the door.

Martín had not seen Jerry Carr since he left for Austin thinking he wanted to join the Texas Rangers. That was about a year ago. He had not seen him since, but heard he came back from Austin. If anyone knew how to find Jerry it was old Charlie down at Hastings Livery. He knew about everyone coming and going in El Paso. Martín stopped at the livery and found old Charlie cleaning out stalls whistling a tune off key.

"Hello Charlie." Martín greeted him.

"Huh," Charlie whirled around startled. "Oh hey thar Martin. Whatcha doin here on Saturdee?" Charlie asked.

"Looking for a friend, you know that boy I used to run with, Jerry Carr. Used to give you some mischief," Martín said.

"Sho, I member dat rascal."

"I heard he moved to town. Do you know where he lives?" Martín asked.

"Sho do, his ma and pa bot themselvees a house on Sixth Street, down by da river."

"Have you seen Jerry lately?"

"Seen him cuple days ago."

"Much obliged Charlie," Martín thanked him and shook his hand.

"Think nuttin of it boy. Dun yew go an git into any trubl with that rascal," Charlie said looking Martín in the eyes. "You bein Mescin and all."

"I know what you mean sir. I just want to see if he'll do me a favor." Martín chuckled to himself as he walked out to his horse.

Once on Sixth Street, Martín found the Carr house by asking an older couple walking home from the market. They told him it was the last house on the street, before the street stopped at the river. The yard was well kept and the house was freshly painted white with blue trim on the windows and door jams. It was a big improvement from the rundown shack on the outskirts of town. When he walked up the path to the front door, he heard gunfire. It was not rapid fire, but more deliberate, like someone taking target practice. He knocked on the door.

"Yes," a woman said when she opened the door. Martín recognized Jerry's mother.

"Hello Mrs. Carr. Is Jerry home?"

"Who yew be?" Jerry's mother squinted at him with her eyebrows furrowed and a none too friendly look on her face.

"My name is Martín. Jerry and I are friends from school."

"Oh shur, yew be that Mescan boy Jerry liked so much. Come on in, he be out back shootin his new gun," she said her voice changing to a friendly tone. She led him through the house to the back door. Martín noticed the house was furnished with mostly new furniture. Somehow, all this did not fit the family he remembered. People called the Carrs – poor white folk.

"Jer, yew got a friend here wants to see yew," Mrs. Carr yelled out the back door and got no response. "Yew go on ahead. He's out thar."

Laughter followed a gunshot and then another gunshot and more laughter. Martín walked nearer the river and saw Jerry shooting at gray egrets and laughing as he made them dance when the bullets hit the mud near their feet.

"Jerry," Martín called.

Jerry turned only his head and looked back hearing his name. "Marty," Jerry used the nickname he had given Martín many years ago. "I'll be damned, whatcha doin here?" Jerry asked as he came up and grabbed Martín in a bear hug.

"Been looking for you. When did you move here?" Martín asked.

"Ah, shucks we moved in here six months ago. Lookee here Marty, look at this beauty." Jerry held up a new Winchester rifle.

"It sure is nice. Can I try it?"

"Shur nuff, here fire at them birds near the bank of the river." Jerry reloaded the gun and handed it to Martín. Taking the weapon it handled much like a GSW with perfect balance. Martín raised it and took a shot toward the river careful not to hit any of the birds.

"How's that feel? She's a beaut, ain't she?"

"Where'd you get that gun Jerry, it looks brand new?" Martín asked handing the gun back to Jerry.

"Cain't tell yew that," Jerry said and winked. "Yew jes let me know and I kin git one fer yew."

"I thought you joined the Texas Rangers?" Martín asked him.

"Shit, I'm still danged pissed off at that deal. I went all the way ta Austin to sign up and after my interviews, a few days later I was rejected. The captain got word from El

Paso, some folks here gave him some bad rumors bout me. Said I was a trouble maker."

"What bout yew Marty, I heerd yew had trouble with them Reynolds and that yer pa got his ranch back."

"Yes, all that is over now. We got our ranch and Roy and Eldon are dead, and so is their pa. My cousin, Rafael, killed them after they burned our barn and shot my little brother."

"Good fer y'all. I coudden stand that Eldon jasper always pokin fun at me and takin my money for that opium shit and callin me Okey trash. Shit, he no betteran me. Wanted to kill im me'self," Jerry spit on the ground as he made the remarks about Eldon Reynolds.

"Roy and Eldon hated Mexicans. They swore no Mexicans were going to live on their ranch after my cousin bought it fair and square when it got foreclosed by the bank," Martín told him. "They shot the sheriff and then tried to burn us out."

"Them no good fer nuttins. They was jes rottin scum."

"Looks like you come up in the world," Martín asked changing the subject and pointing back to the house.

"I bought it fer my ma and pa. Got me some work that pays real good."

"What kind of work?"

Jerry looked sheepish, then grinned. "Cain't tell yew that Marty. It's not kinda legal." Somehow Martín was not surprised. Jerry was not a bad man, but had always been capable of being one step away from the law.

Martín swallowed hard. "Jer, I need to ask you something. You cain't tell anyone."

"Whatsamatter Marty, yew in trouble?"

"No, it's nothing like that. Can you help me buy rifles and guns and get them across the border?"

"What fer, why yew smuggling guns across the border?"

"They're not for me. My cousin wants them to fight people who are taking the poor people's land in Mexico. Can you do it?"

"I might could. Kinda risky, but I know a way. What's in it fer me?"

"They can pay. Well, I don't know how much. They only have about a thousand dollars in gold. They need rifles and pistols. What can you get for that much and keep some for yourself?"

"Let me see," he looked up and Martín could see him trying to figure it out in his head. "Bout ten dollars fer a gun and twenty fer a rifle. That would come to thirty guns and twenty-five rifles and a bunch a bullets. I need bout hunerd fer me an I gotta pay to git em over the border. That sound bout right Marty?"

"I guess so. I need to talk to my cousin about how many rifles and pistols. How do we get them over the border?" Martín knew buying the guns was one thing and getting caught at the border with a load of guns was another. María and Rodolfo would be jailed, if not shot, for such a crime.

"Yew got the money wit ya?"

"No, but I can get it to you. How do you get them across the border? I want to make sure my cousins will be safe."

"Don't yew worry none bout that, I got ways," Jerry said with a grin. "I be rat thar with em. They won't have no trouble. How soon yew needin this dun?"

"As soon as you can."

"Go git the money and meet me at the livery stable in about two hours," Jerry said. "Kin yew do that?"

"Thanks Jerry. I'll be there."

They shook hands and Martín galloped home. Finding María and Rodolfo he told them what they could buy for the thousand dollars through his friend Jerry Carr.

"It will cost ten dollars for a gun and twenty for a rifle. He'll pay off the police at the border and his take is a hundred," Martín told them.

"I want more rifles than guns," Rodolfo said. "What about ammunition, Martín. What did he say about it?" Rodolfo asked.

"The rifles and pistols use the same bullets. He said

ammunition is a dollar a box."

Rodolfo got a pencil and paper and started working on the number of guns, rifles, and ammunition he could buy for one thousand dollars. María watched him writing numbers on the piece of paper in amazement. "I want ten pistols, twenty-five rifles, and two hundred boxes of ammunition. That should be enough," he said and proudly showed his figures to Martín who agreed.

"Bueno. I need to take the gold coins to Jerry at the livery."

"Martín, how do we know we can trust your friend?" María asked and Rodolfo backed her.

"All I can say is Jerry is my friend and has been for a long time. Some people here in El Paso say he is a troublemaker, but he is the only one I know who can do this. I took a chance even asking him, because I just don't know about such things. We have to trust him. He knows people and is not afraid to do what it takes to make it happen," Martín said not knowing what else he could say.

Rodolfo turned to María. *"Querida,* it is your gold. You do not have to do this," Rodolfo said. María handed the pouch with the gold coins to Martín. "Get us the guns."

Martín kissed her on the cheek before he left. "Don't worry. I trust Jerry." He mounted his horse and left heading back to El Paso.

María turned taking Rodolfo by the arm. "How do you know numbers?" she asked him. She knew *peóns* on *don* Bernardo's *hacienda* never went to school and it was so for most *peóns* in Mexico. She could neither read nor write.

"A friend taught me in prison," he said. "I can read some, too."

CHAPTER 36

Rattling bottles and loud voices from the bar downstairs in Lilli Jean's Saloon in El Paso woke Luke Payton. Rolling over he saw Lilli Jean's half naked ample body wrapped in a tangle of sheets, her leg thrown over his. Last evening became a blur after he was thrown out of the card game. Apparently, Lilli Jean took him for a ride.

Luke slowly eased from her embrace. Rising he wobbled over to a pitcher on the dresser and splashed water on his face. The face staring back from the mirror looked bleary-eyed. Lilli opened her eyes hearing Luke moving around in the room.

"It's early, come back to bed," Lilli purred to Luke.

"I gotta git goin. They be gunnin fer me, if they catch me in town," Luke told her.

Last night Luke came back to the saloon and split his winnings with her and it was a little over a thousand dollars. No doubt he may have cheated, but then Mick and the boys were known to be card sharps who would happily roll an innocent player. Lilli sent many to them for a fleecing. Served them right to get a piece of their own medicine.

"Yew got nuff time for one more. Cum back here," Lilli opened the sheets to show her nakedness. Lilli's body was ample and full of womanly curves, more than ample. Luke smiled and walked to the bed. Slowly he lay down beside her.

Later, Luke rose, dressed, and walked downstairs. He needed to find Jed and they needed to get moving.

"Yew seen my friend? The one I came in here with last night?" he asked the bartender.

"I ain't seen him since last night," the bartender said. "He said sumthin bout goin to the opium tent with Maggie, one of the whores."

"Which way is that?" Luke grumbled mad he needed to go find Jed.

"Go down the boardwalk thataway, then follow yer

nose. Yew'll find the Chinee tents," the bartender said and pointed. Following the bartender's instructions, Luke finally found the opium tent. A sweet pungent odor filled the air. Luke had done the smoke several times, but hated the hangover. He found Jed passed out on a small cot and he shook Jed's shoulder several times without any response. Luke groused at the body, "Damn it Jed."

"Hey, whar am I?" Jed jerked and said staring up at Luke's blurry face. Jed's face and hair were wet from the sweats and his mind was cloudy. Finally, he recognized Luke and asked, "What the hell, where's Maggie?"

"Forgit about her, we gotta be moving on to New Mexico. Git yer clothes and boots on, we gotta go." Luke helped Jed up. Still woozy, Jed was unsteady on his feet. Realizing Jed was barely able to stand, Luke grumbled with little patience, "Stay here, I'll go git the horses."

On the way to the livery, Luke thought about just leaving the stupid cowboy behind. His brother was dead, died in New Mexico, so what? It did not really surprise him. Bill was a hothead sometimes. Luke had gotten him out of scrapes with cowpokes and the law more than once when they were young. Still, Luke had been raised on the principle of an eye for an eye. His father always taught them to protect their own. Besides, some damn greaser killed Bill and that was different. No damn greaser was going to get away with killing his brother and live.

Later, getting Jed into the saddle, Luke headed them north out of El Paso. It was well past noon and Luke kept a keen eye out for the gamblers he fleeced. Jed swayed in the saddle near him, but managed to hang on.

"How yew feelin?" Luke asked.

"Alright I guess. Feel kinda numb. I cain't tell what's real and what's a dream."

"Them Chinee gave yew bad shit. It'll pass," Luke said.

It was all Jed could do to nod in Luke's direction. He never did the smoke before, but Maggie got him drunk while he waited for Luke. He remembered following her to the Chinese tent. A tiny bent woman brought two long bamboo pipes with bowls at the far end. Maggie took one of the pipes and the old woman lit it for her as she drew the smoke, then did the same for Jed. Drawing the pungent smoke into his lungs, it burned slightly. At first he felt nothing and Maggie encouraged him to draw another long breath from the pipe. The silks around the ceiling began to flow like waves. Suddenly he was melting into the cushions on the bed, his whole body pulsated with waves of pleasure. A euphoric intensity took him away to another place where he was the happiest he had ever been and then Maggie began kissing him.

Luke saw Jed riding with his eyes closed and barely holding on. "Hey there boy, wake up," Luke yelled at Jed stirring him out of his stupor.

Luke saw a small cantina just off the trail. His stomach was growling and maybe some food would help Jed. He turned off the trail and pulled up at the rail. He helped Jed get down and shouldered him to the doorway. A woven blanket covered the entrance. Luke pushed back the blanket and they walked into the dim room. Inside smelled of roasted meat and chilis, a smell making his stomach growl.

"Hola," a voice said. As Luke's eyes adjusted to the dim light, he noticed several sets of dark eyes staring at them from small tables in the room. It was a short man near the bar who spoke. "Your friend, he don't look so good."

Luke looked around and tried not to visibly show any concern. All the eyes in this cantina belonged to Mexicans. Two men sat a table near the man who spoke wearing tall pointed hats. Dark beards covered their faces. Luke could not see if they were armed. Standing at the bar, a man turned to look at them. He wore a large red bandana knotted around his neck. His chaps had silver hooks up both sides. At his knee a long knife was held by a fringed sash. His spurs were long and pointed and his flat-topped hat sat on the bar.

"We need food," Luke said.

"Sí, we have chili," the short man said and waved

Luke and Jed to a table. Plopping Jed in a chair, Luke scanned the room again. No one seemed to be paying them any mind. Before long the short man brought two heaping plates of meat spiced with chilis and folded tortillas. He placed the plates in front of Luke and Jed and started to walk away.

"Hey, how about a fork?" Luke asked.

"No forks, just tortillas," the man said.

Jed tore a piece of tortilla and grabbed up a hunk of meat. "Use the tortilla like this," Jed said.

Putting the spiced meat into his mouth, the savory flavors burst on Luke's tongue. He was hungry and quickly devoured the meat. It was the best meal he tasted in months. Jed was looking better, less gray, as the food on his plate disappeared.

"You want more, no?" the short man asked Luke.

Sheepishly, Luke nodded yes and handed his empty plate to the man. By the time he was finished with the second plate of red chili, Luke was grinning. "Damn, I didn't know Mescans could cook so good."

Jed shrugged. The meal was tasty and he knew it was good, but his mouth still felt like cotton from the opium. When Luke and Jed climbed back into their saddles, Jed's head was clearing and Luke led them in a gallop north.

CHAPTER 37

Rafe and Carlos arrived early Saturday morning at the fencing school just off the north side of the plaza in the center of Santa Fe. Rafe started taking classes with Carlos last February and found he enjoyed learning the skill of the sword. When Josefina learned Rafe was interested in fencing, she gave him her father's Toledo blade rapier, which had been stored away for years.

When Rafe protested Josefina told him, "My father would be honored to have me pass it on to my son." The long thin blade was made from finely hammered Toledo steel. The silver handle had an intricate S-shaped curved knuckle guard covering the handle and protecting the user's hand. Two crossbars extended from the quillan block at the base of the handle. Even Carlos and the fencing master were impressed with the quality of the sword.

Maestro Luis Aguiler, the fencing master, was sparing in front of a mirror when they came into his training room.

"*Buenos días, Maestro,*" they both chimed at the same time.

"*Buenos días, señores!*" *don* Luis greeted them. "Warm up," he told them.

After touching blades, Carlos and Rafe squared off and Carlos began the attack, lunging forward and then pulling back. Rafe parried the attack easily flicking Carlos' blade down and away. Carlos attacked again forcing Rafe to feint to the left. While Carlos had been training with swords for years, Rafe was still learning the weapon. It took every fiber of his concentration to not be stabbed. They practiced the thrusts and counters until each were panting.

"*Bueno, bueno,*" the Maestro said. "I can see you have been practicing, Rafael."

"Today I want to teach you a very important lesson – the true art of Spanish swordsmanship. The Spanish Circle, sometimes called the Ring of Death, but to the purist it is called *La Verdadera Destreza,* the True Art. *Señores,* the true art of the Spanish Circle has been taught to Spaniards since it was developed by *don* Jeronimo de Caranza in the middle ages. It is based upon an imaginary circle surrounding you," the Maestro said and swung his rapier in circles around himself.

"Caranza's concept was refined by one of his students, *don* Luis Pacheco de Narvaez, and it was he who named it *La Verdadera Destreza*. It is based in concepts of geometry and the mathematical distance surrounding the swordsman."

Rafe and Carlos were intrigued by the Maestro's comments and waited for his instruction. "Now take your rapier and take a step forward with your right foot and extend your right arm as far as it will extend to the right, bend your knees slightly. This is called the *diestro*. Now do the same to your left. Turn to your side and extend, then behind you and extend. Imagine a circle around you where the tip of the rapier extends." The Maestro extended his rapier and showed them how to visualize the circle of reach surrounding them on all sides.

Finishing the moves the Maestro continued. "That *señores* defines the Spanish Circle. Imagine it turning into a multitude of circles which move with you in combat. Your opponent has the same circle. You must learn to protect your circle, while attempting to penetrate your opponents."

"En garde." Rafe and Carlos took opposing positions. Rafe tried to imagine a circle surrounding him extending to the tip of the rapier.

"I want you to face each other with the knowledge of the Spanish Circle in mind. Now practice the *diestro,* moving toward each other and to the right then left and backward. It is like a dance – the Dance of Death." Maestro Luis followed his students as they practiced the *diestro,* injecting instructions as they thrust and parried. Over and over they circled each other with the Maestro using his sword to point to their respective circles.

"Now, begin again and look for some weakness in your opponent's circle," he instructed.

Rafe and Carlos touched blades and faced each other.

As they moved, Rafe could see Carlos moving with his circle. Carlos, a more experienced swordsman, bested Rafe several times entering Rafe's circle. Rafe tightened his jaw and concentrated on his Ring of Death as the teacher called it, but knew it would take much more practice before he could master it.

"*¡Basta! Suficiente por hoy,*" Maestro Luis yelled out for them to stop.

"The Spanish have been the masters of the rapier and creators of the Spanish Circle since the turn of the sixteenth century. Practice the *diestro,* keeping the circles as your guide. I await your return next week." The Maestro bowed and then saluted with his rapier.

Outside the fencing school Rafe and Carlos mounted their horses. Rafe pulled his rapier and called out to Carlos, "*En garde, señor.*" Carlos laughed and pulled his rapier and said. "You are a fool to challenge me, *señor.*"

Rafe urged Rayo and extended his rapier and circled to Carlos' right. "Let us see if you are as good on a horse, *señor.*" Carlos spurred his horse to Rafe's left quickly realizing fencing on horseback was much more difficult than flat on his feet. They crossed swords, parried, counter-attacked, parried, and attacked, being careful not to cut each other. They laughed at each other's feeble attempts to control the horses and their swords at the same time.

Finally, Carlos saluted Rafe and ended the sword game. "Let's go to the plaza. Bibiana and Ana Teresa may be there and we will ask them to have lunch with us," Carlos said.

Bibiana and Ana Teresa walked out of the *Santuario de Guadalupe* just west of the Santa Fe plaza a little after noon. Bibiana was a regular volunteer every other Saturday helping the sisters at the mission of San Miguel feed hungry Indian and *mestizo* children. Ana Teresa agreed to go with her this morning.

It was June and summer was in full bloom in Santa Fe, the trees bright green with new growth and flowers bloomed along the *paseo.* The snow on the top of the Sangre de Cristo Mountains was finally melted. The girls chatted happily as they walked toward the plaza.

Ana Teresa egged her cousin. "What about Carlos? Is he going to ask your father tomorrow for your hand?" Ever since Bibiana shared her secret about Carlos' proposal, the girls whispered in their conspiracy.

"Oh, I wish, but I fear he wants to wait until September when he starts his teaching job," Bibiana said. "I don't care about any old job; he is working with Rafe at the foundry and we could live at the *hacienda.*"

"Your father would never allow it," Ana Teresa responded.

"Then we could live off my dowry," Bibiana protested. "Father must give us that! I don't care where we live as long as I'm with him."

Ana Teresa sighed listening to her infatuated cousin. Bibiana was a dreamer. She had never known hard times. When Ana Teresa's family lost the rancho in California, they were forced to leave everything behind. One of the nicest ranchos in Simi Valley, the de Soto ranch was graciously decorated in heavy tapestries, rich gold-leafed paintings, and hand-carved furniture. Her mother even left the two-foot solid silver candlesticks, which had graced the dining room table for Ana Teresa's entire life. Now it was all gone. The *Americano* government said the rancho and everything in it belonged to them.

One day she had a lovely home, money, a fiancé, and a life in California. The next day everything including her hopes and dreams were gone. Her parents sent her to Santa Fe to live with her aunt and uncle, Bibiana's parents. "You will be safe there," her mother told her. Her parents sailed to Spain. She begged to go with them, but they sent her to Santa Fe. She had not heard from them in more than six months.

Her father promised to obtain copies of the King's land grants for de Soto land here in New Mexico, so they could rebuild here without fear of the *Americanos.* Ana Teresa wondered what was taking them so long to return. Her aunt and uncle were kind to her and she loved Bibiana, but she feared she might never regain her social status. She was not like Bibiana who only wanted love. She wanted the security of status and the money to back it up and she was starting to worry it was not going to happen.

"Tell me more about Diego de la Torre," Ana Teresa queried Bibiana. He came to talk to me last week on the *paseo*.

"Diego's a *picaro*," Bibiana retorted. "Besides he will break your heart."

"Why?" Ana Teresa pouted. "He's not so handsome, but you can tell he has money and status. Do you see the way his friends respect him?"

"Diego is *gachupín* and loves to intimidate his friends. Just because he was born in Spain, he thinks he's better than everyone else."

"Status is still important, Bibiana," her cousin reminded her. "Not everything has changed here in New Mexico. Money is still money and Diego's family is rich, no?"

"Yes, his family is powerful and rich," Bibiana sighed. "Money does not make him kind or special. He is hard and mean, not like Carlos or Rafael. You should think more about Rafael."

Ana Teresa often thought about Rafael, because around him she felt calm and happy. For some unexplainable reason she could talk to him freely and told him about losing her rancho and status. "Well, tell me more about Rafael," Ana Teresa said to Bibiana as they walked.

"Carlos said Rafael saved his life when Carlos' brother left him wounded and dying. Carlos thinks of him as a brother." Bibiana did not share the secret Carlos told her about killing his brother, Benicío.

"Yes, they are always together. Rafael breeds horses and your father says they are the finest he has ever seen," Ana Teresa said with a haughty snit.

"You are being unkind," Bibiana said. "Rafael is a good man."

"Is a horse breeder a man of status?" Ana Teresa asked. "Will he be a *don* someday?"

"I heard Carlos introduce him to my parents. He is

from a *hacienda* in Mexico, so I guess his father is a *don.*"

"He is tall and handsome and those eyes could melt a girl . . . only I need to know if he's wealthy. I'm not like you Bibiana, I . . . I need money," Ana Teresa's voice trailed off.

"If I didn't have Carlos, I would go after Rafael myself. You better figure it out, because some other woman will take him," Bibiana said teasing her cousin.

The Saturday noontime sun shone brightly down on the plaza of Santa Fe. Bibiana and Ana Teresa walked to the corner of Palace Avenue. The plaza was busy with vendors and children of all ages running and playing in the square. As they walked along the street, Bibiana remembered coming to the plaza as a child with her mother. Her mother bought her stick candy and Bibiana remembered being enthralled with the puppet theatres.

Someday she would bring her children here on Saturday mornings, hers and Carlos' children. The thought of marrying Carlos made her tingle all over. Tomorrow he and Rafael were coming to supper and Bibiana was determined to tell her father they wanted to get married. She was sure he would agree. He had never denied her anything she ever wanted.

Ana Teresa tugged on her arm. "There's Emilio to pick us up. We need to go home and get ready for tonight. You promised you'd come with me to the *paseo.* Diego told me he would be riding," Ana Teresa reminded her.

Bibiana was bored with the Saturday ritual of promenading on the *paseo* and talking to the local dandies, especially Diego and his friends. Carlos was her one and true love. No one else mattered, but she promised her cousin to go. "Yes, I'm coming."

Rafe and Carlos rode into the plaza. They circled twice, but did not see Bibiana or Ana Teresa. "We need to come back later for the *paseo,*" Carlos said.

"Why are you so anxious? You'll see her tomorrow," Rafe chided him. Carlos huffed and rode off north toward the GSW ranch. Rafe caught up.

"*Cálmate amigo.* We'll dress and ride to the *paseo*

tonight so you can see Bibiana."

"I want to talk to her tonight about what to say to her father tomorrow. I want to ask his permission to marry her, but . . . "

"Marry her?" Rafe exclaimed.

"Yes, we want to marry as soon as possible, but I'm afraid her father will refuse me. I cannot live without her."

Rafe understood Carlos' feelings. He had felt the same way about Chiwiwi. He wanted to die when she was killed. *"Vámonos,"* Rafe said. "We have work to finish if we want to ride the *paseo* tonight."

CHAPTER 38

Late Saturday afternoon, Diego de la Torre and three of his friends were playing Monte at the Palacio Cantina. Like every other Saturday, Diego was drinking and gambling at the old Spanish cantina. Several white-haired *dons* were playing cards at a table near the back. Virginia had not come down from her room yet. Diego knew she liked to sleep in late and was usually not dressed until later in the evening.

Diego absorbed the sight and sounds of the cantina. It had been catering to the Spanish aristocrats here in Santa Fe for almost one hundred years. Here the old ways ruled and he could forget about *Americanos* and their new laws. He felt at home in the rich European tapestries and huge paintings of the *conquistadores*. In the Palacio, being a *gachupín* still meant something.

Alvaro spent most of the afternoon losing at the game and stood up. "I'm tired of losing to you," he grumbled to Diego. "Let's go to the *paseo*. The *señoritas* will already be there." Diego yawned and stood up. Perhaps the lovely Ana Teresa would be riding tonight. He promised to meet her.

"*Vámonos,*" Diego told his friends.

It was almost dusk when Bibiana and Ana Teresa left the de Soto home for the *paseo*. Ana Teresa was dressed in a stunning dark green and black dress. Bibiana thought her cousin would be the most beautiful girl on the *paseo* tonight.

Their carriage slowly entered the *paseo,* working into line behind other carriages. Cristina Anaya and her younger sister were riding in the carriage just in front of Bibiana's. A young *caballero* rode beside Cristina.

Several dandies quickly surrounded Bibiana and Ana Teresa's carriage, holding out flowers, and hoping to catch the beautiful Ana Teresa's eye. She kept her fan firmly in front of her face, pretending to be disinterested. A young *caballero's* horse on Ana Teresa's side reared, almost knocking the poor boy to the ground.

Diego de la Torre's horse pushed the scared rider out of the way and when Ana Teresa looked up, he was staring intently at her.

"Buenas tardes, señorita," he said and tipped his head slightly. "You are more beautiful than the evening."

"You are most kind, *señor,* but God has made the evening warm and fragrant." Ana Teresa kept her face mostly hidden behind her fan.

"I'm sure your heart is warmer than the evening," Diego said in a smooth tempting manner. Candle lights sparkled off her dark green and black dress. He thought her slim, though her firm breasts swelled against the neckline of the dress below a gold and green necklace. Diego thought the young *señorita* from California was the prettiest girl riding on the *paseo.* She would be a prize catch, except she was penniless. Her lack of status freed his heart for a more lustful purpose. Taking the beautiful *señorita* as a mistress intrigued him. She would have to be grateful.

Ana Teresa enjoyed the bantering with Diego. The exchanges of compliments during the promenade on the *paseo* were orchestrated to have hidden meanings.

"Why is a *caballero* of your stature not married *señor?"* she asked.

"Until now, I have not met a *señorita* of your beauty," Diego flattered her and watched her smile behind her black lace fan as it was fluttered by her quick hand.

"You flatter me *señor,* surely there are many beautiful *señoritas* in New Mexico."

"Sí señorita, there are many beautiful *señoritas* in New Mexico, but none compare with your beauty," Diego continued his flattery.

Ana Teresa enjoyed the banter. She remembered when she had money and a dowry and her fiancé was courting her in California. It was before the *Americanos* took everything. She came to live with Bibiana's parents and she knew they did not gossip about her situation. Only Rafael knew the truth.

Diego continued his sweet talk, manipulating her with

his keen demeanor and was confident he could take this luscious prize for his next conquest. The young caballero dandies he ran with would be most impressed.

"Ah señor usted es demasiado amable," she told him he was too kind. She was enjoying the compliments, though was beginning to worry her cousin was right. Diego was older, in his late twenties or maybe thirty. How could such a *caballero macho* stay single for so long? Perhaps he was a *picaro,* as Bibiana warned.

On the other side of the carriage Bibiana was discouraging a young *caballero* wanting her attention. She kept ignoring him, but Alvaro liked Bibiana and was not giving up trying to talk to her.

Bibiana spotted Carlos and Rafe entering the plaza from the north entrance. "You best be on your way *señor, mi prometido* is coming," Bibiana told Alvaro that her fiancé was coming.

"I am not worried *señorita,* you are not married yet," Alvaro said snickering, but pulled away from her and rode up alongside Diego. When he was beside him, Alvaro indicated with his head toward the north side of the plaza where Carlos and Rafe were riding into the *paseo.* Rafe rode tall on Rayo, a rapier at his side.

Diego acknowledged Alvaro, but kept riding beside Ana Teresa. It was time to confront the *caballero* from Mexico and Diego was ready. Rafe and Carlos rode up behind Bibiana's carriage, Carlos on her side and Rafe on Ana Teresa's side. He urged Rayo between the carriage and Diego. Rayo was several hands taller than the black stallion Diego rode. Rayo snorted as he pushed the smaller horse out of his way.

"Buenas tardes, señorita, te ves hermosa esta noche," Rafe greeted Ana Teresa in impeccable Spanish, telling her how beautiful she looked this evening. He did not acknowledge the *caballero* Rayo pushed out of the way.

"Buenas tardes, señor," Ana Teresa responded fluttering her fan rapidly. She could see Diego was angry and it amused her. Perhaps the intrusion would make him jealous.

"Mi nombre es Diego de la Torre y yo soy un miembro de los

caballeros de Santiago como eran mis antepasados desde que expulsaron a los moros infieles de España," Diego gruffed at Rafe. He blustered about his name, Diego de la Torre, and how he was a member of the Knights of Santiago, as were his ancestors who drove the infidel Moors out of Spain. He expected the Mexican *caballero* to be impressed with his extensive credentials.

Rafe brushed aside the arrogant Spaniard's bona fides by responding with a Texas cowboy twang. "Howdy Diego, glad to know yew. My name is Rafe." He glanced only a second at Diego, then turned his back on him.

Ana Teresa snickered behind her fan watching Diego fume. Diego's blood rushed to his face with rage. The Mexican insulted him and his status. He spoke formal Spanish to Ana Teresa, then sounded like a Texan with no Spanish accent. Diego stared at Rafe's back. On his right hip hung a silver-handled rapier. Diego could tell by the ornate silver handle, it was a fine blade made in Spain.

Confused, Diego's first instinct was to fight, but wondered if the man from Mexico was an expert swordsman. Usually Diego had his dandies fight his fights, keeping his *gachupín* head above the fray. Diego pulled the reins and quickly rode off with Alvaro on his tail. Rafe did not acknowledge Diego's behavior on purpose and kept his attention on the beautiful *señorita* from California.

"Señor, you cannot be driving my suitors away. How am I to know which *caballero* has the best prospects for me?" she teased Rafe smiling behind her fan.

"Perdóneme señorita, but I did not drive him away. He chooses to leave on his own accord," Rafe said acting innocent of driving Diego away. He did not let her see he was annoyed by her attentions to Diego.

By the time Diego and Alvaro rode to the far end of the *paseo,* Diego was in a rage. "Find out about that *cabrón!"* he growled to Alvaro. "I want to know who he is and where he comes from. Do not come back until you know. Go, now."

CHAPTER 39

Sunday after church Carlos and Rafe saddled Rayo and Santiago and rode to the de Soto *hacienda.* Carlos was edgy on the ride.

"What's the matter?" Rafe asked him. "Aren't you happy to see Bibiana?"

"Of course. I'm trying to figure out how to approach her father. I know Bibiana doesn't want to wait to get married until I have the teaching job."

"*Pendejo,* just ask him," Rafe said. "You were educated in Spain and have a future here in New Mexico. You're not a *peón* like me," Rafe said.

"But I have no land or station," Carlos retorted.

"This is not Spain, amigo. Here you can buy land. Look at my horse ranch. Here land is bought and sold, not assigned by a King." Rafe reminded him. Carlos nodded and knew Rafe was right, but Rafe did not understand the way of Spanish fathers. The old ways had not died, even here in New Mexico.

When they arrived at the de Soto *hacienda,* Bibiana came to greet them and walked them inside. *Doña* Agustina greeted them graciously and ushered them into the dining room. The large table reminded Rafe of the one at *don* Bernardo's house in Mexico. Tall candelabras graced each end of the table. A servant was placing platters of food on the table and sideboard.

Sitting at dinner, Rafe thought the talk was not much different than talk around the Summers' dining table. The recent dry weather worried ranchers who wanted more rain. Bibiana's father asked Rafe many questions about the horses and their breeding.

"The Appaloosa you ride is magnificent. What bloodline created such a fine animal?" he asked.

Rafe responded with the horse's bloodline starting with the horses ridden by Hernando Cortés who brought horses from Spain to Mexico. "There were no horses in

New Spain before Cortés. The native Indians had never seen horses and thought the Spaniards on horseback were one being or Gods," Rafe said reciting the history Carlos had taught him long ago.

"Cortés conquered the *Aztecas* with about five hundred soldiers and sixteen horses. Rayo's bloodline is from the original Spanish horses. His sire was named Santiago, after the patron saint."

Don Pedro nodded approvingly and was about to ask more when Bibiana interrupted, "Father, all this talk of horses is boring." She wanted her father to pay more attention to Carlos, while he seemed more interested in Rafael. "Carlos studied in Spain, Father. He was in Madrid for over two years."

"I hear Madrid is hot in the summer," her mother said.

"Yes, quite hot. In fact most of Spain is quite arid and hot, especially in the south," Carlos said. "I studied for two years at the Seminary."

"And how is your family? Bibiana tells us you lost your land grant. It is so with many in New Mexico," her father asked.

"My father, mother, and older brother are dead. My sister, Carolita, is married to a rancher and they have two small children."

"I understand your great uncle Manuel's son, Armando, is regent to our new Governor Giddings?" her father asked.

"Yes he is, but I have not seen Armando in several years." Carlos squirmed in his seat trying to answer *don* Pedro's questions and feeling scrutinized in his eyes.

Rafe watched Ana Teresa through dinner. She sat quietly, but Rafe could tell she was hearing every word spoken. She sat next to Bibiana with her head high and her dark brown hair falling around her face. She wore a simple blue dress with ruffled sleeves, much plainer than the one Bibiana wore, however, Bibiana paled beside Ana Teresa's beauty.

"*Papá,* may we go riding this afternoon?" Bibiana

asked the question to her father in her sweet daughterly voice.

"*Sí mija,*" he replied. "A short ride."

About a half hour later, the foursome left the *hacienda.* Bibiana and Carlos rode ahead.

"You have to ask him, Carlos," she demanded. "We can't wait too long. I'm afraid he will betroth me to another, if you don't ask." Bibiana doubted this was true, however she had no intention of waiting.

"He would not!" Carlos blurted out.

"I'm almost eighteen and he will want to get me married. You must ask him," Bibiana implored him.

"I will," Carlos promised her, feeling like he had no choice in the matter.

When they returned to the *hacienda,* Carlos found Bibiana's father in the parlor smoking a cigar. Bibiana's words gave him courage, but his knees shook.

"*Señor,* might I speak with you?" *Don* Pedro spread his hand toward a chair, but Carlos remained standing. Her father suspected what the nervous young man was about to ask, so continuing to puff on his cigar he sat back.

"*Señor,* I care for your daughter deeply. I come to you to ask for your permission to court her with the intention of marriage."

Don Pedro puffed on his cigar and looked Carlos up and down. He considered giving his permission, thinking about the argument given by his wife about Carlos' solid nature. He wanted his daughter to be happy, while another part of him was enjoying making Carlos sweat.

"You have no land or station. It was taken by the *Americanos.* I want my daughter to have a good life and many children to be raised in the traditional way," he began. "You cannot make a home for her."

Carlos felt his heart falling to the floor. Everything he imagined about the moment was coming true and her father was going to reject him forever. From somewhere deep inside, he heard himself say, "I love her more than life itself. I promise you she will never want for anything as long as I have breath in my lungs."

Don Pedro expected Carlos to rebut his words, but instead Carlos touched the one thing Bibiana's father wanted for his oldest daughter, love. He wanted her to know the kind of love he shared with his wife, Agustina.

Don Pedro smiled, stood up, and embraced Carlos in an *abrazo*. "You have my permission," he said.

"*Gracias,*" Carlos thanked him. "*Gracias, señor.*"

CHAPTER 40

On Monday Ita and María took the buggy into El Paso. María knew it was probably the last time she could shop at a mercantile for basic needs. Martín told them Jerry Carr thought he would have the guns on Wednesday. While Ita chatted about parties and the children, María ordered soap, coffee, several blankets, slab bacon, sugar, lard, flour, candy sticks, several yards of muslin, sulphur salve, and other typical supplies. She used one of the gold coins she kept for herself to pay for the items.

She longed to buy one of the pretty dresses, remembering the fiesta for the fifth of May just a couple months ago, instead choosing a heavy jacket made of wool and a pair of sturdy boots.

"That coat is made for a man," Ita complained to her.

"It is cold at night in the mountains in Mexico," María said to her. "I need a heavy coat." Ita dropped the subject and wandered off to look at baby blankets.

Wednesday morning, María and Rodolfo loaded the old wagon with the supplies and readied to leave. Jose, Lupe, and the rest of the family gave hugs around and wished them well. Jose whispered to María to come back if she needed help when he hugged her. Lupe whispered her love and God's safety for her.

"I will pray to Saint Christopher every day," Lupe told her holding her tightly.

"Don't worry *tía*," María replied wanting to calm her aunt's fears.

Martín made an excuse to ride as far as El Paso with them. He rode alongside the wagon and rode through the American town toward Juárez. He rode with them to a point near the border before he pulled up.

"Jerry will be waiting in a stand of cottonwoods just southwest of the Chapel of Nuestra Señora de Guadalupe," he said and pointed to a tall steeple looming skyward across the river.

María tried to be calm, but her stomach was full of butterflies. They already thanked Martín for helping them and there was nothing else to say. Rodolfo clicked the reins and started the mules toward the border. She noticed he held tightly onto the reins, leaving his knuckles strained. Martín stayed on his horse and watched until they were out of sight, then turned and headed home. Under his breath, he said a prayer for their safety.

The Mexican border guards looked at the rickety wagon and two *peóns* and waved them along. María felt like she held her breath until she saw the Catholic Church of Nuestra Señora de Guadalupe looming skyward up ahead. The small wagon rolled slowly by the church to a stand of cottonwoods just southwest of the chapel.

Jerry waited near a wagon under the cottonwoods well hidden in the trees. He watched the rickety wagon approaching. The wagon was pulled by two pitiful mules looking ready to die and he wondered how the couple on the wagon had any money at all.

Rodolfo pulled up the team and stopped when a young gringo walked toward them. He hoped it was Jerry Carr.

"Howdy, ma'am," Jerry said and took off his hat.

"Buenos días," they each responded. María looked at the sandy haired young man and said a quick prayer. Their lives were in his hands.

Rodolfo helped Jerry load the weapons into their wagon, carefully hiding them under the supplies and blankets. *"Gracias,"* Rodolfo said and shook Jerry's hand.

Clicking the reins of the wagon, Rodolfo started the team. For the next three days they slowly wound their way along rutted bumpy cattle trails, staying away from the main Chihuahua Trail. At night they slept under the stars in each other's arms. Rodolfo made love to María passionately and later more tender. She craved more and more of him as her zest for love awakened. When the exquisite feelings rippled through her body, she felt truly alive. Alone in the desert, they made love over and over again with only the coyotes to hear their screams of passion.

The forth day dawned with orange, pink, and gray clouds on the horizon. As they were packing the wagon, the sound of horses echoed nearby. Rodolfo perked attentively moving toward the wagon where the rifle was hidden under the seat.

Six *vaqueros* rode into their campsite, which was hidden amongst a thicket of trees near a running creek of clear fresh water. The *vaqueros* were all well armed with pistols at their sides. The leader stopped and raised his hand.

María noticed the *vaquero* who slowly rode in last looked wornout and the expression on his face showed he was in pain.

"Hola," the leader said and asked where they were going. *"¿Adónde van?"*

Before Rodolfo could answer, the man asked if they had any food. Rodolfo nodded and said a little coffee, a bit of bacon, but not much else. María did not like the tone of the man's voice and wished they would just leave.

"Stoke the fire and have your woman prepare us food," he demanded. Rodolfo knew these men could kill them both and ransack the wagon at will, so he turned to María and said, "I will get more wood. Unpack the coffee and bacon and the tortillas."

Careful to act subservient, María started cooking. She watched the *vaquero* in pain slide from his horse and limp to a spot where he sat down. After the bacon was cooking, María pointed to the injured man and said, "I can help him."

"He is strong," the leader grumbled and swept his hand toward the men, "they need food."

When the meal was ready, María poured strong coffee in cups and gave the men bacon with a tortilla. When she handed the injured man the food he said quietly, "Please, if you can help me . . . otherwise I think I will die if we keep riding." María nodded to him giving him hope. When the men were all eating, she went to the wagon and found the sulphur powder and muslin. Without asking permission, she walked over to the injured man and knelt down. Carefully she peeled back his shirt to assess his bloody side. Blood crusted around a deep gouge oozing with puss.

"How did this happen?" she asked.

"Chasing strays. One turned and gored me."

"This will hurt," she told him before she scraped the edges of the wound with her knife and used a piece of muslin soaked in hot water to clean the skin. The oozing hole opened to the rib bone. The man grimaced, but did not cry out. Carefully she worked to get as much puss and blood cleared and cut ragged pieces of skin from the edges. The bloody pulpy wound bled easily, and María let it bleed knowing it would clear some of the infection.

"It needs sewing," she told him, "but I don't have any needles. I will have to use fire." She packed the wound with some sulphur powder and walked to the campfire. For the first time, she noticed the leader watching her carefully. His eyes were hard and cold, but he said nothing. She lighted a stick in the fire and walked back to the injured man. She lighted the sulphur in the wound and it blazed brightly. *"Aaaaeeee,"* he cried out at the pain.

María bound the wound tightly with a bandage made from muslin and the man smiled. *"Gracias,"* he told her. *"Eres un ángel."*

Standing up the *vaquero* leader walked toward the small wagon and dug into their food. He grabbed the coffee and the sack of salted bacon. María held her breath as he poked around. If they found the weapons, everything she and Rodolfo had worked for would be lost and maybe their lives. Satisfied with the food, he turned and barked at his men. *"Vámonos."*

The injured man gingerly climbed up onto his horse. María hoped the bandage was tight enough to keep the wound from bleeding. He smiled at her and tipped his hat before he rode off after the others. When they left, Rodolfo gathered María in his arms and held her tight.

"How did you know what to do for that man?" he asked.

"Mi mamá tended to the sick and injured at the

hacienda. I watched her and helped sometimes," she replied.

"It was very brave," he said. "I think the leader may have harmed us, except for your kindness."

Rodolfo stomped out the fire and helped María climb up to the seat. He clicked the reins and the wagon creaked slowly forward following the old cattle trail south.

CHAPTER 41

"I'll tell yew rat now, I'll never do that smoke again. No siree bub!" Jed Clements told Luke Payton again for the umpteenth time. Twenty miles south of San Marcial, Luke and Jed had been riding for three days from El Paso. Jed's head finally cleared from the opium fog yesterday. On top of the wallop of a hangover, Maggie rolled him for all his money.

"Yew wanna go to the ranch first?" Jed asked.

"Naw, let's jes go to town and see if that Mescan's there," Luke replied.

It was just getting dark as they rode down the main street of San Marcial. Jed led the way to Big Ed's Saloon and Hotel.

"Howdy Big Ed," Jed called out as they passed through the batwing doors.

"Hey, Jed. Thought you'd gone back to Texas," Ed said from behind the bar. Several locals stood drinking at the bar and a couple sat at a table. Luke took notice of the large man behind the bar who Jed called Big Ed. Well over six feet and broad across the shoulders, Ed made an imposing form behind the bar.

"Shur did. Brought Luke Payton here, to pay his respects to his brother Butcherknife Bill." Ed knew as soon as the words left Jed's mouth, Luke was not here to pay any respects to his dead brother. He was here to make trouble.

"Welcome to San Marcial, Luke," Ed greeted him trying hard to mask his true emotions. Ed could tell by Luke's swagger and the six shooter hanging low on his hip, Luke was a dangerous man.

"Much obliged Ed. Yew got a couple rooms fer us?"

"Yep, sure do," Ed replied.

"We need food," Jed piped in.

"Got steak and potatoes, that alright?"

"Shur nuff, git us a shot and a beer before yew git our food started," Luke said.

Ed poured the drinks and went to the kitchen to fix up the plates. When he returned, Luke and Jed were sitting at a table. Ed placed a steaming plate in front of each of them, a fork and knife, and walked back to the bar.

Jed and Luke dug into the food. "This here's good," Luke said. "Cept fer them damn greasers over thar, this here is an alright place," Luke commented. "Thought yew said this was a shitheel town?"

"Big Ed's is alright, but the rest of this shitheel town is run by greasers," Jed hissed.

"Tell me about that Ed feller," Luke asked Jed after draining his glass of beer.

"His name is Ed Seeley. He's a good ol' boy retired from the Union Army at Fort Craig. After he mustered out he decided to stay here and open this here saloon and hotel. Always treated us Texans right well," Jed said.

"What about the rooms, they passable?"

"Dun know, never been in one. We stayed out in the bunkhouse at the ranch," Jed grumbled remembering the cold nights and drafty, poorly-built bunkhouse. "Biggest problem, Ed don't run no whores."

Luke looked around the room and realized there were no women. "What kinda saloon dun have no whores," Luke sneered.

"Git used to it Luke. Tol ya this here's a shitheel town. That's why I went back to Texas." Jed thought about Texas and wished he was back there and not here in San Marcial with Luke.

"More beer?" Ed asked walking up to their table.

"Naw, jes bring us a bottle," Luke ordered.

"Coming right up." Ed brought a full bottle and sat it on the table. "That'll be five dollars each, including the meals and the rooms," he said to Luke.

Luke thought the price was steep, but did not argue. He pulled some bills from his vest pocket and counted out ten dollars.

"Take any of the rooms upstairs when you're ready. There's a stable out back for your horses," Ed told them.

After their meal, Luke pulled a deck of cards out of

his vest and dealt a friendly hand of five-card draw between him and Jed. Ed Seeley stood behind the bar and watched Jed and Luke nurse the bottle and play cards. He knew Jed was one of John B. Sutton's cowboys from Texas. Jed said Luke was Butcherknife Bill's brother. After Sutton and Bill were killed last fall, Jed went back to Texas. Jed was one of the cowboys who had refused to continue on for Cynthia Sutton, John's widow, and left rather than work along side of the local Mexican cowboys.

Ed studied Luke. He did not look much like his brother Bill – taller and less weathered. He did not look like a cowboy either, and Ed suspected he might be a gambler or gun hand. Luke and Jed stayed at the table drinking until the bottle was gone and the saloon was empty. When they went outside to collect their gear and stable the horses, Ed started closing up.

"Hey, I ain't dun drinkin," Luke groused when he walked back into the saloon. Ed could see Luke wobbling a bit and his words slurred.

"Sorry boys. I'm closing up for the night."

"I said I ain't dun drinkin," Luke growled and started toward the bar. Ed moved slightly and reached for his shotgun under the counter.

"Cum on Luke. I'm tired. We got a long day tomorrow." Jed pulled on Luke's arm, but Luke jerked away. "We got us a greaser to hunt down tomorrow," Jed hissed to Luke. "Cum on."

Luke did not like being told what to do, but saw Ed Seeley holding a shotgun in his right hand and said, "Ah, I'm just foolin round."

Ed watched the two climb the steps to the upstairs rooms. Things had been quiet in San Marcial since Rafe killed Butcherknife Bill, Ponyboy George, and John B. Sutton. Most of the cowboys stayed and were working along with locals for Cynthia Sutton, John's widow. Now, trouble had come back to San Marcial, Ed knew it, and their names were Jed Clements and Luke Payton.

CHAPTER 42

It was Wednesday afternoon at the Palacio Cantina and Diego de la Torre and several young *caballeros* sat around drinking and playing cards. Diego had been fuming mad since Saturday when the young Mexican *caballero* riding the Appaloosa insulted him on the *paseo*. The drinking and lustful sex with Virginia Barceló Verdugo, the owner of the Palacio, only briefly calmed his rage.

"The *pendejo* did not speak in Spanish and when I told him my ancestry, he just ignored me and continued talking in Texas English," Diego complained before he slammed down another shot of tequila. *"El hombre me insultó.* He speaks like a *Norte Americano* and not like a Mexican; he cannot be a *caballero,"* Diego continued venting.

His friends listened to him grumble since last Saturday and knew to nod and agree. Diego was in a dark, hateful mood and his friends knew to keep their distance.

Diego got up and wandered to the Monte table and sat down. Perhaps playing would take his mind off of the strange *caballero*. The beautiful *señorita* from California was a prize catch, if only for a conquest. Rafe pushed him aside, and Diego was never pushed aside by anyone. If he had to do battle with Rafe, he would gladly do so. After all, Diego was an excellent marksman and even better with the rapier than anyone in Santa Fe.

He told Alvaro to find out about the man riding the Appaloosa and to not come back without news. That was four days ago and Alvaro had not come around. An hour later, bored and angry from losing, Diego stood up and said to his *compañeros, "Vámonos."*

Wednesday afternoon Rafe was on his way to the tack shop located on the central plaza to get Rayo fitted with a new saddle. Esteban, an older man who worked for George Summers for many years, rode alongside him on Lolo's mare. George sent Esteban with Rafe to fetch the new saddle he ordered for the mare.

The saddler was now making American saddles, as well as Spanish saddles, and Rafe was anxious to try an American saddle on Rayo and was bringing Rayo in for a fitting. When they arrived at the saddle shop, Esteban took a hold of both horses' reins, while Rafe entered the shop.

"*Buenas tardes, Timoteo,*" Rafe greeted Timoteo Florentino, the owner.

"*Buenas tardes,* Rafael. I see you've brought Rayo for a fitting."

"Yes and George sent Esteban to pick up the mare's saddle."

"Ah yes, bring the horses around to the shop in back," Timoteo said.

In the shop at the back, Rafe dismounted and pulled the Mexican saddle off of Rayo. Timoteo grabbed a leather measuring tape and began measuring the Appaloosa. He wasted no time scribbling figures as he worked around the tall horse. Once done, the saddle maker helped Rafe resaddle Rayo. "Bring him back next week so I can test the seat," the saddler said. Timoteo took the mare's reins from Esteban and told him to wait outside while he made the final adjustments on the mare's new saddle.

Rafe and Esteban walked out of the saddle shop, Rafe walking Rayo by his side. "Can you get the old saddle back to the ranch?" he asked the older man.

"*Sí,* I can tie it to the new saddle," Esteban responded.

"Tell *don* Jorge I will be home later to help him finish the last of the guns for the shipment to Albuquerque," Rafe told Esteban using George Summer's Spanish name.

Rafe mounted Rayo and headed down the street to see *don* Luis, the fencing master, leaving Esteban standing in front of the saddle shop. He had some questions about the Spanish Circle or the Ring of Death, which the Maestro taught him last Saturday.

Alvaro and Benjamin were riding on the plaza when Benjamin spotted a man standing by an Appaloosa in front of the saddle shop. "Alvaro, is that the *caballero* Diego is looking for?" Benjamin asked pointing toward Rafe talking to another man.

"*Sí,*" Alvaro responded looking toward the saddle shop.

They watched as Rafe mounted the Appaloosa and rode away toward the plaza. Alvaro told Benjamin, "Follow him, I'm going to talk to that old man."

Reaching the shop, Alvaro jumped from his horse. Esteban was leaning against the outside wall of the shop waiting for the mare to be fitted.

"*Hola,*" Alvaro greeted Esteban. "That man, the one who rides the Appaloosa, do you know him?"

"*Sí, es Rafael,*" Esteban responded.

"He is your *jefe?*" Alvaro asked thinking the man must work for the *caballero.*

"*No, señor,*" Esteban replied politely to the young *caballero.* "He lives with *Señor* Summers at the GSW foundry and we work for *Señor* Summers."

Work? Alvaro knew no *caballero* would work in a foundry. Calmly Alvaro asked, "Is he from Mexico?"

"*Sí,* he came to live with the Summers a number of years ago. He is from Mexico." Esteban shortening the story George Summers had told him many times.

"Where in Mexico?"

"Torreón."

Esteban thought it odd Alvaro wanted to know about Rafael. The stableman, he worked with Rafael for the past five years. Rafael was a good worker and a good man. Esteban knew George Summers was proud of Rafael and treated him like a son. He assumed most of the town knew the story of how Rafael came to Santa Fe.

"He has a *hacienda* in Torreón?" Alvaro asked.

"No, no he is not a *haciendero,* he's a *mestizo.* He did not own the *hacienda.*"

"Why did he come here to Santa Fe with *Señor* Summers?" Alvaro asked still processing the news the man on the Appaloosa was a *mestizo.*

"Rafael saved *don* Jorge's life. He was fleeing from a *haciendero* and found *don* Jorge dying in the Texas desert. *Don* Jorge loves him like a son for saving his life."

"Where did he get such a fine horse?" Alvaro asked trying not to show his glee at the information about Rafael's true identity.

"He took it from the *hacienda* in Torreón," Esteban explained.

"What do you mean he took it?"

Esteban did not like the questions Alvaro was asking, but felt obliged to answer. "He just took it *señor*. I know nothing else." Esteban hung his head sorry he answered any of the rude *caballero's* questions.

Alvaro allowed the story to sink into his brain. The man on the Appaloosa was no *caballero,* he was a *mestizo,* just a *peón* from Mexico pretending to be a *caballero.* Alvaro turned on his heels without acknowledging the old man. Walking to his horse, he saw Benjamin approaching from the plaza and mounted up to go meet him.

"He's at the fencing school," Benjamin told Alvaro when they met up.

"*Vamos.* Let's go get him." Alvaro said.

Rafe entered the fencing school and found *don* Luis kneeling and facing a statue of Santiago Matamoros, Saint James, the Muslim slayer. The statue depicted a knight atop a white horse yielding a fiery sword. Rafe waited until *don* Luis finished his prayers before he approached him.

"*Buenas tardes, Maestro,*" Rafe greeted *don* Luis.

"*Buenas tardes, Rafael,*" *don* Luis replied. "Why have you come today? It is not your lesson day and you did not bring your sword?"

"*Maestro,* I am intrigued by the Ring of Death. Will you explain it to me again? I believe I can visualize it, but I lose track when I put it into action."

"Ah, the Spanish Circle allows you to know the effective range of your weapon and use it to your advantage. Each swordsman is different in size and reach. You must envision the effective range of your sword to include a small step or lunge toward your opponent. This range forms circles around you, protecting you as well as defining your limitations. Come let me show you again."

Rafe picked up a sparring sword and stood facing the

master. *Don* Luis took a step forward and at arm's length he placed his rapier over Rafe's head. He explained a sword's effective range would be a distance or a chord measured from the base of the leading foot to an arm's length over the fighter's head, as he demonstrated.

"Here, I will lend you my copy of the book *Libro de las Grandezas de la Espada,* by the master, *don* Luis Pacheco de Narvaez. Study it and we will discuss it at your next lesson."

"Muchas gracias, Maestro," Rafe thanked him and took the book. Outside, he placed the precious book into his saddlebag and climbed up onto Rayo's back. He decided to stop at the mercantile on the plaza to buy the children, Antonio and Alicia, their favorite stick candy before he headed home.

Alvaro and Benjamin rode toward the fencing school near the plaza. Benjamin pointed to the back of a horse and rider far down the street. "There he is." Alvaro thought about riding to get Diego, but decided to confront the *peón* himself. Diego would be impressed if Alvaro bested the scoundrel. Alvaro and Benjamin rode up behind Rafe as he reached the mercantile.

"Eh, peón, you do not belong on the *paseo,"* Rafe heard a gruff voice call out behind him. "And you will not speak to our Spanish women anymore."

At first the comment did not register in Rafe's mind. *Peón?* Rafe looked up as two young *caballeros* rode up on either side, blocking him.

"What are you talking about?" Rafe responded cringing inside being called a *peón.*

"Your kind are not allowed to ride on the *paseo* and talk to our women. You are no better than a dog. Do not show yourself on the *paseo* again, or we will kill you," Alvaro warned him.

Rafe reached to his side and then remembered he left his pistols at the ranch. "You best be careful who you threaten to kill, *baboso,"* Rafe said calling Alvaro a drooling idiot with a defiant tone.

The two on horseback edged closer. Rafe yanked

hard on Rayo's reins and Rayo jerked backward making Alvaro's horse buck and pushed Benjamin's horse back. Rafe quickly turned Rayo and pulled away from the two. Several people walking on the boardwalk stopped to stare at the commotion.

Alvaro saw red and pulled his rapier. *"Hijo de puta!"* he yelled, calling Rafe a son of a whore.

Burning with ingrained rage from his years at *don* Bernardo's *hacienda,* Rafe turned Rayo charging directly at Alvaro. Alvaro raised his sword skyward. Rafe thought about the Circle of Death picturing the circles around him. Could it keep him safe when he held nothing to defend himself? Rayo, several hands taller than the young *caballero's* horse, was a born leader. Other horses sensed Rayo's power and as Alvaro's horse approached it shied and turned aside, but Alvaro's sword swung and was able to knick Rafe's arm as he whirled.

"Cabrón," Alvaro swore at him, turned his horse again, and headed toward Rafe wielding his sword straight in front of him.

From somewhere deep in his subconscious, Rafe heard the Aztec Healer's voice. "Clear your mind of rage and hate and your perception will be keen. Do not lose sight of your senses; be aware of everything around you," the old Healer had taught him.

Turning Rayo, Rafe stood his ground as Alvaro and his horse charged. Yanking on the reins, Rayo reared and the smaller horse spooked and bucked Alvaro off the saddle.

Rafe calmed his rage not wanting to lose his temper and jumped off of Rayo. He picked up Alvaro's sword and walked to where the young *caballero* lay in the dirt, pointing the sword at his throat.

Benjamin saw Alvaro on the ground and the *peón* holding the sword to his throat and fled the plaza. Rafe circled Alvaro holding the rapier near his throat. Rafe was furious at the unprovoked attack. Most of all he hated being called a *peón* – he swore a long time ago he would never let anyone treat him that way again.

Rafe saw the fear of death in Alvaro's eyes. He thought he recognized the young *caballero* from the *paseo* last Saturday. He was with the *caballero* named Diego – the one talking to Ana Teresa.

"Why did you attack me?"

"You are a *peón*. You do not belong on the *paseo*, only *caballeros* are allowed," Alvaro tried to sound brave.

"This is New Mexico, *pendejo*, not Spain. Here we are equals."

"Diego will take care of you," Alvaro sneered. Rafe pointed the tip of the rapier into Alvaro throat until it drew blood and Alvaro flinched.

"Never call me a *peón* again. If you do I will kill you, not with a sword, but with my guns," Rafe growled at him. "Do you understand?"

Alvaro, red faced and scared, nodded his head only slightly.

"Now get away from here and you better not let me ever see you again and if I do, you better be carrying a gun," Rafe told him throwing the sword far across the road. Rafe climbed up onto Rayo and kicked him hard in the ribs. Rayo took off like a shot.

Picking himself up from the dirt, Alvaro cursed at Rafe's back. *"¡Cabrón!"* He jumped up to his horse's saddle and rode hard to the de la Torre *hacienda*. The nick on his neck stung, but not as much as being bested by the *pinche peón*. Riding into the courtyard, Alvaro yelled out for Diego, who came striding out of the house, with Vicente and Armando following behind him.

"Diego, that *cabrón* with the Appaloosa is a *peón* from Mexico. He is no *caballero*," Alvaro said.

"¡Peón!" Diego let the information sink in. "Are you sure?" he asked Alvaro.

"Sí, amigo. He came from Mexico and works at the Summers' foundry." Alvaro related the story told by the old man at the saddle shop.

"How did you get cut on your neck?" Diego asked Alvaro seeing the blood crusted on his collar. Alvaro was ashamed about being bested by the *peón* and lied, "He attacked us, that *pinche peón* attacked us," he told Diego. Alvaro was angry at Benjamin for leaving him at the plaza and would deal with him later.

Diego bristled at the news of the *caballero* who was just a *peón*. *"Me cago en el hijo de puta,"* he swore he would someday shit upon the son of the whore. No *peón* would attack his friends and tarnish the reputation of the *paseo*.

CHAPTER 43

"Hola Ed," Tomás Armijo called to Ed Seeley as he walked into Big Ed's Saloon and Hotel for his frequent morning breakfast. Tomás Armijo was the mayor of the small village of San Marcial, New Mexico, located along the west bank of the Rio Grande, elected because his family had been one of the original settlers.

"Hey, Thomas. When did you get back from Socorro?" Ed always called Tomás by his English name of Thomas.

"Late last night. Your light was still on and I was going to stop by, but I thought Teresa was probably already worrying."

"How did it go?"

"I made my plea again to get a deputy permanently assigned here, but the sheriff says there isn't enough work to keep a deputy busy here and he can handle it from Socorro."

"That's too bad Thomas."

Tomás Armijo was the only law in the town of San Marcial, the mayor, not a lawman. Last fall John B. Sutton bought a large spread south of town and brought thousands of head of cattle and thirty Texas cowboys to run them. Up until then, San Marcial was a sleepy hamlet of mostly the descendants of the original Spanish settlers. They were farmers and small time ranchers. The cowboys swept into town with an attitude against Mexicans, making San Marcial a powder keg of trouble.

The cowboys shot up the town and terrorized the locals. Two of the cowboys, Butcherknife Bill and Ponyboy George, raped and killed a young Mexican woman. She was the wife of the carpenter building Sutton's new ranchhouse. While Tomás was trying to solve the murder, the cowboys continued to plunder the town for supplies, taking what they needed at gunpoint. Tomás needed help and he was disappointed the sheriff would not appoint a deputy to San

Marcial.

"Is the coffee hot?" Tomás asked.

"Sure." Ed pulled a cup onto the bar and poured hot coffee to the top. "Go sit at a table and I'll bring us breakfast."

Ed went to the kitchen to scramble some eggs and returned, sitting two plates of eggs, bacon, and toast on the table where Tomás sat drinking his coffee. When they finished the food, Ed quietly said, "Butcherknife Bill's brother, Luke, is upstairs. Came in last night with Jed Clements. He said he wants to pay his respects to Bill's grave, but I doubt that's the reason."

Tomás stared at Ed as he let the news sink in. Jed had come back and brought Luke Payton and there could be only one reason, revenge. He did not need Ed to tell him there was going to be trouble.

"Does Mrs. Sutton know?" Tomás asked Ed.

"I doubt it. They just came in last night. I'm planning on going out to the Sutton ranch this morning and talk to her."

"Good, she needs to be warned, though I doubt they will do anything to hurt her. Still they may stir up trouble with her men."

"I agree. I was thinking the same thing. I hope they don't start trouble between the Texans and the locals," Ed said.

"I'll send a telegram to Socorro and ask for the deputy to come," Tomás told him. "Let me know if they cause any problems."

"Sure thing Thomas."

Tomás Armijo left the saloon walking into the bright morning sun. It was a beautiful summer day in the Rio Grande valley. The weather had been mild and the farmers were happy with a bumper crop of grain.

Life had returned to normal in San Marcial after the killings last winter. Rafael Ortega, a friend of Tomás' cousin Carlos, killed Butcherknife Bill and Ponyboy George, two of John B. Sutton's Texas cowboys. The two bushwhacked him as he left San Marcial for Santa Fe. The one called Ponyboy was also the murderer of Carmen Gomez, the carpenter's wife. He raped and murdered the poor woman and hid the body near the river.

Not all the Texas cowboys were bad, but those two were scum. They bushwhacked Rafael, underestimating his ability with firearms. Not only was Rafael a gun maker, he was an expert with a gun. When he brought the pair of dead cowboys back to town, he confronted Sutton in the saloon. Butcherknife told Rafael before he died, they had bushwhacked him because Sutton wanted his horses. Sutton called Rafael a liar and pulled his gun, before Rafael shot him dead. The court cleared Rafael of any wrongdoing.

Since the killings, Cynthia Sutton, John's widow hired a number of locals to work with the cowboys and life calmed down in San Marcial. Some cowboys stayed and some, like Jed, went back to Texas. There had been no trouble for many months. Now, Jed was back with Luke Payton.

After Tomás left, Ed picked up the breakfast dishes and walked back to the kitchen. It was still early and those two upstairs would probably sleep late. He started to clean up the kitchen, planning on riding out to see Cynthia. As Ed washed up the breakfast dishes his mind drifted to Cynthia and the events over the past months.

She and her husband had been living at his hotel while their ranchhouse was being built in the months before her husband was killed. It surprised him she wanted to stay after John's death. She finished the ranchhouse, hired locals, and did what her dead husband had not – made the ranch a viable business. Everyone was amazed, but no one more than Ed.

When she first stepped off the stage from El Paso, the new bride of John B. Sutton was the picture of elegance. Dressed in the latest style, Cynthia's auburn hair fell around her face and her emerald green eyes flashed in the sunlight. Ed remembered he thought she was the prettiest woman her had ever seen.

After Rafe killed her husband, Cynthia and her ill

mother continued to live upstairs at Ed's hotel. He got to know her well over many dinners and they often talked late into the night. Ed helped her manage her mother who was senile and dying. It was Ed who found her mother dead one afternoon when Cynthia was out at the ranch.

Ed helped her make arrangements and held her hand through the funeral. She cried on his shoulder. Sometimes Ed imagined she held him a bit too tight, moving her body close to his so he could feel her breasts against his chest. He smelled her perfume in her hair when he was near her and maybe she flirted with him, or maybe he was imagining it.

Finally when the ranchhouse was finished, Cynthia moved from the hotel and Ed remembered being disappointed. He hated to admit it, but he loved her and had not wanted her to leave. He wanted to ask her to stay, to stay with him and he wanted to marry her. After she moved to the ranchhouse, Ed saw her in town shopping and she always came to the saloon to say hello.

Several weeks after Cynthia left the hotel for her newly constructed ranchhouse, one of the local New Mexican wranglers working at her ranch stopped at Big Ed's and left a message addressed to him. Ed still had the note pressed between the pages of his Bible.

Dear Ed,
Please come to supper at my ranch tomorrow at 4:00 pm and bring a bottle of your good wine, and we will dine on beef and potatoes with a yellow squash soup.
You have been so good and kind to me through all my troubles and I feel it is time to reward you with good home cooking.
Best Regards,
Cindy

Ed remembered reading the note over and over. He tried to tell himself it was a friendly invitation, just repayment for his kindness to her, not love. Over the next day he read her note memorizing the words by heart. He had thought about being alone with Cynthia since the day she stepped off the stage in front of his saloon. Her beauty awoke something in him, which stayed hidden since he joined the U.S. Army at the age of nineteen, but it was her quiet strength he loved even more.

The following day seemed to come slowly. Ed tried to keep busy while the hours ticked by slowly. He closed the saloon early and took a long hot bath. He wore a blue checked shirt and a black bandana knotted around his neck. At over six feet tall, Ed was a big man and he had put on a few pounds around the middle. He slicked back his sandy hair and put on his best hat.

Ed reached the Sutton ranchhouse just before four. It was late March and spring was beginning to show itself in the lower Rio Grande valley. Cynthia planted flowers around the house which were starting to bloom. As he dismounted from his horse, he took a long breath to calm his nerves.

"Good evening Ed," Cynthia startled him from the porch. She was dressed in a tan taffeta dress with red ruffled trim. The low cut dress exposed her slightly bulging breasts. She wore little make up, just enough to give her face a bit of color and her lips were colored a deep red. Her auburn hair cascaded down her shoulders and curled around her face. Ed's heart jumped in his chest.

"Thank you for inviting me, Cynthia," he stammered.

"I've told you to call me Cindy," she reminded him. "Cynthia is so formal."

Ed struggled trying to make conversation. Normally they talked freely and easily, but tonight he struggled to find words.

"I've been looking forward to spending time with you," he said trying hard to not let her beauty rattle him. He followed her to the parlor just off the dining room where she had a bottle of rye and two glasses. After she poured, she handed him one.

"Here's to you Ed, for all you have done for me," she raised her glass to his. "I hope you like my cooking," she teased. She clinked her glass with his while looking straight into his eyes. Her eyes stood out like bright shiny emeralds when she looked up at him.

"Here's to you Cindy. You are the strongest woman I know." Lame he thought. He wanted to tell her how beautiful she looked. Cindy heard his compliment; he thought she was strong. Most days she felt lost and vulnerable, wondering why she thought she could ever run a cattle ranch.

He saw her eyes moisten and she put down her glass. Rising on her tiptoes, she embraced him. Her tears flowed and she cried loudly, letting out all the pent-up emotions. He held her close allowing her to release the emotional flood along with buckets of tears. She held on to him like a vulnerable little girl, then she tipped up her head.

She came up from his shoulder and kissed him tenderly. He responded with a ravenous hunger and she responded equally as hard. They kissed and did not stop until he lifted her and carried her into her bedroom.

She relished feeling safe and secure in his arms. Part of him wanted to ravage her, while the other wanted to make sweet love to her forever. He could feel her respond to his touch. Slowly she unwound the black bandana from his neck and unbuttoned his shirt. A mass of curly brown hair covered his chest. She ran her hands over his shoulders and kissed his chest.

"Anybody here?" he heard a voice yelling from the front room of the saloon.

"Yes, coming," Ed responded drying his hands and shaking out of the sweet memories.

Three strangers stood in front of the bar. "Can we get some grub?" one of the men asked. Ed wanted to tell them the bar was closing, but it wasn't good business.

"Sure, eggs and bacon? Help yourselves to coffee," he said putting three cups on the bar.

Ed headed back to the kitchen to make the breakfasts. He would have to go later to warn Cindy about the two upstairs.

CHAPTER 44

When Diego de la Torre heard the news from Alvaro and Benjamin about Rafe, he wanted to kill the *mestizo* on the Appaloosa pretending to be a *caballero*. The *cabrón* insulted him and tarnished the Spanish tradition on the *paseo*. In Diego's mind, that tradition was an exclusive right of the Spanish aristocracy.

He wanted to kill the *cabrón* and be done with him. In the old days aristocrats would severely punish or kill such a *mestizo* without rebuke, but under the new *Americano* laws Diego might be jailed or hanged for killing him. Instead he wanted Rafe to suffer in humiliation, to be shunned forever from society, and he wanted to see the abhorrent look in Ana Teresa's eyes when she realized Rafe had tricked her. As much as Diego wanted to outright kill Rafe, moreover he wanted him to suffer in disgrace and he had a plan.

The following morning Diego dressed in his formal *traje* and rode to the de Soto *hacienda* to pay *don* Pedro a call.

"Diego," the *don* greeted him.

"Buenos días, don Pedro."

"What brings you to my door. A call on my beautiful daughter or Ana Teresa, perhaps?"

"I came to warn you *don* Pedro."

"Warn me? Warn me about what?"

"The *caballero* named Rafael is not what he seems. He is no *caballero*, he is a *mestizo* from Mexico. He has only been pretending to be of noble birth."

"¡Mestizo!" *Don* Pedro gruffed at the words spoken by Diego. Carlos brought the young man to their family's fiesta and introduced him as a man from Mexico, a horse breeder. *Don* Pedro assumed he was a *caballero*.

"He is from Mexico and rides a fine horse. His horses are better than any in Santa Fe. How can this be true?" the *don* asked.

"He attacked my two friends in the plaza. The Appaloosa he rides was stolen from Mexico. I swear on my honor this is true. Ask Carlos the truth about his friend, Rafael," Diego told him.

"*Gracias,* Diego. You are a man of honor. You are welcome here at anytime."

"Perhaps I have your permission to call on your niece, Ana Teresa?" Diego asked.

"Yes, you are always welcome," *don* Pedro responded thinking Diego would be a good catch for Ana Teresa.

After Diego left the *hacienda, don* Pedro sent a servant to fetch Carlos. "Bring him to me immediately," he told the servant.

The servant from the de Soto *hacienda* went to the GSW foundry and asked for Carlos. "*Don* Pedro summons you to come, *señor,*" the man said and Carlos had to oblige. Riding to the de Soto *hacienda,* terrible scenarios played in Carlos' mind. Bibiana was sick or dead or her father changed his mind and cut off the engagement. Dread felt like a knot in his stomach.

When he reached the de Soto *hacienda,* Carlos found *don* Pedro, Bibiana's father, in the parlor. He did not look happy and did not rise to greet him.

"Carlos, your friend Rafael, he is a *caballero* from Mexico, no?" *Don* Pedro waited for an answer. Carlos felt the room shrink around him. The tone of the *don's* voice was hard and cold.

"*Señor,* he is from Mexico, but he is not a *caballero.*" Carlos could not lie. "He is George Summers' adopted son and a horse breeder."

Relieved Carlos did not lie, the *don's* tone softened a bit. "You brought him dressed as a *caballero* to my home and he has been seen riding on the *paseo.* I allowed him to ride with the girls."

"*Señor,* I am sorry if you believed he was a *caballero.* Rafael is a good man. He saved George Summers' life and mine . . . he is a good man . . . " Carlos could not finish the sentence.

"Diego de la Torre told me your friend, the *mestizo,* attacked two *caballeros* on the plaza yesterday and his Appaloosa is stolen. Is this true?" Carlos was confused.

Rafe did not tell him anything about an attack yesterday.

"I know nothing about an attack, *señor*. Rafael rode the Appaloosa from Mexico. It belonged to the *haciendero* who raped his younger sister."

"A *peón* riding an Appaloosa from Mexico that belonged to a *haciendero* sounds stolen to me," *don* Pedro said gruffly.

Carlos could not dispute his words. Yes, Rayo was stolen. Stolen from *don* Bernardo's *hacienda*. "The *haciendero* is dead, *señor*."

Don Pedro sat quietly for several minutes. Carlos wanted to say more, but held back seeing the look in his eyes. He feared *don* Pedro would end the engagement and throw him out on his ear.

Bibiana's father was conflicted. Carlos spoke the truth when asked directly about Rafael. Although he brought the *mestizo* to their fiesta, he had at no time introduced him as a *caballero*. If Carlos was to be his future son-in-law, at least he now honored him with the truth, even if he showed poor judgment in his choice of friends.

"You are forbidden to bring Rafael to this house again. He cannot speak to or see Ana Teresa and I will make sure he does not ride on the *paseo* ever again."

"*Gracias, don* Pedro. It will be as you wish." Carlos bowed his head in a movement of respect to the older man and started to turn away.

"Carlos?" the *don* said as Carlos turned to go. "You said he saved your life? How so?"

Carlos decided to tell the *don* everything. He wanted no more secrets with the man who would be his father-in-law. "My brother, Benicío, left me dying on the Chihuahua Trail after he robbed a wagon train. Benicío became an outlaw after we lost our land to the *Americanos*. He was leaving me to die, knowing I was still alive. My brother was a bad man *señor*. Rafael found me and took me to the Isleta pueblo where he asked the *Indios* to treat my wounds and care for me. He saved my life," Carlos repeated.

"And your brother?"

"I killed him *señor*."

"You killed him in revenge?"

"No, I killed him when he tried to kill Rafael. He killed the woman Rafael loved." Carlos explained briefly.

Don Pedro said nothing more and Carlos took his leave. When he was gone, *don* Pedro pondered the information. Carlos was an honorable man. It was honor which bound Carlos to the man named Rafael and *don* Pedro understood honor.

Carlos left the *hacienda* in a rage and on a gallop. He knew exactly where to find the scoundrel Diego. Diego and his friends were playing Monte at the Palacio Cantina, as was often their usual afternoon activity. Vicente and Alvaro were sipping tequila and laughing while they stood at the long bar. Virginia, the beautiful owner of the cantina, was sitting next to Diego. It was unusual for her to be downstairs so early in the day and she was serving them tequila and enjoying the conversation between the *caballeros.*

"Virginia, come spend time with us and leave those whelps to their Monte," *don* Daniel Archuleta bellowed across the room. *Don* Daniel was one of the older and wealthier *caballeros* in the cantina. He was most respected by his *compañeros* for his distinguished family's Spanish ancestry. Virginia excused herself and sauntered over to grace her presence with the old gents, but before she left she whispered into Diego's ear, "I will meet you later in my bedroom."

Diego smiled at Virginia's invitation. He was no longer angry at being insulted on the *paseo.* He set in place a plan to discredit Carlos' friend, the *mestizo,* and *don* Pedro had all but given him a blessing to begin courting Ana Teresa. On Saturday he would ride the *paseo* and have his free will in enticing the beautiful *señorita* from California.

He was spreading the lie about how the *mestizo* assaulted his friends at the plaza. Virginia believed him, of course. She wanted the *mestizo peón* caught and punished for what he did to the young *caballeros.* When Diego finished spreading the rumors, most every prominent family in Santa Fe would be insulted how the *peón* pretended to be of the aristocratic elite.

"Diego!" Carlos' voice startled him. His back was to the door and he did not see Carlos enter the cantina.

"*Qué, ¿Quién eres? Ah, Carlos, Qué tal, amigo.*" Surprised, Diego sputtered then recognized Carlos and asked what he wanted.

"Diego, why are you spreading lies about Rafael?" Carlos demanded.

"Who? Rafael?" Diego smiled an innocent smile at Carlos.

"You are spreading lies saying Rafael attacked two of your friends."

"What are you talking about? I have spread no lies about Rafael, I have only told the truth."

"You told *don* de Soto he attacked those two sitting there with you." Diego had sworn Alvaro and Benjamin to lie if ever asked about who did the attacking and who was attacked.

"Ah yes, your amigo, the *mestizo,* did attack these two for no reason. I think he did it because he is a *peón* and does not like pure-blooded Spaniards. You must tell him he has broken a long standing rule about *peóns* attacking their masters," Diego warned Carlos.

"You forget Diego, we are not in Spain or Mexico. New Mexico is now an American territory and the Spanish *casta* system means nothing according the United States Constitution – everyone is equal," Carlos said defiantly.

"*Me cago en la Constitución de los Estados Unidos,*" Diego cursed against the United States Constitution saying he would shit upon it. "*Un peón o mestizo* will never be the equal to a pure-blooded Spaniard, never."

"Rafael is a man you will not intimidate, Diego. If they are still walking, he bested your two friends after they attacked him and sent them home to lick their wounds. Someday you will have to face him alone, without your dandies to protect you. You think about that, before you spread more lies about him," Carlos warned.

"You tell the *mestizo,* he is not welcome on the *paseo* and he is not welcome at the de Soto's. Ana Teresa will look to me now that she has been disgraced," Diego said standing and walking toward Carlos until they were almost nose to nose.

"You have been warned, Diego. The old ways are dead here in New Mexico. Rafael is not a *peón* and you are not a *haciendero*. Rafael is a man with land and a horse breeder. You are a scoundrel pretending to be an aristocrat," Carlos said, turned, and left the cantina.

Virginia watched Carlos confront Diego, hearing most of the conversation from where she sat with the old *caballeros*. "Oye, ¿Qué está pasando con esos dos hombres?" *don* Daniel asked Virginia. *Don* Daniel's hearing was almost gone and all he could tell was two men were arguing.

"*Nada, don* Daniel. They are arguing about a girl," she told him.

"*Ah, las cosas del corazón,*" *don* Daniel chuckled saying it was the way with things from the heart. He and the other old *caballeros* laughed and sipped their brandy.

Virginia walked to Diego. She tried to put her arm in his, but he pushed her aside and grumbled at her. No one pushed Virginia aside.

"Who was that man named Carlos? He is handsome even with the scar, in fact, I find it dashing," Virginia egged Diego.

"You can't be serious. He's a *criollo!*" Diego growled and gave Virginia a disgusted look. He pushed her away in a rage. He would get more than even with Carlos and Rafael. He would make them pay the highest of price.

Carlos spurred Santiago away from the Palacio Cantina and headed north to the Summers' ranch. It was almost dusk when Carlos arrived home. He rode directly into the horse barn and saw Rafe's head poking above Rayo's stall. "Rafe!" Carlos bellowed slipping off of Santiago. Rafe was in Rayo's stall brushing the Appaloosa down when he heard Carlos call.

"Over here," Rafe answered.

"Why didn't you tell me you attacked two *caballeros* on the plaza yesterday?" Carlos groused at him as he walked up.

"Me attack? They attacked me for no reason."

"What?"

"I was in front of the mercantile and they called me a *peón*. They told me to leave the plaza."

"Then you attacked them for calling you a *peón?*"

"I wanted to, but I was unarmed. The one called Alvaro attacked me with his rapier," Rafe said simplifying the encounter.

Carlos let the story sink in for a moment then smiled. "You bested them unarmed?"

"Yes. One of them rode off and I told Alvaro never to call me a *peón* again or to bring his gun."

Carlos was not surprised Rafe was able to best Diego's two friends. Most *caballeros* in Santa Fe were not as skilled and brave as they acted.

"Diego is spreading lies about the attack and told *don* Pedro you are not a *caballero."* Carlos avoided using the word *peón.*

"What?" Rafe stammered stunned at the news.

"I think Diego de la Torre orchestrated the encounter with his friends to dishonor you."

"Why would he do that? I don't even know him," Rafe asked.

"Diego is *gachupín* and hates *Americanos* and believes in the *casta* system, the purity of blood. I think it is all about Ana Teresa. He wants her and wants you out of the way. By exposing you as a *mestizo,* the upper class Spaniards in Santa Fe will treat you as an outcast, a man not fit to be around their daughters. He has done a good job of it already. *Don* Pedro has forbidden you to see or speak to Ana Teresa again," Carlos told him the bad news.

A knot twisted in Rafe's gut and a hot rage spread to his heart. "Carlos, we are not in Spain or Mexico. None of that class ugliness matters here in the territories. I will not stop seeing Ana Teresa, no matter what they say."

"I am afraid it matters here in Santa Fe, Rafe. Those old customs are held onto by the Spanish. *Don* Pedro will be true to his word. He will not allow you to see Ana Teresa."

"What about you and Bibiana?" Rafe asked realizing

he may have put Carlos' courtship of Bibiana in jeopardy within the old *casta* system.

"The *don* did not cut off the engagement, although he was very angry because I misled him. I have not spoken to Bibiana yet . . . " Carlos' voice trailed off. He hoped Bibiana would understand and not be angry at him.

Rafe threw the horse brush at the stall's wall in anger. Rayo snorted and whinnied at the sudden noise, shuffling side to side in the stall. "They cannot stop me. This is New Mexico and I will not live like a *peón*. Those days are over."

"I'm sorry Rafe. *Don* Pedro will forbid Ana Teresa and she will have to follow his bidding."

"I don't care. I will not stop seeing her. She will have to tell me she does not want to see me." Rafe gripped the pitchfork and raised it in anger in the air.

CHAPTER 45

Jed Clements heard laughing and woke up with a hangover in a small room in San Marcial's only hotel at Big Ed's Saloon. It was a whiskey hangover, not opium, and Jed was glad about that. The sun shone brightly in the window and Jed thought it must be late. Luke brought him back to this shitheel town to find Bill's killer, but Jed had no idea where to find the greaser. He was hoping now they were in San Marcial, Jed could leave Luke on his own to find the Mexican who rode the Appaloosa and Jed could go home to Texas.

Jed pulled on his boots and opened his door. The laughing came from the bar downstairs. Looking over the railing, Jed saw three men eating breakfast. He banged on Luke's door until he heard the big man yell something from inside.

When Luke finally opened his door and walked down the stairs, Jed was already sitting at a table. "I tol Big Ed to make us sum breakfast," Jed told him. A few minutes later, Ed delivered plates heaped with potatoes, bacon, and eggs.

Luke wolfed down the food. "So where do we find the greaser?" he asked Jed.

"I'll ask Ed iffin he knows." When Ed returned to pick up the empty plates Jed asked, "Ed, you seen that greaser who kilt Bill and Sutton?"

"No. He doesn't live in San Marcial," Ed responded.

"If he dun live here, where's he live?" Luke demanded.

"Santa Fe." Ed thought about lying to Luke, but thought better of it. Santa Fe was a big town and likely they would never find Rafe there.

"Who'd know where?"

"Well, the mayor might know." Ed hoped Tomás would be smart enough not to tell Luke and Jed where to find Rafe.

"So, where kin we find him?" Luke grumbled.

Ed gave Luke and Jed directions to the Armijo *hacienda* near the Rio Grande, hoping Tomás was not at home. When Luke and Jed knocked on the door at the Armijo home, Teresa, Tomás' wife, answered the door. *"No se, Tomás no está en casa,"* she said in Spanish shaking her head at the two men. They asked her again, but Teresa spoke no English and repeated Tomás was not at home.

"Cum on," Jed pulled on Luke's arm. "He ain't here. We'll go to the Sutton ranch and talk to the boys."

Luke and Jed rode south out of San Marcial. It was July and the summer blue grama grass was abundantly growing in the valley. The midday sun was warm, not hot, and hawks circled lazily in the turquoise sky.

"I kin see why Sutton picked this place to raise cattle. The valley is lush with grass and thar is plenty of water," Luke commented. Though not a cattleman, Luke had been around the critters all his life and knew good cattle country when he saw it.

"Yew be right bout that, but it ain't Texas. The whole damn territory is run by Mescans. I didn't like it one damn bit," Jed complained.

Jed led the way to the Sutton bunkhouse. In the distance, they could see cows loose on the escarpment and some down near the river. There were several cowboys rounding up strays, keeping the herd from straying too far on the unfenced land.

As they rode along the road to the Sutton ranch, Luke took in more of the surroundings. The river flowed wide and shallow in the lush valley edged by tall cottonwoods. Flat-topped hills ran along the western edge of the valley, the river to the east, giving the valley definition. Luke had wondered why a good Texas cattleman would leave Texas for the New Mexico territory. Now, he thought Sutton was a smart man. Too bad he got himself killed; he would have made it big here with the good grasslands and water.

As they rounded a corner, the bunkhouse came into view. Jed was surprised when he saw the new bunkhouse made of fresh lumber. It looked solid and had a rock fireplace chimney on the far end. No one was around, but there were a few horses in the corral. They dismounted and went into the bunkhouse where they found Rusty, the cook cleaning up after the breakfast meal.

"Hey Rusty!" Jed called out.

"Hey Jed! How the hell yew been? What yew doin back here?"

"Ah, jes came back to make shur yew galoots don't turn Mescan on me," Jed teased laughing.

"Tain't never gonna happen," Rusty gruffed back at him.

"Rusty, meet Luke Payton, Butcherknife Bill's brother," Jed said nodding over to Luke.

"Yew don't say. Glad to meet yew Luke. Bill was a good friend and I's sorry he got hisself kilt by that curlywolf Mescan. We shur do miss im round here," Rusty said and Luke could tell he meant it.

"Yeah, well I'm here to be takin care of that damn greaser. I'm gonna plug im good with sum lead fer what he did to my brother," Luke swore.

"Yew bess be good mister, cause that greaser is lightnin fast," Rusty warned him.

"Hell, I ain't never seen no greaser warn't scared of a Texan. They just start shakin and shit themselves, when they come up against a Texan with a gun," Luke bragged.

"They say this'n ain't scart. He's mighty fast," Rusty said.

"Don't yew worry none. Ain't gonna take long to take care of that greaser, once we find him," Luke assured Rusty.

"Say Rusty, yew seen that greaser round here lately?" Jed asked.

"Naw, ain't seen him since the trial. I heerd he went back north." Luke was disappointed to hear the greaser was not around San Marcial. He was getting pretty damn tired of traipsing around looking for him.

"Anybody know where he went?" Jed asked.

"I think he's related to the mayor, his cousin or

sumthin. Yew could ask him," Rusty replied.

"Yew seen the mayor tday?"

"Naw, he never comes out here. Try the Sutton lady's ranchhouse. Sometimes the mayor brings sum new workers for her to hire. Maybee he's over ta the house," Rusty said.

"Much obliged. Tell the boys I'll catch up with em later on," Jed told him and led Luke out the door.

Jed and Luke mounted and Jed led the way. Jed pondered what to do as they rode to the Sutton ranchhouse, never having any contact with Sutton's widow. He had only seen her from afar when she was riding with the boss man, John B. Sutton, and at the funeral and trial. He never even spoke to her when he left for Texas, only telling Jack, the new foreman. The only thing he knew for sure was a rumor about her being a whore in Austin. The boys used to grouse about it after old man Sutton brought her here as his wife. Jed could remember Butcherknife Bill saying, "Hell, Sutton's the only one what's got a whore in this here shitheel town."

"Anybody ta home?" Jed called out after he knocked on the ranchhouse door. There was no answer. They walked around back to the kitchen door where they found an elderly Mexican woman pumping water into a bucket at the well outside of the kitchen door.

"Howdy. Is Musses Sutton ta home?" Jed asked the woman.

"No, la señora no está en casa." Jed understood enough Spanish to know Missus Sutton was not at home.

"Donday?" Jed asked, where, in broken Spanish.

"No lo sé," she said she did not know shaking her head side to side.

"She doesn't know where she is," Jed told Luke as they mounted up and rode away.

"Damn Mescans cain't talk right," Luke grumbled. "She's probly lyin."

Jed and Luke mounted up and rode out to high ground to have a better view of the range. Luke saw the valley below filled with cattle. Thousands of head grazed peacefully along the lush grasses near the river.

"Wheeeuuuwwww," Luke whistled when they stopped to overlook the herd. In the distance they could see men on horseback working through the herd and riding on the fringes.

"Mighty fine lookin herd, Jed. Mighty fine. That Sutton widder must be one rich woman."

"Yew got that right. Too bad this here's greaser territory. I still dun understand why ol' man Sutton left Texas for this shithole," Jed grumbled.

"Yew got shit for brains, Jed. Look at the grass and water and those fat critters grazing down there. Sutton had a great idea bringing his herd here. That widder's goin be one hellava rich woman. I cain't wait to meet her."

CHAPTER 46

Ana Teresa sat alone in her room after a day which brought nothing but perplexity to her life. Her uncle summoned her and told her she could not speak to or see Rafael. He was not a *caballero,* he was a *mestizo* from Mexico. She was stunned. It was like the bottom dropped out of her heart and yet she was more angry than hurt. It was the same feeling as when her fiancé told her he was stopping the engagement because the new American laws took her family's land and wealth.

The complexity of the situation frustrated her. She was angry with Rafael pretending to be what he was not, though he never lied to her. Was she any better pretending to be a rich *señorita* from California, when she was penniless and without a dowry? She was struggling with her feelings for Rafael, then again she did not like being told she could not see him.

A knock on her door brought her back from the heavy thoughts disturbing her young, innocent life. *"Ana Teresa, ¿Puedo entrar?"* Bibiana asked if she could enter.

"Sí."

"I brought food and lemonade for you."

"Gracias," Ana Teresa took the tray and sat it beside the bed. She picked up the glass of lemonade.

"I can't believe Carlos brought a *mestizo* to the fiesta. It is his fault and I plan to let him know how mad I am," Bibiana said snottily.

"You are a fool, Bibiana. You took me to the fiesta and I am penniless. Rafael has land, a horse ranch, and a future here in New Mexico. Am I better than he, just because I have pure Spanish blood and he has something else?"

Bibiana was surprised. She expected her cousin to be angry. Of course pure Spanish blood was better than mixed blood.

"My father says *mestizos* are inferior. They are born

that way. It is not their fault. Spaniards are just better."

"Bibiana, what if you found out Carlos was a *mestizo,* would you suddenly not love him?" Ana Teresa asked her. Bibiana scrunched her forehead. Carlos was not *mestizo.* Ana Teresa was being silly.

"Do you love Rafael?"

"I don't know. I do know if I did love him, it would not matter he was not pure-blooded."

"Father said Diego asked to call on you. He is the most eligible bachelor in Santa Fe," Bibiana tried to change the subject.

"You said he's a *picaro.*"

"Well yes, but he is very rich and a true *caballero.* You should be honored."

"Go away Bibiana. I'm tired hearing about money, *caballeros,* and status. I need time alone to think."

The following morning, Diego de la Torre rode to the de Soto *hacienda.* When a servant ran to fetch Bibiana and Ana Teresa, Bibiana was excited. "He must be here to begin courting you," she said to her cousin.

"Tell him I'm dressing and I'll come down shortly." Ana Teresa purposely made Diego wait for her. It was typical for a Spanish woman to leave the man waiting. When she finally walked down the stairs and out to the veranda, Diego was pacing.

"Diego, how nice of you to come," she said.

"You look lovely *señorita.*" He bowed to her and she extended her hand. Studying Diego, Ana Teresa noticed he was shorter than she expected. He looked taller on horseback. His nose was a bit hawkish and his face pocked on both cheeks. When he smiled, his teeth were crooked and yellowish.

"I have kept you sitting too long. Perhaps you would like to walk in the garden?" She took Diego's arm and they walked across the courtyard to the planted gardens on the south side of the house. Ana Teresa pointed out some of her favorite flowers to him.

Diego was stiff, formal, and not a man of small talk. He thought her beautiful and tried to act interested in what she said.

"Your uncle said I should call on you because of the dishonor caused you by the *mestizo*, Rafael," he said.

"Dishonor?" Ana Teresa certainly did not feel dishonored.

"The *mestizo* dishonored you on the *paseo, señorita*. You must feel disgraced by his presence and know you need to be seen with a *caballero* to regain your status. Your beauty will not stop rumors from hurting you. Being seen with me will dispel any fears you have been tainted." Diego voice was syrupy and condescending.

Ana Teresa thought it ridiculous anyone would think she was tainted and wanted to scream at him, but instead said contritely to Diego, "You honor me, *señor.*"

"Spaniards cannot allow *mestizos* to forget their place. It is the stupid *Americanos* who have given the *mestizos* respect. They deserve nothing."

Ana Teresa had heard similar words and ideals spoken most of her life. Her father treated *mestizos* not much better than slaves at their rancho in California. Her childhood nanny was *mestizo* and treated her lovingly. While her mother spent most of her time fussing over dresses, parties, and furnishings in the house, Ana Teresa's nanny tended her when she was sick, brushed her hair for hours, and held her when she was sad. Ana Teresa grew up playing with her nanny's daughter, Rosa, They were more like sisters.

"The stupid *Americanos* allow people who are inferior to think they can be free. Spanish *conquistadores* conquered this land and only Spaniards deserve the bounty it holds," Diego continued blustering about the past.

"*Americanos* believe everyone is free to own land and no one is forced to be a slave. They fought to abolish slavery for *negros*. Does that not apply to *mestizos?*" Ana Teresa said. Well educated she knew about the Civil War and its outcome.

"*Señorita,* there is no difference between *negros* and *mestizos*. They are no better than dogs and cannot be allowed to soil our precious Spanish women, such as yourself. *Americanos* will rue the day they gave freedom to *negros* and *mestizos.* "

Tired of listening to his arrogance, Ana Teresa steered Diego toward the house. When they reached the steps to the veranda, she turned to him. *"Gracias señor* for your visit. Will I see you tomorrow evening at the *paseo?"*

"I would be honored to ride beside you, *señorita."*

"Until tomorrow," Ana Teresa said seething at Diego's egotistical attitude, but maintaining a formal gracious facade.

Walking into the house, she met Bibiana in the hallway after Diego left. Bibiana had watched the two walking in the garden from the upstairs window. "You are lucky to have his attention," she told her cousin. Ana Teresa was not so sure she was lucky.

CHAPTER 47

Tomás Armijo, the mayor of San Marcial, left the saloon and rode out to meet with his foreman on the far side of the river. Tomás inherited the Armijo *hacienda,* one of the bigger ranches in the Rio Grande valley, after his grandfather passed away a number of years ago.

Since the killing of her husband last fall, Tomás watched Sutton's widow assume command of the large Sutton cattle operation. She had a strong will and a natural ability to bring the Texans and locals to an amicable relationship. Nothing about the woman now surprised him.

San Marcial was thriving these days, the local businesses providing the supplies needed for the ranching operation and Cynthia providing fresh beef for the local population. She was enticing some of the small ranchers to combine their herds with hers, work with her, and reap a higher portion of profit. Tomás was absolutely sure her dead husband would never have thought of such an ingenious plan. Sutton hated the locals and made his disdain of Mexicans obvious. He allowed, if not encouraged his Texas cowboys to wreak havoc on the small hamlet, shooting up the town on a regular basis.

Tomás was riding back to town when he heard someone yelling at him.

"Mr. Mayor!" Jed shouted out when he and Luke saw Tomás Armijo riding down the road back to San Marcial. He slowed his horse and looked behind him. They called to him again and he stopped in the road and waited.

"Yes, what can I do for you?" Tomás asked as they pulled up. He did not remember Jed, but he had no doubt in his mind these were the two Texans Ed told him about this morning.

"Mr. Mayor, this here's Luke Payton, his brother was Butcherknife Bill. Yew know, the cowboy shot last fall by that Mexican *pistolero.* Luke wants to know where Bill is buried sos he kin pay his respects." Jed asked for the information respectfully, but Tomás did not like the look of Luke Payton. His eyes were cold and hard and he had the look of a gunslinger, not a cowboy.

"My condolences for the loss of your brother, Mr. Payton. Your brother is buried in the cemetery next to the church. It has a wooden marker put there by the town," Tomás said addressing Luke directly. Luke returned a steely eyed look – a look meaning trouble.

"I understand he was kilt in cold blood by a Mescan?" Luke sneered the comment as a question.

"No, you have been misinformed. Your brother and another cowboy bushwhacked the man on his way out of town. The man killed your brother in self defense," Tomás told him.

"Ain't nuttin fair bout gittin kilt."

Tomás saw Luke's eyes flicker with hate and he could feel it crackle in the air. "Again, I am sorry about your brother, Mr. Payton."

"I was tol yew know that Mescan and where he might be." Luke looked hard at Tomás.

"I know his name, Rafael Ortega, but I only know he lives in Santa Fe," Tomás replied. Luke's hand moved to his side and he fingered the trigger of his gun. He thought the mayor was probably lying, but threatening or killing the unarmed mayor would not help him find the greaser. There would be other ways to get information.

"Much obliged, mayor," Luke replied and without another word he turned his horse and headed down the road to town with Jed on his heels. Jed caught up with Luke and they rode into town. They were almost to Big Ed's Saloon, when Jed spotted Cynthia Sutton getting off her wagon in front of the mercantile. "Lookee here, thar goes the lucky widder," Jed told Luke pointing toward Cynthia Sutton as she walked into the mercantile. Cynthia was wearing denim jeans and shirt, her curly auburn hair was pulled back into a ponytail. Luke stared at the woman's face. She looked very ordinary in the working clothes, but there was no doubt she was a beautiful woman. It took a minute for Luke to recognize her. It was Cinnamon Baker, the high priced whore from the Chrystal Palace in Austin Texas. He was sure.

"That's the widder?" Luke asked with a smirk. Apparently Jed did not know her past, or if he did he said nothing. "Gad damn if it ain't Cinnamon Baker from the Crystal Palace."

Jed knew of the rumor Sutton brought his whore from Austin as his wife, but had never heard her name. "Yew know her?" Jed asked. "I heerd she was a whore frum Austin, everyone knew, but ol' man Sutton woudda kilt us fer talkin bout it."

Riding on, they stopped at the church and found the wooden marker for Bill. Jed thought it was pretty nice for a bushwhacker. He was also surprised when Luke knelt and said a silent prayer.

Cynthia parked her wagon at the mercantile and went in to give Arturo a list of supplies she needed. She came to town on several errands.

"Buenas tardes, Señora Sutton," Arturo the mercantile owner greeted her.

"Good afternoon Arturo, I got your note saying the china I ordered arrived."

"Sí, come let us open the crate to make sure it is not damaged," Arturo said and led her to the back storage area. Arturo pried open the top of a wooden crate and carefully began removing the china out of the straw. They unwrapped and inspected each piece.

"Thank you Arturo. Have it loaded on my wagon along with this list of goods," Cynthia said. She was happy about the china and was looking forward to using it when Ed came for dinner.

"I am going to the dressmaker. I won't be gone long," she told Arturo and left. Arturo climbed up onto Mrs. Sutton's wagon and drove it around to the back of the store where loading the heavy supplies would be easier.

For a good while at the cemetery, Luke stood above his younger brother Bill's grave with hat in hand and said nothing as he thought about his brother. Bill was really dead – buried here in the New Mexico Territory and not in

Texas. Bill would not have liked it and neither did Luke.

He fingered his pistol as he thought about plugging the greaser who did the killing, then spun around and headed to his horse. "Cum on let's git outta here."

"Whar we goin?" Jed asked as they mounted up.

"We're gonna find the widder. I wanna talk to her," Luke growled back.

When they got back to the mercantile the wagon was gone and Cynthia was nowhere to be seen. Luke finally decided she went back to the ranch. "Yew kin go do sum drinkin. I'll meet yew thar later," he told Jed. "I'm gonna go find that widder; she and I is good old friends."

Jed was glad to go to the saloon and be away from Luke. He watched Luke head south on the road to the Sutton ranchhouse, before he headed into Big Ed's. Jed was tired of not knowing what was coming his way next. All he had wanted was a job when he went to Round Rock, now here he was back in this shitheel greaser town again. Jed just wanted to get back to Round Rock, back to cow punching, and back to Bonnie Brunel. He sure did miss her. He had to find a way to get Luke to hunt for the greaser without him, because he sure as hell did not want to go to Santa Fe.

"Howdy Big Ed," Jed called out to the bartender.

"Hey there Jed, where's your friend?" Ed asked. He planned on keeping a close eye on Jed and Luke while they were in San Marcial.

"Went to ask Mrs. Sutton bout that Mescan who kilt Bill and her husband."

Ed tried hard to not react. The thought of Luke Payton going to talk to Cynthia alone scared him.

"What'll you have?" Ed asked Jed.

"Give me a bottle and a beer. Whatcha got fer vittles?"

"Same as always, steak n taters."

"Give me the drinks and git some meat a cookin."

Ed went to the kitchen to grill up the steak. He was cooking a big pot of potatoes on the stove. A knot twisted in his stomach. Luke Payton was going to the Sutton ranch to see Cynthia. He looked up at the clock. It was a little after three. Breathing a bit easier, Ed knew her housekeeper would still be there. At least she would not be alone when Luke came to call.

Picking up two hot plates, one with the thick steak and the other a mound of potatoes, Ed carried them to the front room. Jed sat at a table by himself. The beer glass was empty and the bottle of whiskey was already down a couple inches.

"So, your friend Luke went to pay a call on Mrs. Sutton?" Ed asked as he walked up.

"Yeah, he's on his way to talk to Sutton's widder. Say's he knew her as Cinnamon Baker, some high-priced whore in Austin," Jed answered then downed another long swallow of whiskey.

Feeling hit like a thunderbolt, Ed's hand drooped with the heavy plate and the steak dropped on the floor. He bent and picked it up brushing it with his apron, then flopped it back on the plate. "What did you say?"

"Luke is on his way to see the Sutton widder," Jed answered.

"No, no . . . a . about the whore," Ed stuttered a bit.

"Well, Luke tol me he thought he rekenized the widder as a whore he once knew back in Austin. He's goin to talk to the widder an find out what she knows about the Mex. Me, I don't give a hoot about all that. I jes wanna git back to Round Rock, Texas," Jed talked, not caring one way or another what he said about the widow. The rot-gut whiskey fogged his brain and loosened his tongue.

Stunned, Ed tried to process Jed's words. "Is Luke a gunman?" Ed asked.

"Sur is, rode with the Sam Bass gang in Texas," Jed answered.

Ed undid his apron on the way back to the kitchen. He grabbed his holster and pistol before he rushed out the door to the mercantile across the street. Finding Roberto, Arturo's janitor who helped him out at the saloon from time to time, he asked him to go work the saloon while he took care of some business.

Working as quickly as he could, Ed fumbled trying to saddle his horse. Mounting up he headed south out of town toward the Sutton ranchhouse, still stunned and feeling numb with what Jed just told him. Cynthia Sutton was a whore and it made no sense to him. If he was any judge of character, John B. Sutton would never have married a whore. It did not seem to fit Sutton's moral fiber and Ed had not heard talk from the cowboys at the saloon.

Regardless, if she was a whore or not, the thought of Cynthia alone with Luke scared him. Damn it, he should have ridden out to warn her this morning. Ed urged his old horse to a gallop.

CHAPTER 48

Late on Saturday afternoon Bibiana and Ana Teresa were dressing for the *paseo*. Ana Teresa sat in front of the oval mirror meticulously brushing her hair trying to stall, not really wanting to go. When she told Bibiana to go alone, her cousin bristled.

"You must go. Diego promised to ride beside you," Bibiana reminded her.

Ana Teresa was not sure if she was afraid Diego might be right and people would shun her, or whether she was dreading seeing Diego again. Her thoughts remained conflicted. After brushing her hair, she tried on several gowns – the blue one felt too tight, the red had a small tear in the hem, the green and black one she wore last week.

"Hurry up," Bibiana groused. "Carlos will think I'm not coming and leave."

"I thought you were mad at him?"

"Well, yes I am. He lied to me and I want to make him jealous with the other *caballeros,*" Bibiana huffed. Ana Teresa knew she was lying.

Ana Teresa finally buttoned up the blue gown. She picked up her fan and a lightweight shawl. The girls walked to the waiting carriage and the driver clicked the reins.

Finishing cleaning the stalls in the horse barn, Rafe saddled Rayo late Saturday and mounted the Appaloosa. Kicking him hard, Rayo flew toward the foothills down a familiar path. Rafe knew Carlos was getting ready to go to the *paseo,* leaving him behind. *Don* Pedro de Soto forbade him from speaking to or seeing Ana Teresa. Rafe toyed with the idea of ignoring the *don's* decree. This was America and no one could tell him what he could or could not do. He was not a *peón* anymore, but Carlos begged him to honor *don* Pedro's command, for his sake. If Rafe insulted the *don,* he could refuse to let Carlos marry Bibiana.

"I'm sorry Rafe, please," Carlos begged. "Diego will have the *paseo* watched. If you are seen, *don* Pedro will be told."

"I want to see Ana Teresa," Rafe said. "Ask Bibiana if she can arrange something." Carlos agreed to try, but saw no point in asking as *don* Pedro would not allow it.

When Rafe reached the lower foothills, he slowed Rayo to a canter. The night was warm and Rayo broke into a sweat. Rafe leaned down and patted the horse's neck. "Easy boy."

Entering the *paseo* in their carriage, Bibiana and Ana Teresa began the slow circling carriage ritual. Young available girls rode in the fancy carriages and available *caballeros* vied for their attention. It was an age-old tradition of Spanish aristocracy, one performed in Spanish cities and towns across the world. Normally, Bibiana's carriage was surrounded by young suitors, but tonight none came near. Ana Teresa could see Bibiana tighten her grip on her fan and nervously flutter it.

They were on their third circling, when a young *caballero* headed their way. Bibiana released a deep sigh. When he was almost at their carriage, the young man jerked his horse and veered off.

On the far end of the *paseo,* Diego watched Bibiana's carriage circling alone. It was as he commanded. None of the *paseo* dandies were to engage the two lovely *señoritas.* Diego ordered it, and the young *caballeros* complied.

Reaching the *paseo,* Carlos quickly spotted Bibiana's carriage. No *caballeros* were riding beside them. Riding up he startled Bibiana. *"Buena noches, querida,"* he greeted her affectionately.

"Oh Carlos. Come ride beside us." Bibiana completely forgotten she was mad at him.

"Buena noches Ana Teresa," he said and she only nodded a response. He noticed she looked less than happy. The three of them circled several more times and still no other *caballeros* came near them.

"Carlos, why are we shunned?" Bibiana finally asked.

"This is Diego's work. He has spread rumors about Rafael and knowing Diego, he probably told everyone to shun you and Ana Teresa," Carlos told her.

Seething, Ana Teresa only nodded in agreement with Carlos' accusations. She would not put it past arrogant Diego to orchestrate such a deed.

After Carlos rode beside the carriage for several rounds, Diego rode up beside Ana Teresa's side of the carriage. *"Buena noches, señoritas,"* he greeted them ignoring Carlos.

"You look lovely tonight Ana Teresa," Diego complimented her. He deliberately directed the *paseo* dandies to shun Bibiana and Ana Teresa's carriage to make his point. He controlled the *paseo,* and he controlled Ana Teresa's chances of marriage here in Santa Fe. None of the local *caballeros* would try to court her; he would make sure of that.

"Gracias, Diego," she accepted his compliment graciously, still seething inside. As they circled the plaza, Diego made small talk and Ana Teresa obliged answers. He was acting gallant, though she now knew it was just an act.

When the evening was drawing to a close he said, "Until we meet again *señorita.* Perhaps I will come calling and we can take a ride." His syrupy, aloof tone made her skin crawl, but she knew he was suddenly in control over her future here in Santa Fe. "I will look forward to it, *señor,"* she lied.

Carlos followed their carriage to the edge of the de Soto *hacienda,* before he said goodnight. When he was gone, Bibiana turned to Ana Teresa and groused at her, "You were very rude to Diego."

"Me rude? Diego made us the laughing stock of the *paseo.* Why are you defending him?"

"You should have been gracious with his attention. After all, it is your honor Rafael tarnished."

"My honor has not been tarnished," Ana Teresa responded tartly. "Diego is the one with no honor."

"He is trying to protect you from the *mestizo* and dishonor," her cousin argued. "You must be nice to Diego."

Ana Teresa only huffed at Bibiana. Her cousin was blinded by tradition, thinking the ways of the past were right and just. Ana Teresa did not have to kowtow to Diego's demands, no matter what. Perhaps the *Americanos* who stole her family's land in California also stole the blinders from her eyes. She no longer felt the binds of the Spanish traditions. She was a free American and could marry anyone she wanted, and Diego would not dictate her future.

Continuing with his devious plans, Diego had his friends watch the de Soto *hacienda* from a small knoll not far away. Ana Teresa was not very friendly to him and he was worried the *mestizo* would try to see her. He thought she would be an easy conquest after the *mestizo* tarnished her reputation, gratefully accepting his advances, realizing she needed him. Expecting her to meekly submit to his advances, she did the opposite – she was headstrong and aloof to him. At first he was affronted, now it made the hunt of the conquest even sweeter. When he deflowered her and then left her, she would know her rightful place as a penniless girl.

On Wednesday afternoon, Bibiana went to town with her mother to shop for lace for her wedding dress. *Doña* Agustina was hoping to order Venetian needle lace from Madrid for her daughter's *mantilla*. After they left, Ana Teresa saddled the brown mare and quietly slipped away from the *hacienda,* alone.

Benjamin and Vicente were watching the de Soto *hacienda* from the small knoll and saw her riding north alone. "Go tell Diego," Vicente ordered Benjamin. "I'll keep an eye on her."

Benjamin rode the short distance to the de la Torre *hacienda* and found Diego. "She is riding alone. Bibiana and her mother left earlier in the carriage," he told Diego.

"Did you see the *mestizo?*" Diego asked.

"No."

Ana Teresa thought riding would be a good diversion from the boring days stuck at the *hacienda* while Bibiana was excitedly planning the details for her wedding to Carlos. She was happy for her cousin and Carlos was a good man, but the extensive details did not interest her. The July day was sunny and warm and her lungs enjoyed the smell of the fresh air.

So many thoughts buzzed through her mind. She knew she should be honored Diego was showing her any attention. He was the most eligible bachelor in Santa Fe, well at least the most eligible Spanish aristocrat. He was not very handsome, although it did not bother her as much as his arrogant manner. She wanted someone honest and kind, like Rafael. Someone who would be true to her, and she knew Diego would have several mistresses to appease his every whim.

She rode north, not really paying much mind to where she was going and enjoying her freedom. The horse slowed and Ana Teresa saw she was in the treed grove near the stream. It was the grove she, Bibiana, Carlos, and Rafe had ridden to several weeks ago. Dismounting, Ana Teresa walked along the stream watching the stones shine under the water when the sun struck them.

All of a sudden she heard hoofbeats nearby. A lone horse and rider galloped into the grove. It was Diego de la Torre.

"Buenas tardes, señorita," he said as he jumped down from his horse.

"Buenas tardes, señor," she replied.

"You should not be riding alone," he said. "There may be thieves or *Indios* about."

"I have nothing to steal and I have heard of no *Indio* attacks in Santa Fe." Her response was haughty and cool. "How is it you knew I was riding alone?" Ana Teresa asked and skirted him, as she continued walking along the stream.

Diego did not answer and strode after her. No woman left him standing. Grabbing her arm the sleeve of her dress tore exposing her undergarment. Diego smirked as he whirled her around to face him with the bodice of her dress drooping. "You are forgetting yourself, *señorita.*"

"And you have no manners," she tested him knowing it was an insult. Blood rushed to his face. How dare she act this way with him. He was *gachupín.* She was *Californio,* not much more than the stupid *mestizo.* Perhaps she was not even of pure Spanish blood.

Fire raged inside Diego's gut, but blood rushed to *garrancha*. No one was around – no one to hear the beautiful *señorita's* screams when he speared her.

Ana Teresa saw the fire in his eyes. She knew her words and the tone of her voice was offensive to him, especially from a woman. Suddenly, she wished she was not alone with him. Trying to calm him she said, "I am honored you came to my rescue. Perhaps, you are right and there are *Indios* lurking in the hills."

Diego ignored her comments. Grasping her bare arm tightly with one hand, he used the other to pull her chin up toward his face. Ana Teresa saw rage in his eyes and a vein throbbed in his temple. "You have nothing. No money, no dowry. The only thing you have is the softness between your legs." Diego brought his lips to hers in a hard and angry kiss, grabbing her by the hair and keeping her lips against his.

Squirming, she tried to break his grasp, but it made him clench her arm harder. *"Pendeja,"* he growled. "You are no better than the *mestizo* who soiled you. When I am done with you, I will kill him slowly for the insult."

"He is a better man than you," she spit the words at him.

His hand under her chin moved down to her neck and he wrapped his fingers around her throat squeezing hard. It must have been instinct which made Ana Teresa jerk her knee into his groin. She heard a grunt as he loosened his grip and backed a couple of steps. Running for her horse, Ana Teresa grabbed the reins and jumped up. Kicking the horse in the ribs, she begged God to make the horse go faster. She did not look to see if Diego was coming after her and just kept kicking the horse as hard as she could.

CHAPTER 49

Cynthia Sutton finished unloading the wagon with help from her housekeeper. It was late afternoon and she told the housekeeper to heat up some water for a bath. She hoped Ed would be able to leave the saloon and come for dinner, which was often their way now.

Stretching back in the hot tub of sudsy water, Cynthia relaxed. For the first time in her life, since she left her home in Cincinnati, Ohio, as a teenager, she felt what she thought was love. She loved her father, as every little girl does, and she loved her mother. There was still an empty spot in her heart since her mother's death five months ago. She had felt puppy love for a boy in her eighth grade class, named Kenny. That was before she and her girlfriend left Cincinnati on a river boat bound for New Orleans and Cynthia ended up a whore. She learned to make love with her body, but not her soul. It was all about the money and she was good at her job.

When John B. Sutton, a long time client asked her to marry him, she refused the older man at first, but he promised to care for her and her mother in New Mexico – a new start. It was only after Madam Marta fired her from the Crystal Palace, she reluctantly accepted John B's proposal. After he defended her honor at Lilli Jean's Saloon in El Paso when a cowboy called her a whore, Cynthia tried to make John happy. It was not love with John B, it was respect. Her new life with John was just starting when he was killed in the gunfight with Rafael Ortega.

Cynthia harbored no blame against Rafael as John B was no saint. John had killed one of his cowboys in cold blood, maybe more than one, and ordered his men to steal from the local merchants. He disliked Mexicans and gave them no respect. Apparently, two of John's men bushwhacked Rafael on the road out of town, wanting to steal the young Mexican's horses. He killed Butcherknife Bill and Ponyboy George in the fight and brought their bodies draped over their horses back to San Marcial. Before he died, Butcherknife Bill told Rafael they bushwhacked him to steal the horses for John B.

When Rafael confronted her husband in the saloon, John pulled his pistol on the young Mexican. Rafael shot him through the heart. It had been a hard number of months since then, trying to keep the cattle ranch running smoothly. Ed Seeley was her support, helping her with her dying mother, holding her hand during the funeral, allowing her to stay in the hotel without paying until the ranchhouse was finished, and talking to her over many long dinners at the saloon. He helped her to understand how to work with the cowboys and listened to her complain.

He became her lover in April. Theirs was a sweet and gentle relationship, and now she was sure her feelings for Ed Seeley was true love. It made her giddy like a little girl.

"*Señora,* there ees sumwan at thee door," the housekeeper said in broken English disrupting Cynthia's bath.

"Who is it?" Cynthia asked.

"*No lo sé, un hombre,*" she said she did not know, but it was a man.

"Show him in. Tell him I will be right out," she said and got out of the bathtub and put on a bathrobe. It must not be Ed for the housekeeper knew him. It could not be one of the cowboys, as the housekeeper knew most of them, too. Cynthia walked from the bathroom off the kitchen and hurried to the front room.

"Yes, can I help you?" she asked the man. The tall well dressed man held a black flat-crowned hat in his hand. His ruffled white shirt was open at the neck with a black silk kerchief knotted around his neck. A patterned red vest stopped just above his waist and a long black duster hung to below his knees to where his pants were tucked into his shiny black boots. She recognized the man as a gambler. She had seen many of his kind when she worked at the Crystal Palace in Austin

Luke stared at Cinnamon dressed only in a bathrobe. She was even more beautiful than when she was all painted up at the Crystal Palace. Her auburn hair was pulled up and held by a large silver clasp.

"Ma'am, my name is Luke Payton. My brother Bill was head wrangler for Mr. Sutton. Bill was kilt here in San Marcial and I was wonderin why. Do yew have a few minutes to answer some questions for me?" Luke asked acting as polite as possible.

"Well, I don't know how much I can tell you. I'm sorry about your brother. I didn't know him, but my late husband often told me how valuable his foreman was to him," Cynthia told him.

Cynthia led Luke to the parlor where afternoon sunlight brightened up the room. Luke sat and waited while Cynthia went and ordered the housekeeper to bring out a pitcher of cool lemonade. She thought about changing from her bathrobe, but assumed the man would be gone shortly. She knew little about his brother or the killing, only what she knew from the trial. Sitting opposite Luke while the housekeeper served them the lemonade, Cynthia looked more closely at Luke. He looked vaguely familiar, probably looked like his brother.

"Tell me ma'am, how did he git kilt?" Luke asked. He already knew, but was just biding his time until he would bring up the Crystal Palace. It was obvious Cinnamon did not recognize him, so he decided to play her for a while.

"All I know is your brother and another man called Ponyboy George tried to take some blooded horses from a man and he shot them," Cynthia said. "Your brother believed my husband wanted the horses, and they planned on stealing them for him. Apparently, my husband tried to buy the horses and the owner refused to sell."

"Yew mean the Mescan refused to sell?" Luke asked.

"Yes, the man was a Mexican."

"I heerd that Mescan kilt your husband?" Cynthia did not like the way he referred to the man as that Mescan, with disrespect. It reminded her of the Texas cowboys and of John B.

"Yes, the same man accused my husband of sending the two cowboys to bushwhack him and steal his horses.

My husband was insulted and drew on the man, but the man was faster and my husband died," she continued and looked down at the floor wanting to avoid eye contact with the stranger.

"I'm sorry to hear that ma'am, about yer husband and all. My brother was handy with a gun and I suppose yer husband was too. Hard to believe some Mescan gunned them both. Does he live round here?"

"His name is Rafael Ortega and he lives in Santa Fe." Cynthia was sorry when she said it. She should have lied to this man. It was suddenly becoming obvious he planned on avenging the death of his brother.

"Santa Fe? I guess I'll have ta go on up there and see ta that Mescan," Luke said. "First, seems like we's met somewhere afore."

"I don't know, you don't look familiar to me," she replied taking a closer look at him, but did not recognize him. Then a knot turned in her stomach, thinking he might have been one of her customers at the Crystal Palace.

"Have you been to Round Rock, Texas?" he asked still playing her.

"*Señora,* I go home now. Do you need anything else?" the housekeeper interrupted. She wore her coat and her handbag was in her hand.

"*Bueno,* Consuelo. This gentleman is just leaving. See you tomorrow," Cynthia answered and got up and walked her to the door.

Turning and speaking to Luke she said, "I'm going to ask you to leave now. There is nothing more I can tell you about your brother's death." Watching Consuelo ride away in her buggy, Cynthia became apprehensive finding herself alone with Luke Payton. There was something ominous about his eyes. His voice sounded friendly, but his eyes betrayed his mannerism.

Luke slapped his thigh getting up from the chair. "I member now, it was at the Crystal Palace in Austin. Why yew was the best looking whore there and yew was good, real good," Luke said walking over to Cynthia. He wrapped his arms around her tightly and pulled at her hair to bring her face up to look into her green eyes. "Seein yew's a widder and ain't got no husband anymore, maybee I wouldn't mind gittin some rat now."

"I don't know what you're talking about. I never worked in a saloon," she lied pushing away from him and fighting to maintain control over the situation.

"Don't yew member, Cinnamon? Yew tol me I was the best yew ever had, biggest too," Luke sneered not letting go of her.

Cynthia cringed when he used her whoring name of Cinnamon. It proved he did know her from the Crystal Palace. "Let go of me!" she demanded. "I'm not this Cinnamon person."

"Don't yew lie to me girl. I'll whoop yew til yew member," Luke hissed and pulled on her hair tighter. "So you think you're an all high and mighty rich widder now and too good fer the likes of me?"

"Don't, stop, don't you're hurting me," Cynthia demanded.

"Yew bess be good to me, real good to me. I's thinkin of gettin me a fancy spread like this one. Now, there's an idee. Yew cut me in on this here spread or maybee I'll ruin yew here in New Mexico. Bet the mayor and his friends would be real interested in a whore runnin this here big cattle spread."

"That's blackmail. I don't care what anyone thinks. I'm not Cinnamon and I'm not a whore." Cynthia slapped at the big man and wished she had John's gun handy. It was sitting in the drawer in the dining room.

Luke knew he had the upper hand. Cinnamon was alone, way out here in the middle of nowhere. He slapped her across the face leaving an ugly red welt almost knocking her off her feet.

"Get out!" she screamed at him.

"Not afore I get what I cum fer," he said sternly and picked her up like a sack of potatoes.

"NO! DON'T!" she screamed knowing there was nobody near to hear.

"Go ahead and scream. Ain't nobody gonna hear

yew," he told her as he carried her down the hallway searching for a bed.

"NO! NO! NO!" she kept kicking and screaming.

Luke found a bedroom down the hallway and threw her on the bed. "Let's see if yew's as pretty as yew's afore." He yanked off her bathrobe exposing her nakedness. Scrambling to cover herself with the bedcover, she watched him pull off his duster. A pistol hung low on his right hip. He unbuckled his gun belt, dropped it on the floor, and then unbuttoned his pants. His erection stood straight out of a matting of sandy hair. Cynthia grabbed the bedcover around her body and jumped off on the far side of the bed wanting to distract him and get to his pistol.

Cowering in the corner, Cynthia screamed as loud as she could, hoping somehow, someone would hear her. Luke came around the end of the bed with a leer spread across his evil face. "Cum on Cinnamon. Jes yew be nice to me, like yew used ta," Luke said.

"I'm not Cinnamon anymore. Get out!" Cynthia spit at him. As Luke rounded the end of the bed, trapping Cynthia in the corner, she jumped onto the bed and hopped across to the other side. She saw the gun lying at the foot of the bed and made a dash for it. Luke laughed and kicked it out of her reach as he grabbed her arms.

Caught, Cynthia spit in his face. Yes, she had been a whore, had serviced many men, probably him, but she would now rather die than allow this man to fuck her. Kicking him hard in the shins, she struggled with all her might to break free of him.

Luke laughed at her. "Yew always was a spitfire." Cynthia could feel his erect penis pushing around her hips as they fought. Backing up a step she cocked her knee and drove it as hard as she could between his legs.

Pain shot through Luke's groin. "Yew fucking bitch!" Rearing his right hand back, he slugged her across the jaw with a force sending her sprawling across the bed. Just before Cynthia blacked out from the searing pain, she heard Luke's evil laugh.

Ed Seeley urged his horse to a fast gallop. Old Morg,

the Morgan mixed with a Mustang he took with him when he left the Army, was up in years and not used to the speed anymore. Ed urged the old horse, and luckily old Morg was still willing. Ed knew riding him hard for the ten plus miles to the Sutton ranchhouse would hurt him, but the horse gave Ed all he could.

He passed Consuelo on the road. She was driving the buggy home from the ranchhouse. Ed knew it meant Cynthia was alone with Luke Payton.

It was getting near to sundown when Ed rode up to Cynthia's house. He noticed Luke's horse tethered to the hitching post at the front of the house. Anger flushed Ed's face when he saw the horse and he fought to remain calm. It would not help him, if he flew into the house in anger. Jed said Luke rode with the Sam Bass gang, a notorious outlaw gang in Texas. No doubt Luke knew how to use the gun he wore low on his hip.

Ed pulled his old Army revolver out and checked the loads, all good. Creeping up the front steps, he listened for voices. Then he heard a loud thump and a moan. He did not bother to knock before he opened the door and stepped silently into the house.

All was quiet except for muffled sounds coming from the bedroom at the far end of the hallway. Ed slowly and deliberately made his way to the doorway. Cautiously, he poked his head into the open doorway. Cynthia lay naked on the bed, dead or unconscious. Luke was pulling her by the ankles toward him. In the dim light coming through the window, Ed noticed an angry red welt on Cynthia's jaw.

"Get away from her!" Ed yelled at Luke.

"W . . . what," was all Luke got out, before Ed smashed him on the back of the head with the butt end of the revolver. Luke fell over Cynthia, but quickly rolled off as the glancing blow only dazed him for an instant. Luke struggled to get on his feet. Ed came after him, but Luke braced himself and delivered a mighty blow into Ed's stomach sending Ed's pistol flying across the room. Bending over and gasping for air, Ed felt a blow to the back of his neck throwing him to the floor.

He heard Cynthia moan on the bed. He knew in an instant, if Luke reached a gun first, both he and Cynthia would end up dead. He rolled over and kicked Luke's legs out from under him as Luke reached for the gun.

Jumping up, Ed got to his feet. Luke's hand was on the pistol. All Ed could think about was Cynthia lying naked on the bed, hurt. He saw Luke turn, pistol in hand. Ed stretched his six foot two inch frame to the max and threw himself on top of Luke and the gun, feeling the hard steel of Luke's gun push into his ribs.

Luke growled at Ed. "Fucker." Grappling, the two rolled over on the floor. Luke tried to thumb the hammer of his pistol, but could not pull it while wrestling with the bigger man. Luke rammed an elbow into Ed's ribs, but Ed rolled back over on top of Luke shoving his right hand into Luke's neck squeezing his throat in a death grip.

Luke's free hand held his pistol. Desperately he was trying to thumb the hammer. The big man had him by at least sixty pounds of pure dead weight. If only he could thumb the hammer he'd have him dead to rights, but the big man grabbed his thumb with his left hand.

Ed's fingers squeezed Luke's throat. The pistol waved away from them while Ed kept squeezing. Slowly, Ed felt Luke's arm begin to droop, but in his rage Ed would not let go of Luke's throat, until finally Luke slumped, dead.

Ed slid against the bed sucking in air. Luke's lifeless eyes stared at the ceiling. Ed sat looking at Luke thinking how he had never killed a man with his bare hands. Only once before when he was a corporal at Fort Craig had he grappled with an Indian with a knife. One of his officers shot the Indian dead.

After catching his breath, Ed got up and looked at Cynthia. She was still unconscious, oblivious to the fight he had with Luke. He went to the kitchen and came back with a wet towel, and placed it on her jaw. She stirred a bit, and then flayed her arms at Ed, lashing out.

"It's alright Cindy, it's me, Ed." Wrapping the bedcover around her, he pulled her to him and held her gently. "It's all over. He can't hurt you anymore."

"Oh Ed, Ed . . . " Cynthia cried holding on to Ed's wide chest. He let her cry and just held her. The thoughts about a whore, Cinnamon Baker, and a brothel called the Crystal Palace nagged at him, but he loved her. He did not care about the past. Only the future was important.

He would never ask her if it was true. Luke Payton was dead and Ed would make sure Jed would be leaving for Texas. She was Cynthia Sutton, soon to be Cindy Seeley, if she would have him.

CHAPTER 50

"What's wrong with you?" Bibiana complained to Ana Teresa on Wednesday evening. She and her mother spent most of the day in town shopping for laces. "All you have been doing is brooding today." Ana Teresa had not shared the violent encounter with Diego earlier in the day with her cousin.

"Nothing is wrong," Ana Teresa responded. Bibiana began to talk excitedly about the upcoming Saturday ritual on the *paseo* sorting through her dresses and picking the one she would wear.

"You should wear your green dress," Bibiana turned and told Ana Teresa. "I think Diego likes that one. You want to look pretty for him." The thought of seeing Diego seared through her and Ana Teresa burst into tears.

"What's wrong?" Bibiana implored her cousin seeing her in tears.

"Diego, Diego attempted to violate me," she blurted out.

"Violate?"

Ana Teresa told Bibiana of the encounter with Diego in the grove of trees. She explained how Diego grabbed her and showed her the dress he tore when she fought him off and fled. "He is not a man of honor. He only wants his way with me."

"I heard he was a *picaro,* but I did not think he would try to violate you," Bibiana replied.

Ana Teresa fell into her cousin's arms and wept. All afternoon she thought about Rafael. She did not care if he was a *mestizo,* he was kind and she knew he had a good heart. Her run in with Diego, only confirmed what was truly valuable in life. Rafael knew what it meant to be penniless and yet he was now a horse breeder, a man with an honest future, not like the *caballeros* who thought money and station was their right.

"Can you get a message to Carlos? I want to see

Rafael," Ana Teresa asked her cousin after her tears subsided.

"Rafael? But, father has forbidden you to see him."

"Yes, and it is your father who thinks Diego is a saint."

"Carlos told me to tell you Rafael wanted to see you. He mentioned it last Saturday as we rode the *paseo,* but I didn't tell you." Bibiana waited for an angry response.

"I understand, but now can you send a message to Carlos?"

Bibiana agreed and the two girls talked about what to say in the letter. Bibiana warned her cousin – she must not be seen with Rafael. We have to meet him someplace hidden. She remembered an old abandoned *hacienda* near the river which was hidden by a large stand of trees. The girls decided to set the meeting for Saturday morning, as it was a time when they usually went to feed the poor with the nuns at the mission of San Miguel. "The nuns will not miss us and my parents will not be suspicious," Bibiana said.

Carlos received the letter from Bibiana on Thursday morning and went to find Rafe.

"Here, read this," he said handing the letter over to him.

"Ana Teresa wants to see me?" Rafe was happy, but surprised.

"Yes, on Saturday morning." Carlos knew Saturday morning was their fencing lesson so he preempted Rafe's thoughts, "I will tell Maestro Luis you have been detained at the foundry." Rafe smiled at his best friend who knew him so well.

Ana Teresa was perkier on Thursday. She and Bibiana took a long walk in the gardens, enjoying the spectacular summer weather. Deep purple, white, and pink cones of the foxglove hung heavy on stalks shooting upward toward the sun. Dahlias burst in multiple colors. The smell of lavender filled the garden. The girls talked and giggled about the secret meeting on Saturday morning.

Later, Ana Teresa sat down and wrote a letter to her

father and mother in Madrid, Spain. She had not heard from them in several months. She told her parents she was well, safe, and happy. She told them of life here in New Mexico, of the flowers, the mountains, helping Bibiana feed the poor children, but not about Rafael. She knew her father, like her uncle, would not agree to let her marry below her class.

When she finished the letter, she pondered what she would say to Rafael on Saturday. She would ask him if it was true he was a *mestizo*. She wanted to know more about his past. When she thought of him, she smiled. Tall and broad shouldered, his skin was golden bronze. His eyes were several shades of soft brown. When he talked to her, his eyes looked at her and into her soul. He had a quiet way, not loud and braggadocious like Diego.

Bibiana said Rafael saved Carlos' life and they were obviously close, like brothers. *Don* Pedro said he bred some of the finest horses he ever saw here in Santa Fe. He was obviously well educated, speaking both Spanish and English. How could he do these things if he was a lowly *peón?*

Later that day, Ana Teresa and Bibiana were sewing when horse hooves clattered in the courtyard. The servant came into the room and announced Diego. Ana Teresa's stomach turned into a sour lump.

"Buenas tardes, señoritas," he purred in his arrogant manner striding into the room.

Bibiana rose to leave and Ana Teresa almost growled, "Look Bibiana, Diego has come to call on us . . . " Shooting a look to her cousin, Ana Teresa used her eyes to beg Bibiana to stay.

"Yes Diego, it is an honor," Bibiana replied sitting back down next to her cousin.

Ana Teresa sent the servant to bring refreshments, wishing Diego would leave, but knowing she must pretend to be gracious. Diego was angry with Ana Teresa and had hoped to get her alone to berate her for her insolence in the grove. He nervously strutted back and forth in front of the stone fireplace, trying to make small talk. Ana Teresa never stood up and continued her sewing, which infuriated him even more. No woman would best him, especially one bankrupt and desperate.

As Diego paced the room trying to make small talk to the women, he swore he would make the California *señorita* pay for her disrespect to him. He would take her and soil her to his pleasure like a *puta*, and then leave her, spreading the truth and soiling her reputation. Everyone would believe him after her flirtatious ways with the *mestizo*.

CHAPTER 51

Saturday morning dawned clear and warm. Bibiana and Ana Teresa were up and dressed early, which was their normal schedule to go to the mission to help the sisters feed the poor children. By ten o'clock, Bibiana asked to have the buggy readied. She kissed her mother and father before they headed to the courtyard. "We'll be back later," she said brightly.

Alvaro, Benjamin, and Vicente were sitting on the hill watching the road leading to the de Soto *hacienda*. They saw the girls leaving in the buggy and followed them at a distance keeping out of view.

Bibiana drove the buggy to the outskirts of town and then turned heading west along the Santa Fe River toward the abandoned Archuleta *hacienda*. Ana Teresa's stomach turned in knots with excitement. Bibiana pulled up to the abandoned main house and Ana Teresa jumped down from the buggy.

Rafe nervously waited with Rayo tethered to a nearby tree at the abandoned *hacienda* as indicated in Bibiana's letter. Hearing a buggy approaching, he stayed out of view until he was sure it was the girls. Recognizing Ana Teresa's hair glinting in the sunlight, Rafe stepped out from behind the trees and walked the short distance to where she stood. Bibiana drove the buggy a short distance away from the house to give them privacy.

Ana Teresa stood in the middle of the abandoned courtyard, proud and unafraid. Though dressed in a simple checkered summer dress, Rafe's heart thumped a beat faster at the vision of her standing in the sunlight. She saw Rafael walk toward her. His stride was confident, though not aloof. A broad smile washed across his tan face, showing his straight white teeth.

"Good morning, Ana Teresa," he greeted her. Rafe could see her hands were trembling.

"Why are you trembling?" he asked her. "Are you

afraid of me?"

"No, I am not afraid of you. I am afraid of Uncle Pedro and of Diego, if they find out I am here," she told him.

Rafe took her hand in his. It trembled, but was warm. "I will protect you always," he said and she fell into his arms. Feeling his strong arms wrapped around her, Ana Teresa felt safe for the first time since she left California. She did not have to hear Rafael tell her he loved her. She knew it without the words. She no longer cared if he was *mestizo*. He was a man and a man who would protect her and love her.

From a short distance away Alvaro and his companions saw Ana Teresa standing and talking to the *mestizo*. "Let's go get Diego," Benjamin said. When Alvaro looked back, Ana Teresa was in the *mestizo's* arms.

"No, we must do this now. We can beat the *mestizo*, three against one," Alvaro told his friends. "Diego will reward us if we do this. Come let's get him." Not waiting for an answer, Alvaro spurred his horse toward the abandoned *hacienda* and the other two young *caballeros* followed.

Rafe heard the horses and the *caballeros* yell, *"Aaayyee."* He pushed Ana Teresa aside. "Go to Bibiana and get out of here," he yelled to her.

They came riding into the courtyard on a gallop. Alvaro's horse brushed Rafe and he swung his riding quirt at Rafe's head. The blow hit Rafe square on the temple and momentarily stunned him as it was a heavy Spanish quirt used to slap cattle to get them moving. Rafe staggered a bit to his right, but managed to keep his balance. Rafe almost sidestepped Benjamin's horse, but the horse's flank knocked his shoulder hard as it went by. The sting on his head and pain in his shoulder enraged him. He looked up and saw only hate in the eyes of his tormentors. It brought back images of *peóns* being teased and tormented by *vaqueros* at the *hacienda* where he grew up.

Two of the *caballeros* were the ones who had attacked him on the plaza. No doubt they all were friends of Diego.

Rafe whirled around in time to see Alvaro coming for another pass with his quirt raised high. He knew he was defenseless. His GSW pistols hung on his bedpost at home. He deliberately did not wear them, thinking it would scare Ana Teresa. His rapier and shotgun were stowed on Rayo's saddle.

Suddenly the Spanish Circle of Death flashed in his mind. He tried to draw the circles around him. He feinted right as Alvaro approached, ducking from the quirt as it swung in the air. He did not hear Vicente's horse behind him until it was too late and the horse's flank knocked Rafe down to the dusty ground.

Rafe jumped up and staggered a bit. A sixteen hundred pound horse was a mighty weapon against an unarmed man on foot. Rafe looked for Rayo, his only route of escape. The Appaloosa was tethered to a tree in the grove, what seemed like a million miles away. Whirling in circles, Rafe tried to calm his mind. He tried to concentrate and remember the circles.

Alvaro, Benjamin, and Vicente rode around Rafe trapping him. They swung at him with their quirts. Vicente pulled his rapier and slashed in the air.

"Hijo de puta," Alvaro screamed calling Rafe a son of a whore. "You cannot touch our women, you mestizo dog."

The caballeros dismounted and circled their prey. They stood around Rafe laughing. Alvaro spit and yelled a Spanish curse at him, "Me cago en el hijo de puta."

They surrounded him and he had little room to move about. Benjamin attacked first, raising his rapier and thrusting toward Rafe nicking him on his right arm as it swung down. Blood seeped from the slash in Rafe's shirt. Benjamin laughed and the others cheered him. Vicente, a bit more cautious, tried to whip Rafe across the face with his quirt. Rafe feinted to his left and the quirt only found air.

Bibiana and Ana Teresa watched from the trees in horror as the caballeros surrounded Rafe. Ana Teresa was sure it was Diego's friends. She and Bibiana were standing near the buggy in the trees, near where Rayo stood patiently tethered. On Rayo's back, Rafe's rapier and shotgun were secured to his saddle.

Rafe knew it was only a matter of time before the three bested him. Without any weapons, Death was stalking him and this time Rafe thought the *desgraciados* would kill him. He ducked under the tip of Vicente's sword. Not too far away he saw Ana Teresa standing in the trees. He wished he had told her he loved before Death took him.

Rafe moved erratically, making moves to confuse the three men. Benjamin slashed at him again and missed, but Alvaro slashed him across his shoulder. The three laughed and jeered. Benjamin moved again and slashed Rafe's thigh, almost buckling his legs from the pain. Blood squirted from the gash and soaked his pants leg. Alvaro swung high and crashed the butt end of his sword into Rafe's skull, knocking him to the ground.

Seeing Rafe on the ground and defenseless, Ana Teresa grabbed Rafe's rapier from Rayo's saddle and strode toward the men. *"¡Basta!"* she yelled at them to stop it.

Alvaro looked at Ana Teresa approaching with the rapier drawn. "This does not concern you *señorita,"* Alvaro told her. "This is man's business. We must teach this *peón* a lesson. We cannot allow this *mestizo* to touch our women."

"No, you will leave now," Ana Teresa got between them and Rafe bleeding on the ground.

"Step aside *señorita,* we do not want to hurt you," Alvaro warned her. He was surprised when the beautiful *señorita* took the rapier and expertly thrust it toward him, making him jump back. Ana Teresa had taken fencing lessons in California most of her life. She whipped the slender blade close to the men, but did not strike.

Rafe struggled to get up, then kept his head down as Ana Teresa swung his rapier at the *caballeros.* He noticed the three seemed unsure about what to do with the sword-wielding *señorita.*

Encouraged by Ana Teresa's daring, Bibiana ran to Rafe's horse and pulled the heavy shotgun from the saddle. She came into view of the others carrying Rafe's shotgun out in front of her. "You heard what she said, stop it, and leave now." Rafe doubted Bibiana knew how to fire a shotgun, and hoped she would not kill them all, if she did. Alvaro looked at Bibiana and backed away. "Now get on your horses and leave or I will kill you," Bibiana warned them. They saw fire in her eyes and assumed the shotgun was loaded.

"*Vámonos!*" Alvaro called out and the three mounted up and rode off. "You will pay for this *señoritas,* you and that *mestizo* dog."

Bibiana and Ana Teresa helped Rafe to the buggy and tethered Rayo to the back. The cuts on his shoulder and arm were not too bad, but the leg was seeping a lot of blood. "We cannot take him home with us," Ana Teresa said.

"Take me to my home," Rafe moaned.

"No, it is too far. We'll take him to Genoveva, the *curandera.* She will know how to treat the wounds," Bibiana said with butterflies still fluttering in her stomach, thinking of carrying the heavy shotgun toward the *caballeros* and threatening them.

Ana Teresa and Bibiana helped Rafe onto the buggy and sat him between them. Snapping the reins, Bibiana started the horse to a fast pace away from the abandoned *hacienda.* The *curandera's* house was only a few miles away.

"Where did you learn the sword," Rafe asked Ana Teresa.

"My father taught me. I never used it in battle before, only lessons." Ana Teresa felt exhilarated. She had not only defended Rafe's life, she defended her honor. She would not be scared of Diego or the *caballeros* ever again.

"You were magnificent," Rafe told her.

"Shhhh, rest," she replied and smiled at him.

Riding away from the Archuleta *hacienda,* Alvaro, Benjamin, and Vicente groused at each other.

"You let a girl best you," Benjamin goaded Alvaro.

"I did not let her best me. I could not hurt the girl," Alvaro retorted.

"That girl had the tip of her sword at your neck," Benjamin kept needling him.

"*Cállate,*" Alvaro growled back telling Benjamin to shutup. "You never drew your sword, just like the last time when you left me alone with the *mestizo* on the plaza. You are a *culón.*"

"*Pendejo,*" Benjamin groused back, but he knew his comrade was right. He was not brave, nor was he very good with a sword.

"Quit arguing," Vicente yelled at them to stop. "What are we going to tell Diego. If he finds out we ran from two girls and left the *mestizo* standing, he will kill us."

"We will not tell him. Only the girls and the *mestizo* know what happened. They will not talk, and if they do no one will believe them," Alvaro said. Benjamin nodded his head in agreement.

Leaving Ana Teresa and Rafael at the *curandera's,* Bibiana drove the buggy to the Summers' ranch to find Carlos. Pulling in the courtyard, a servant came to greet her.

"*¿Dónde está Carlos?*" she asked where to find Carlos. The servant told her he was in the horse barn.

Whipping the buggy horse, Bibiana drove into the barn.

"Carlos, Carlos! You must come with me, Rafael is hurt," she said excitedly half sobbing.

"*Cálmate, querida,*" Carlos asked her to calm down. "What do you mean, hurt?"

"Alvaro and his amigos attacked him and cut him." Suddenly the events of the day overwhelmed her and she was having trouble getting the information out about Rafe.

"What happened?" he asked as he pulled off his work gloves and helped her down. Bibiana excitedly told Carlos how the *caballeros* must have followed her in the buggy to the abandoned *hacienda.* They rode in and attacked Rafael. He was unarmed and they surrounded him. "Ana Teresa grabbed Rafael's sword and defended him and then I grabbed his shotgun and told them to leave."

"You threatened the *caballeros* with Rafael's shotgun?"

"Yes," Bibiana said proudly. "I scared them and they left." Carlos marveled at his soon-to-be wife. She had never seemed so brave, and he was very proud of her.

"Where is he?"

"We took him to Genoveva, the *curandera*. Ana Teresa is with him," she told him as he held her. "His leg was bleeding badly."

"Go back and wait for me there. I'll get there as quickly as I can." Carlos helped her back up to the buggy seat. "Bring clothes for him," she said before she rode off.

Carlos rushed to the house for his gun and clothes for Rafe. Luckily he did not see George, Josefina, or the girls. Quickly saddling Santiago, he rode the stallion hard to the *curandera's* house.

No doubt this was Diego's work. Diego must have watched the road to make sure Rafe did not go to the de Soto *hacienda*. Carlos cursed at himself for not realizing how devious Diego would be and for letting Rafe go alone today.

Carlos arrived at the *curandera's* house rushing in without knocking. Rafe was lying on the kitchen table with his head resting on a pillow. The *curandera* was wrapping his leg. Rafe was alert, smiling, and holding Ana Teresa's hand.

Relieved at seeing Rafe in good spirits Carlos quipped, *"Eh, pendejo.* What did you get yourself into?" Carlos called him a dummy and saw Rafe grin.

"The *señoritas* came to my rescue. Those *culóns* ran off when Bibiana pointed my shotgun at them," Rafe told Carlos.

"What about me?" Ana Teresa complained. "I bested them with your rapier."

"You saved my life," Rafe told her squeezing her hand.

More seriously, Rafe told Carlos of how the three must have followed the girls and swooped down on him in the courtyard. "I was unarmed. If the girls were not so brave, I would be dead."

Rafe remembered what the Aztec Healer had told him, "Death will stalk you and take you when you least expect it," Well, today Death stalked him and left an indelible stench, but Death was thwarted by the girl's bravery.

"It was my fault. I wanted to see Rafael and I did not understand the lengths to which Diego would go to hurt me," Ana Teresa spoke up.

"Hurt you?" Rafe asked. "Why would he want to hurt you? He hates me. I am *mestizo* and he has sworn to be rid of me to protect women like you." It was the first time Ana Teresa heard Rafael use the term *mestizo*. Yes, he was a *mestizo* and she a penniless *señorita* from California.

"Diego has no honor toward me. He tried to violate me last Wednesday at the grove by the stream. Diego just wants to disgrace me and then he will humiliate me to his friends." Rafe was amazed at how matter-of-factly Ana Teresa told of Diego's plans. She was not ashamed.

"*Desgraciado,*" Rafe growled and tried to get up, but the *curandera* and the girls pushed him back down. "As soon as I can get back on my horse, I'll just go and tell *don* Pedro what Diego has done and what my intentions are for Ana Teresa. I want to marry her," Rafe said, then turning his head to look at Ana Teresa directly he asked, "Will you marry me?" She stared into his eyes and nodded her head up and down, trying to stop tears from running down her face.

"No Rafael. My father will never allow it," Bibiana told him. "He will tell Diego to kill you next time."

"Yes, it is madness," Ana Teresa agreed, but her heart was breaking. "Please don't do it, my love. I don't want you to get hurt or killed because of me," Ana Teresa pleaded with Rafe.

"I cannot let this stand. This is New Mexico and we have the right to marry if we want to. If I don't confront Diego, you know he will never let us live in peace. We'll see what kind of man he really is. So far, he has sent his *compañeros* to do his fighting for him. I'll meet him on his terms and I will best him." Rafe said.

Chapter 52

When Rafe and Carlos arrived home, the wounds on Rafe from the fight at the abandoned *hacienda* could not be concealed from his father and adopted family. Everyone was worried about him and George Summers was angry with him for not telling him about the other encounters with Diego de la Torre and his amigos.

"What were you thinking? How could you think you could pass as a *caballero,* and you Carlos why did you let him do it?" George admonished them in his office at the foundry a couple days later.

"Yes, it was stupid of me to talk him into this charade," Carlos admitted.

"Not your fault Carlos. I did this on my own. It would have been nothing, had I not fallen in love with Ana Teresa," Rafe admitted.

"Carlos, you should have known better. You know how the Spanish feel about purity of blood," George continued reprimanding them.

"*Don* Jorge, purity of blood should not matter here in New Mexico. Here we are free to marry who we love," Rafe grumbled. "Why did you bring me here, if I will forever be a *peón?*"

George's heart ached for his adopted son, who was caught in between the two worlds – Spanish traditions and American freedoms.

"Son, traditions won't die easy for the Spanish. They are a proud people and the Spanish *casta* system has been followed for centuries. You lived it in Mexico where even though Mexico is free from Spain, the aristocrats carry on their Spanish traditions. It is the same here in New Mexico, though here we have freedom as Americans. It will not change quickly," George said as a matter of fact.

"But, I love Ana Teresa and she loves me. We want to marry."

Rafe's problem hit only too close to George's heart.

Once he was young and in love and once he had the same problem. "I had the same problem with Josefina's family in Toledo, Spain," he admitted something he never told Rafe before. "We fell in love, but I was an *Americano*. Her father did not give us permission to marry, but Josefina came here to New Mexico with me. Her family disowned her and it took them many years to forgive her," George continued.

Stunned by this revelation, Rafe smiled. Here was a solution to his problem. Ana Teresa's parents were in Spain. If they married here before her parents returned, there was nothing they could do to reverse a consummated marriage under the eyes of the church.

"Gracias, don Jorge. I have things to do." Rafe hugged his father and bounded out of the office. George tried to stop him, but knew it would be useless to dissuade him from following his heart.

Rafe was elated by George's admission about Josefina's family. He would have his say with *don* Pedro and ask for his permission, though he doubted he would get it. Then he would go face Diego de la Torre, if need be. First, he needed to wait for his wounds to heal and spend time with the builders who were well on their way to finishing his ranchhouse. He wanted the home to be finished and quickly. With his home and horses, he could marry Ana Teresa, as well as have a place for his mother and María's children.

Several weeks went by as Rafe healed. Carlos saw Bibiana at Mass on Sundays and started an official courtship. Rafe asked Carlos if he saw Ana Teresa and Carlos reported she was only at Mass with the family. "She is not riding the *paseo,"* he told Rafe. "Bibiana says she is very unhappy."

"Do you think *don* Pedro knows about the fight with the *caballeros* at the abandoned *hacienda?"*

"No. Bibiana said nothing has been mentioned at home. If he knew, I'm sure *don* Pedro would have said something. He would not let Ana Teresa's disobedience go unpunished." Both Carlos and Rafe were surprised Diego had not gone to *don* Pedro with the news, if he knew of the fight.

Rafe spent several weeks with the builders and nursing his wounds before he felt strong enough to pay a visit to the de Soto *hacienda*. It was Saturday morning and Carlos was going to Maestro Luis's fencing class. Rafe lied to Carlos, telling him he did not feel strong enough, yet, and not telling Carlos of his plans.

He dressed in his finest American style suit and tie, along with his black Stetson hat. This time when he went to meet *don* Pedro, he would be a New Mexican man. He strapped on his gunbelt and slid a GSW pistol into the right side and on the left side he hung the rapier *doña* Josefina gave him. Late in the morning he mounted Rayo and took his time riding to the de Soto *hacienda,* mulling over in his mind what he would say to *don* Pedro.

He wanted to confront the old man and take Ana Teresa with him now, but knew it was an unlikely scenario. Most of all, he wanted just to see her and know she saw him. He wanted her to know his feelings had not changed.

He arrived at the main house and a servant came out to greet him. Rafe dismounted and held on to Rayo's reins. *"Yo soy Rafael Ortega de Estrada y quiero hablar con don Pedro,"* he told the servant his name and said he wanted to speak with the *don.*

"Sí señor," the servant said and ran toward the front door.

Suddenly from the veranda, Rafe heard the *don's* voice. *"¿Qué es lo que quieres, sabes que no está permitido aquí, en mi casa?"* the *don* growled. The *don* made it clear Rafe was not welcome here at the *hacienda* and to leave immediately. *Don* Pedro stood with his hands on his hips and a scowl on his face. Across the courtyard, a well-heeled *vaquero* was walking toward Rafe with his right hand resting on the butt end of a pistol.

"Señor, first, I give you my heartfelt apology for having deceived you in any way. I am a New Mexican horse breeder and not a *caballero* from Mexico. I meant no disrespect to you and your family and I see now I insulted you. For that I am truly sorry. Second, I want your

permission to marry Ana Teresa. I have no disguises with me. What you see is who I am. This may not sound true to you after what I have done, but I am a man of honor and will give her a good life," Rafe said proudly and unafraid.

From the window on the second floor, Ana Teresa and Bibiana peered out the shuttered window. Ana Teresa opened the shutters to see Rafe more clearly. She could hear Rafe's words and *don* Pedro shout back at him. He still wanted her to marry him. He came to confront her uncle for her hand. Her heart sang with joy and she wanted to go out on the balcony and show herself to Rafael, but Bibiana held her back.

"You are a lying *peón*. Get off my *hacienda* now or I will have Ignacio shoot you like the dog you are," the old *don* yelled at Rafe pointing a long finger at him.

From the corner of Rafe's eye, he saw Ignacio reach to the gun butt on his hip. "I would not pull that gun if I were you, *señor*. I am an excellent shot and my double-action revolver will be fired before you thumb the hammer on that *pistola* of yours." Rafe shot a quick look directly at the *vaquero*. The hesitation on the *vaquero's* face told Rafe he would not be shooting.

Turning back to *don* Pedro he said, "I will not leave until I talk with Ana Teresa. It is her decision to make, not yours."

Stunned at the young *peon's* impudence, *don* Pedro quickly tried to think of a response. His stupid *vaquero* was afraid of the *peon's* pistol and he was standing here unarmed. Being responsible for his brother's child grated on him. He had not heard from her parents in over six months. She did not have a dowry and he was certainly not going to pay for her marriage, if her parents did not return. If it was not for his own social standings, *don* Pedro would throw his penniless niece to the *mestizo* and be done with it.

Instead he lied. "You are wasting your time *peón*. Ana Teresa has been promised to Diego de la Torre," *don* Pedro said and he gloated when he saw Rafe's face darken. Rage churned in Rafe's chest as he tried to remain calm.

"Again, I ask you politely, may I speak with Ana

Teresa? I await her decision, *señor*, not yours," Rafe asked controlling his anger.

In the upstairs bedroom, Ana Teresa turned and headed down the long hallway. She wanted to show herself to Rafael and tell her uncle she wanted to marry him. Bibiana trailed after her. "My father will turn you out," Bibiana implored her cousin.

"No!" *don* Pedro screamed. "You will have to kill me to get into this house. You will never have Ana Teresa. She will marry Diego," the old man said puffing out his chest defiantly. Rafe thought about Death. Death was teasing him again, this time to kill an old man, because of love. Death pushed him to do it, but Rafe wanted no innocent blood on his hands. Instead, Rafe mounted Rayo.

"I am sorry for you *señor*. Ana Teresa is innocent and deserves better than Diego. If Ana Teresa will have me, we will be married." Rafe turned and kicked Rayo into a gallop riding from the *hacienda*. As Rafe rode away, Ana Teresa reached the veranda where her uncle stood. It was a lie, she was not betrothed to Diego de la Torre, and she would rather die before marrying him. She loved Rafael. Sinking to her knees, she looked up at her uncle and screamed at him. "Why?"

The metallic taste of adrenaline filled Rafe's mouth — the taste of Death was with him. He did not want to kill the old man or the *vaquero,* but would have if the *vaquero* pulled his gun. Again Rafe faced Death head on, and he knew this time it would not have been his, rather an innocent man doing the bidding of a crazy old man.

Rafe swore to himself to find a way to see Ana Teresa. He could not believe she wanted to marry Diego de la Torre. Rafe knew she loved him and he would not allow her uncle to marry her against her will to the *desgraciado*. He was sick of the stupid Spanish caste system, which perceived *mestizos* to be inferior. It was not true. There was nothing special about Spanish blood. It flowed red from a bullet hole just like his.

Rafe rode toward the *barrio de Analco* heading to the Palacio Cantina, hoping Diego and his amigos would be there. Diego would not marry Ana Teresa without a fight from him. This time he would surprise them and be in control. He had his weapons and he knew Diego would be no match for him. Knowing Diego would be there with several of his companions, Rafe wished Carlos was by his side, but did not want any harm to come to his friend. This was not his fight.

Rafe rode into the *barrio*. He circled a few streets until he found the Palacio. Tethering Rayo to the front post, Rafe checked his pistol. He did not want to kill anyone. He only wanted to put a stop to the madness, but if Diego forced his hand, he would send him and his friends to their *jefe* in hell and Death would be satisfied.

Casually he pushed open the front door and strode into the cantina. Once inside he was surrounded by an opulent setting. Large paintings of Spanish *conquistadores* hung on the walls, as well as bronzes statues of the heads with Spanish *conquistador* helmets. Rafe recognized most of the images. Thick European rugs lay on the floors and heavy embroidered tapestries hung by the windows. There were several card games going on and many older *caballeros* sat around tables drinking and talking. Through the thick smoke of cigars, a lovely woman walked toward him.

Virginia Verdugo looked at the *Americano* with a pistol on one hip and a rapier on the other who just walked into her cantina. His lean tan face was handsome and strong.

"What do you want here," a beautiful woman dressed in a traditional Spanish red satin dress trimmed with black silk edges asked him in broken English. On her head was a tall *peineta* comb with a black *mantilla* made of lace draping past her shoulders. As she walked closer, Rafe saw her beauty was not a young beauty, but the beauty of an older woman.

"I'm sorry to disturb you ma'am. I'm looking for Diego de la Torre," Rafe said. He thought about speaking Spanish and then decided against it.

"You are not permitted here. You must go now," she said pointing to the door.

"I will not leave until you tell me if you know where Diego is," Rafe said stubbornly.

"Diego is not here, you must go," she said. Several older *caballeros* watched the *Americano* come into the cantina. Several rose and moved in behind Virginia with hands on their swords. Rafe tipped his Stetson, turned, and strode out the door. He was satisfied Diego was not there, and scoffed at the sight of the old *caballeros* wanting to get up and throw him out.

By the time he reached the main plaza in downtown Santa Fe, he willed himself to be calmer and tried to clear his mind. *Don* Jorge taught him never to fight angry. "In anger you will make mistakes," he had told him. *Don* Luis taught the same philosophy in fencing.

It was late Saturday afternoon on the *paseo*. A few carriages carrying *señoritas* were circling the plaza and several young *caballeros* strutted their horses alongside wanting to attract their attention. Especially today, the Spanish ritual reserved only for the Spanish aristocracy grated at Rafe. A part of him wanted to disrupt the ritual, riding wildly and cursing to drive away the young *caballeros,* but instead he looked for Diego.

Shortly after Rafe left, Diego and his *compañeros* stopped at the Palacio Cantina for a few drinks before joining the ritual on the *paseo*. Virginia rushed over to him.

"Diego, Diego, there was an *Americano* here looking for you," she said excitedly.

"What do you mean an *Americano?*" he asked, confused about what she meant. *Americanos* were not welcomed at the Palacio.

Virginia described Rafe and before she finished, Diego knew it was the *mestizo.*

"He is a *mestizo*, a *desgraciado mestizo,*" he told her. "Where did he go?" he asked Virginia.

"I don't know. I told him to get out."

"The *paseo,* he will look for you at the *paseo,*" Alvaro spoke out.

"Let's go take care of that *peón,*" Diego said waving an arm at his friends. He pushed Virginia aside as they rushed out of the cantina.

Approaching the *paseo* cautiously, Rafe cleared his mind. While part of him just wanted to kill Diego and be done with it, he knew nothing good would come of a *mestizo* killing a *gachupín,* even here in Santa Fe. If he bested Diego, then *don* Pedro might reconsider Diego as a suitor for Ana Teresa, or perhaps Diego would drop his contract for marriage.

Diego and his amigos were nowhere to be seen, so Rafe strutted Rayo around the plaza several times daring anyone to run him off. Dressed in his American clothes, people on the plaza stared curiously at a stranger, though no one challenged him. On Rafe's fourth time around, Diego and Alvaro rode into the *paseo* coming from the opposite direction. Rafe spotted him instantly.

"There he is," Alvaro yelled spotting Rafe on the tall Appaloosa.

Diego growled as he drew his rapier and spurred his black stallion toward Rafe. Rage filled him with bravado against the *mestizo.* Rafe saw him coming, moved away from the carriages, and drew his sword. Diego's black stallion brushed Rayo's shoulder while Diego slashed at Rafe. Rafe parried the strike easily flicking Diego's sword away and turned Rayo to defend the next attack.

"Hijo de puta, you were warned not to show yourself on the *paseo,"* Diego screamed after him, turning the black horse to attack Rafe again. Rafe envisioned the Spanish Circle of Death, trying to feel the circles protecting him. Again the black came at Rayo and bumped the Appaloosa on the shoulder while Diego slashed wildly at Rafe. Surprisingly, Rafe thought Diego looked unwieldy slashing his rapier from the horse. Diego seemed surprised Rafe could defend himself with the sword.

Rafe felt Rayo's powerful flanks under his thighs. The Appaloosa was used to responding to even the slightest nudge from Rafe's legs or foot. They rode as one against the black stallion, allowing Rafe to use his nerve and a hand on his sword freely.

As Diego came near again, Rafe yelled at him,

"What's the matter Diego? Can't you beat a lowly *mestizo?*" Diego heard the *mestizo's* words and rage filled him even more. Rafe could see the rage building in his opponent, and though he knew Diego was fighting in anger, Rafe was sure Diego still had an advantage. No doubt Diego was trained in the sword since he was young.

"Aaayyeeee," Diego screamed as he came on Rafe's left side, farthest from Rafe's sword. As the black horse passed near, Rayo turned his head and bit the black on the rump as it went by. The black let out a howling whinny.

Diego rode past then turned the black around to attack at Rafe directly. As the black horse and rider approached, Rayo lifted on his hind legs and thrashed his front hooves at the black. Suddenly, both horses were standing up on their hind legs, hoofs pawing and punching each other.

Drivers of the carriages carrying screaming young girls whipped their horses to safety away from the battling stallions. A crowd gathering around the plaza was cheering at the two men on horseback.

Carlos stayed later than usual at the fencing academy working one on one with Maestro Luis. When he finally walked out the door, he could hear shouting coming from the plaza. Hopping up on Santiago, Carlos rode the two blocks to the plaza. A carriage careened by him carrying two girls screaming and crying. He rode to the corner of the plaza opposite from the church. In the middle of the *paseo,* Rafe and Diego clung to their wild horses. Rayo reared up his front legs and punched at Diego's black stallion. Diego swung his sword wildly holding the black's reins in the other hand.

Rafe whirled Rayo around trying to calm the horse. He had never seen Rayo behave aggressively. Diego rode a few yards away and was turning around.

"Diego, you don't want Ana Teresa. Go tell *don* Pedro you don't want to marry her. Break the contract and live," Rafe yelled at him.

Diego processed the *mestizo's* words. He would never marry Ana Teresa. He had no contract with the *don,* but the *mestizo* could not have her. "She can never marry you, *mestizo*. No one here will ever allow it," Diego growled.

Diego tried to ram his black horse at the Appaloosa. Slightly smaller the black shied at the last minute and Rayo crashed his big head into the black's flanks. The smaller horse jerked and Rayo pushed again almost knocking Diego off the saddle.

Rayo's nostrils flared. Rafe could feel the big horse panting and straining for breath. Diego turned and charged again, sword drawn high. Rafe readied his rapier and envisioned the circles surrounding him. This time Diego brought his horse close and swung his sword at Rayo, nicking the Appaloosa on the shoulder. Rayo screamed and bucked kicking his hind legs at the black.

Diego felt his advantage. He knew he was a better swordsman than the *mestizo*. He was *gachupín* and in his world he always won. It was the *mestizo's* horse, which gave the Mexican an advantage. Several hands taller than his black stallion, the Appaloosa was a superior horse.

Rafe struggled to calm both himself and Rayo after Diego cut Rayo's shoulder. *"Cálmate,"* he whispered to Rayo. Diego had an advantage on Rafe's novice experience as a swordsman and Rafe knew it. As Diego attacked, Rafe struggled to defend himself. Diego delighted in seeing the *mestizo* struggling with the sword and grew more confident at each pass, laughing as he swept by.

"Give up and go back to Mexico *mestizo* where you belong. You are no match to me," Diego sneered at him. However, he had no intention of allowing the *mestizo* to leave. He would kill him here in a fair fight for all to see. He would be celebrated by the *caballeros*.

Alvaro and Benjamin were not far from the fight, sitting on their horses watching the two men fight. Alvaro was ready to attack in case Diego needed help besting the *mestizo*. Carlos rode up behind the two. So engrossed in the fight, they did not hear him coming up behind them.

"Don't interfere or I will shoot," Carlos told them. Pulling his GSW pistol, he pointed it at their backs.

Rafe allowed Diego to rush him over and over,

defending each strike and protecting Rayo from Diego's sword. He thought about the GSW pistol in his holster and how he could kill Diego in an instant, but there was no honor in it. Death was stalking him again, and this time Death's name was Diego.

Diego felt the win was his and urged the black stallion to rush at Rafe for the kill. As he approached, he pulled back on the black's reins forcing the smaller horse to drive into the Appaloosa's shoulder, hoping to knock him down. Rayo saw the smaller horse coming at him and held his ground and pushed him aside. As the black slid by, Rayo feinted to the right, reared up and kicked the black with his hind hooves on the black's flank crushing into Diego's leg caught in the stirrup. Diego screamed in pain pulling on the reins held tightly in his hands.

The black whinnied and snorted, pulling around and came back at Rayo. Both horses reared up and clawed at each other with their hooves. Rayo, taller than the black, pawed at the black horse's face. Neither Rafe nor Diego had much control of the fighting horses. All they could do was try to hang on.

Rayo's hoof struck the black square on the forehead, stunning it for an instant and Rayo bit the black's neck. Rafe saw fear in Diego's eyes. He saw him fighting for control over the black stallion, still holding his rapier in one hand. Rafe threw his rapier far across the dirt and grabbed onto Rayo's saddle with both hands as Rayo reared and bucked.

Rayo turned and kicked the black with his hind hooves, over and over. Diego dropped his sword and clung to the black's reins with all his might, pulling on the bit forcing the black up on his haunches. As if in slow motion, Diego slipped from the saddle and fell to the ground. The weight of Diego falling off his back still pulling on the reins tipped the black horse backward. It fell back landing on Diego, sixteen hundred pounds crushing him to death.

A large crowd gathered on the grassy plaza to see the men and horses fight. Rafe calmed Rayo, riding him slowly until the horse calmed. Rafe looked up surprised to see

Carlos not too far away holding a gun on two *caballeros*. Several men ran and pulled the frightened black horse off of Diego and checked to see if there was any life left. There was none.

Rafe was exhausted. He did not want to kill Diego, but in the end Death won and took another soul. This time Death took a twisted soul to its master in the fires of hell.

CHAPTER 53

After the fight with Diego, Rafe and Carlos rode back to the horse barn at the Summers' ranch. Rafe looked for Pablo in the barn. Rayo needed treatment for the wounds obtained in the fight, the worst of which was the slash from Diego's sword. While Pablo and Rafe checked over Rayo, Carlos went to the house to find George. He wanted the family to know what had happened on the plaza. Although everyone saw it was a fair fight and Diego's horse killed him, not Rafe, Carlos was concerned there would be repercussions.

George, Josefina, and Celiá were in the kitchen. Carlos explained about the fight on the plaza and how Diego was killed. "Is Rafe hurt?" George demanded.

"No, but Rayo took some cuts and bruises."

George and Celiá hurried out to the barn, finding Rafe with Pablo working on Rayo. George grabbed Rafe in a bear hug, then admonished him, "Whatever were you thinking having a sword fight with a *caballero?* It could easily be you who is dead."

"I'm sorry father. I had to try and earn my right to marry Ana Teresa. I am an American, a businessman, and yet I have no right to be her husband by the Spanish caste system. I could not let that stand without a fight."

"I understand, but killing Diego will not help."

"I didn't kill him. I asked him to refuse *don* Pedro's contract to marry Ana Teresa, and he attacked me. He only wants to violate and dishonor her, not marry her. *Don* Pedro is forcing the marriage."

"Still, it is not a reason to attack him," George said.

"He attacked me because I am *mestizo,* calling me a son of a *puta."* Rafe knew the words would hurt his mother standing near him.

Celiá heard her son's words and cringed. Yes, he was a *mestizo,* that would never change, but he was the son of a *haciendero.*

Pablo listened to Rafael tell George about the Spaniards here in Santa Fe. It sounded not much different than life in Torreón, Mexico. The Spanish upper class ruled in Santa Fe just as they do in Mexico, keeping *mestizos* subservient. However, laws and customs were changing slowly, both in Santa Fe and in Mexico. Here a *mestizo* is an American, capable of owning land and being free, and in Mexico a bastard *mestizo* could now inherit land.

"You must accept *don* Pedro's reasons," George told him. "He is responsible for Ana Teresa."

"*Don* Pedro betrothed Ana Teresa to Diego against her will. Now Diego is dead and he will have to reconsider. I will prove to him I am worthy," Rafe said.

"I'm sorry son, but I doubt you can change his mind. You would have to be a *haciendero*," George said.

Celiá fought with herself. She and Pablo discussed the issues about the inheritance of the Reyes *hacienda* and of Rafael's birthright several times over the last weeks. Celiá thought she could not stand telling Rafael the truth, but hearing her son's despair, she spoke up. "Rafael, you are a *haciendero*."

At first no one heard her or responded. George had a hand on Rafe's shoulder and was about to say something when Celiá's words sunk in.

"What did you say, Celiá?" George asked. All eyes in the barn turned to her.

"*Mijo,* what I am going to tell you will hurt you and you will hate me, but you must know," Celiá said nervously while tears trickled down her cheeks.

"*Mamá,* what is it?" he asked. Her face clouded and the tears ran harder down her cheeks. Rafe walked to her and gently held her by her shoulders. Celiá looked up into his eyes.

"*Mijo, don* Bernardo was your father. He raped me, like he raped your sister, and after I became pregnant I married Antonio. The only one I ever told was Pablo," she admitted falling into her son's arms sobbing. "*Lo siento, lo siento,*" she cried out she was sorry, over and over.

"*Qué, ¿Qué estás diciendo?*" Rafe asked what she meant,

not believing what she was saying to him. *Don* Bernardo could not be his father. All the past swept through his mind – the evil looks *don* Bernardo gave him when he was a child, the way Pablo helped him as a child, the day the old *don* raped María, the image of *don* Bernardo falling when he shot him in the bedroom for raping María, and the day *don* Bernardo shot him in the canyon and left him for dead.

Suddenly he remembered the picture of *don* Bernardo's grandfather, *don* Rafael, hanging in the stairwell of the Reyes home. The picture looked familiar to him, like looking in a mirror. If *don* Bernardo was his father, then *don* Rafael was his great-grandfather.

Rafe remembered the day he came back to the main house to kill *don* Bernardo for shooting him and leaving him for dead in the canyon. They stared at one another and then *don* Bernardo fell, not by a bullet from Rafe's pistol, but from heart failure. As Rafe bent over the dying *don,* the old man whispered something to him before he died and Rafe thought he said, *"Mijo,* my son." Rafe thought he heard it, but was not sure and dismissed it because it made no sense to him.

Now, his mother was telling him the truth, a truth that would no doubt turn his life upside down. Most of all a pain shot through his heart for his mother. She had kept this secret all these years. Pushing her gently away from him he dried her cheeks with his fingers.

"Why are you telling me this, now?" he asked.

"Rafael, we tell you because the *hacienda* will be turned over to the government, if a proper heir does not claim the property. The laws in Mexico have changed, and now even if the first born is a *mestizo,* he is allowed to claim the property. The *hacienda* will belong to you. It is your birthright. Your mother and I think you should claim it and let María and Rodolfo live there to keep them out of trouble," Pablo stepped up and told him.

"But, how can we prove I am *don* Bernardo's son?" Rafe asked.

"The day you were born, I went to padre Andres and told him what happened to your mother. He made a record of it and the day you were baptized he made a separate baptismal record, a hidden record acknowledging your real name, Rafael Reyes de Estrada. Before I left Torreón, I verified with the padre and he still has the records. The painting of *don* Bernardo's grandfather has a striking resemblance to you. I stored the painting at the house of a friend. We have enough proof," Pablo declared.

"You named me after my great-grandfather?" Rafe asked his mother.

"*Sí, mijo.*"

Rafe looked at his adopted father, George Summers. All his life he believed his father was Antonio Ortega, but it was *don* Bernardo Reyes. *Don* Bernardo raped his mother and created him, Antonio gave him a home and a legal name, and then George gave him a life, a new life as an American man.

"*Mamá,* it is not your fault. I have a new life here in Santa Fe. It does not matter who my father was. I am alive and free now and so are you. I will go with *don* Pablo to Mexico and see about the property and find María and Rodolfo. If what *don* Pablo says is true, then I will inherit the *hacienda* and give it to them and the children and if you want you can live there too."

FIN

Please continue reading a preview of the next Young Pistolero Series adventure by Robert J. Alvarado, *Legacy for the Young Pistolero*, due to be released in 2016.

CHAPTER 1

On an early evening in July of 1871, Rodolfo Guerrero urged the old and tired mules along a rutted cattle trail in the hills northeast of Torreón, Mexico. María Ortega sat on the seat of the rickety wagon by his side, her long dark hair whipping around her face in the wind. They had been on the trail from El Paso, Texas, for over two weeks, slowly winding their way south toward Torreón on forgotten dirt paths through the rural countryside.

Almost a month ago they left a ragtag band of *bandidos* in the hills not far from the abandoned Reyes *hacienda,* while they traveled to El Paso to buy guns. On this return trip, tucked safely under other supplies, the guns and ammunition were a precious cargo. Discovery by the authorities would mean immediate arrest, if not execution.

Despite the danger and long hours bumping along on the broken down wagon, the last month with María renewed Rodolfo's spirit. He loved to watch her genuine excitement of each blazing orange, pink, and gray sunrise as they lay in each other's arms waking to glorious mornings. Her strength and practical ways amazed him and made him proud. Though raised a *peón* on *don* Bernardo Reyes' *hacienda,* she was smart and knew of plants and herbs in this part of Mexico using them for both cooking and healing.

Rodolfo, the leader of a loosely bound band of *peón* outlaws, left Javier in charge of the group when they left for El Paso, without any specific plan as to how to find them on his return. He found himself fretting, wondering if he would be able to locate his amigos. Although he knew the hilly escarpment was a safe location with a view of the valley below and a rock overhang for protection from the weather, it was not normally possible for the band to stay put for any length of time. Slowly he drove the wagon on, hoping he could find the campsite before nightfall.

About an hour later, Hector, one of the lookouts for the *bandidos,* came running down the path from the abandoned logging road waving to Javier. "A wagon is coming," he yelled. "A wagon with two people."

At Javier's signal, several men picked up heavy clubs. Women and children scurried under the overhang, leaving the cooking fires unattended. Javier hoped it was Rodolfo and María returning, but learned how to protect the group over the last month. He wanted to show Rodolfo he was a responsible man who followed orders and had kept the group safe, though worried what Rodolfo would say about the new people who joined the group in his absence.

Winding up the trail, Rodolfo's nose caught the scent of roasting beef in the wind. He let out a big sigh of relief knowing they were almost home. María was half asleep and leaning on his shoulder when they pulled into the campsite. "María, wake up. We're here." Rodolfo nudged her awake as he stopped the wagon.

"Jefe, bienvenidos," Javier shouted out a welcome, recognizing Rodolfo driving the old wagon. *"Muchachos,* help Rodolfo put the mules away," he bellowed to the other men.

"Gracias Javier, help María get down," Rodolfo told him. Exhausted from the last leg of the trip, Rodolfo climbed down from the seat. Behind him he heard giggling and a woman's voice. Turning around he watched in amazement as six women and a group of children ran out from under the overhang of rock. The women smiled at him and walked to the cooking fire. The children happily ran off playing with sticks. Walking out of the dim light of the overhang, Rodolfo saw more than ten men standing quietly.

"Jefe, today is a good day. We have a calf on the spit and we will all eat well tonight," Javier said puffing his chest out proudly hoping the man he considered the boss was pleased.

"I smelled it coming up the road, Javier. María and I need a good meal and rest," Rodolfo told him noticing his friend's pride.

"*Sí, jefe.* You look tired. I hope all went well in El Paso," Javier commented. He led Rodolfo and María to a large rock where he told them to sit.

"Benita, bring food and water," Javier ordered one of the women.

A woman, unknown to Rodolfo, brought them each a large tortilla stuffed with meat mixed with wild onions and peppers, while another woman brought cups of water. Rodolfo and María nodded to the women with thanks and hungrily ravished the meal. Over the long weeks on the trail, they had eaten mostly meager rations. The tortilla and meat was a feast.

Javier sat beside them eating a stuffed tortilla. "Javier, what are all these people doing here?" Rodolfo asked.

"I was going to ask you the same," María chimed in. When they left, she was the only woman of the group of thirteen men.

"*Jefe,* this is your doing," Javier answered.

"My doing! Why do you say that?" Rodolfo asked.

"Yes, you shared what we stole with the poor people and word got around. They found us and want to be here. Now, we have many mouths to feed. I have done the best I can, but the *hacienderos* are watching their stock more carefully and it is harder to steal a steer now. Today we got lucky," Javier told him. Though proud of how he had managed, Javier was glad Rodolfo was back to take the responsibility of these people off his back.

María looked around and asked, "How many new people are here?"

"Fourteen men, six with wives and children. Just this morning a man and his woman with two children found us. She is pregnant. All total we are twenty-seven men, six women and eight children," Javier explained.

"What, what the hell are we going to do with all those people?" Rodolfo tried hard not to shout.

"*Cálmate mi amor,*" María said trying to calm him.

"I will not calm down. I cannot be responsible for the women and children," Rodolfo huffed.

"I am a woman, Rodolfo," María reminded him, "and we have the guns. We can take what we want from the *haciendéros,*" she spoke of the rich landowners.

"Look at them María, do they look like fighters?"

María looked around and saw men in dirty cotton peasant clothing wearing leather sandals and well-worn straw sombreros. The women wore simple shirts and skirts with their long black hair braided down to their lower backs. The children ran around barefooted, some half naked. They were not fighters; they were *peóns,* simple peasants, people who never owned anything in their lives. *Peóns* worked like slaves for *haciendéros,* the land owners of the large estates, as both she and Rodolfo had on *don* Bernardo's *hacienda.* These were simple working people, who needed much and asked for little.

"How are they able to find us when *la policía* and the *haciendéros* cannot?" Rodolfo asked wondering how it was possible.

"I was as curious as you," Javier said. "I asked some of them how they knew where to find our campsite. They told me *peóns* know about us and the word has spread that we are the only *bandidos* who help them. You know how *peóns* pass information, but they keep our whereabouts a secret, *jefe.*"

"It is as you dream," María said to Rodolfo. "The *peóns* will rebel against the *haciendéros* for their freedom."

"They say there are many other *bandido* gangs around who only take for themselves and kill anyone who gets in their way. They report those *bandidos* to *la policía.* We are the only ones who help them and they will do what they can to help us," Javier informed Rodolfo as he finished his tortilla. "Did you get the guns in El Paso?" he asked changing the subject.

"Yes we got the guns. I will show them to you in the morning. María and I are tired and need rest." Rodolfo took María by the hand and led her to the spot where their bedrolls and belongings had been placed away from the main campsite. On the way the people looked at them and smiled. Some bowed and some of the children ran alongside of them and giggled and screeched as they touched them before they ran back nearer the fire.

Exhausted from the trip Rodolfo lay down and María curled up in his arm. Around them the night critters resounded in the monotonous symphony with no conductor, the natural rhythm of the shadow of night. "María, what are we going to do with these people?" Rodolfo whispered to her and in his voice she heard an uncertainty she had not heard before.

"I do not know, *querido*. You are the *jefe*, and you will figure it out. Sleep now my love, things will look better in the morning," María said before falling asleep in his arm.

Glossary of Spanish Words:

Italicized Spanish words used repeatedly throughout the series which do not have an English counterpart, such as important = *importante* or Mama = *Mamá*. Other infrequently used words, phrases, and sentences written in Spanish are immediately explained within the text itself.

abogado: a lawyer, attorney at law
abrazo: a hug
abuelo; abuela: grandfather; grandmother (m;f)
adios: goodbye
alcalde: the mayor of a town or city
amigo(s); amiga(s): friend (m;f)
anglo(s): a word to mean a white man, an American
ayúdame: help, asking for help
baboso(s): drooling idiot (a slang or curse word)
bandido(s): a bandit or outlaw
bueno: good
buenos días; tardes; noches: good day; evening; night
bienvenido(s): welcome
cabrón: asshole or bastard (a curse word)
caballo(s); caballero(s): horse; horseman or gentleman
cállate: shutup or be quiet
cálmate; cálmese: be calm or calm down
camisa: a blouse or top
casita; casa: small home, home
chaqueta(s): jacket or suit coat
chico(s); chica(s); chiquita: young boy or young girl (m;f)
chingado: shit or fuck (a curse word)
Chino(s): people of Chinese heritage
cojones: slang for a man's testicles
compañero(s): companion, friends
criollo(s): pure-blooded Spaniard born in the New World
ciudad: a town or city
culón: a chickenshit (a curse word)
desgraciado(s): a miserable wretch or terrible person
Dios: God
don; doña: title for nobleman/woman
gachupín(s); peninsulares: pure-blooded Spaniards born in Spain
garrancha: means sword, slang for penis
gracias; muchas gracias: thank you; many thanks
grandee: Spanish nobleman, aristocrat (i.e. dandy)

hermano; hermana: brother; sister (m;f)
hacienda: a large plantation or estate
haciendero(s): the nobleman owning the hacienda
hola: hello greeting
huaraches: sandals
Indio(s); India(s): means Indian (m;f)
jacal(s): small ramshakle house of mud and sticks
jefe: the boss man
machismo: very manly
mañana: tomorrow or the sometime later
maricón: slang for a homosexual man
mestizo(s): man of mixed blood, Spanish and Mexican Indian
mestiza(s): woman of mixed blood, Spanish and Mexican Indian
mierda: same as shit (a curse word)
mi hijito; hijo; mijo; hijita; hija; mija: my son; daughter (m;f)
muchacho(s); muchacha(s): like saying 'the guys' (m;f)
nada: no or nothing
Nana; Tata: common nickname for grandmother; grandfather
padre: head friar, monk, minister, priest
pantalones: pants
paseo: the road, boulevard; place to stroll or ride
patrón; patróna: formal for a boss; a mistress (m;f)
pendejo(s); pendeja(s): slang for asshole (a curse word) (m;f)
pene(s): slang for a penis
peón(s): a peasant
peso(s): Mexican money
picaro: a womanizer
pinche: fucking (a curse word)
plata: silver
primo(s); prima(s): cousin (m;f)
pulque; pulqueria: a poor man's drink in Mexico
puta(s): a whore (a slang or curse word)
que?: what or why
querido; querida: affectionate meaning my dear (m;f)
rayo: thunderbolt
sarape: cape, loose coat or blanket
señor(es); señora(s); señorita(s): like saying Mr. or Mrs. or Miss
sí: yes
tío; tía: uncle; aunt (m;f)
traje(s): ornate Spanish aristocrat's style of suit
vaquero(s): livestock herder or cowboy
vámonos or vamos: let's go, get out of here

Made in the USA
Coppell, TX
13 September 2020

37863163R00175